PRAISE FOR JOHN MARRS

"What a twisted and sinister book that was. Loved it."
—Peter Swanson, author of *The Kind Worth Killing*

'Whatever you do, don't read this in the dark . . .'
—Cara Hunter, author of *Close to Home*

'Really clever concept and some great characters and twists. It's a real joy to read something totally original, smart and thought-provoking'
—Peter James, author of the Roy Grace series

'One of the most exciting, original thriller writers out there. I never miss one of his books'
—Simon Kernick

'Gorgeously written, and pulsing with heart'
—Louise Beech, author of *The Mountain in My Shoe*

'. . . This is a superb heart-pounding chiller of a thriller'
—*The Sun*

'A brilliantly inventive thriller'
—*Good Housekeeping*

'Gripping from the start and full of surprises, this kept us up long after lights out'
—Isabelle Broom, *Heat*

'A compelling read . . . intriguing ideas'

KEEP
IT IN
THE
FAMILY

ALSO BY JOHN MARRS

KEEP IT IN THE FAMILY

JOHN MARRS

THOMAS & MERCER

Text copyright © 2022 by John Marrs
All rights reserved.

Published by Thomas & Mercer, Seattle

www.apub.com

Amazon, the Amazon logo, and Thomas & Mercer are trademarks of Amazon.com, Inc., or its affiliates.

ISBN-13: 9781542017275
ISBN-10: 1542017270

Cover design by Blacksheep

Printed in the United States of America

KEEP
IT IN
THE
FAMILY

PROLOGUE
THIRTY-NINE YEARS EARLIER

I pluck up the courage to make my move and begin my ascent of the staircase. I know this route well so I avoid every creaky floorboard.

Keeping an arm's length from the door I've been approaching, I lower myself to my knees and freeze when they crack like the snapping of dry twigs. If I've been heard and the handle turns, I'm done for. Such a violation of the rules could place me inside the room next time.

Even knowing the stakes, I can't stop myself from wanting to be out here, close to the action.

When I've convinced myself it's safe, I lie my whole body down before the door. My warm cheek presses against the cold floorboards until eventually I hear him. His voice is more muffled and muted than it was this morning. Then, he was banging on the floor with his fists and feet, his screams and pleas to be set free bouncing off the walls and ceiling. This didn't last for long, as he rapidly fell silent when they stormed up the stairs to confront him.

Now I'm squinting so hard at the gap under the door that my eyes burn. It's daylight outside but shadowy in there, so the curtains must be drawn. A pointless precaution, as no other structures look down upon this one. Outside lies only a private, walled garden and a modest orchard of cooking-apple trees. A disused farmyard separates us from the nearest neighbour a quarter of a mile up the road.

Eventually, I make out a pair of bare feet. His soles are arched but they're not connecting with the floor, so he must be standing on his tiptoes. He is likely being held upright by the rope attached to the ceiling hook. They must've loosened his gag, as I can just about make out words such as 'home' and 'let me go'. His desperation will delight them.

He isn't the first to be caught in their web and he won't be the last. Most of them beg for mercy but they are all wasting their time. There will be no change of heart because there never is. No one under this roof believes in compassion. Empathy is an alien emotion here.

My thoughts drift from him to them. Theirs is a mismatched partnership, yet they're made for one another. Only together can they be their true selves. Outside in the real world, where they have no control over their environment, they are forced to adapt and perform. They are quiet and unassuming and I expect most people forget who they are soon after crossing paths with them. They get away with what they do by hiding in plain sight and by being ordinary. Nobody sees in them what I see because they have no reason to look. Only I notice the hollowness of their eyes.

A dry cough within the room jolts me back to attention, swiftly followed by desperate, choking gasps for air. Then a shaft of light appears inside and my previously splintered view coheres: he's balancing on the tips of his toenails. But even in the face of certainty, he doesn't give up. 'Please,' he pants. 'Don't do this.' He is more persistent than I gave him credit for.

Like those before him, he holds on to the hope of a miracle. He doesn't realise that, to them, he is not human. He is an everyday, ten-a-penny object. And it doesn't really matter how carelessly you treat an everyday object, because if it breaks, it is easily replaced. That's what *will happen to him. It might take them weeks or months, but eventually, another one just like him will come along. One always does.*

The rustling of a plastic bag tells me they have all but finished playing with him. Then in one swift manoeuvre, his feet leave the floor and vanish upwards, as if the angels have carried him away to heaven. They haven't, of course. This is a place even angels avoid. A violent thrashing sound follows, accompanied by more rustling and muffled cries, before the room falls silent.

Now all that remains is a thin veil of cigarette smoke seeping under the door.

It's my cue to leave. I rise as slowly and silently as I arrived, pad along the corridor until I reach my room, and close the door behind me. I'm lying on my bed with an open book in my hands when, soon after, they approach my door.

She is the first to speak, a sing-song inflection in her voice. 'You can come out now,' she chirps. She is only ever this upbeat in the aftermath.

When I don't reply, the footsteps stop. My door slowly opens and both are standing in the doorway. His hair is ruffled and there's a deep-red lipstick mark on his neck. She wears the same satisfied expression as when she has taken the first puff from a cigarette. 'Did you hear me?' she asks.

'Yes,' I reply and muster a disingenuous smile. 'Sorry.'

She regards me for a moment before they move on, leaving the door ajar, and I return to the book I'm not reading.

Once I am sure they have returned to the ground floor, my morbid curiosity urges me to return to the room. It wants me to look under the door again and locate his body because I've never seen what they do when they have no more use for them. I've imagined it though. Frequently. However, I talk myself out of going. No, I think, I've pushed my luck enough today and the reward isn't worth the risk or retribution.

3

It won't be long until this latest disappearance is made public. It might remain in the newspapers or on the television for a few days, or even a week. Then something fresher and more pressing will replace him. Everyone except their families soon forgets about a missing child. And me. I remember every one of them.

Because I am the bait that lures them here.

PART ONE

TRANSCRIPT OF ANGLIA TV NEWS INTERVIEW WITH KATE THURSTON, HIGH STREET, STEWKBURY, BEDFORDSHIRE

It's the kind of house you don't notice, even when you've been living in the village for years. It's right on the outskirts and is so overgrown you can't see it through the trees and the bushes. The last time anyone lived here was over thirty years ago – an elderly couple who I think were joined later on by a young family. Then a few years later, they all did a moonlight flit. Nobody knows why or where they went. Anyway, I'd never seen anyone come or go from it until that new couple arrived. We were all wondering who'd take on a place like that. We thought they must have deep pockets and a lot of time on their hands.

CHAPTER 1
MIA, 2018

Sitting inside Finn's van, we stare at the property to our left. He turns off the ignition and the silence is palpable. Neither of us knows what to say first.

'So,' he eventually begins, 'this is going to be our home?'

It's as if he wants me to confirm information he already knows. I try to muster up something suitably enthusiastic, like, 'We're going to be so happy here' or 'This is our dream home', but my reply is more succinct than reassuring. 'It is,' I say.

He responds with a slow nod as he tries to comprehend what we have done. Then we fall silent again as the enormity of the task before us sinks in. I feel nauseous.

I catch a glimpse of the rest of the high street in the wing mirror. We walked and drove along these roads a handful of times over the last year agreeing it was exactly the kind of village we wanted to move to. Our criteria were straightforward: the place could be no more than a fifteen-minute drive from the town centre and train station, it must have shops and a pub, it couldn't be too overlooked and had to be surrounded by plenty of long countryside walks for when we get that dog we're always promising ourselves. Stewkbury ticked each box.

The only sticking point – and it was a biggie – was property prices. If you don't want to live in an identikit new build, then be prepared to pay for the privilege. And we didn't have that kind of money.

Neither Finn nor I had noticed this two-storey, five-bedroom, detached Victorian house in our previous recces. It only appeared on our radar when my monster-in-law saw it advertised in an online auction-house brochure. She and my father-in-law were going to put a bid in to renovate it themselves, but it was perfect for Finn and me. And after a fair few arguments, they eventually – albeit reluctantly – agreed to let us make an offer for it.

And before we knew it, we were sitting in a draughty hall bidding on it against half a dozen strangers.

When the auction began, Finn's knuckles were as white as his face. It was as if he was having a premonition of what lay ahead of us. Tearing apart and rebuilding this house was going to put an end to our Mr & Mrs Smith boutique hotel weekends away, my spa breaks with the girls, his Sunday morning football league with the lads, along with gigs and overpriced gym memberships. Goodbye fun, hello hard graft.

House buying hasn't been an easy process for us. When we married five years ago, we sold my flat in London and moved into Finn's terraced house in Leighton Buzzard. But the two-up two-down wasn't spacious enough to start a family. So we sold it and moved in with his parents, Dave and Debbie, while we waited to find somewhere. Four times we had an offer on a house accepted, but four times we were either gazumped or the owners had a change of heart. So, throwing caution to the wind and without even seeing this house in person or organising a surveyor, we found ourselves the last ones standing at the auction.

Now, I look towards Finn, his gaze fixed on the house like he's a rabbit caught in the headlights. I can't let him know I too have doubts. My next question invites criticism, but I ask it regardless. 'Is it better or worse than you thought?'

'It's hard to say,' he says. He's choosing his words carefully. I can almost hear the cogs in his brain turning as he prioritises the work required. Finn is the pragmatic sort, and possesses a natural talent for solving problems. I suppose that's what makes him a good plumber and all-round handyman. He can look at an object and instinctively know how it works or how to repair it. I'm the opposite. I look at something and it falls apart.

'But you and your dad will do a lot of the work, won't you?'

'I hope so.'

We exit the van. 'Shall we go inside?' I wrap my hands around his arm. He's as tense as a hostage negotiator.

We've always been 100 per cent honest with one another, but today I hold back on sharing what I'm really thinking – that we've made a bloody huge mistake and we are so far out of our comfort zone that we can't even see it from where we're standing now. But this is the only way to get what we wanted – a house in the country for a fraction of the price, and to escape living with his parents. He may be close to them, but I am most definitely not.

This place could be good for us, I tell myself. *It could be just what we need.*

My positivity lasts for as long as the thought does. And then I'm back to feeling nauseous again.

CHAPTER 2

FINN

What the fuck have we just done? What the *actual fuck?* My heart is beating twenty to the dozen and it's all I can do to stop myself from blurting out how I really feel to Mia.

We've always said that we'd tell each other the truth no matter how much it might upset the other one, but when it comes to this house, I've bottled it. From the moment we stepped into that auction place to when we picked up the keys an hour ago, my gut has told me we are making a massive mistake. We have sunk our life savings into a building we've not even been inside, and it's stressing me out how much cash it will drain.

I just didn't actually think we'd go ahead with it. The rule of thumb is that if Mum loves it, Mia will hate it. Only this time, Mia really wanted it and wasn't going to take no for an answer. My parents were planning to flip it and now I feel like crap for taking the opportunity away from them, because they really need the money.

Even when our highest bid was accepted, I still thought that something would happen last-minute. But now here we are, keys in hand, our name about to be added to the deeds. And I'm crapping it like I've necked a handful of laxatives. A quick once-over from outside tells me it's even worse than I imagined. But for Mia's sake, I've got to act like it's all going to be okay. She's had enough bonfires pissed on without me joining in.

Perhaps I'm misreading my wife, but something tells me she's not as into this place as she's letting on. When she's anxious or freaked out about something but doesn't want to admit it, she rubs her thumbs and index fingers together. Today she's moving them so quickly she's in danger of giving off sparks.

Mia crosses the road first; I'm close behind. She opens a rusty metal waist-high gate and we fight our way through a driveway so overgrown, it's hard to see where it ends and the garden begins. 'It's like *Jumanji*,' I say. 'I'm half expecting Dwayne Johnson to appear on a motorbike.' My joke falls on deaf ears.

The front door and ground-floor windows have been secured with metal sheeting, but the windows on the first floor are still visible. Some are broken, either by time and the weather or vandals, while others are hanging on by a thread in their rotten frames. I've never seen a wisteria grow this big – its trunk is like a small tree's, and it stretches all the way up to the roof. Two chimneys and much of the brickwork around the door frame needs repointing and the wooden fascias are rotten. It isn't a doer-upper, it's a knock-down-the-whole-damn-thing-and-rebuild-it-from-scratch-er.

Only we don't have the money to do that. The plan is to do as much of the work as we can ourselves. I'd never say it out loud, but thank God Dad's business has gone down the drain, because otherwise, he wouldn't have the time this house needs. Unpaid invoices and work drying up forced him to close his construction business, so now he survives on odd jobs and by labouring for others. He doesn't talk to me about how difficult it is for him. We rarely talk about anything worthwhile.

Mia uses the keys to open the padlocks on the door and we make our way inside. The boarded-up windows make it dark in here so I return to the van to grab a couple of torches from the toolbox. I also start recording on my phone to watch again later, calculating what to prioritise.

'Can you remember how long it's been empty for?' I ask.

'I think the auctioneer said forty-something years.'

The kitchen is our first port of call. It's made up of wood-panelled walls, and cupboards hidden by half-curtains or doors. It's all so dated. The dining room, lounge, bathroom and reception area aren't any better, and we make our way carefully up the staircase, being sure to tread on the sides of each step or risk falling through a weakened middle. We are just as careful with the floorboards along the landing that leads to all five bedrooms. With no condition report or building survey, we could be tiptoeing across matchsticks as far as we know.

Mia walks ahead of me and opens the last door. Inside is an empty bedroom containing a hook screwed into the ceiling and a rope attached to it. It looks like a noose or something, which is a pretty dark thing to leave behind. I pre-empt what she's thinking. 'I'm sure it's kids having a laugh,' I say, even if I don't necessarily believe it. She isn't convinced either.

Back downstairs, I'm tapping on walls to discover which are load-bearing and which we'll be able to knock through for open-plan living. It's going to take us years to get this house how we want it, but it's doable, I'll admit.

'We've done the right thing, haven't we?' Mia asks.

I wrap an arm around her shoulders. 'Time will tell.'

'If that's supposed to comfort me, it's a poor effort.'

'Look, I can't say hand on heart that this is going to work out for us. It might be a complete disaster. But we can only give it our best shot and keep our fingers crossed.'

'Funny, that's what I was going to say in my wedding vows,' she jokes.

'Ladies and gentlemen, my wife, the comedienne,' I deadpan. 'Anyway, who'd have believed you and Mum were fighting to get your hands on the same thing?'

'She and I have been doing that ever since I met you.'

'I meant the house. You two finally have something in common. They say that men marry their mothers.'

'I'll remind you of that comparison the next time you're begging for a fumble under the duvet. I'll even let you call me Mum if you like.'

'You win,' I add, and shake the image she's just created from my head.

CHAPTER 3

MIA

'The house is all ours.' I hold up the keys and jangle them.

'Congratulations,' says Debbie, but her smile doesn't reach her eyes.

She hugs her son and I get a pat on the arm. This level of intimacy suits me just fine. 'You didn't mention the auction was today,' she says.

'We didn't want to say anything and jinx it,' Finn replies. 'You know how many times we've been let down before.'

'And we've wasted enough time living here,' I add. 'We are grateful for everything you've done for us but we need to get on with our lives.' I look only at Debbie. 'Just Finn and I.'

I swear there's a part of her that shrivels up like a slug doused in salt each time she is reminded that Finn married me. But only I ever pick up on it. From the moment I met her and she spotted the tattoos on my wrist, ankle and back, my card was marked, even though her son has a sleeve of inkings, including one with his ex-girlfriend Emma's face that he has yet to have lasered despite my nagging.

There's a small, silly, insecure part of me that wonders if he's still not let go of her completely, which is why he's kept it. Debbie certainly isn't willing to wave farewell to Saint Emma. She keeps a framed photograph in the dining room of them at their high school prom. Emma's wearing a silver gown and Finn's dressed in a smart suit and tie. I assumed she'd eventually replace the photo with one of our wedding pictures, but no. Every time I'm in there, I swear to God that girl's eyes follow me around.

'There's a lot that needs to be done but we're willing to put in the hours,' I say.

Debbie lets out a half-laugh, half-pig-snort. 'Oh Mia, wandering around John Lewis picking out bedding and matching curtains isn't "putting in the hours". It'll be Finn and his dad doing most of the work, won't it?'

I love my husband and I accept that sometimes he's caught between us, but there are times like this when I need him to grow a pair and stand up for me. I bite my tongue and wonder how I've managed to put up with living under her roof for the last fourteen months. I am sure I'd have gone mad had we not had the Annexe to ourselves. It's compact but comes with its own bedroom, living area, kitchenette and bathroom. It's served us well, except it doesn't stop the out-laws from entering whenever they feel like it.

I divert my attention away from her and towards Dave. I can't help thinking how much he has aged over the last year. He remains broad but is less muscular than he was even a few months ago. The grey in his hair is now the most dominant colour and it's receding, so he can no longer hide with a fringe the deep-red port stain that covers half his forehead and part of his eyelid.

'It's certainly a good-sized place,' Dave says. 'There's a lot of scope to put your stamp on it.'

'It's just a shame you won't be able to fill all those bedrooms—'

'Debbie,' interrupts Dave, and he's not the only one who can't believe what his wife has just said.

'Oh, I'm sorry . . .' she begins, but her face says something different. And now I'm exiting the room and making my way back to the Annexe. She knows the exact place to punch me for it to hurt the most. As I leave, I want to hear Finn giving her both barrels, telling her how thoughtless that was. But he simply follows me.

I slam the Annexe door behind me but it reopens just as quickly. 'Babe,' he begins, but I don't want to hear it.

'Don't you dare make excuses for what she said.'

'She said it without thinking.' I brush off the hand he has placed on my shoulder. 'You know what she's like.'

'I certainly do. She can't stop herself from trying to make me feel worthless. I see how she looks at her defective daughter-in-law. Well I'm glad I've got broken bloody ovaries because that means she'll never get to sink her claws into a grandchild.'

'You don't mean that. I'll talk to her.'

'Don't bother because she won't listen,' I say. 'She's being a spoiled brat because she knows we deserve that house and she doesn't.' Even as I slide a suitcase out from beneath the bed I know I'm being completely unreasonable, but I can do nothing but roll on. 'Let's just pack our clothes and some toiletries and get a room at the Travelodge. We can collect the rest of our things tomorrow. I'll call the storage company to give notice and arrange to have it delivered to the new house.'

'It's uninhabitable, Mia. You know that. Let's sleep on it and then we'll talk about it in the morning. And if you are still dead set on us leaving, then we'll find somewhere to go.'

I know he's only pacifying me, just telling me what I need to hear. I allow him to pull me to his chest. We both know that when morning arrives, this foul mood will have passed. But for tonight, I intend to have loud, passionate sex with Debbie's son and scream the sodding roof down if I have to, and I don't care who hears. If I can't give him a baby, I'll at least give him the time of his life.

16

CHAPTER 4

DAVE

Debbie and I are awake long into the night once again discussing the pros and cons of Finn and Mia buying that house. She's convinced that if she can get Finn alone, she can talk him into selling it to us after all. But Mia has the same fiery determination that I've seen one too many times in my wife. When they put their minds to something, it isn't easy talking either of them out of it. I fear this isn't a battle Debbie can win.

Earlier we had words over her comment about them starting a family. I know Debbie didn't mean it to come out as it did, and had Mia not stormed out, she'd have heard Debbie apologise. Sometimes she says things without thinking but she means no harm. However, Mia is a hothead and their spat will make the atmosphere around here awkward for a while.

Truth be told, I think Mia was gunning for an argument. There was something combative about the way she jangled their house keys in front of us. She wasn't just celebrating the purchase of a home, she was celebrating getting one over on Debbie.

'Wouldn't you rather the house belonged to one of us than someone else?' I ask.

'I suppose so,' she concedes, but she hates losing.

I also warned Debbie that if she doesn't start trying to win Mia round and make her realise she's not the enemy, then she will lose Finn. He will choose keeping his wife happy over pleasing us, as is the natural way of things. But Finn has also got his work cut out for him because Mia isn't always the easiest girl to please. He calls her ambitious and opinionated, but I'd describe her as pushy and always wanting something she doesn't have. It's probably hereditary. I've only met her parents a handful of times but they give the impression they're never happy with their lot either. Perhaps that's why they're on a five-year global sailing adventure: they want to see for themselves if the grass is greener on the other side of the world.

I'd never admit this to Debbie but I'm a little envious of Mia's mum and dad. I've thought about escaping many a time when the weight of my worries pushes me deep into the ground. In those moments, I'd give anything just to disappear. But in reality, I wouldn't do it. I couldn't leave Debbie alone unless I absolutely had to. We need each other too much.

There's a gnawing physical pain in my stomach tonight that won't go away, so when Debbie eventually drifts off to sleep, I pad out of the bedroom, make my way downstairs into the dining room and take a couple of tablets from a bottle hidden in the drinks cabinet. Then I wash them down with a neat Jim Beam bourbon whiskey. It's now early morning and, at this time, it's either my last drink of the day or my first. I don't feel so guilty when I think of it like that.

I don't have a problem with booze, but I also know that it's become more than a habit lately. My reliance on it to remove all the sharp edges from my life began soon after Debbie's diagnosis. Then it heightened when the business started slipping away from me.

Bigger, better, cheaper construction companies came along with lower overheads and quotes and there was no place for craftsmen like me.

I pour another dram and promise myself that it'll be the last for today. I'm not sure if it's the alcohol or my secret stash of pills helping my stomach pain to ease. Either way, it's a temporary fix – especially when I unplug my phone from its charger and press play on the video that Finn sent me. The hairs on my arms rise as he walks through each room and I set to roughly calculating the work that needs to be done. Finally I give it up. There's too much to distract me. I need to see it in person.

There might be a silver lining amongst all this cloud though. Perhaps this project will be what Finn and I need to bring us closer together. The distance between father and son began the day he arrived in our world, and I admit I'm partly at fault for that.

I place my phone back on charge, enter the bathroom and clean my teeth for the second time tonight, taking a long swig of mint-flavoured mouthwash until I can't taste the bourbon any longer. Then I quietly slip back into bed with Debbie.

I place my arm over her chest as it rises and falls. For all her faults, I could never be without this woman. She came into my life at a time when I needed someone to be on my side, and she has never left. I would die for her, without hesitation. In fact, if it wasn't for her, I would probably be dead already.

CHAPTER 5

I cut a casual figure as I approach the house on foot. I cast my mind back, trying to recall when I was last here. It must have been some thirty years ago, when curiosity got the better of me. But before I even reached the driveway that day, each young face from my chequered childhood appeared behind the weather-stained windows like they had all been waiting for my return. Unprepared for such a confrontation, I beat a hasty retreat.

Today, that apprehensiveness returns. My pace slows as I watch a truck driver with a cigarette dangling from his mouth attach netting to the top of a skip crammed full of old bricks, plasterboard and a familiar bathroom suite. Next to it is an empty skip, ready to be filled with more remnants of the home I once knew. I imagine there will be very few of the original fixtures left by the time their work is complete.

A car pulls up ahead and I stop in my tracks, anxious not to be seen. I hide behind trees on the opposite side of the road. As the new owners wait for the truck to reverse from the driveway, they crane their necks upwards and stare at the roof. My eyes follow the direction their heads move in.

This place was pristine back in my day, a far cry from how it appears now. While Dad kept up with the indoor maintenance, the garden was Mum's domain. I can still picture her out here, floral gloves on, a pair of secateurs in her hand and a bag full of pruned twigs and stalks by her feet. She looked at peace in nature. However, towards the end of our time here, even that wasn't enough to satisfy her.

Today, there are no such things as flowerbeds or lawns; they have all bled into a sea of green. Weeds stretch towards the pale blue sky from the second-floor guttering.

I am too young to recall exactly how we ended up living here or where we were before. But my brother, George, would tell me stories of our family's incessant journeys before we settled here, always on the move, rarely remaining in one flat or house for more than a few months at a time, and always living with others much older than Mum and Dad. I vaguely remember two adults already being in this house when we first arrived, but they didn't stay for long. Soon we had it all to ourselves to explore. 'Dad says we are cuckoos,' George explained, but I didn't know what he meant.

My eyes gravitate now towards the two bay windows, where all six panes of glass have been boarded up to keep out trespassers, I assume. I look to where the lawn was, half expecting to see the remains of the chair that I hurled through one of those windows. Then more memories and long-buried emotions return in waves so high that they threaten to knock me off my feet. I know that I wear a different, tougher skin now to the one I was born into, but scratch beneath the surface and below I am that same, frightened child.

As the lorry pulls away and the new guardians of this house leave their vehicle, my attention gravitates towards her more than him. Her head is held straight, her shoulders are thrown back and her stride is self-assured. But her confidence is undermined by the way she clings to his arm for dear life. She is an actress. She needs him more than he needs her.

I think of how fortunate they are to be unaware of this building's history. Even though I haven't set foot under that roof for decades, I am forever part of its fabric. I'm the mortar that binds the bricks together, the pipes linking each tap, the wooden beams that hold up the roof. I have never truly been able to escape it. I am it and it is me. Good or bad, it has made me the person I am today. To some, I'm a saviour, but to others, I'm a monster. I know what my work has been about, all the souls I've saved from torment. It's part of the bargain that I can never share my role with the world. There'd be no hope of them understanding. Blinkered as they are, I could only be a monster.

BEHIND THE HEADLINES PODCAST

EPISODE 4/6

PARTIAL TRANSCRIPT OF AN INTERVIEW WITH GABBY GIBSON, RESIDENT AND LANDLADY OF THE WHITE HART PUB, STEWKBURY

Can you tell us when you first became aware of work being carried out at the house?

The first of the lorries started thundering through our narrow village lanes about a fortnight after the sold sign went up. The noise made my windows rattle. I thought we were having an earthquake.

As their nearest neighbour, what could you see?

Nothing from here, but I'd get a better view when I took the dog for a walk. After they spent a few days hacking the garden down you could finally see what had become of the place that'd been hidden all those years. It was a hell of a project to take on.

You grew up in the village. Can you tell our listeners what you remember about the house?

I've never known it to be occupied. The back garden is enclosed by walls and it isn't overlooked. So as teenagers, it was the perfect place to skip school, spend the day getting stoned and drinking cider, before sobering up and going home. But none of us ever tried to go inside. There was something so creepy about that place that not even a group of pissed-up teens were stupid enough to break into.

How did the rest of the village react to what was later found inside?

As you'd expect, with total shock. It's worse than any of us could have imagined.

CHAPTER 6

MIA

Dust clouds hover in every room we enter. It's a good job we bought a job lot of masks from eBay or we'd be coughing up our lungs by now. I run my fingers through my hair and wish I'd worn a hard hat because it already feels dry and powdery and I've only been here an hour. I'm going to give it the conditioning of its life tonight.

The last time I was standing in this kitchen it was galley-shaped, dingy and ridiculously small for a house of this size. Two days later and it's missing a load-bearing wall and metal poles are propping up the ceiling. The RSJ delivery is due tomorrow. I almost sound like I know what I'm talking about, I think. But I've had to learn a lot in the two months since work began. Dave has been project-managing while doing a lot of the renovation work himself. If there's a workman on site, then so is Dave, following him like a shadow and making sure everything is just how we want it.

I have very definite opinions of what I want and don't want from these rooms once they're complete. As part of my public-relations job in London, I've organised dozens of photoshoots in homes I've hired to show off my clients' products. And socially, with my ex, I spent a lot of time in the houses of celebrities who'd employed interior designers to turn neglected period homes into palaces. So I know what I'd like to replicate, albeit on a much tighter budget.

It's probably the dust and this mask making me queasy, but I'm not entirely convinced the sick feeling isn't all just in my head. It hits me with alarming frequency whenever I'm here, even if it's during a lull in the demolition work. It's the constant reminder of how much money we are ploughing into this, with so much yet to be done before we can even think about moving in. Maybe we should've let Debbie and Dave buy it after all.

I have been within a hair's breadth of throwing in the towel many times. Like when most of the upstairs bathroom ceiling collapsed thanks to a leaky water tank. Or when we turned up on the first week of work to discover the storm had left the top half of the chimney lying on the bottom half of the driveway. Then, I'd wanted to hurl the house keys at Finn, turn around and never set foot in here again.

But what's the alternative? If we give up now, we'd be leaving it in an even worse condition than when we bought it. And who'd want to take it off our hands? Plus the financial impact would cripple us. We are already cutting back on all spending. Much to my parents' disappointment, we've cancelled our plans to meet them in Long Island and spend a week sailing down to Florida with them. Our belts are drawn so tightly, mine feels like a corset.

I'm really lucky because my boss, Helena, doesn't need me commuting to the capital five days a week when I can get just as much work done from home. So if I'm not working on my laptop in the Annexe, then I'm rotating my way around a bunch of different coffee shops and cafés in town. You can take a girl out of London but you can't take a large triple-shot latte with nutmeg sprinkles out of her hand. Not without a crowbar, anyway. My sweet tooth and increasing intake of pastries is actually starting to give me a paunch, or what Finn calls a 'food baby'. It's meant as a joke but it's a little insensitive, considering. Or maybe I'm still a little touchy.

As I head towards the front door, I catch Debbie shuffling her way up the drive with her walking stick. Her leg looks particularly cumbersome today. She doesn't know I can see her, so perhaps I'm wrong to think sometimes she exaggerates it for sympathy. I duck, hurry through the house and leave via the huge hole in the wall.

It's great timing because now I can work from the Annexe knowing she's not lurking around in the main house, waiting to waft in like a bad smell. She has never understood my job or the point of PR. She thinks it's a made-up, emperor's-new-clothes career created to fill a gap in the market that doesn't really exist. And it kind of is. But who cares when it pays so well? I'm sure Finn has told her how much I out-earn him in my 'made-up job'. Which has probably only caused her to resent it even more.

My friends and colleagues were speechless when I told them I was giving up my flat in Hoxton to live out here in the sticks. A handful even held what they semi-jokingly called 'an intervention' to persuade me to change my mind, reminding me I shouldn't give up anything for a man, let alone one with a job as ordinary as Finn's. 'He's just a plumber,' more than one of them said. And once upon a time I'd have probably said the same.

But by the time we met, I needed more than the superficial boys I was used to dating. Finn wasn't a fashion photographer with a man bun and a contacts book that could get me into A-list parties; his parents weren't titled and living in a country pile; he didn't spend his weekends bar-hopping with the Chelsea set. He was regular with a capital R. And I was beginning to realise I liked normal. Even now, when we hear Pulp's song 'Common People' playing, he tells me it's like Jarvis Cocker is singing our story. There's enough of a grain of truth about that to make me laugh.

I started feeling sick again so, now that I'm outside, I slip off my mask and take some deep breaths. I climb into the car, turn the ignition on and Daft Punk's 'Get Lucky' appears on the radio. I smile as I blast it out. It was playing the night Finn and I met. I was at my friend Priya's hen night at the W Hotel in Leicester Square, not long after I'd broken up with Ellis. We were in the bar when this strapping six-footer with lashes I'd kill for and eyes as dark as his hair caught my attention.

I couldn't stop staring at him. He was standing with a group of his friends and, emboldened by Prosecco and encouraged by the girls, I made my approach. He was a little younger than me, I guessed, and more softly spoken than I imagined. I assumed he'd be nothing more than a drunken snog, or at a push, a one-night stand if I was so inclined. Even now, Finn likes to remind me that I thought I was being sexy and seductive when, in reality, I was slobbering all over him with the grace of a Saint Bernard as he politely fended me off. But even my clumsy, gin-soaked haze wasn't enough to dampen the spark between us.

There was something a little bit different about him. Finn was – and still is – an open book, and admitted straight away that he had a girlfriend, Emma. Yet I still grabbed his phone from his pocket and typed my number into it. I justified it by telling myself the Girl Code only applied if I knew the competition personally. *Not cool, Mia, not cool.*

We began texting in the days that followed – instigated by him, I might add – and then he FaceTimed me – accidentally, he claimed. The call lasted almost two hours. The next day, he caught a train to London just to take me out for a coffee during my lunch-break. Soon after, he ended it with his childhood sweetheart. In less than six months, I'd sold my flat and moved to Leighton Buzzard.

Soon after, we married on the beach in the Maldives. We got a huge discount through a client but Debbie and Dave couldn't afford to join us on this once-in-a-lifetime trip. I expect she has never forgiven me for 'making him' do it abroad. And when my parents joined us, it only rubbed salt deeper into her wounds. The framed photographs we gave her of us saying 'I do' on the beach have yet to make an appearance anywhere in her house.

Finn and I began trying for a baby almost immediately. The first year passed unsuccessfully and it wasn't until my doctor sent me for scans that a specialist diagnosed me with endometriosis in both ovaries. Three years later, and after an operation, two free NHS IVF rounds, two private fertility clinic transfers and three miscarriages, we were no closer to having our much-wanted child. My guilt over not being able to give Finn children was, at times, all-consuming, and I wondered if our marriage could withstand it.

Over and over again I'd ask Finn if he'd have married me knowing what he knows now. Yes, he kept reassuring me, of course he would have. But it was never enough to put my mind at rest. I'd stare at the photograph in Debbie's dining room of him and Emma on prom night, telling myself how much happier he'd be with her, not someone as broken as me. This was the universe punishing me for stealing another woman's man.

I even snooped around his phone, reading his text messages and emails and scanning his social media accounts to see if they were sliding in and out of each other's direct messages. But I found nothing. Finn wasn't having an affair with anyone, but I risked pushing him into someone else's arms if I continued behaving like a madwoman. Once I learned to let go of what I couldn't have, I appreciated what I did have. Finn. My Finn. He was enough. And I stopped behaving like the child I was unlikely to have.

Child. I repeat the word to myself. *Child.* The notion is fleeting, but it's there nonetheless. 'Child,' I say aloud.

Jesus! This isn't why I've been feeling sick lately, is it? I can't be pregnant, can I? No, our last round of IVF was months ago. My periods have always been erratic, but now I think about it, I haven't had one in ages.

I run my fingers through my hair and more dust comes out. Minutes later and I'm driving towards the town centre to find a pharmacy. I need to know for sure whether I'm imagining this or not. Because if I am finally pregnant, this is the best news ever but at the worst possible time.

CHAPTER 7

FINN

There's something wrong with Mia, I can sense it. She hasn't come out and said there's a problem, but for the last few days, she's been distant with me. I'm well practised at hiding things from her, but she's usually pretty vocal if something's pissing her off.

We're now eleven weeks into the renovations, but it must feel like an eternity for her, as she's the one juggling a full-time career and an evening job managing the money. The thing is though, I know that her enthusiasm is waning – if it was ever totally there in the first place – while mine has done a one-eighty. The first thing that crosses my mind when I wake up in the morning is no longer *What the fuck have we just done?* Instead, I'm thinking about what I need to do today to help us inch towards the finishing line. I see it like this: we have a once-in-a-lifetime opportunity to turn this place into something special. And the more time I spend working my arse off toiling over each pipe, fitting, floorboard and brick wall, the quicker it is going to happen.

I'm watching Mia from the end of the aisle in the tile warehouse. She's turning the display boards as we try and settle on a design to use above the sink and the range cooker now the kitchen is closer to being fitted. I want those timeless, white Metro-style tiles, but she has her heart set on a colourful Moroccan design she saw on Pinterest. She'll win. She always does. My mates take the piss out of me, saying I'm so henpecked that I might as well build myself a roost in the garden. If Mia wants to think she wears the trousers and knows everything about me then I'm not going to try and persuade her otherwise. I have bigger fish to fry.

She's very different from anyone else I've dated. It was a big jump, moving from the girl I was with throughout my teens and early twenties and knew inside out, to someone completely new. But that was part of the appeal. Emma was sweet and kind and would do anything I asked of her, but our relationship was claustrophobic. She insisted we did everything together, which I know is important, but not 24-7. I was already looking for a way out the night Mia and I met. She was a funny, confident force of nature and drunk as a skunk. Oh, and as fit as you like.

There's something special about a girl who won't follow the crowd, refuses to jab herself with Botox and lip-fillers and doesn't only eat salads to stay Instagram-skinny. Mia doesn't care that she's not a size six. And that blonde hair and blue eyes still light something inside me that burns all these years later. She also values her own space, which means I get time to myself and that suits me down to the ground. I have a life away from my marriage.

I'd never heard of her before we met because I don't read celebrity gossip magazines, but my mates' girlfriends recognised her immediately. Her ex was a soap actor when he won *Strictly Come Dancing* and became a household name overnight. It meant Mia was also thrown into the spotlight. I googled her recently and it was weird seeing a younger version of my wife on the cover of magazines. She and Ellis were all set to get hitched when he was caught out dirty-dancing behind Mia's back with his professional partner. Mia dumped him and his loss was my gain.

Mia picks up a box of tiles but the cardboard base can't have been secured properly because they fall to the floor and shatter. Swearing, she sets about picking them up, then cuts her finger and curses again, sucking on the bleeding tip. I'm carefully picking the rest up when I notice she's been silently crying. It can't have hurt that much.

'It's okay, they're only tiles,' I say.

'I'm pregnant,' she blurts out. I'm thinking I must have misheard her but she doesn't give me time to consider what else she might have said. 'And I know that it's bloody awful timing as we have so much work to do on the house and living with your parents and everything, but . . .' Her sobs return, and this time she can't keep them quiet.

This is the last thing I expect to hear. 'How long have you known?' I ask.

'About three weeks,' she replies wetly. 'I went for a scan at the hospital yesterday and the sonographer says I'm twelve weeks gone.'

She knew about this for weeks and didn't tell me? Perhaps she's better at keeping secrets than I've given her credit for. 'Why didn't you say anything? You shouldn't have gone for the scan on your own.'

'I didn't want to get your hopes up in case there was something wrong with it.' She backhands her nose clear and takes a deep breath. 'I couldn't bear to see the disappointment in your face again.'

'And is everything, you know, alright with it?'

Only when Mia nods do I give up my smile. 'It's perfect,' she replies, and places the palm of her hand on her stomach. 'It's absolutely perfect.' Then she reaches into her handbag and pulls out a black-and-white ultrasound photograph. She has to point out precisely where the baby is because, to me, it resembles a blob in an ocean.

She rises to her feet while I remain literally and figuratively floored, trying to figure out what this means for us. 'So what do you think?' she asks.

I stand up and draw her head closer to my chest. 'It's absolutely brilliant.'

The timing is going to be tight, but there's no better motivation for completing a house than not wanting your newborn baby living on a building site. We make our way to the car having made no decision about tiles. She's talking, but I'm not listening. Instead, I'm trying to get my head around the news that she is going to make me a dad. I'd come to terms with children not being on the agenda for us. And if I'm being honest with myself, it didn't take that much doing. It was always Mia who was desperate to start a family, much more so than I was. Not that I ever told her that.

As exciting and life-altering as this news is, it's going to stretch me thinner than tracing paper. And it'll mean I will need to keep my eye on the ball, much more so than I ever have before. Because if I don't and I slip up, Mia will never forgive me.

CHAPTER 8

DEBBIE

Mia and my son are sitting on the opposite side of the wooden table to Dave and I in our local pub's beer garden. She and Finn have returned from the bar with a tray of drinks. I think she always offers to help him so that she isn't left alone with us. I can't blame her for that; I'd rather not be alone with her either. No matter what I say, it's always the wrong thing.

I am really trying with her after Dave suggested it would be in everyone's best interests if I made more of an effort. 'You two don't have to be friends,' he said, 'but you need to find a way to make it work.'

Of course I'm protective of my son, but that doesn't mean I'm unwilling to share him. I want to like Mia as much as Finn does: Emma and I got on like a house on fire, so I know it isn't me. Mia just doesn't want to be my friend. I have tried and tried with her but she never meets me halfway and there's only so many times you can keep going down that road only to be caught in a cul-de-sac. 'I'll do my best,' I promised him.

I lift my half-pint of lager shandy and it feels heavy with my weak wrist. My occupational therapist has put me on a new medication. It's supposed to help relax my muscles and relieve spasms. It works intermittently and the side effects aren't pleasant – diarrhoea and a sore throat when I wake up most mornings. If I mix the tablets with too much alcohol, I end up forgetting things. And I can't afford to do that.

This is Dave's third beer, I've been counting them. And I suspect this isn't the only occasion alcohol has passed his lips today. Though he arrived at the pub straight from the building site he's been labouring at, I'm sure I smelled beer on his breath when he kissed me. I'd be lying if I said I wasn't concerned about how often he's been using drink to get him through the day. I've noticed the whiskey in the booze cabinet has slipped down to just below the label. It was still above it earlier in the week.

He also doesn't know that I've found the bottle of prescription tablets he hides in there. I don't recognise the name on the label – Antoni Kowalski – and I had to google the words *Leki Przeciwbólowe* to discover it was Polish for painkillers. It's not like Dave to keep something from me. For the time being, I've held off asking why he needs them but I'm sure it'll be his back that's causing him trouble. The older he gets, the less willing he is to admit work is taking its toll on him.

A sharp cramping seizes my left leg and I press hard into the flesh at its source. It really hurts, as if someone has stabbed me with the red-hot blade of a knife then left it embedded. I stop myself from yelling, so my family and Mia are none the wiser. The worst part is that I know this is only going to get worse over time. I'm only in my early fifties, but feeling increasingly like a knackered old horse heading for the glue factory.

I have been relying more on Finn for help recently. To be honest, I don't always need him, but show me a mother who doesn't want to spend time with her son and I'll show you someone who hasn't raised him properly. Then my heart sinks when I remind myself of the time limit my diagnosis set upon us.

'We have something to tell you,' Finn begins, pulling me away from my pity party. He removes a white envelope from his back pocket and slides it across the table. 'Open it,' he says.

Inside is an ultrasound image. Clear enough, but it still takes a moment for it to register. 'You're pregnant?' I say to Mia and she nods.

I look to Dave, who's as shocked as I am. 'How?' I ask them.

'I hope I don't need to explain it to you . . .' Finn chuckles.

'The natural way,' Mia says. 'After the operation and all the IVF attempts, nature won in the end.'

'And you're sure?' I ask.

'Fourteen weeks,' she says and clutches my son's arm tighter, like a boa constrictor wrapping itself around its prey.

As Dave rises and shakes our boy's hand, I offer her a polite hug neither of us can wait to break from. But when I get hold of my son, I don't want to let go.

'I'm going to be a granny,' I say, scarcely believing my own words.

Mia, Finn and his dad continue to talk but I've vanished into my own little world again. I'm picturing how our lives will alter with a new addition to our family. I can see myself pushing a pram with my grandson inside it; I'm texting photos of him to my friends; I'm watching as Finn holds him as preciously as I did that first time with him. Then I realise I've already allocated this child a gender.

Reality bites hard and fast. *I won't get to be a grandmother for long*, I think and the wind leaves my sails. Dave's right. I'm going to need to work much harder on my relationship with Mia if I'm to make the most of the time I have with my grandchild. I have to find a way to make her realise I can be her friend and not her enemy. I can only hope that she does the same with me.

TRANSCRIPT OF INTERVIEW CONDUCTED WITH JILL MORRIS, FRANCHISEE OF COSTCUTTER SUPERMARKET, STEWKBURY

I was on my way to the shop to cover the lunch-time shift when the first responder's car passed me. It pulled up outside the house where all the work was being done and I assumed there'd been an accident. An ambulance followed a minute or so later with its blue lights flashing, and I wandered down the road to see what was going on. And not long after, they came out with someone lying on a stretcher, their head and shoulders in one of those cervical collars and arm in some kind of splint. There was so much blood on their face that I couldn't even tell if it was a man or a woman, but they were definitely unconscious. That was probably for the best, judging by the state they were in.

CHAPTER 9

The patio door is carelessly unlocked and glides open with ease. I only slide it a fraction, just enough to slip through the gap. Once inside, I move quietly into the lounge and take in my surroundings. The furniture is too large for the compact space, leaving little room to manoeuvre, but the open curtains and almost-full moon outside enable me to see well enough to avoid bumping into something and attracting attention.

On the rare occasion I'm required to break into a property, I remain still and silent as a statue upon entering, as the house talks to me. I listen patiently to differentiate between the noise of a person, of floorboards creaking or the rumbling belly of a heating system. Once I am sure I'm safe, I go about my business. Tonight, heavy breaths lure me towards a partially opened door. I walk slowly across the carpet until I reach it.

She is here and she is alone. She lies in the bed, oblivious to my presence, on her back and deep in slumber. Her throat makes a cackling sound as she breathes in and out. It reminds me of a death rattle, something I have heard – and instigated – many times.

Without warning, the outdoor intruder lights switch on and illuminate the room's interior more brightly. I glare at her, expecting the lustre to wake her up, but she doesn't so much as twitch.

Through the window I spot a vixen with her cub, foraging around for food in the flowerbeds. And here inside, I see this woman clearly. She is like my mother, a pretty woman who hides an ugly heart. Her looks will soon fade and her soul will only grow more grotesque. But my intervention can stop that.

Her neck is slender and I instinctively move my hands towards it, hovering so close to her skin that I can feel the heat she radiates on the palms of my hands. I wonder how much pressure I would have to exert to rupture her windpipe and choke her to death. Only a fraction, I think. My skills are well honed.

She has pushed the duvet down to below her waist, and I can clearly make out the rise and fall of her swollen, pregnant belly under her T-shirt as she inhales and exhales. My hands move towards it, gradually drawing closer until finally, they are resting on it. She doesn't stir as my skin touches hers.

They rest upon a section above her navel. It's firm to the touch and I assume that, under the surface, her unborn child's back is pressed against it. It sleeps like its mother, unaware of my presence, oblivious to the danger it faces. Now I contemplate the strength needed to push a blade into her doughy flesh and the depth required to penetrate the womb. I imagine the warmth of her wound against my cool skin as I slice her open, push my hands inside her, feeling my way around until I can locate and pull out its contents. I have never taken an unborn before, but for her, I am willing to make an exception. The innocent need protecting, no matter the age.

Now I am standing over her, my face directly above hers, my mouth next to her nose. I gently exhale so that she breathes me in and I become the oxygen that fills up her lungs and feeds her baby. Then I open my mouth and allow the thinnest line of silvery saliva to drip from my mouth, thread-like, and on to hers. She unconsciously runs her tongue over her bottom lip and I am inside her.

Experience has taught me never to outstay my welcome, so I begin making my way out of the room as slowly as I entered it. After only a few steps, the garden lights extinguish. I pause and peer back into the shadows, taking one last look at the woman who is now responsible for the house that made me. 'I'll come by again soon, Mia,' I whisper.

CHAPTER 10

MIA

Finn pushes his knuckles into my shoulder as I lie on our bed in the Annexe. The iPad reads 5.17 a.m. The slow, pulsing thrum of a knot woke me up, and I woke him in turn. 'Harder,' I say. He does his best, but just can't undo what's trapped deep under the surface.

On the bedside table is a framed 4D scan taken a fortnight ago to mark our thirtieth week. It's remarkably detailed. You can make out the cupid's bow of our son's lips and cleft of his chin. I'm as nervous as hell about being a mum, but so excited at the prospect of meeting our little miracle man.

As Finn works his way around my shoulders and back with the precision of a man much more experienced with a pregnant woman's body than he should be, I remain lying on my side, propped up with an elbow and putting this early wake-up call to good use. I'm scrolling through Excel spreadsheets, prioritising which bills to pay first. I can never find time to chill out like my midwife advises.

It hasn't been the easiest pregnancy, especially now I'm a month into the last trimester. Aside from the haemorrhoids, swollen ankles, bladder the size of a marble and the fact that it looks as if I'm smuggling a hippo under these pyjamas, the hospital's Maternity Assessment Centre has me recording my rising blood pressure twice a day and going for baby scans once a fortnight. I keep telling them, after three miscarriages, it's the waiting that's making me a bundle of nerves and encouraging its climb. But they're having none of it.

I should be cutting down my working days but that's out of the question now that mine is the only wage coming in. Finn is working sixteen-hour days, installing two new bathrooms and helping his dad outside with masonry repairs and the removal and installation of windows. Their work has saved us a small fortune. But we'll be living on our credit cards if I go on maternity leave now.

Even Debbie is making an effort, which is disconcerting. She left a vase of yellow lilies in the Annexe kitchen for me last week, along with a pregnancy pampering kit containing moisturisers and a scented candle. It almost feels as if we might've drawn a line under everything that came before the pregnancy. Either that or she's hired a bloody good surgeon to repair the bite marks in her tongue. I can't lie and say a small part of me isn't waiting for her to slip up.

She's only irritating when she insists on being involved in everything baby-related. Again, Finn thinks I'm exaggerating, but she invited herself along when we went shopping for nursery furniture and had an opinion on each cot, changing table, baby sling, monitor and pushchair. Then when Finn spotted one too many of my side-eyes, he interjected, supporting me over her on my choice of breast pump.

I've stopped telling my friends on our group WhatsApp chats about how she irks me because they think I'm ungrateful. Even when I recall the passive-aggressive things Debbie's said, such as 'I wish I could eat like you without feeling guilty' or 'It's nice to see a girl of your age who's not obsessed with her appearance', they tell me I'm reading too much into it. And the friends who've also been pregnant tell me she sounds like a godsend for wanting to be so involved.

Anyway, it will be impossible to finish the whole house before the baby arrives two months from now, so we have split it into sections. Phase one is the lounge, kitchen diner, downstairs cloak-room, office, upstairs main bathroom, our bedroom, the nursery and rear garden. When we can afford it, we'll make a start on the rest.

'Ow! That hurts!' Finn's knuckles have finally pinpointed the exact location in my shoulder causing me the most angst.

'It's supposed to,' he says, digging deeper and moving the knot in a circular motion until it eases. Then he starts massaging my shoulders before his lips brush against my neck and ear. I'm tired and I ache and I want to protest but he knows exactly the right buttons to press no matter how shattered I feel. And before I know it, the iPad falls to the floor and, despite my considerable size, I'm straddling him and my hips are moving like Shakira's.

I have the day booked off work, so after breakfast I grab a lift to the house with Finn. On our way he talks about what else the nursery needs, suggesting stuff I'd never considered like a thermometer for the bath, a nappy bin, brushes to clean out milk bottles, Sudocrem for nappy rashes, never-ending packets of wet wipes, muslins and a blackout blind. How does he know all this stuff? He must have done his research. He's going to make a fantastic dad.

As our due date approaches, I've found myself missing my own parents. We have never been as close as he is to his, which is not necessarily a bad thing for me as I couldn't stand an overbearing mother like Debbie. But there have been occasions when I've quietly envied what the three of them have. Finn and I are both only children but I was raised to be independent from an early age. I'd make my own evening meal before Mum and Dad returned from work; they didn't chase me to do my homework and allowed me to pick my own clothes. For the last five years of my education I chose to go to boarding school and got the attention I needed from those I surrounded myself with. I didn't rebel in my teenage years because I had nothing to rebel against. Soon after Finn and I married and Dad won his prostate cancer battle, they announced an around-the-world sailing expedition. 'It's our time now,' Dad explained. I resisted asking, 'When wasn't it?'

When they failed to return after my first two miscarriages I didn't bother telling them about the third. And while they were delighted to be told via Skype that I was pregnant again, they failed to commit to a date on which they'd be coming back to meet their only grandchild. Sometimes I worry if their apathy might shape my attitude to parenthood.

Finn pulls up outside the house next to two vans. Dave and Debbie are already here. We really aren't far from the finishing post of this phase of work. Am I actually starting to see it as our home? An unexpected warm flutter appears in my stomach. It's either the baby moving or something inside me is shifting when it comes to this house.

I make my way upstairs to what will be the nursery. A painter-and-decorator friend of Finn's is coming tomorrow to strip the walls of this 1970s-style brown and yellow patterned wallpaper and to sand the floor and skirting boards. I have the new wallpaper picked out and some glow-in-the-dark stars to arrange across the ceiling.

The vibrations coming from the hammering downstairs go straight through me so I close the door, which mutes it slightly. The carpenter has done a great job of restoring the door's broken lock and handle. The sun pours through this window and is now able to bathe every nook and cranny in light since we had the apple trees pruned and conifers removed. It really is quite beautiful.

I suddenly remember the curtain fabric swatches I left in the back of Finn's van, but as I make my way towards the door, ripped wallpaper by the skirting board catches my eye. I get the urge to tear off a strip and it's as satisfying as pulling off sunburned skin. There's more wallpaper underneath it so I tear off a little more from down by the skirting board.

It's then that the sun highlights something I hadn't noticed before. There are lines, etched into the skirting board's paintwork. I move closer and it looks as if they make up the letter W. I rub a little of the dust off with my hand. There are more letters. There's a backwards S and a P. Actually, it's a word – it reads 'Save'.

Outside, a cloud appears and the room darkens. With the sleeve of my jumper, I hesitantly wipe more of it away until, eventually, I see a whole sentence. The letters are childlike in their appearance.

I squint just as the sun blooms and now I can read the whole thing.

I WILL SAVE THEM FROM THE ATTIC.

CHAPTER 11

FINN

'Finn! Come here!'

Straight away I assume the worst when Mia yells my name from upstairs. Our consultant's warning about her high blood pressure flashes in my head and I hurry up the staircase and meet Mia halfway.

'What's wrong?' I ask and look to her stomach. She's holding it and I panic. We've never even come close to reaching the seven-months mark with any of our other pregnancies but I thought we were home and dry with this one. *Not now*, I say to myself.

'I need you to look at something,' she says.

'Should we call an ambulance?'

'What?' She's confused. 'Oh God no, no, I'm sorry, it's not the baby.'

I let out a long breath. 'Jesus, you scared me to death.'

She apologises again. 'I found something in the nursery, words carved into the skirting board.'

Mum and Dad have joined us now, having heard her cries.

'Is she okay?' Mum directs this to me, and I nod.

'Words? What are you talking about?' I ask Mia.

'Someone's etched something into the skirting board behind the door: "I will save them from the attic."'

'It's someone's idea of a joke,' Dad says dismissively.

'I'm not so sure,' Mia adds. 'What does it mean? Who are "them" and why are "they" in the attic?'

I shrug.

'If the last people living here had kids,' continues Dad, 'it's probably one of them with an overactive imagination. Remember what you were like when you were young, Finn? You convinced yourself you had an invisible sister and insisted we bought her Christmas and birthday presents.'

I cringe. *Tan-Tan.* I'd forgotten about her.

Mia's expression tells me she's not convinced this message is as innocent as my make-believe sibling.

'Finn,' Dad says, 'we need to get back to plastering before the wall starts drying out.' He starts to head back downstairs, but stops when nobody joins him.

I follow Mia into what will be our son's nursery. 'See?' she says and points to the skirting board. I lower myself to my knees and wipe away a little more of the dust. I read it aloud – it says just what she said it did – and turn to her.

Mia is clutching her belly again as if protecting our baby from an unknown threat. I need her to stay calm. I know what she can be like when she winds herself up. Last month she watched a documentary on YouTube about a brother and sister who went missing from their garden years ago and were never found. It was all she could talk about for days. 'How are we going to keep our baby safe?' she kept asking, but nothing I said assured her.

'What do you think?' she asks now.

'Dad's right,' I say. 'It's just kids messing around.' I look to Mum. She's usually as cool as a cucumber but even she looks a bit spooked by this.

'We need to go up there and look,' Mia says determinedly.

'The attic?' says Dad. 'There's only a couple of packing cases up there, isn't there, Finn?'

'Packing cases?' she repeats. 'What was in them?'

Dad shakes his head. 'We didn't look. There was no need to.'

'Until now.'

'Whoever wrote that is probably just talking about some old toys they didn't want their parents to get rid of,' Mum says. 'I put Finn's Buzz Lightyear and cars in our loft when he grew out of them. They're still up there somewhere. We should dig them out for the baby.'

'So Buzz and Woody are leaving messages for us on skirting boards, are they?' Mia snaps. 'Finn, I'm not going to rest until I know what's in those cases.'

And if I know my wife like I think I do, she won't.

CHAPTER 12

MIA

Finn takes a metal pole with a hook on the end and detaches the latch on the attic door. The hinges creak as it opens and we all duck as a wooden ladder falls with alarming speed until it hits the floorboards.

It wobbles as Finn climbs it, followed by Dave. Debbie waits with me at the base and we both stare up at the dark hole they disappear into. She clutches my hand; I flinch but she doesn't let go. Perhaps she's human after all. Above us, one of them flicks a light switch but, a second later, there's a ping and the bulb blows.

'Do we have any bayonet lightbulbs left?' shouts Dave, and Debbie calls back that she doesn't think so. They use the torches on their phones instead.

'I don't like this,' says Debbie nervously. She raises her voice up into the hole above us. 'It's an old house, Finn; it's not safe up there. You should come down. We should wait until we know the floorboards are secure and then look around.'

'Don't worry,' Finn shouts back and I hear him shuffling away from the hatch and along the ceiling directly above us. 'Okay, I see the packing cases,' he shouts, 'but the lids are nailed shut.'

I grab a screwdriver lying on the floor and begin to make my way up the ladder.

'What are you doing?' asks a horrified Debbie.

'It's fine.'

'Darling,' she protests. I hate that she's started calling me this. 'You're more than seven months pregnant. You can't be climbing up there.'

I'm not used to her caring about my welfare, but regardless, I can't stop myself from staring at her walking stick and sniping, 'Well you certainly can't.' I continue my ascent. 'I'll stay at the top, I won't go inside,' I concede. 'You stand on the bottom rung and keep it steady.'

I pass the screwdriver to Finn, who opens his mouth to complain about my stunt but knows from the look I shoot him that it'll fall on deaf ears. Not only that, now that I'm here I'm staying put until I know for sure if I have blown that skirting board message out of all proportion.

He passes his phone to his dad and I take out mine from my pocket, turning on the flashlight and setting the video to record. Finn pushes the tool under the rim of the packing case and prises it open. He repeats the action on the next side. The torchlight catches the first few raised nails and it takes all his strength before it lifts. We look to one another through the gloom. I don't know what I'm expecting to find in there, but my imagination is in overdrive. Every horror film that scared me to death as a girl is flashing before me, from clowns in drains to burns victims with razors for fingers. A tense Finn then pulls the lid off as his dad shines the light inside. They go quiet and my heart wants to beat its way out of my chest.

'What is it? What's in there?' I ask. An eternity passes before he answers.

'Just old rolls of wallpaper and cans of paint,' Finn says, and my relief is palpable.

'And the second one?'

That opens more easily. 'Same,' he says, and I now feel utterly stupid for making them go up there. I blame my bloody pregnancy hormones for having me up and down like a yoyo. I don't like looking irrational in front of Debbie, but to be fair, she was every bit as anxious as I was.

'Okay,' I say as Finn turns around. His torch catches the corner of the room, a wall, but there's an odd, small gap where it reaches the roof. He doesn't appear to have noticed it but I have. 'What's that?' I ask and grab my phone.

'What's what?'

'Behind you, direct your light in the corner like I am.'

He does as I ask. It's more obvious with a third beam. 'Huh. The house doesn't end there,' he says. 'Dad, does that wall look like it's been added?'

'Maybe, but if it has been then it's probably for insulation purposes,' says Dave. 'Back in the 1950s it was common to reduce loft space or lower it to keep it warmer.'

I'm not convinced and neither is Finn as he moves towards this additional wall and starts pushing at it with the palm of his hand.

'We shouldn't be messing around with that until we know how secure the floor behind it is,' Dave advises. 'You don't want bricks crashing through the ceilings of bedrooms we've only just re-plastered.'

But Finn is now equally as keen to discover what lies behind it as I am. Eventually he finds one loose brick and dislodges it. It falls into the other side, landing with a thud.

'What's happening?' asks Debbie below me, startled by the thump.

'It looks like another room,' says Finn, flashing his light into the hole. 'And there's something in there.'

'Please come down, Finn, it's not safe,' Debbie says.

'What's inside?' I ask.

'I can't quite see.'

Finn follows me down the ladder to borrow a mallet and a lamp from one of the workmen in the lounge. Debbie makes one more attempt at talking her son into not returning as he ascends it again but he's not listening. And neither am I when I too reach the top rung. I point my phone at Finn as he sets to work demolishing enough wall for him to enter and for us to see inside. The light from the lamp illuminates this hidden room. The first thing I notice is a chimney breast with missing bricks, creating a hole in the centre. Then I focus on several rectangular objects, standing on their sides on the floor. The closest one has a pair of others just like it set behind it, with a row of four arrayed beyond those two in the same fashion. The formation spreads out into a V, like a flock of geese mid-flight, only the objects are positioned on the floor.

'Are they suitcases?' I say, squinting.

'I think so,' Finn replies and I notice him inch away from them.

There's seven of them. It's hard to tell under so much dust, but they appear to be different colours, though all are the same size. And there's a red letter embossed on each of them, a P.

'What's that in front of them?' Before each suitcase is a small pile of something.

'Clothes,' says Finn. He turns to his dad, who's now as apprehensive as his son. Finn picks up a bag and the dust makes him sneeze. 'Kids' clothes in a shrink-wrapped bag,' he says sombrely.

'Perhaps we should go back downstairs and leave this until another time,' suggests the normally unflappable Dave.

I feel myself becoming light-headed. I can't be sure if it's my blood pressure or if I'm just winding myself up. Like Finn, the heavy air starts making me sneeze.

'We need to look inside one,' I say.

'Why?' he asks.

'Because they're in our attic. Open one.'

He reluctantly fiddles with the catches of one case until eventually it pops open. However, the lid is so tight and won't budge no matter how hard he tries to pull it. In the end, Dave takes hold of the case while Finn yanks it. Then the top opens up but with such force that Dave lets go and loses his balance, falling to his knees.

There's an immediate smell of decay, but it's not overpowering. Finn shines his light into the case but, to begin with, neither of us can work out what we are looking at. It's a large, solid lump of something, dark brown in colour, almost black. Then I recognise fur and assume it's a cat or a dog. No wait, is that hair? Yes it is. And I see it's attached to a skull. A human skull, only small. It's then that I realise it belongs to a child.

I'm looking at the mummified remains of a child.

My legs start to shake uncontrollably and I drop the phone on the rim of the loft hatch. But before I can steady myself, I'm falling backwards, all the way down, my wrist hitting the ladder before I land on the floor below with a heavy thwack and everything turns black.

PART TWO

CHAPTER 13
ONE YEAR EARLIER

'You're the last one,' I whisper as I stare deep into his lifeless grey eyes. His limbs are flopped by his side and his skin is warm to the touch as my hands glide across his face and arms. The pinky-red impressions left by my fingers around his neck are beginning to fade. I stroke his hair before finally, I hold his hand. It feels so small in mine.

My swansong needed to be someone special. And when I saw a boy with dark-blond curls, a freckled nose and cheeks, walking home alone from school, I instantly knew I had found who I was looking for. He was the spitting image of my brother George. And for the first time in all these years, this child's circumstances were of no consequence. I was not trying to save him from anything. His death was a selfish one. I killed him because I wanted to.

This moment marks the end of an era.

I'm on my knees amongst the golden wheat fields on this beautiful afternoon. The crops ahead of me stretch far into the horizon and it won't be too long before the farmers begin their harvesting. The beauty that engulfs me will vanish and so will the boy. But both will live on inside me.

The location wasn't an easy reach. First, I had to drag him through woodland, wincing and cursing as the sharp prickles of bracken tore at my bare arms. But the colours surrounding us are so vivid and the landscape so perpetual that it was too enticing to ignore. I am blessed that I get to share these final moments with him here.

I palm his eyes shut and begin to carefully strip him down to his underwear.

◆ ◆ ◆

Weeks ago, when the familiar urge escalated from a nip to a bite, I chose my location in a Bristol housing estate and wore a police officer's uniform I bought in a car boot sale a couple of years back.

I approached another young boy not entirely dissimilar to this one in a park and asked his name. 'I'm glad I've found you,' I said and informed him with urgency that my colleagues and I had been out searching for him as his mum had been rushed to hospital after being hit by a car. He trusted me immediately and, with tears pouring down his cheeks, we hurried in the direction of my parked vehicle.

'Everything alright, Connor?' a woman asked as she appeared from nowhere with a child of her own. *Damn it*, I thought. *She knows him.*

'Mummy's in hospital,' he sobbed.

The woman turned to me. 'What's happened to Sue?' asked the panicked friend. 'Is she alright?'

'I need to get my radio from the car,' I informed her. 'Can you keep an eye on Connor for a moment?'

'Sure,' she replied, her confusion outweighed by her need to comfort the boy.

Once out of sight and back at my vehicle, I drove away.

It had been a close call and was reported in the news the next morning as a 'failed abduction'. To my relief, the police artist's impression of me could have been anyone.

There had been a handful of other failures over the years, but that one left an indelible impression on me. If I don't stop now, then it's a certainty I'm going to get caught soon. I have escaped capture for so long thanks to thorough preparation and determination – plus a little good fortune thrown in. But modern technology and streetwise children are also making it harder for me to do this.

Take that girl in North Yorkshire last year, for example. I was forced to hurry my final ritual after her watch made a pinging sound. I'd already disabled her phone, thinking that was enough to keep her off-grid. But I hadn't considered there might be a tracking device on her smartwatch too. I had barely spent any time with her when someone tried to locate her. If I hadn't sped up my process, she'd have soon been reported absent and the police would've used cell towers to pinpoint her last location. I will forever regret being unable to treat her with the respect she deserved.

I'm also calling time because my judgement isn't what it used to be. I researched that girl's watch afterwards – someone had paid more than £300 for it. She was not as impoverished as her appearance suggested. Then I think about the child I picked out in Devon because of the holes in her jeans and pastel shades in her hair, like paint that hadn't been washed out. She too looked as if she came from nothing. But when her disappearance made the news later that week, I learned her mother was a company director and her father a pharmacist. Appearances are now so deceptive.

There are of course other ways for me to find children than to break cover and go scouting for them. I'm internet savvy and I can confidently work my way around message boards, chat rooms, social media and direct messaging. I once attempted to meet with a child who thought I was a ten-year-old girl he'd been messaging on Snapchat. I watched from a distance as he waited in playing fields but something about it didn't sit right. It felt I was cutting corners to lure him there. At the very last minute I walked away, and by the time I reached the car, I'd deleted all trace of my online presence.

Some technology, however, benefits me. For years I relied on maps and newspaper clippings on library microfiches to narrow down areas to strike in unfamiliar towns. Now, property apps and online street views give me a flavour of a location before I even travel there. But no matter where I visit, CCTV is the enemy. Cameras keep a record of where I have been and how long I was there. Car parks remember my number plate; buses, motorbikes and cyclists can all be fitted with helmet or dashboard lenses, and even my own car works against me with its onboard computer system recording every journey I take. It's all just too exhausting.

So for that and all the other reasons I have mentioned, I am bidding farewell to this life while it still remains my decision to make.

My attention returns to completing the task in hand. Rigor mortis typically sets in after three to four hours, so while he is still malleable, I take his limp, feather-light body and gently fold his torso and legs in half, bending his arms and neck so that he fits inside my suitcase. I hear the crack of his wrist as it snaps in two and I apologise to him. I close the lid, and for the final time, fresh air brushes across his skin. Then I leave his clothes stacked neatly in front of it and sealed in a shrink-wrapped bag.

I take several steps back and stare at the beauty I have created for long enough to ensure every inch of this scene is framed and sealed in my memory. In the future, each time I return to this moment, I will remember it in miniscule detail. Nothing will escape me, from the shape and shade of the clouds above us to the direction in which the suitcase casts a shadow. Each rock, each stone, each branch of the trees ahead of us will feed me for the rest of my days.

Finally, when I have taken everything I need from the moment, I pick up the suitcase and the boy and I leave as we arrived. Us together but me alone.

CHAPTER 14
MIA, 2019

I can just about make out the sound of a siren and I awake with a start.

I open my eyes but my vision is blurred so I don't recognise what I can make out of my surroundings. *Where am I?* I rack my brain.

My last memory, it occurs to me with a desolate feeling, is of regaining consciousness on a stretcher in the back of an ambulance, an oxygen mask strapped to my face and my brain throbbing like it wanted to burst out of my skull. When I tried to move, I realised I'd been strapped in and my head and neck were tightly packed. It was only when a sharp pain jabbed me in the stomach that, to my horror, I remembered I was pregnant.

'Please don't panic,' said Finn, his words undermined by his terrified expression. He was sitting with me, jammed into a tiny seat with his back to the ambulance's side.

'The baby,' I gasped before I blacked out again.

So it makes sense that I've woken up in hospital, I think.

'You're safe,' comes Debbie's voice. I open my eyes further and through the fog of pain medication I now see her sitting next to my hospital bed. My unborn baby boy is the first thing on my mind. Debbie's hand is resting on my arm but I yank it away to feel my pregnancy bump. It isn't as firm as it was. But before I can cry out, she says, 'He's okay, darling,' and smiles, and I feel a warmth radiating from her that I don't recognise. 'You've had a caesarean,' she continues. 'He's only a wee thing at three pounds eight ounces, but the doctors say he's healthy. Finn is with him now in the special-care baby unit.'

'I want to see him,' I say groggily.

'You will, just not yet. You need to rest. I'll stay with you.'

My body refuses to play ball when I try to shift myself along the bed and prop myself up with my elbow.

'You need to be careful,' she warns. 'Your body has been through trauma. You're lucky – it could have been worse.'

'What's wrong with me?'

She tells me I have two broken ribs and bruising to my spine and head, and then there's the caesarean. I've also got multiple fractures to my wrist and I'm going to need an operation to set it properly in a couple of days. Only then do I spot the plaster cast. 'But the most important thing is, despite what you did, my grandson is okay,' she says. 'He is very lucky.'

I pause to absorb her words. *Despite what you did.* The sincerity in her timbre suggests she isn't deliberately apportioning blame, but even if she was, she'd have every right to. I almost killed my son, her grandson. The fact he is still alive has nothing to do with me but the surgeons who have cut him out of me and saved his life. Debbie passes me a tissue from her handbag along with my mobile phone that I'd left on the rim of the loft hatch.

'The suitcases,' I ask. 'Were there bodies in all of them?'

She bristles as if even the thought of it makes her queasy. 'We don't know, the police are there now. It's all just too horrible to contemplate. But please, don't think about that now. Close your eyes and relax.'

I do as she asks and I'm soon back under a heavy blanket of painkillers.

Later that night I awake again, and after a tearful reunion with Finn, he and a nurse settle me into a wheelchair and he pushes me along to the neonatal unit to meet our little boy. To begin with, all I can focus on is the plastic incubator shielding him from the dangers of the world – like me – then the beeping and flashing lights of the heart monitor attached to his toe and the tube giving him fluids intravenously. I can barely look at him. He is so, so small, skinny and vulnerable, and I did this to him.

'He'll be staying in here for a couple of days while they monitor him,' Finn explains. 'But from what they've seen so far, the doctors say he's doing great. They might even let us have skin-to-skin tomorrow.'

I hope Finn didn't see me recoil at that suggestion. The last thing our fragile baby needs is me anywhere near him. I'm a risk to him. I don't deserve him.

Later, two police officers appear in my room – a uniformed officer whose name I don't catch and DS Mark Goodwin, a detective investigating the bodies in the attic who has also been appointed as our family liaison officer. They take my statement and I tell them everything I can remember.

'What do you know?' Finn asks them when I have finished.

'For now,' says DS Goodwin, 'all I'm allowed to say is that the deaths are historic and appear to have been deliberate.'

'Are they all children?' I say.

'It's likely, yes.'

I close my eyes and shake my head. For now, I don't want to know anything else.

BEDFORDSHIRE POLICE PRESS CONFERENCE TRANSCRIPT

MEDIA BRIEFING LED BY DETECTIVE SUPERINTENDENT ADEBAYO OKAFOR

Good afternoon everyone and thank you for joining us. I will begin by reading out a brief statement of the facts as we are aware of them so far. As widely reported, human remains of seven individuals have been located in the attic of a property at 45 High Street, Stewkbury, during renovation work. Today, Scenes of Crime officers remain at that location in their search of the property. Officers will continue to gather evidence from the scene for some time to come. Bones from the remains have been examined by a Home Office pathologist and we can now establish all the victims died between the late 1970s and early 1980s. We can also confirm that all of the victims were children – three male and four female. DNA is being recovered from their remains and will be entered into a database of children who went missing over that time period. I will now open up the floor to questions from members of the press.

Have you identified any of the children yet and have their families been informed?

No, not yet. This won't be an overnight process as we are working from a time before DNA testing.

Several families have come forward, convinced their children were in that attic. How much longer will they have to wait?

I'm sure that we all want these questions answered, especially those families. However, to establish what happened, we need to go through the procedures with our dedicated team so that no mistakes are made. As soon as we have the information, the families will be informed before anyone else.

Do you know how the children died yet, and was it on the premises?

The cause of deaths will be revealed in the pathologist's full report which we expect to receive in a fortnight or so and which we will release soon after.

Have the previous occupants of the house been located yet?

We are following up a significant number of leads after a response from both current and former villagers, alongside calls to our dedicated hotline. But as of now, the search continues.

Thanks for your attendance today, a further news conference will be held tomorrow to update you all on the progress of the investigation.

CHAPTER 15

MIA

It's the first time we have returned to the house since our discovery three weeks ago. I didn't know if I was ready to go back inside, but to my relief, the police have taken that decision out of our hands.

I'm clutching Finn's hand so tightly I'm worried I might break his fingers. But I'm scared that by letting go, the tornado that swept us off our feet might come back and finish us off. Ahead of us are police officers, CSI investigators, photographers, camera operators and forensic teams. Away from here we've had to deal with the endless questions from friends and turned down unrelenting requests for interviews with journalists and TV shows. It's all just too much.

Finn and I don't say anything. We simply stand here and take in the crime scene. Large white perimeter boards and fencing hide the house itself from public view. Even the garden is mostly out of sight. From where we are standing up against the police tape, I can just about see an orange mechanical digger. I assume that's for the garden.

Sonny sneezes in his sleep and brings us out of our contemplative quiet. Our baby is strapped to his father's chest in a grey wraparound sling. He is tiny and it dwarfs him. Finn turns to look at me, as if expecting me to be the first to say something. But I'm at a loss as to how to express myself now that we're here. There's no rulebook for a scenario like this. He squeezes my hand back more gently, as if it might offer me some comfort. It doesn't. A phone pings and I realise it's mine. The screen reveals it's a message from Debbie that simply reads *Be strong*, followed by a heart emoji. I text back thanking her.

My pulse thrums as a uniformed police officer checks with his superiors that we are who we say we are. He pays me more attention than Finn, likely taking in the faint remains of the bruising scattered across my face and arms from my ladder fall.

He lifts up the blue and white tape, allowing us to enter this cordoned-off section of the road. We are greeted by DS Mark Goodwin, who has been keeping us up to speed with developments and invites us to join him inside a blue tent erected in a corner of the garden. We are alerted to a faint buzzing sound in the sky and all three of us glance upwards. It's a drone circling the property.

'Is that one of yours?' Finn asks.

'No, that one is most likely press or the public,' he replies. 'It's annoying but, legally, there's nothing we can do.'

Inside the tent are plastic seats and tables, plus tea and coffee caddies. 'Our CSI team take their breaks in here,' he continues and beckons us to sit. As if on cue, two figures appear, dressed head-to-toe in white polythene suits, two pairs of gloves on each hand, plus foot and head coverings. Only when they strip off their protective suits and bin them can I tell they're male. They sit down and talk as they tuck into pre-packaged sandwiches like it's an ordinary day at the office.

Mark, as DS Goodwin asks us to call him, is friendly but professional and seems sympathetic to our situation. He's taller and broader than Finn, likely around our age but with a salt-and-pepper beard. He is what my mum would refer to as 'a safe pair of hands'.

'As I explained to you on the phone, I can't take you inside the house because it's an ongoing investigation,' he begins. 'But as you were keen to try and understand what's been happening, my senior investigating officer has said I can at least play you video footage we have recorded as we've worked. I know the press is keen for any new angles on the story but we prefer to control the narrative where possible, and I'd appreciate it if you kept what you're going to see to yourselves. I should also remind you of the extensive search going on in there. Our team of officers are specially trained to be absolutely thorough, so this might be upsetting.'

Finn and I nod and DS Goodwin removes his phone from his pocket. He keeps his hands on the device as if we're readying ourselves to snatch it away from him. The footage begins at the front door and, from what I can see, the porch remains the same. But the entrance hall now has virtually no floor, just gaping holes with planks of wood to walk across. The wall between the dining room and the lounge no longer exists and I can't recall whether we took it out or if it's something they've done. In the upstairs bedroom where I found the message etched into the skirting board, there are little yellow plastic markers scattered about the floor, each of them numbered. I shudder as to how many children were hurt in a room we planned for our nursery.

There are several sheets of paper taped to the walls containing plans of the house and someone is also measuring a wall. 'We use structural engineers to measure the inside and outside to see if they are the same length and width,' DS Goodwin says. 'It saves having to tear them down.' *Small favours*, I think.

It continues like this from room to room until I become desensitised to the chaos. There are more drilled holes in the lounge floor and walls; DS Goodwin explains it's so they can insert endoscopic

69

cameras to search inside for remains. Our new plasterboard looks as if it's been used as a firing range.

I'm momentarily distracted by an itch under the plaster cast that covers my wrist and forearm. Three silver metal pins are poking out, keeping four separate fractures in place as they heal. I've already undergone two operations and I hope to have the cast removed within the month.

The camera snakes its way up the staircase and along the landing. It points upwards and, for the first time, I'm aware that several sections of ceiling have been taken down. I can now see directly to the underside of the roof. A cold shiver runs through me when I recall the moment the first suitcase opened to reveal the mummified body of a child.

I reach out to stroke my sleeping baby's head as he leans on Finn's chest, but withdraw it sharply before I make contact. If Finn notices, he says nothing.

CHAPTER 16

FINN

Mia tightens her grip on my hand when the police footage reaches the attic. I don't stop to think before I blurt out loud, 'Well at least we don't have to go far to get new luggage.' By the time Mia glares at me I already know it was a stupid thing to say. Gallows humour, I think they call it. Neither of us is thinking straight. Stress and sleep deprivation are messing with our heads. Now that copper is looking at me like I'm a dick, and it's not for the first time. If he's not directing most of what he says to Mia, then he eyeballs me like I'm guilty of something.

We watch as the camera operator returns to where the footage began, in the porch. The parquet flooring stacked up in piles triggers something and my eyes unexpectedly start filling up. That flooring was an eBay find and I travelled more than a hundred miles to pick it up from the stately home that was getting rid of it. Then, for the best part of a week, I spent every night sanding, varnishing and slotting each piece together. Now I see some of them are broken, scarred or chipped from where they've been jimmied up to look underneath. All that wasted effort. I wipe my eyes with my free hand.

I watch as another CSI drills into the wall and a dog handler appears with a springer spaniel on a lead. It sniffs the hole briefly then wanders off. I assume that means there's nothing – or no one – in there.

'When do you reckon this will all be over?' I ask Goodwin.

'Not for some time, I'm afraid,' he says to Mia, not to me.

'How much is some time? A couple of weeks?' I persist.

When he shakes his head, I know I'm not going to like his answer.

'Finn, an investigation like this involving multiple historic homicides can take months. We are in it for the long haul.'

'Months?' I repeat. 'But this is our house.'

'I know that, but our warrant allows us, by law, to take every step needed to ensure we are one hundred per cent confident there are no more bodies inside.'

'Can't you bring in more people to speed it up?'

He looks at me as if I'm an idiot once again. 'Because there's so much evidence to gather and preserve in a place this size, it's a job that requires specially trained, licensed officers. There is no urgency here.'

'Not for you, mate, but there is for us.'

He returns his attention once more to my wife, as if she's capable of being more rational than I am. He wouldn't be thinking that if he'd been around her twenty-four hours a day for the last few weeks like I have. She's had more ups and downs than a bucking bronco.

'If we cut corners or try and speed things up then we are at risk of making mistakes,' he adds. 'We can't risk missing anything.'

I know that he's right, but it doesn't help our circumstances. I just want shot of this place, but I can't see that happening any time soon. In my naivety I contacted an old schoolmate who works as an estate agent to see what the chances would be of a quick sale once this is over. He laughed, then asked me, 'Who in their right mind would want to buy a house where seven kids were murdered?' He reckoned we should consider tearing it down and rebuilding it or selling the land instead. Goodwin has already told us the Home Office will pay for all repairs if we decide to stay. But we can't afford to build another place here, and selling the land means we'd take a massive financial hit. We're fucked if we do, fucked if we don't.

Personally, I reckon I could live here. I don't believe in ghosts. Once we put our stamp on the place, it'd feel less like a morgue, I'm sure. However, when I suggested it to my horrified wife, she made it clear pretty quickly that she wasn't having any of it. Perhaps in time she might change her mind. But from what Goodwin says, it's not a decision we're going to need to make in a hurry. So, for now, we've no choice but to live with my folks.

Mia asks Goodwin for an update about the bodies again, but to be honest, I've had enough of hearing about it for today. I know that sounds harsh but Mia and I need to focus less on the dead children we never knew and more on the living one I'm holding. My family is my priority, not them.

She tried to bring it up with me earlier this morning when she saw on the breakfast news that one of the kids had been identified. But I'd already tuned out. I don't know if it's a boy or a girl. I don't even care. I'm trying hard not to let these murders dominate our lives but they're coming between us a lot lately. She accused me of being cold and unfeeling but I'm not. I'm just better at compartmentalising than her. Whereas everything in her head lately is untethered, as if her thoughts are colliding with one another like bumper cars in a dodgem ride. I get it, I tell her – what she saw, then her fall and our baby coming early, has hit her hard physically and emotionally. But she's not alone. It has been tough on us both.

And now she needs to see that we have someone else to prioritise above ourselves.

Every time I look at my son I think of how lucky he is to be alive. When Mia fell off the ladder and smacked her head hard on the floorboards I was convinced I was going to lose both of them. I was totally helpless in the back of the ambulance watching as she slipped in and out of consciousness, and for the first time in my life, I prayed. God, if He or She or it exists, must have been listening because here we all still are.

Goodwin slips his phone back into his jacket as two more forensic CSIs enter, removing their plastic head coverings and mopping their brows. Goodwin grins at Sonny as my boy turns his head to gauge his surroundings. I find myself clutching Sonny a little tighter to my chest and moving my body so that he is out of Goodwin's line of sight. Then a sickly sweet, familiar smell grabs my attention and I know it's nappy time. I don't bother asking Mia for her help as she is preoccupied. So I take Sonny to the corner of the tent to change him.

When we return a few minutes later, I don't think she even realised we'd gone.

CHAPTER 17

MIA

I pull the duvet up close to my chin. I've started sleeping with the bedside lamp on and a Spotify playlist of ambient music playing in the background. If I'm not distracted, then I cannot stop thinking about the children in the attic. In the dark silence of my bedroom, I can hear as clear as day the click of the suitcase latches opening. I can smell the decay seeping from it and I can see the shape of that poor mite's skull.

It's selfish, I know, but the only positive outcome of my fall from the ladder more than two months ago now is that I didn't have time to make sense of anything else up there. Poor Finn saw those remains for longer than I did. He hasn't told me if that image haunts me like it does me and I haven't asked. We used to talk about everything but now we brush so much under the carpet there's an elephant-shaped lump there.

I toss and turn, unable to find a comfortable position. The painkillers I took earlier for a persistent headache must contain caffeine because, when I turn the music off, my active brain moves up a gear and I'm staring into that suitcase again. It's not just at night when I'm like this. I can be looking at Sonny's outfits and they'll bring back images of shrink-wrapped children's clothes placed in front of the cases. Or if I close my eyes in the shower my legs feel as if they're about to buckle and I'm going to plummet down that ladder again. My brain is trapped in a moment it won't let me leave. I obsess about those children more than I do about my own son. And Finn knows it.

I see how he looks at me when I'm with Sonny; appraising me, studying me to see if my baby and I have connected as we should have. But I don't think Finn has ever once asked himself why I am so distant. He has never tried to understand what's turned me into someone who's only going through the motions of being a mother. He doesn't know I'm like this because I spend my life in perpetual fear. I'm so scared that if I allow myself to completely fall in love with Sonny, I'll make another careless mistake and something even more terrible will happen to him. The weight of responsibility feels like too much so I am keeping him at arm's length for his own sake. Through my own stupidity I brought him into this world too soon. I couldn't live with myself if he left it just as quickly. It would break me.

Debbie has been an incredible support. I'm not sure what I would do without her. 'I'm sure you're doing the best you can,' she tells me. But her encouragement falls on deaf ears. With my wrist still in plaster and my caesarean wound still fragile, I struggle to even pick him up, so she changes Sonny's nappy and clothes, comforts him when he cries, and feeds him milk I'm expressing into bottles because I'm too frightened to allow him to latch on to my breast in case I fall asleep and he chokes. I witness her do all of this without complaint and with the ease of a seasoned pro. And I worry, when I'm healed, will I ever be the mother Sonny needs? She is more of a parent to him than I am.

I've come to realise that I misjudged her. I based what I thought I knew about parenting on my own mum's hands-off approach. I thought Debbie's behaviour to be extreme, but this is how mothers are supposed to be, protective of their brood even way into adulthood. They fight your corner.

My body will soon be mended, but my head is in far from normal working order. Debbie is right when she says Sonny is a miracle baby and lucky to be alive considering how he came into the world. And I'm forever reminding myself of the stupid risks I took with him before he was born. My only job was to grow him and protect him and I was too selfish and stubborn to get that right. I didn't cut down on my working hours despite my high blood pressure, and then I almost killed him by climbing that ladder.

I don't know how I'm ever going to be the mum he needs or deserves. I'm just grateful I can trust Debbie to help me.

CHAPTER 18
THREE YEARS EARLIER

Today marks 372 days since my last kill. And if I don't strike again soon, I fear for my sanity. It's begun to consume my days, thinking about all those poor souls out there who need me and who I'm letting down on this self-imposed sabbatical. By doing nothing, I am as complicit as everyone else.

Until recently, it wasn't an urge that controlled my everyday life. I didn't pass schools or trawl shopping centres targeting the next one. I went about my day the same way as Joe Public. I admit there were times, back in the late 1990s, when I gave in to my urges more frequently, and struck twice, and even three times, in a calendar year. Not now. I have limited myself to helping one child per year, because if I spread myself too thinly, I risk being exposed. Multiple disappearances of children with similar profiles within too short a time or close a radius creates a pattern. And as more police forces work together and share information, red flags are raised and my safety is compromised.

But I can't ignore these visceral urges. They've started targeting me at night when I'm at my most vulnerable and there are fewer opportunities to distract myself. In the darkness, I relive how I have helped the others, recalling each scene with clarity. However, it's no longer enough. The need to deliver the worthy into a better world is like having rats under my skin. They claw at my insides and tear at my flesh until they break through the surface.

So I cannot turn the other cheek any longer. This afternoon, I will do what I am trained to do. And the anticipation alone is enough to unleash a river of adrenaline coursing through me, rendering me light-headed and dizzy, almost. Every part of me is awakening.

You might not think it, but I possess enough self-awareness to question what I do. Many a time I have wondered if I'm fooling myself into believing I do it for the victims' sake when it's actually for my own satisfaction. I can't deny there's a small, selfish element to taking a life, a physical release that is hard to explain. But it's a by-product of what I do, not a reason. In doing one thing, I am enabling another. It's no different to giving money to charity. By helping someone in need, I feel better about myself.

I find myself sitting on a bench opposite a playground in Newmarket, and sipping coffee from a flask. I check the news headlines on my phone and take a bite from an apple. It's the nearby community centre I'm here to watch. Today it's a polling station and is buzzing with voters deciding whether our country should remain in or leave the European Union. I eye the centre up and down. Half of its windows have been boarded up and a CCTV camera above the door is dangling from its brackets. The housing estate behind it has also seen better days. It's a good location.

I'm counting on the high footfall working to my advantage because there's nothing memorable about me. I don't stand out and I'm not behaving oddly. My clothes are ordinary, my expression calm. I have made blending in an art form. No one will recall me.

Some of the children brought here today have been left to play outside as their parents put an X in a box. But they're rarely inside the centre long enough for me to make my approach unobserved. One lone boy, however, garners my attention, and I stare at him long and hard. He is short and bespectacled, his frame is slight, and headphones filter out the noise and presence of anyone around him. He fits the bill. I'll keep my eye on him. He arrived alone but if I take the right approach, we will leave together. He is already making my skin prickle.

It's in moments like these I can't help thinking how nice it would be to have a like-minded soul to enjoy these experiences with. I thought I had them once. I shared everything I knew with that person, I trusted them with my life and my freedom. But it takes strength, resilience and conviction to be someone like me, and as much as I wanted it for them, ultimately, they didn't have it in them.

I sank into a deep funk after we parted ways, something I managed to hide from all those around me. Eventually I dusted myself down and returned refreshed and rebooted – if a little bruised – but with the same purpose.

Watching parents come and go from here makes me dwell on my own. It's only as an adult and with the benefit of hindsight that I recognise how twisted and cruel their behaviour was. Yet there were glimmers of normality if you knew where to look. Along with my brother George, we celebrated Christmases, Easters and birthdays together, and like other families, we enjoyed spending the summer months on caravan holidays.

It was always just the four of us. There were no visits from aunts, uncles or cousins. I didn't even know if I had any. And I had no relationship with my paternal grandparents until I was twelve. From what they told me later, they had disowned my father for marrying Mum. I've considered this a lot over the years and I wonder if it was because they saw a darkness in her that my father didn't. I will never know who damaged who or if they met on a level playing field. All I can be sure of is that for the first decade of my life, they shaped me into the contradiction I am now. I am not like them yet I am them. I kill as they killed but not for the same reason. I kill to save others, not punish them. I walk my own path yet I am always aware of the outlines of my parents' footsteps before me. Killing is as natural to me as walking or blinking. It's like bursting a blister or taking a tablet for a headache.

Only, here in this playground, there will be no footsteps today, not mine and not my parents', because a television camera and reporter have arrived to interview voters. I don't need to be caught by a lens. So I screw the top of my flask on tightly, take my phone from my pocket and examine a map of this partially familiar town.

I'll drive to another area where the pickings may be richer yet poorer. Then I hesitate, taking one last look at the boy with the headphones. He will never know how unfortunate he is not to have met me.

CHAPTER 19
FINN, 2019

I am in a foul mood by the time I return to Mum and Dad's house.

I've just got back from an early evening emergency call-out to a boiler that had lost its pressure. It wasn't that urgent a job but they were insistent I came straight away, despite my higher call-out charge. I need the money so I was hardly going to refuse. Immediately, I could tell there was something a bit iffy about the job. The boiler was a brand-new model and the tap that controlled the pressure gauge had been turned to the off position. It was too stiff for it to have been accidental.

The customer was as fit as you like and really friendly when she ushered me in. I gave the boiler the once-over to make sure there were no other issues, but this woman wouldn't stop hovering while I worked. By now, she wasn't trying to hide that she knew who I was. She kept trying to get me to talk about the tough time we must've had lately, if I'd been inside the house since the bodies were found, how it had affected Mia and me. And she wasn't taking the hint from my one-word answers. They were the kind of questions a mate might ask you, not a total stranger, even if she's hot. She had a hidden agenda and I'd had enough.

'Who are you really?' I asked, squaring up to her.

'What do you mean?' She was a poor actress and easily intimidated.

'Cut the bullshit.'

She continued to protest as I packed up my tools and headed for the front door.

'My name is Aaliyah Anderson and I'm a freelance journalist,' she admitted finally. There was an air of desperation in her voice, as if she was seeing the biggest scoop of her career slipping through her fingers. 'Look Finn, people just want to hear your side of the story; what it was like being in that house, how it feels knowing all those kids' bodies were a few feet above you.'

'No comment,' I muttered and began walking up the driveway.

'How's Mia coping? I hear she's back in touch with her ex, Ellis Anders. Do you feel threatened by that?'

Without warning, a photographer appeared from behind a parked car and started clicking away, blinding me with the white of the flash. I pushed my way forwards and he wouldn't stop, which is when I really lost my rag. I grabbed the camera out of his hands and hurled it to the ground, breaking it. He called me all the names under the sun, but he was only a scrawny fella and didn't try and fight back, which I was grateful for because the mood I was in, I'd have kicked the shit out of him. I rummaged around the camera's debris until I found the memory card and snapped it in two. 'Come on, that's my livelihood!' he said, exasperated. But I was not feeling charitable.

I'm still angry now as I lock up the van on my parents' drive. My time has been wasted on a non-existent job I haven't been paid for and I've not eaten since lunchtime. Even from here, my stomach growls from the smell of meat cooking on the barbecue in the back garden. Before I join my parents, I stop at the Annexe to see if Mia and Sonny are there. I can't remember a time when she last met me with a kiss or even a 'How's your day been?'

I hear Sonny bawling before I open the door. It's funny how quickly you recognise what he wants by just his cries. This one is high-pitched and desperate and tells me he's hungry. *I know the feeling, son.* I call my wife's name but she doesn't answer. I find them both in the bedroom, her curled up in a foetal position on the bed, cradling her belly and wearing her headphones. Tinny music and drumbeats come from them. She has her back to Sonny, who lies in his carrycot next to her, his face bright red and his cheeks wet with tears. He's been crying for a while.

'Mia!' I say, picking up Sonny and repeating myself twice more before finally she blinks and sees me.

'Oh, hi,' she replies and slips her headphones off. Her smile is weak and forced.

'Didn't you hear him?' I don't disguise how pissed off I am. The bottom half of Sonny's Babygro is sodden. 'When's the last time you changed him?'

'Um . . .' She thinks. 'Earlier this afternoon.'

'It's almost eight o'clock! You need to stay on top of these things.'

'I'm sorry. I fell asleep, I was just waking up when you arrived.'

She's lying but I don't argue the point. I set about stripping off Sonny's clothes, throwing them into an overflowing wash basket and pulling a fresh nappy and clothing from the drawers under the changing table.

I glance at knackered Mia. Dark rings surround her eyes and her skin is pale. I keep telling her that she needs to go outside and get some sunlight but she doesn't listen. 'Did you get much sleep last night?' I ask.

'No.'

84

'Have you tried the tablets I bought?'

'I can't take them if I'm expressing.'

'Well maybe you should rethink not using formula. I bet Sonny won't notice the difference.'

'Of course he will.'

For the last week, I've been sleeping on the sofa bed in the lounge. Mia's constant tossing and turning and then waking up to feed Sonny means neither of us are getting any sleep, and I need my wits about me at work. I can't be bothered to argue tonight so I change the subject. 'Are you coming outside for dinner? Mum and Dad are doing a barbecue.' I hold a fresh and clean Sonny up in the air. His eyes are as brown as mine and I catch my reflection in them. He appears content.

'Do I have to?'

'It would be a nice thing to do.' Mia makes no effort to get off the bed. 'Are you coming then?'

She sighs and tells me she'll meet me outside once she freshens up. I take Sonny and a bottle of milk with me.

The sky is darkening when Mia finally appears. She's put a little make-up on. She ignores the cooked burgers and hot dogs cooling on the rack and gravitates towards the salad. She hasn't once acknowledged Sonny, whose head is peeking over his grandmother's shoulder.

'You should have a burger,' Mum says to her. 'The iron will do you good.'

I wait for Mia to argue. Instead, and without looking at Mum, she says, 'Okay,' and takes one. She barely nibbles at it.

'So, your text message earlier,' I direct to Dad. 'You said you wanted to talk to us about something?' He's not a great texter, or a great communicator, period. So he must have something important to say. He rests his bottle of beer next to a handful of empty ones on the table. He's started early again tonight, I think.

'Your mum and I want to help you,' he begins. 'We had a telephone conversation yesterday with the bank and they've given us the go-ahead to remortgage our house if we want to. It means we can lend you what you need to buy somewhere new.'

Their offer takes me aback and I remind them that, because the killings are historic and nothing to do with us, the Home Office will fork out for all the repairs.

'Yes, but that could take months and months,' Mum adds. 'I don't want to see you go, but you're going to need a place of your own sometime. This means you can buy it now and you can pay us back when you sell the other house.'

Mia looks up but I can't read her.

'Shouldn't you be putting that money back into the business?' I ask them.

'You and Sonny are our priorities,' Mum explains, before realising who she has excluded. 'You as in you and Mia, of course. There's a place just down the road that's up for sale and definitely worth a look.'

'The Michaels' house?'

Mum nods. 'It's in immaculate condition; they've only just had one of those Shaker-style kitchens fitted. And there's plenty of space outside for Sonny to play.'

This could be the answer to all our problems but I doubt Mia will see it that way. She'll tell me they're trying to control us.

'Well?' I ask her tentatively. 'What do you think?'

'It sounds great,' she says with a thin smile.

Mum and Dad glance at each other, then at me. We're all as surprised as one another.

'I've actually made an appointment to view it tomorrow afternoon,' Mum says, 'just in case you were interested. Because, mark my words, it'll go quickly.'

'We can do tomorrow, can't we?' I ask Mia.

'You go. You don't need me there.' Then she pushes the remains of her food to one side, tells us she's tired and heads back to the Annexe, leaving Sonny out here.

None of us is quite sure what to say next. Mum recently confided in me that she thought all wasn't right with Mia. I dismissed it because, to be honest, mental health is a minefield and I'd have no clue where to begin in helping her. But I'm starting to agree with Mum. It's more than just headaches and a lack of sleep that's troubling her.

CHAPTER 20

DEBBIE

'Tell me if I'm being daft,' I ask Dave once Finn retires to bed, taking my yawning grandson with him. 'But I'm worried about Sonny.'

'Why?'

'It's as if Mia is on autopilot. There's nothing there.'

'Can you blame her, after what she's been through? She just needs a little more time to adjust.'

'Maybe, but I can't shake the niggling feeling that there's more to it than that. I remember how intense and exhausting those first months of motherhood are. And she has the look of a woman who's really struggling.'

'Is there something else we could be doing?'

'Well, I already have Sonny with me most days, as I'm worried just how much attention he'd get if I wasn't there to pick up the slack.'

Dave gets up to take another beer from the cool box. His face looks pale, making the crimson birthmark on his forehead more striking. The outdoor lights illuminate his silhouette, and as they shine through his T-shirt, I'm alarmed by just how much weight he has lost. I need to bring it up with him. And perhaps I'll mention his alcohol intake too. But not tonight, because just now I'm more concerned by my daughter-in-law's behaviour.

'I've been reading up on it,' I add. 'And I'm convinced she's either got postnatal depression or she has a head injury from that fall.'

'She's had brain scans, and apart from the swelling that gives her the headaches, they found nothing wrong with her.'

'Yes, but doctors don't know everything, do they? I hate to say this, but what if Sonny isn't safe with her?'

'Debbie, it's great that you two are getting on so well and I see how much you're supporting her, but you have to give Mia the time and space to find her feet. Eventually she'll stop relying on you and she'll find her confidence.'

I refrain from admitting that I'm dreading that moment. 'You saw her tonight. She needs more than just space. We offered to buy her a bloody house and her response was nothing short of apathetic. She'd have been just as grateful if we'd offered her a cup of tea.'

'Perhaps you need to concentrate on your own health rather than Mia's,' he says. 'You know that stress and pushing yourself to the point of exhaustion can bring about complications.'

I roll my eyes. He's not listening to me. I don't need reminding that, physically, I'm already running on half the speed I should be. Three years ago I was diagnosed with Motor Neurone Disease. The fatigue and leg stiffness were so gradual that I dismissed it as the early onset of arthritis. But it all came to a head when I was shopping for the buffet for my fiftieth birthday party. My legs gave way for no reason and I fell to the floor in Aldi. It was Dave who insisted I saw my doctor. She sent me to a neurologist who, over the following months, tested and scanned my brain, took samples of spinal fluid and scanned my nerves and muscles. Eventually I was told it was MND.

It made for grim listening – a future filled with balance issues, increasingly stiff and weakening muscles, muscle cramps, an uncontrollable bladder, slurred speech and a rollercoaster of emotions as, gradually, my body shuts down. Then, eventually, it will kill me. My particular type, Primary Lateral Sclerosis, is rarer and slower than other versions and I should be grateful that I might live ten years if I'm lucky. Now I have seven left. Every day, the ticking of the countdown clock used to drown out almost every other sound. Then my grandson came along and now he is all I hear.

We make our way into the kitchen with crockery in hand, and I scrape uneaten food into the compost bin and load the dishwasher.

'I'm going to talk to her in the morning,' I say. 'I'll suggest Sonny moves in with us for the time being. We can put his carrycot next to my side of the bed.'

'And how is that going to help her in the long run?'

'Sonny is my priority, not Mia.'

'They come as a package.'

'There have been some women with undiagnosed postnatal depression who've killed their babies, you know. What if she's a danger to him? You've seen her with Sonny, there's a disconnect, isn't there? She isn't as hands-on as other mothers are.'

'Be fair. There are metal pins in her wrist and she's had a caesarean. She's limited with what she can do.'

'Stop defending her!' I snap. 'This isn't about not picking him up or changing his nappy. She sleeps too much during the day, she's distant and she's always in tears. I've caught her crying when she doesn't think anyone's watching. And she looks anywhere else in the room but at her child. Do you remember what I was like when I first brought Finn home? I couldn't stop staring at him.'

'You still can't.'

I allow his dig to pass. 'I can't just sit back and watch my grandson being neglected.'

'*Our* grandson.'

'Don't be pedantic.'

'And if that is the case,' he says, 'then I'm sure Finn is aware of it and handling it himself. Give them time. This is his family.'

'Or he could take your approach and spend his life with his head buried in the sand.' I shut my eyes tight, wishing I hadn't just said that.

'Then let's hope he learns from my mistakes,' Dave says, and then leaves me alone, smarting from his parting shot.

CHAPTER 21

EIGHTEEN YEARS EARLIER

I stop the car by the side of the road and turn the ignition off, but leave the radio on. Two politicians are tearing each other to shreds in a heated debate over whether Britain should join forces with America and start bombing the hell out of the Middle East in retaliation for 9/11.

When I think about the thousands of armed forces personnel who might one day be shipped off to fight if we ever go to war, it makes me think of George. As children, if we weren't playing football and cricket together then we were pretending to be soldiers. He'd create army assault courses for us in the garden, with strawberry netting to crawl under and golf clubs to carry instead of rifles. We'd smear our faces in wet soil for camouflage and use an egg timer to see who could complete it in the fastest time. I would give it my all to try and impress him but didn't care that he always beat me. I just wanted to be with my brother.

Some of my earliest memories are of that garden, of helping our father dig long, deep holes by the wall when we first moved in, of climbing the apple trees or playing hide and seek in the unused farmyard next door.

'Six years left to go,' George would remind me. 'Then I'll be old enough to join the army without Mum and Dad's permission and I'll never have to live in this house again.'

I hated it when he spoke like this. 'What will happen to me when you've gone?' I'd ask. He could never give me an answer.

It's George's birthday soon and I try to imagine how he might look now. Do we still resemble one another? Maybe he's still in the forces, his dark-blond curls now greying and cut military-grade short, his freckles perhaps fading with age. I picture him in his uniform, shiny medals with colourful ribbons attached to his jacket, rewards for successful tours of duty. But while I might no longer recognise him if he stood in front of me, I'd like to think that he is every inch the hero to others today as he was to me back then.

A little voice inside gnaws at me. *That's wishful thinking*, it whispers. *You know what happened to him*. I shake my head to silence it. I once hired a private detective to try and locate George. But several months and a few thousand pounds later, there was no proof that he ever existed beyond my memory. Not even a birth certificate, even though I have one of my own. Sometimes I wondered if he was a figment of my imagination; if I'd made him up to make life at home bearable.

'Are you okay?' my passenger asks me. They're sitting next to me in the front of the car.

'Yes, why?'

'You went quiet.'

I return to the present and contemplate the sprawling housing estate before us. 'We are best to avoid places like that,' I say.

I'm pointing to a Safeway supermarket and continue the lesson I've been teaching all morning. 'It's likely to have security cameras inside and out. They've also started attaching them to lamp posts in car parks. So it's important we do our homework before we decide where to target.'

My passenger nods as if making mental notes.

'It's also vital that you adapt to your environment, which means you must plan what you're going to wear. Don't stand out from the crowd. I keep a completely different set of clothes for days like this. Never wear the same outfit twice and always destroy what you've worn afterwards. Our own DNA is our biggest threat.'

On-the-job training, I guess that's what you might call this. Although you won't find the apprenticeship I offer advertised on a Jobcentre wall. I have years of experience to share with the perfect student. And I think I've found them.

'If you're targeting an estate then choose it carefully,' I continue. 'I avoid middle-class new builds and roads with large, expensive houses or ones that have two or more cars on the drive. It's unlikely you'll find who you're looking for playing in their streets. Instead, choose areas with average or smaller homes – or even better, council estates. The more neglected the better. Look out for graffiti on the walls, overgrown gardens and discarded bin bags. If a tenant can't be bothered to look after their house, they probably can't look after their children either. And they are the ones who need saving the most.'

I turn the ignition and do my best to answer their questions as I drive to our second destination. I've only visited this area twice before, but I've put to memory certain places.

'Why do you strangle them?' This is just blurted, out of nowhere. 'You've never told me.'

The question alone makes my fingertips tingle . . . the softness and pliability of their necks, the warmth of the blood flowing close to the surface, their palpitating, escalating pulse, their small, hopeless hands grabbing at mine . . . there is no feeling that will ever replicate it. 'It's clean, quite painless and you don't need to rely on a weapon,' I say instead. 'And if you know what you're doing, they can fall unconscious in seconds and stop breathing within just a couple of minutes.'

I park in a free space under a block of flats. Beer cans and smashed glass bottles are scattered about. 'Weekdays are a good time to visit places like this,' I explain. 'There are plenty of children playing truant. Most parents either don't know or don't care. So they make for successful targets because their absences aren't immediately noted. But don't be opportunistic. We must always be in control; always be in mind of our safety above all else.'

A young girl wearing tight jeans and a crop top draws our attention. She can't be more than eight or nine years old, but she walks and dresses with the confidence of a teenager. I dismiss her, reminding my passenger not to choose anyone who might fight back. A boy on the opposite side of the road catches my eye next. He is small and rake-thin and lost in his own little world.

'There!' I say. 'He's the perfect example of everything I've been telling you.' We exit the car and I look at my watch. 'It's 10.25 a.m. and he should be in school.' We pick up the pace and I lower my voice. 'His trainers are unbranded and falling apart and his football shirt has faded so it's probably fake.' The boy entertains himself by dragging a stick against a set of metal railings he passes. 'He's taking his time because he has nowhere in particular to go.'

We follow him to a park a little further down the road. The seesaw and slides have all been vandalised so he takes up residence on the one working swing. There is nobody else around. He is as vulnerable as they get. This boy is unloved and uncared for. He needs us to help him. An image of my parents briefly flashes into my mind. They are why I do this. To protect him from people like them.

'Are you ready?' I ask. When they nod, a rush of endorphins energises my body.

'Can I watch this time?' they ask as we exit the car.

'Which part?'

'When you kill them?'

I hesitate as I consider it and eventually decide against it, but without offering an explanation as to why. The moment is too personal to be shared. They don't protest. Instead, we concentrate on moving in different directions until they reach our target first. I watch from a distance as my instructions are followed.

This is all I have ever wanted, someone who shares my beliefs and who is committed to the cause. They have also helped me recognise how lonely this hidden part of my life has been until now. On paper I have everything I could ever need, but deep down, this part of me has been so isolated. I used to feel like the only person on earth who cares with such intensity about the well-being of others. But now I have found a kindred spirit who believes the same. I cross my fingers that this will be a long and fruitful working relationship.

Now I must focus. The skinny boy leaves with my accomplice and I know that, soon, I will have framed another mental picture. Only this time I will have someone else to share it with.

EXCERPT FROM CHANNEL 4 DOCUMENTARY *WRONGLY ACCUSED*. INTERVIEW WITH DS MARK GOODWIN

At what point during the investigation into the murders at Stewkbury did the accused appear on your radar?

It wasn't someone we had a reason to be suspicious of so we didn't dig into their background.

In retrospect, do you wish you had considered them a suspect earlier?

With the benefit of hindsight, there is a lot we could have done differently if we'd had the evidence. But there was nothing to suggest they were involved in the unlawful killings.

What were you focusing on at that point?

Identifying and interviewing known child sex offenders in that area at the time of the murders, as well as current and former neighbours and relatives of the deceased children. But the crimes were so historic and appeared to end so suddenly that it was also possible the killer or killers could have died decades ago. It was an exhaustive, massive search with huge public interest and very few leads. And at that time we had no idea the case was about to expand into something broader than any of us could ever have imagined.

When did that happen?

The afternoon of the incident in question, when we were called to the warehouse following a fatal altercation.

Can you elaborate on what you mean when you say 'the incident'?

When more bodies were discovered and the person we believe responsible was found with their throat slashed.

CHAPTER 22

MIA, 2019

The email link to the house down the road that Finn and Debbie went to look around today remains unopened on my iPad. He tells me that while it's a world away from the house from hell we own or our preferred style of property, we won't have to do anything to it before we move in. When I told him I was happy to go along with whatever he thought best, I sensed it wasn't the right thing to say.

'It's not just my decision though is it, Mia?' Finn sighed. 'This is for all three of us. You could at least pretend you're interested.'

'I'm sorry.' My eyes filled, and he retreated to the lounge. I feel so guilty for making Finn sleep on the sofa bed in there. To make matters worse, I've asked him to take Sonny with him tonight. I've barely seen my child all day, as he's been with Debbie again, and now I'm palming him off on his dad. But I'm feeling particularly fragile today.

I'm so grateful for Debbie's help though. She doesn't think to question me when I ask if she can have Sonny, she just has an instinct for when it all gets too much for me. And in those moments, she'll come in with cups of tea or coffee or food to make sure I'm okay.

I know I'm a bad wife and mother for pushing a good husband and child away. But I can't help it. Finn wants the woman he married to return but I don't know how to be her again. I'm better on my own, away from him and away from his baby. Here, alone in my room, I can't hurt anyone.

I don't just fear my own behaviour though: I'm equally as frightened of strangers on the rare excursions I'm outdoors with Sonny. I don't trust anyone who shows an interest in him. I haven't put any photos of him on social media because I don't want him to be the focus of anyone's attention, even for a second. Seven children were stolen from their parents and killed in our house, and something similar could happen to Sonny if I'm not careful.

Thinking about those poor babies preoccupies much of my night-times. I spend hours trawling the internet when I can't sleep, searching for all the information I can find about them. The police have only released one name so far, a little boy called Nicky Roberts who vanished in 1979 from Northamptonshire. The media has gone to town with its coverage, tracking down his parents, extended family and former school friends from forty years ago. I wonder if it was his body I saw. In an online cloud folder I've titled 'PR Images', I have a secret file dedicated to him. It contains school portraits and photos from holidays and birthday parties. My heart breaks for all he left behind and could have done with his life.

Finn knows nothing about this folder or the e-books I download about serial murderers. By reading biographies about child killers Fred and Rosemary West, Ian Brady and Myra Hindley, I hope to understand more about what motivated the killer of the children found in our house. So far, all they have done is petrify me regarding what people are capable of.

Sometimes I'll distract myself from all the doom and gloom by scrolling through my iPad catching up on my social media, envying my old friends in London living their best, carefree, filtered lives on Instagram. I've ignored almost all of their concerned messages and removed myself from WhatsApp group chats. I can't face interacting with any of them at the moment. I want everyone to forget about me.

I return to my bookmarked pages, all stories related to the murders, just as a Google alert bell chimes. I click on the link – a second child has been identified. Frankie Holmes was seven when he vanished in 1977 from his home in Berkhamsted, about thirty miles away from here. There's a quote from his sister Lorna and a photograph. I hesitate, and then take a second, more careful look at her picture.

I know her!

Or at least I knew her for a while. It's been years since we shared some of the same university lectures, and if I remember correctly, she dropped out of uni after only the third term.

I catch up on the last few weeks of her life on Facebook, as her settings are public. Going by the number of posts she's written recently about her missing brother, she has been waiting for today to come. Her most recent post is a photo of a grinning little boy with a shock of red hair and a broken heart emoji as its caption. I have no recollection of her ever mentioning anything about a missing brother when we were friends. But then why would she?

An idea appears from nowhere, but before I act on it, I weigh up the pros and cons. In the end, I can't help thinking that in helping her, might she be able to help me?

CHAPTER 23

FINN

She is fast asleep but I'm far from it. It's been ages since we last found the time to have sex, and I know that I'm just as much to blame because I'm never here. But tonight, I escaped from work early and, before I knew it, we'd done it twice in a couple of hours. I'm absolutely knackered. Post-shower, I'm sitting in the lounge in my boxer shorts while she remains out for the count in the bedroom. I look at the time – it's past midnight.

I question if we'd still be together had she not fallen pregnant. I hate to say it, but no, probably not. It was an accident, albeit a happy one.

I scroll on my phone through the photo album of Sonny that Mia and I share. There are hundreds of photographs I've taken of him since he was born three months ago. From the very first one in his incubator to him behind me in his car seat yesterday morning, the novelty of being a dad to that little man still hasn't worn off. For the first time I notice that of all the pictures I've taken, Mia features in only a handful. That can't be right, can it? I check to see if she has created a separate photo folder of just the two of them together, but unless they are only stored on her phone, then no, there are definitely only four of mother and son.

I can't keep ignoring that there's something not right with her. Mum reckons it's the head injury from her fall or postnatal depression, and she sent me the links to the NHS websites that list the symptoms. Mia ticks more boxes than I'd like. Mum says I need to go to Mia's doctor and get her on medication ASAP. 'Make her more manageable,' she says. Of course I want her to get better, but I didn't marry her because I wanted someone I could manage. I married her because I loved her and I wanted someone independent so that we could both lead our own lives as well as share one. My best mate, Ranjit, tells me I'm playing with fire in wanting the best of both worlds, marriage and freedom, and I guess he's right. But I can't see myself stopping unless I get burned.

I look at my watch again. I'll be pushing my luck if I stay here much longer, so I return to the bedroom and quietly slip on my jeans, T-shirt, overalls, socks and boots. I pause for a moment like I always do to check that I haven't forgotten anything, and glance at my phone again for messages. Mia knows I've been subcontracted by a plumbing firm, taking on emergency call-outs at stupid hours. She doesn't know I'm not on a call-out now. And she doesn't know how much I lie to her or who I'm with now. I intend to keep it this way.

Fifteen minutes later and I've returned to the family home, tiptoeing into the Annexe. A light is shining from under Mia's bedroom door and I wonder if I should go in, even if it's only to say hello. But she's probably surfing those bloody murdered-kid websites again. She doesn't think I know of her obsession, but with our shared internet account, I can see on my phone what she looks at when I'm not around. I also know she's downloaded at least half a dozen books for her Kindle about serial killers. To live the way I want to live means knowing everything about her life, even when she doesn't have the first clue about mine.

I decide I'm too tired for her now. I'll see her in the morning. I stretch out on the sofa and stare at the ceiling as I get my head together, straightening my stories, preparing for tomorrow, planning for all eventualities. It takes a lot of forward thinking to be me.

CHAPTER 24

MIA

Somebody's shadow moves behind the frosted glass panel of the front door and, losing my nerve, I hesitate before ringing the bell. I take a couple of deep breaths and watch as the taxi driver who brought me here from Berkhamsted's train station pulls away. I have to stick to the plan.

I release the tension building up inside me by flexing and unflexing my fingers like the hospital physio showed me last week after my plaster cast was removed. My wrist and forearm are still too stiff to turn a steering wheel, hence the train and taxi instead of driving myself. The headaches following the fall are becoming less frequent but one has appeared this morning that I'm struggling to shift.

When I told Debbie that I was going out to meet a friend for coffee, I was only partially lying. I hate not being honest with her after all she's done for me but I couldn't admit to her or Finn the truth of where I was really going, or they'd have tried to talk me out of it. They wouldn't understand my necessity to be here, and to be honest, I'm not sure I do either. Instead of pushing the bell, I swipe to the photos folder on the phone in my hand and re-read the headlines of old articles I found on the *Hemel Hempstead Gazette*'s website. The image of the class photo is blurry and the print quality poor but readable. 'Parents of missing boy make anniversary appeal', reads one.

I steel myself. It's now or never.

I brace myself as Lorna Holmes opens the front door. We haven't seen each other for more than twelve years but she is well aware of our more recent shared link. She catches me off guard with a bear hug that belies her skinny appearance, almost winding me. I feel how bony her shoulders are as she pushes them into me.

'Thank you for agreeing to come,' she says, her gratitude genuine.

'How are you?' I ask, quickly aware of how pointless the question is.

'Okay, considering.'

I take her in properly. Back when we shared the same media studies classes at the University of London, she was a mature student, quite a few years older than the rest of us, a larger-than-life party girl who wanted everyone's attention with her skimpy outfits and outrageous antics. Today she's conservatively dressed and her make-up is minimal. She's always been a lot slimmer than me and I'm reminded of the rumours that she had an eating disorder, and I wonder if it contributed to her dropping out after the first year. Regardless, I find myself holding in my post-baby paunch.

Lorna beckons me into the hallway and takes my coat. The light catches her arms and I notice scarring on her wrists. I choose not to ask about them. 'I used to read about you in *Heat* and *OK!* magazine,' she recalls, and I feel my cheeks blush.

'That seems like such a long time ago,' I say. 'As does uni. When we'd hang out, I had no idea you had a missing brother.'

'I didn't tell anyone. I wanted to be someone different from the person I was around here, not just the sister of the kid who disappeared. So I rebelled. I drank a lot and well, you know, the rest. I was more than aware of how quickly life can come and go and I wanted to make the most of mine. Only I took it too far and made myself ill.' She doesn't go into specifics and she doesn't need to. 'When did you learn Frankie was my brother?'

'The same day I messaged you on Facebook. And thank you for inviting me over. I wish that we could have met again in different circumstances.'

'You have nothing to be sorry for,' she replies. 'It's no surprise that Frankie's passed. I wasn't even born when he disappeared, and from everything my mum and dad told me about him, he'd never have run away. He was a real home bird.'

'How are your parents dealing with the news?'

'Okay, I guess. They're looking forward to meeting you.'

'And me them.'

I'm not really; in fact I'm as nervous as hell. I follow Lorna along a corridor and into the kitchen. We pass a room where condolence cards cover a sideboard and dining room table. There are vases of flowers everywhere. She opens the kitchen door and the air is thick with cigarette smoke. Lorna introduces me to Pat and Frankie Snr, who rise from behind a kitchen table and embrace me every bit as tightly as their daughter did. The whites of Pat's eyes are spotted with red as if she's cried so hard that she has burst blood vessels. Her face is lined and some auburn flecks remain in her grey hair. There's a yellow nicotine stain in the centre of Frankie Snr's white moustache.

'Thank you for finding our son,' Pat begins, her voice brittle. *You're welcome* doesn't feel like an appropriate response. She beckons me to sit. 'What . . . what was it like up there?'

'In the attic?'

She nods. 'I asked our family liaison officer, but she said it was best I didn't see the photographs.'

'I wasn't there long,' I say. 'But it looked . . . for want of a better expression . . . peaceful.' I recall how tidily and carefully arranged the suitcases were, one behind the other, forming a V-shape.

'The police brought round photographs of his Cub Scout uniform for us to identify,' Pat continues. 'I'd forgotten how small they were. He was only a wee thing, smaller than his friends. I often wonder if that's why he was taken from us, because he wasn't strong enough to fight back.'

We sit quietly and I give them the time they need without interruption. I reflect again on why I agreed to Lorna's invitation. I reach the conclusion that I'm here because witnessing those mummified remains, followed weeks later by their grainy faces in newspaper photographs, isn't enough to make those children real to me. I need to find a way to humanise them; I need to meet the families who loved them, to see how pined for they've been all these years. Then perhaps I'll understand how fortunate I am to have a living, breathing child of my own, and allow myself to love Sonny properly and not be frightened of how I or others might hurt him.

Frankie Snr removes a roll-up cigarette from a tobacco pouch and lights it. He takes a deep drag and chooses his words carefully. 'You expect your son to be with you for the rest of your life. But when he's taken away from you, it changes everything. All you once felt is replaced by fear and confusion and, above everything else, anger. Because the someone . . . the some*thing* . . . that stole him can't see the boy that you knew inside and out. All they see is an object they want to destroy. And they have no right to do that, no right at all. I'm not a violent man but when they catch him, I will happily rip him apart with my own bare hands.'

I don't doubt him for a minute.

'Even when we took part in a TV appeal soon after he vanished, I knew in my heart that we'd lost him,' adds Pat. 'I couldn't feel him inside me any more.' She points to her heart. 'I hoped it wouldn't be long before they found his body, but the days spread into weeks and months and we never got the call. Eventually, we gave up hope of ever being able to say a proper goodbye.' She places her hand on my recently repaired wrist. The pressure she exerts to demonstrate her sincerity hurts but I don't yank it away. 'He was our life. Without him, the soul was torn from our family.'

Lorna inches back in her chair and I wonder what that's like to hear, knowing that, even now, she will never be enough to complete her parents. Her childhood was stolen along with her brother's; only, she was the one who had to carry on. She puts a kettle on the hob as Pat leafs through the pages of a family photo album, showing me faded pictures of Frankie taken up until a few weeks before he vanished. The pages at the back of the book have been left blank, and I realise that after Frankie vanished, they stopped taking photographs. There are none of Lorna.

Later, and when it feels like the right time to leave, I say my goodbyes and Lorna escorts me to the front door. We hug each other and promise to stay in touch. I mean it.

I need a little quiet time to clear my head so I make my way to the train station on foot, following a map on my phone. I text Debbie to see how Sonny is. She sends me a picture of him lying on the lawn, his feet kicking up in the air and smiling. Without warning, my eyes start brimming. A young boy waiting at a bus stop gives me a puzzled look so I lower my head and quicken my pace until I pass him.

This visit has helped me a lot, I think. Pat and Frankie Snr don't have a second chance with their son like I do with mine. Being with them has made me understand just how much work I need to do to get out of this depression. I was raised by my parents to be independent and to solve my own problems, so I'm not used to asking for help. But I don't think I can sort myself out on my own. This is too big for me to handle.

There's just one more place I need to visit before I can draw a line under this terrible chapter in my life and be a better mum and wife.

CHAPTER 25
TWENTY YEARS AGO

Amongst the acrid stench of stale urine in the room is the lingering smell of damp. I hold a tissue over my nose and mouth, but it only keeps in my nostrils what I have already inhaled.

Circular blobs of black mould have gathered at the bottom of the walls and are inching their way up towards the ceiling like ivy. I spot a gold-framed painting of a colourful and serene Jesus nailed to the wall. There's a luminous halo hanging over his head and he holds out his hand as if offering hope or forgiveness to those who need it. He's wasting his time; I need neither.

There are a couple of mattresses on the floor with so many stains it's impossible to know what the original pattern was. Dozens of empty cans of supermarket own-brand cider are scattered across the floor, along with discarded plastic needles, scorched tin foil, cigarette lighters and cracked plastic pipes. Beneath the mould are fine lines of a brown spray, likely blood ejected from the syringes. This could easily be a set from that *Trainspotting* film. Yet amongst all this dereliction, I have created beauty.

Somewhere in this tower block is a stereo blasting out Prince's song '1999'. We might be on the cusp of a new millennium but if I never hear it again it will be too soon. I turn to stare out from the cracked window, partially covered by a solitary curtain hanging off the track. The city of Sheffield lies beyond it and I feel as if I know it well, even if I only came here a couple of times before today. It's amazing what you can learn about an area from only the photographs people have uploaded on to the World Wide Web, isn't it? I've grown to love the home computer I bought on a whim in the New Year sales. Once you turn it on, it only takes a few minutes to connect before you have the world at your fingertips. My only fear is that it's going to be damaged by the millennium bug they're all talking about.

My attention returns to the suitcase in front of me, a tan-coloured one with two copper catches. The leather is tough, taut and built to last, and its framework is more than strong enough to support the dead body of the girl inside it.

She posed little challenge, God bless her. One of the forgotten children, I assume, the ones whose profiles are crammed inside a folder somewhere in a social services department's 'at risk' filing cabinet. Budget cuts meant she probably wasn't monitored as regularly as staff might have liked. If George and I had been on a register that people had paid attention to, then things might have turned out very differently for us.

I estimate the girl was eight, perhaps nine, and a sliver of a thing. Blink and you'd miss her. Undernourished, sapling arms and legs, a dirty Britney Spears T-shirt and unwashed hair. I doubt she had been to school in an age. Here, in the slum she called home, she was the queen of the concrete corridors as she glided up and down on her chipped pink scooter. She was too young to understand that this kind of living was not the norm.

She is better off where she is now, with me. I have saved her from a lifetime of poverty, misery and repeating the mistakes of her parents.

On a previous recce I'd followed her and the man charged with her care back to their home from a little further beyond the estate. Her father scratched constantly at his groin and I assume he either had a sexually transmitted infection or had run out of veins in his arms and legs and was now using anything left to inject. He had bought tobacco, rolling papers, lighters and a bottle of vodka. His daughter skipped as she carried the alcohol home. Their front door was broken and partially boarded up, as if once the target of a police raid.

Earlier today, from where she played alone in the car park, I lured the girl into this empty flat by telling her Daddy was poorly and needed help. She followed me without question, suggesting this was the norm. Once we were alone I wrapped my hands around her neck and wasted no time in doing what I came here to do. Afterwards and with a firm click, I locked the suitcase and dragged it into the centre of the room, directly below the window. Then I placed her clothes in front of it.

Now, I carefully kick away from the case the beer and food cans, discarded newspapers and needles, making sure their sharp points don't penetrate my footwear. Finally, she has a clean patch surrounding her. Then I stand in the doorway and relax my mind and body and score the scene to memory.

However, this tried-and-tested process is not coming to me as naturally as it usually does. I'm distracted. I can't be sure if it's the lighting or another part of my staging that is askew. Whatever the reason, I'm transported back some twenty years, and instead of the suitcase, I'm staring at my parents from the doorway of their dining room. I'm unaware of the context of their conversation but I distinctly recall my father telling my mother that he forgave her.

Then he held her hand and kissed her. It was an unusually tender moment between them, at least in front of my brother and in front of me. The affection George and I required from them was less forthcoming.

Prior to me attending a comprehensive shortly before my thirteenth birthday, Dad homeschooled us as we moved from area to area and house to house. He was evidently an educated man, judging by his firm grasp of most subjects. He used long words and taught us how to phrase and verbalise our thoughts and questions more poetically than other children might. But when in the company of our peers, he insisted we mirror their language and behaviour so as to blend in.

He loved the English language but art was his favourite subject and he'd spend hours encouraging us to draw and paint.

'Whatever it is you're sketching, be it a tree or a person or something abstract, always remember to frame what you want the viewer to see,' he would remind us. 'You must control their focus . . . burn it into their memories so they can close their eyes and return to it whenever they want to.' He is long gone but his advice remains.

George and I might have been too young to understand the complexities of the family we'd been born into, but we were still able to pretend to be like normal children when the opportunities arose. We'd take ourselves to the play park in the grounds of the village, but hide in the bushes if other kids arrived because we were only allowed to befriend children at youth and social clubs and church events of our parents' choosing. The sole purpose of that was for us to bring them home to play. Then our part was complete and our parents took charge. One boy, Martin Hamilton, jumps out from my past and into the present so suddenly and with such clarity that it's as if he is here in the room with us. He remains long enough for me to recall the day he tore our family apart. I shake my head and he vanishes like a fine mist.

I need to start making a move from this flat. After I'm finally able to frame the girl in the suitcase and take my mental snapshot of the image I'll return to, I ready myself to leave. But before I carry her away with me, a sudden burst of light appears through the grey skies and settles on the painting of Jesus. I release a smile. He is offering me forgiveness again. *Sorry Jesus, you are wasting your time. It should be me who is forgiving you for ignoring us all those years.*

CHAPTER 26

DAVE, 2019

I haven't prepared for this. I'm normally a cautious man who prefers to think about my actions first and plan for all eventualities. But sometimes I find myself caught in a moment and I need to act. Like now. I'm on the move, following her taxi, stalking her like prey.

Mia has no reason to believe that I'm behind her. It helps that I'm not in the company van, I'm using Debbie's car, which is about as generic as vehicles get. I also have plenty of surveillance experience and am adept at keeping a low profile, so I leave a stretch of distance between us to remain unseen.

We've already been on the road for ten minutes, and the longer this journey continues, the more my pulse jackhammers. The only reason I have an idea of what she has planned is because I overheard her talking to Finn in the kitchen shortly before she left, and even then, I only caught a few words. But they were enough to concern me.

Finn seemed to be suggesting it wasn't a good idea but she was digging her heels in and refusing to back down. I don't want to lose track of her because I need to see for myself what she's up to.

How does that old saying go? 'Take charge of your own destiny or somebody else will.'

Her taxi pulls over at a small branch of Waitrose and she exits, wearing her black suit and sunglasses. She disappears inside for a few minutes, reappearing with a bouquet of white lilies which she peels the label off as she walks back towards the vehicle. Then their journey continues.

The car remains at a steady speed until we reach the first of a series of roundabouts that Milton Keynes is infamous for. Then a further fifteen minutes pass before we arrive in the north of the town and now we are following signs for Crownhill Crematorium. There's a sour taste in my mouth. Eventually, the taxi pulls into its car park while I remain outside at the kerb. She takes the flowers and, as she closes the door, she pats out the creases from her dress.

She makes her way towards the arched glass and brick building and I turn my engine off. I pull a can of lager from my toolbox, sink into my seat and watch Mia approach a group waiting outside the main entrance. She stops short before she reaches them and stands alone, suggesting she doesn't know them.

Without meaning to, I've already finished my drink and I curse myself for it. Lately, the contents of these cans are barely touching the inside of my mouth before I've drained them. I'm aware of a sudden sharp, burning pain in my gut and I don't have my pills with me. I make a mental note to text Jakub to bring me more on site tomorrow. I don't know or care where he gets them from but they're much stronger than the over-the-counter painkillers I've used in the past. For now, I reach for another can, to at least soften the jagged edges these episodes bring.

Then I take my phone from the dashboard stand and go online to visit the Milton Keynes Citizens' Births, Deaths and Marriages section. I'm slow to read it, stumbling over the words and speaking them aloud.

DOUGLAS – ABIGAIL (ABI) Born 1968. Returned to her loving family after a long absence on August 8. Much-loved daughter of parents Geraldine and the late Sidney, dearly missed sister of Steven and Michael. Funeral to be held at Crownhill Crematorium, Milton Keynes, on August 22 at 11.30am. All invited. Flowers welcome or donations can be made to the charity Missing People. 'Your wings were ready but our hearts were not. Fly high with the angels, darling Abi.'

I know the name. She is the third child found in Finn's attic to have been formally identified. But why the hell is Mia going to her funeral?

A hearse pulls on to the crematorium's driveway. I slip on my glasses and get a better look at the girl's name spelled out in the white carnations leaning against a white, child-sized coffin. I briefly picture my own name inside a hearse next to my coffin and I wonder what flowers Debbie will choose for me and whether they'll spell out Dave or David.

A restlessness rises up and through me and I know that I have to leave. I turn the ignition and within seconds I re-join the flow of traffic, leaving behind my none-the-wiser daughter-in-law.

CHAPTER 27

MIA

The golf club's function room is a large, open space and not really suited to the intimate nature of a wake. Below rows of photographs of stern-faced former captains are pockets of mourners talking amongst themselves. Being around so many unfamiliar faces makes me nervous but I'm at least grateful nobody has recognised me from the newspapers.

Five months have now passed since the bodies in the attic were found, but as the owners of the house, we are still getting media attention. I'm sure they'd have left us alone by now had they not realised early on who my ex-boyfriend was. 'Ellis Anders' Ex Caught Up In House Of Horrors', 'Ellis's Former Fiancée In Babes In The Attic Terror' and 'House Of Horrors Mum Was Engaged To Ellis Anders', read some of the headlines, all illustrated with historic photos of us together. Ellis and I split up what feels like a lifetime ago and I'd assumed my fifteen minutes of fame by proxy were over and I'd been forgotten about. I was wrong.

We have all been forced to change our telephone numbers to stop the press from contacting us despite the police informing them we didn't want to make a statement. Most weeks, they're still pushing notes through our door offering us money for our story or for photos taken inside the house. When I'm wearing my PR hat, I understand they're only doing their job and perhaps giving them one interview might shut them up. But Finn and his parents were adamant that we didn't. I also appreciate the money would be useful, as almost every penny we have is tied up in a house we can't live in. But we can't in good conscience cash in on those children's deaths.

My eyes flit around photos of Abigail Douglas in a framed montage. Next to me is a pile of orders of service with her black-and-white image on the cover, alongside her date of birth, but the date of her death is absent. I guess it's unlikely her family will ever know exactly when she died or how much she suffered. That must be one of the hardest parts of coming to terms with your child's murder, I think, not knowing if it was swift or cruel and drawn out.

There must be around eighty people here, a good turnout for a little girl who made more of an impact in death than life. I wonder how many mourners are family members and former school friends or who, like me, don't belong here.

A cold shiver creeps up my back when I contemplate whether the killer is also here amongst us. If some murderers get their kicks from attending search parties for their victims, then it stands to reason they'll gain something from attending a funeral too. And now my imagination is doing somersaults, questioning if they've also been to our house – perhaps even when we were working inside it – to relive their crimes. I do a headcount and there are at least ten men in this room who would've been the right age in the 1970s and 1980s. *No*, I tell myself, *I'm being silly*.

I try to redirect my thoughts by picking up the order of service again. The ceremony at the crematorium took around half an hour. It was difficult not to be moved by the vivid recollections of Abigail by her two older brothers. Her father died soon after she vanished and their use of phrases like 'never forgave himself' and 'couldn't live without his daughter' suggested he either died of a broken heart or took his own life. Like my old friend Lorna Holmes's family, they too have been irreparably damaged.

By the time Abigail's coffin disappeared behind the curtain to the sound of her favourite song, Michael Jackson's 'Don't Stop 'Til You Get Enough', a huge hit at the time, there wasn't a dry eye left in the building. I know I'm never going to hear that song again without thinking of a little girl I never knew.

From a selfish perspective, I hope that witnessing her being laid to rest will help bring an end to my preoccupation with this case. I want to move forwards, so I've googled therapists and have a shortlist of half a dozen I'm going to look into.

I gravitate towards two women who, like me, appear not to know anyone. Their faces share a similar shape and I assume they're related. I envy the older one's beautiful, unblemished skin. Since having Sonny, my cheeks and forehead have been prone to acne break-outs. It's hormonal, but along with the extra weight I'm still carrying, it doesn't help with my self-confidence. The other woman is much younger and in a wheelchair. She stares into the distance, her limbs twisted and a faint transparent thread of saliva dripping from the corner of her mouth.

'Hello,' I begin. 'Do you mind if I join you? I don't really know anyone here.'

'Please do,' the older woman says warmly in a lilting Caribbean accent. She introduces herself as Jasmine Johnson and her daughter as Precious.

'Were you at the crematorium?' I ask.

'No,' says Jasmine. 'There are certain situations Precious struggles with and I thought that might be one of them. It wouldn't have been her fault, but I didn't want her to make a scene and take away from the family's grief.'

'I understand,' I reply. 'How did you know Abigail?'

'She and Precious went to the same school. Although Precious was a different girl back then to the one you see now.'

'How so?' I ask before realising how nosey that might've sounded. 'If you don't mind me asking,' I add quickly.

'She vanished at the same time as Abigail,' Jasmine says so matter-of-factly that I think I've misheard.

'Vanished?'

'Three days after the girls didn't return from choir practice, my daughter was found by the side of the road with head injuries, a broken leg and pelvis. Hit and run, the police reckoned. She'd also suffered an extensive bleed to the brain, and when she came out of her coma, she was as you see her now. And she was never able to tell us what happened to her and Abi or how she ended up where she was found. Everything she knows is locked inside her head.'

When I tell her that I don't recall reading about this, Jasmine says it was barely reported on. 'Back in the early 1980s, if it was a choice between putting a blonde, blue-eyed pretty little white girl on the front of a newspaper or a little black girl, you can guess which one was going to sell more copies. Even though she isn't the same girl as she was, by God's good grace she's still with us. Despite what happened to her, I give thanks every day that my daughter survived.'

When she asks why I am here, I feel embarrassed, ghoulish even. 'It was my house where Abigail's and the other children's bodies were found,' I say quietly, hoping I haven't been overheard.

Jasmine cocks her head, regards me more closely and then nods slowly, as if she now recognises me. She picks up a school photograph from the table, a picture of Abigail and Precious's class lined up in two rows, one behind the other. She points out her daughter, a wide-eyed, vibrant twelve-year-old. Her hair is tied into bunches and she wears a school uniform with pride. 'Isn't she beautiful?' she says, and I nod.

I examine the rest of the photograph when a face in the row behind Precious and Abigail catches my eye.

'That little boy looks like my father-in-law,' I say.

'Which one?' Jasmine asks and I point to a child with a port-wine stain on his forehead and eyelid. 'Oh, you know Davey Hunter?'

I take a short gasp of air but, before I can reply, a sudden, high-pitched noise rings out around the room, snagging everyone's attention. Only when it's followed by a thumping sound do I realise it's Precious, banging her fists against the armrests of her wheelchair. Her squeal is as shrill as a smoke alarm.

'Whatever is the matter?' her mother asks, and her knees crack as she kneels down to calm her daughter. It has little effect. Instead, Precious takes to jerking her head back sharply again and again. 'She gets like this sometimes.'

Jasmine hands me the framed photograph and turns her daughter's chair around, offers her apologies and tries to say goodbye but it's hard to hear her above the screaming. Precious accidentally bats the picture out of my hand as she passes and the glass shatters as it hits the floor.

As mother and daughter leave, I pick up the shards and place them into a napkin. When I decide that everyone has at last ceased staring at us, I slip the photo into my handbag. I'm thinking about my father-in-law, racking my brain to recall if Dave ever mentioned, when her name was released to the media, that he went to school with one of the missing children. I know that I've been in a fog lately but I'm sure I wouldn't have forgotten something that important. And if Finn knew, he would definitely have brought it up, as he tells me everything. I'm adamant Dave has said nothing.

So why would he deliberately keep this quiet?

CHAPTER 28

DEBBIE

'Morning,' I say, and then open the lounge window in the Annexe. This room hasn't been aired for a while and it smells musty in here and of dirty nappies. I take a can of Febreze from the cupboard under the sink and spray the curtains, sofa and even the carpet with a fine linen-scented mist.

There doesn't appear to be any sign of Mia wanting to move out of our house. Finn has declined our offer to give them the money to buy somewhere, explaining it's not the right time for them. He stopped short of blaming her. So it doesn't look as if they are going anywhere in a hurry. I won't lie and say this doesn't please me.

Mia exits the bathroom and looks at me in a way that I can only interpret as awkward. Typically, each morning she'll give me a heartfelt smile and she'll thank me in advance for taking Sonny back into the main house with me for the rest of the day. We've got into quite the routine, he and I, playing out in the garden if it's warm enough, or holed up in the playroom I've created for him in one of the spare bedrooms. I'll feed him, change him and will only bring him back when Finn has texted to tell me he's on his way home from work. The upside of whatever it is that's wrong with Mia means I get to spend all my days with my grandson.

Mia has already changed out of her pyjamas, her hair is washed and she looks almost guilty for having made the effort. She holds her head down a little and doesn't make eye contact when she asks me how I am. Is she hiding something or am I misreading her?

'I'll keep Sonny here with me today if that's okay?' she says.

'Really?' I ask. 'Why's that?'

'It'll give you a break.'

'Oh I don't need one, I'm fine. Besides, I was taking him to show off to my friends at lunch.'

'You've been having him loads lately, you could do with a rest.'

This time her smile is artificial, as if there is something else going on behind it.

'Is everything okay?' I ask.

'Yes, it's absolutely fine, honestly. I just think it'll do him and me some good having a bit of time together.'

'Well, if you're sure you can handle it. It's been a while since you've had him for a whole day. He can be quite demanding if you don't know what you're doing.'

'Yes, I'm sure.'

'Maybe I'll pop by at lunchtime and make sure he's okay.'

'Honestly Debbie, there's no need.'

'Right then,' I huff, and kiss my grandson's forehead before leaving them alone. I turn one last time to look at them both. He remains on his play mat but she has yet to approach him.

This development doesn't sit comfortably with me one little bit. I'm not going to be pushed out of his life just because Mia has suddenly decided she wants to play at being Mum.

CHAPTER 29

TWENTY-FOUR YEARS EARLIER

The interior of this vehicle suddenly feels very, very enclosed. It's as if I'm inside the jaws of a junkyard compressor, about to be crushed into a cube.

I distract myself by looking at the *Daily Mirror* newspaper on the passenger seat. It contains an interview with a woman who believes she once escaped the clutches of Fred West, who killed himself a few months earlier. While we have one obvious thing in common, he and I couldn't be any more dissimilar. He was a sick, twisted man, and it rankles me that if I'm ever caught, people might lump us in the same category. I do what I do for the greater good. He did what he did for his own perversions. I'm glad he's dead. People like him have no place in this world. I throw the paper into the footwell.

Desperate to feel fresh air against my face, I open the door and check my watch, confused as to why I am here so early. Then I remember: I only wound the clocks in the house forward after the weekend's winter change, and not the clock in the Mondeo. It's 2.30 p.m. and I don't need to be here for another hour.

I've been haunted by this claustrophobic feeling for a week now and I know what it means. I need to distract myself from the nagging voice that wants to be heard, so I make the most of the mild weather and extra time and take a walk along the path by the canal instead. Perhaps revisiting that spot will be enough to take my mind off my intrusive thoughts. Who knows? I'm in uncharted territory here. I've never taken such a long break between kills before.

The last time I was here, I was thirteen years old. I remember it as if it was yesterday because you never forget your first premeditated murder. His name was Justin Powell and he was a year or two older than me and much bigger. He wasn't somebody who needed saving – his death was to save someone else and redirected the course of the rest of my life.

I had followed this tall, stocky lad with hair combed into a quiff from the school playground to the barely lit canal path. I used dusk as a cloak to hide me, and by the time he'd turned to see where the rapidly approaching footsteps were coming from, he was already falling into the freezing water.

As he slipped beneath the surface, I took one of the rocks lying by the footpath and held it above me. And the moment his head emerged from the water gasping for air, I brought it down upon him with all my might. I can still recall the crunch it made as it collided with his skull and how he disappeared again into the water. It was a good twenty minutes before he surfaced again, face down and motionless. It was too dark to see his blood in the water so I had to use my imagination instead.

The bench I'm sitting on now wasn't here all those years ago. Back then, I watched the next morning from my standing position a distance away as police swarmed over the canal and surrounding parkland, investigating the body of a teenager discovered wedged between two moored canal boats. I had been trained never to show emotion at the fate of strangers, so there was no panic, no regret and certainly no guilt attached to what I'd done. In killing him, I'd taken control of a situation and helped someone who had helped me.

I spent most of that day there, taking in every second of the aftermath, framing images to bring back to life as I am today. For a moment I wonder how my world might have been had I not killed Justin that day. But I'm convinced that, if not him, it would've been somebody else. There's only so long you can fight nature. Lately, this is something I am being reminded of every hour of every day.

The last time I acted on my urges was exactly five years ago today. I thought the many distractions of my new life might be enough to occupy my time and give me all the fulfilment I required. But I've grown to realise that when I don't have blood on my hands, they are uncomfortably dry.

I check my watch again and start making my way back to where I need to be. Ahead, a small crowd has gathered, some chatting with one another, and all with a common purpose. I wait on the other side of the road, watching them, and wondering how many hours I have spent hovering around school gates resembling these. A bell sounds and, moments later, dozens of pairs of small feet come running out of the door to greet their parents. When most of them disperse, I spy the one I have been waiting for. They search for the familiar, only encountering it when our eyes lock.

I make my way towards them and their embrace is tight. It fills me with light. Then I take their hand, ask about their day and we begin to walk to the car before I drive us home.

This is what normality tastes like. I only wish it was enough.

IPSWICH HERALD, 1990

POLICE LAUNCH MANHUNT FOR MISSING SIBLINGS

BY JIMMY SHAKESPEARE

A one-month-old baby boy and his big sister were snatched from their front garden in broad daylight yesterday, sparking a major police hunt.

Infant William Brown and his four-year-old sister, Tanya, were abducted after their mother left them alone to prepare her son's bottle. Detectives admit fears for their safety are growing as specialist teams hunt for the missing siblings.

A police spokesman said they are becoming 'increasingly concerned' for the children's safety and have deployed a large number of officers around Stoke Park, Ipswich.

Hundreds of local residents in the estate have joined the hunt, with many continuing their efforts overnight.

CHAPTER 30

MIA, 2019

I'm finally alone with my father-in-law and I'm so nervous my armpits are damp.

Considering we share the same house, it's been near impossible to get Dave on his own lately. It's as if he knows I've discovered he was in the same class as two kidnapped kids and doesn't want to be alone with me. He has been working longer hours than usual, and when he returns, he either heads straight to bed or he's with Debbie. And this isn't a conversation I want to have in front of her. That's why I've had Sonny for the day and waited until she has gone out with friends before I approach him.

When I spy him from the Annexe alone in the garden, I grab my opportunity. He is sitting on one of the patio chairs, making the most of the afternoon sun. I pick up a sleeping Sonny from his carrycot, hoping not to wake him, and quietly hurry across the lawn so as not to warn Dave I'm approaching and give him an excuse to leave.

'Hello, Dave,' I begin and he flinches, but tries to disguise it. His face looks gaunt, almost as if it's haunted. Or maybe I'm reading too much into it. 'Day off?'

'Mia,' he replies, and gives me a brief smile. He glances over my shoulder as if he is hoping Finn will follow. When he realises I am on my own, his eyes flicker, which tells me he is already uncomfortable. Now I'm sure he knows what I know. 'Yes, I'm not needed today.'

'It's a beautiful afternoon.'

'It is. We have been lucky. It's been a good summer.'

'Not for everyone,' I reply, thinking about the families of the murdered children. A still-sleeping Sonny makes an unfamiliar squeaking sound and I don't know how to respond. I gently rub his back and he stops. 'There's something I need to talk to you about.'

'Oh, yes.' He doesn't phrase it as a question, but as a statement. And as if he has been expecting it.

'Last week, I went to one of those children's funerals. Abigail Douglas.' I allow her name to hang between us. He takes a swig from his can of beer and stares ahead to the copse at the end of the garden. But he doesn't respond. 'When I went to the wake afterwards I met a woman called Jasmine and her daughter Precious,' I continue. Again, there's no reaction. 'Jasmine remembers you. Precious, Abigail and you were all in the same class, weren't you?'

I don't give him time to deny it. From my pocket, I pull out the photo I stole from the wake and show it to him. He takes it in his hand and looks it over. Finally, he nods his head.

'I'm confused, Dave. Why didn't you think to mention it?'

'I discussed it with Debbie,' he says and takes another sip.

'What about Finn? Did you tell him? And why not me?'

He shrugs. 'I didn't see the point. And you've been . . . distracted lately.'

My nerves make way for irritation. 'Yes, but it was my house where Abigail's body was found and you were in her class. Don't you think I deserved to know?'

'Know what? That I barely knew her? I was hardly in school then. I was spending most of my time with older lads and getting into trouble.'

'So you don't remember Abigail?'

'Like I said, I barely knew her.'

'What about Precious?' For a split second, I catch his eye twitch again. He rubs at it.

'What about her?'

'Do you recall her too? She went missing at the same time.'

'Vaguely.'

'Do you know what happened to her?'

'I heard she was in an accident. It was a long time ago so I don't remember the ins and outs.'

When he doesn't enquire as to how she is now, I can't decide if he is detached from his former classmates because he is telling the truth, or because he is hiding something.

A sudden squeal from Sonny brings the conversation to an abrupt halt. I will him to be quiet but the cries that follow are ones of hunger. Only a bottle will calm him down.

I reluctantly take him back to the Annexe to feed him. From here, I watch Dave through the window opening another beer and drinking most of it in a series of long gulps. The way he stamps on the empty can with force tells me he is angry and that he's a liar.

He knows much more than he is letting on.

CHAPTER 31

DAVE

I wait until I hear the door to the Annexe close before I drain my last can of beer. But my frustration gets the better of me and I drop it to the floor and stamp on it. Perhaps I'm being paranoid, but something tells me that Mia is watching me right now. No, it's not paranoia. I'm sure she is. Because if the roles were reversed, I would be doing exactly the same thing to her as she is doing to me. Watching and waiting to see how I'll react, because we're only ever our true selves when we think we are alone.

Maybe I should have told Mia the whole truth rather than the abridged version. It's difficult to know what to do or say for the best. So instead, I played it safe and gave her snippets – not lies, but not the full story either. However, she's not the kind of person who's satisfied with a half-truth.

Abigail Douglas. Precious Johnson. I didn't know either girl well, that much was true, but I recall them being kind to me. And I guess back then, my definition of kindness was kids who didn't yell 'dumb shit' at me because of my poor reading and writing skills, or

'Two-Face' from the *Batman* comics for the vascular birthmark on my forehead and eyelid.

It's no wonder that from the age of twelve, when everything at home was gradually worsening, I spent much of my time sneaking out and hanging around with a gang of older boys on the old rec. I might have been the youngest, but puberty had arrived early, giving me height and breadth. My need to belong somewhere was so strong that it didn't matter if it was a group that didn't have my best interests at heart. With these fellow outcasts, I was accepted. We wasted many of our nights drinking cheap alcohol or sniffing glue or the contents of aerosol cans sprayed into empty crisp packets. It didn't matter where the buzz came from as long as it carried me away from my miserable reality.

I'd do anything to fit in or impress. I'd volunteer to shop-lift booze or snacks from the supermarket, and when that wasn't enough to satisfy my craving for their approval, I took it further with burglary and theft. But I was always careful never to get caught. And then one summer's afternoon, my luck ran out.

Finn knows very little of my childhood. He has no idea of the lengths I have gone to – and continue to go to – in protecting him from the truth. The first day I held him in my arms, I was unsure of his arrival in our world. But I vowed he would be better than me. I even pinned my hopes on him being the Band-Aid with which Debbie and I would cover the wounds of the past and stop the infection from returning. But it didn't work. *He* didn't work. I failed him. And God only knows what damage has been inflicted on him that the eye can't see.

For most of his life, Debbie has made me feel as if I was intruding on the two of them. I don't think she even consciously meant to. But there was not enough of Finn to share, so I backed off. First and foremost he is her son, and then he is mine. One of the biggest regrets of my life – and I have more than most – is that I didn't fight harder for him.

It was only when we were renovating his cursed house together that we really started to get to know one another. Until we found what we found in the attic. Now we are back to working in our own fields and we are as far apart again as the sun and the moon. He doesn't know that our time together is running out. I wish that I could be honest with him about everything. But I can't place that burden on his shoulders. It's unfair.

I hear a car pulling into the drive so I pick up my can and push it deep into the bin with the others and where Debbie is unlikely to find them. She approaches me, leaning heavily on her stick. As each month passes, she becomes that bit less mobile. We both know it but we rarely address it. There is so much that we keep from one another.

'Hi,' she says and gives me a peck on the cheek.

'How were the girls?'

'Same as ever,' she says. 'Lots of moaning about husbands and work.' She sees through my smile. 'What's wrong?'

I clear my throat. 'Mia knows about Abigail, Precious and I.'

She arches her eyebrows, lowers her voice and looks towards the Annexe. 'Exactly what does she know?'

'That we went to school together.'

'How?'

I explain how I followed her to the crematorium. She's surprised I went to such lengths but doesn't question me. 'She has a photograph,' I add.

'Of what?'

'Of the girls and me in the same class.'

Debbie makes no attempt to hide her annoyance. 'Why didn't you tell me about any of this sooner?'

'I didn't want to worry you.'

She shakes her head vigorously. 'Dave, I need to know sooner in future. If Mia is poking her nose in business that doesn't concern her, you have to tell me immediately so that I can protect you.' She hesitates and I give her the time she needs to consider our options. 'What did you tell her?'

'That I barely knew them.'

'And did she believe you?'

'Yes, I think so,' I lie.

'Well, that's something, I suppose. But you have to promise you won't keep anything else from me. This family only works when we are united. We cannot let her interfere with that.'

'Okay.'

She rests her stick up against a patio chair and takes a seat. She's quietly working out her plan of attack, so I give her space. I let out a long, beery breath from the far corner of my mouth, conscious of how much I've drunk today. I stare at the woman I have spent most of my life with, hoping to spot glimmers of the girl I fell in love with. I'm not usually an emotional man, but the urge to cry and hold on to her for dear life threatens to consume me. Because it won't be long before she is forced to manage alone all that life throws at her.

I grit my teeth and vow to protect her for as long as I can. I also need to keep a closer eye on my daughter-in-law. If she continues to poke at the wasps' nest, she will end up getting stung.

CHAPTER 32

FINN

I'm apprehensive as I return home from work because I can never be sure which Mia I'll find when I walk through the door. Sometimes it's weepy Mia, who I can make cry just by looking at her. Other times it is frustrated Mia, who can't find satisfaction in anything I say or do and flips out at me for no reason. But more often than not, it's can't-be-bothered-to-feel-a-damn-thing Mia. That's the one who scares me the most, because she's like an empty shell of who she used to be. I miss the sarcasm, her keeping me on my toes, me telling her when she's getting London-y. I'd cut her down to size and she'd hit back at me with something cheeky and we'd have a good-natured laugh at each other's expense. That's the Mia I miss the most. The one who laughs.

Sometimes, and I hate to admit it, she behaves like she doesn't love Sonny. I catch her staring at him like he belongs to somebody else. And that scares me.

I'm losing grip on my wife and I can almost measure the distance between us. We don't talk any more, and in the moments that we are together, I get the feeling she'd rather be in her own little online world, surrounding herself with stories about dead kids, than with me. I've tried asking her what's wrong but she tells me I wouldn't understand and shuts down the conversation. And instead of pushing it further and upsetting her more, I've left it at that.

Mum's taken me aside a couple of times, asking me what I'm doing about getting her help. I keep repeating that she's okay and she's got a lot to process but I know Mum's right. The truth is that I'm scared I might be the root of Mia's problems. That if a therapist pokes around inside her head, Mia will realise she deserves better than me and my family and leave. Sometimes I think I might wake up and find she's moved back to London because the life she had there is better than the shitstorm we're living in now. Maybe that's why she's not the only girl in my life: subconsciously I keep a spare as I don't want to be left on my own. Perhaps I'm the one who needs therapy, not Mia.

So tonight, as I walk through the door and shout my hellos, I'm as ready as I'll ever be for who I'll find. Only, it turns out it's none of the above. Mia is waiting for me in the lounge, Sonny is gurgling on his play mat and squeezing the life from a toy Igglepiggle by his side. She is dressed in dark jeans and a long-sleeved T-shirt, and she's wearing make-up. It's the first time I've seen her out of her sweatpants and not barefaced. Five months after her accident, have we reached a turning point?

I speak too soon, though, as when I go to kiss her, she turns her head so my lips land on her cheek, not her mouth.

She's cordial, asking me about my day, and I give her the bare bones of it. She doesn't need to know where I've really been this afternoon. I want to tell her how great she looks but I decide not to draw attention to it in case she thinks I'm having a dig at how she usually appears these days. Her thumb and forefinger are doing that rubbing-together thing again, so something is on her mind.

When I ask if everything is okay she says yes, but I don't believe her. 'Is there something you want to talk about?' I ask her.

She hesitates before she replies, then heads into our bedroom. I follow her in and realise it's been days since I was last in here, a further reminder that she and I aren't living a normal marriage. When she just stands there with her back to me, I say 'Mia', more firmly. 'What's going on?'

'It's your dad,' she replies.

'What's he done?'

'Do you know that he went to school with one of the children in our attic?'

'He did what?'

'Abigail Douglas . . . Dave was in the same class as her. And he knew another girl who vanished at the same time but was found alive, although barely.'

'Who told you this?'

'Jasmine, the surviving girl's mum.'

'And how do you know her?'

She pauses before she replies. 'I met her at Abigail's funeral.'

'What? You went when I asked you not to?'

'Yes.'

'Why?'

'Because I'm not a child and you can't tell me what not to do.'

'I can't believe you went behind my back.'

'Finn,' she says, 'you are missing the point. Your dad knew one of the victims and he never told us.'

'This Jasmine woman has him mixed up with someone else.'

'I saw a photograph of them together when I was at the wake . . .'

'You went to the wake as well? Jesus.' I'm genuinely lost for words. For weeks she has walked around this house like an extra from *The Walking Dead*, unable to give our son much affection

140

or attention while my parents and I pick up the slack and tiptoe around her. Now it turns out she's been sneaking out to the funerals of dead children she never even knew. Who else is she putting above her family?

'Look.' She delves into her handbag and rummages about but comes up empty-handed. So she picks up a black coat and rifles through the pockets instead. Again, she doesn't find what she's looking for. 'I had a school photo of them and your dad together,' she says, puzzled. 'I swear it was in here.'

'It must have been someone who resembled him. I mean, how do you know what he looked like as a kid? He doesn't have any photos from his childhood.'

'I'm not stupid, it was definitely him. Jasmine mentioned his name before I did. And the boy had the same birthmark on his forehead. So why didn't he tell us he knew one of the victims when she was named?'

'Maybe he didn't remember her or he didn't know she'd been identified.'

'It was all over the news. He deliberately kept it quiet from us.'

'There'll be an explanation for it.'

'Well, he didn't sound very convincing.'

I frown. 'Have you spoken to him about this?'

'Yes,' she admits sheepishly. 'Yesterday.'

'Mia, what the hell are you doing?' My temper is beginning to fray. 'I thought things were getting better between you and my parents. Mum and you have been getting on brilliantly.'

'Finn!' she exclaims, dismayed. 'Again, you're missing the point. This has nothing to do with your mum. Dave told me that he barely knew the girls because he didn't go to school very often.'

'You knew that already. He could barely read or write until he met Mum.'

'I think he kept this from us for a reason. He knows more than he's letting on. Look how they reacted when we told them we wanted the house. They kept trying to talk us out of it.'

'You're saying he knew there were bodies inside? Don't be so ridiculous. You were there. They were as shocked as we were. I think there's another underlying problem here.'

'At last!' she says jubilantly. 'Now we can agree on something. So you'll ask him about it then?'

'I don't mean with Dad, I mean with you.'

'Me?'

'You kept this from me, you obsess about the police investigation, you're not connecting with Sonny like you should be . . . I'm just saying that perhaps it's time we got you some help, because I can't mend you on my own.'

'*Mend me?*' she says slowly. 'You can't *mend me?*'

Wrong turn of phrase, I think. 'I mean we should make an appointment for you to see a doctor because you have all the symptoms of postnatal depression. It's not your fault, I know that. Plenty of women suffer from it. But Mum thinks . . .'

I stop. I'm digging myself an even deeper hole.

'Your mum thinks, does she?' Mia growls. 'Well, if Doctor Debbie has diagnosed a problem then there *must* be something wrong with me. Remind me which medical college she graduated from? Holby City or Grey Sloan Memorial? How dare you, Finn, how fucking dare you talk about me to your mum like that.'

'I was worried about you . . .'

'Then try *listening* to me! Try *talking* to me about what we went through at that house, how I almost lost Sonny, how knowing what happened to those kids is making me petrified that the same thing might happen to him. Talk *to* me, don't talk *about* me.'

'I'm sorry,' I say. 'I just want my old Mia back.' I pull my phone out of my pocket and show her some screenshots I took of various

142

medications I found online that can help with PND. 'If you don't want to talk to someone, we can get you some tablets. Look.'

'Oh, this just gets better.' She lets out a sharp, humourless laugh. 'Now you all want to drug me into being the dutiful little wife and daughter-in-law.'

'That's not what I meant.'

Sonny reminds us he's here by reacting to our raised voices with a whimper. 'Perhaps you should deal with your son,' she snaps, 'because clearly I'm too shitty a mother to go anywhere near him.'

I follow her again as she storms out of the bedroom and into the lounge. She grabs her coat and the car keys, but before she leaves, a presenter on the early evening news catches our attention.

'And we have some breaking news regarding the Leighton Buzzard Babes In The Attic killings where the bodies of seven murdered children were found.' We stop as if someone has pressed pause on us. 'This morning police have confirmed two more bodies have been found at the property.'

CHAPTER 33

MIA

I've grown used to uncomfortable silences and conflict in this house, but it has never felt as awkward as it does this morning.

I lead DS Mark Goodwin from the front door into the kitchen of the main house, where Finn and his parents await us. He's the only friendly face I've seen in days and I'm glad he's here. Finn and I have barely spoken since our row two days ago, and Dave and I aren't making eye contact. I'm not picking up a vibe from Debbie, so I assume neither of them have told her about our conversations. Perhaps Dave lied when he told me that Debbie knew he went to school with those girls.

'Firstly,' Mark begins as he takes a seat, 'I want to reiterate how sorry I am that you found out about the latest development from the media and not from me. I had a couple of days' annual leave and it was a breakdown in communication between departments that meant it was released publicly before anyone briefed you.'

'Do you know who those bodies are?' I ask.

'All I can say – and as always, this goes no further than these four walls – is that two adult skeletal bodies are with the Home Office pathologist.'

'Adults?' I repeat. 'Not children?'

'No.'

A knot unravels in my stomach. I don't know why it makes such a difference that they're adults, as they are still two more victims. But it does.

'They were discovered buried in the garden, by the rear wall,' Mark continues. 'We believe them to be male and female, but they are missing body parts.'

'Which parts?' asks Finn.

'Their heads.'

I shudder.

'Could they be the previous owners of the house?' Mia asks.

'It's a line of inquiry we are looking into,' Mark says. 'The former residents disappeared, quite suddenly by all accounts, back in the 1970s. We haven't been able to trace any living relatives, so confirming them via a DNA match might take a little time.'

Debbie turns to Dave but his gaze is now fixed to the floor. She takes a tissue from a packet and dabs at her eyes but she's not quick enough to catch her tears. 'I'm sorry,' she says. 'Everything about this story is just so awful . . . those children missing for so long, their poor parents and now two more bodies . . . Sometimes I wonder if this is ever going to end. Every day, that house and what it's been hiding is all I can think about. I just want this to stop.'

Dave places his arm around her shoulders. I'm a little taken aback by her emotion because I don't recognise this Debbie. I've never given any thought to how the discovery might have affected her.

When Mark leaves soon after, I miss his calming presence in this turbulent environment. It's like, when he appears, everyone is on their best behaviour and I can pretend we're all normal, when in reality, we are far from it. Or maybe I'm not ready to admit to myself I like being around him more than I should. There's a warmth about him that makes me believe, one day, this nightmare will come to an end. God only knows how high the body count will be by then.

We retreat to our own corners of our private, messed-up worlds. Dave heads to work; I've told Debbie I'm having Sonny again today, so she's off running errands in town; and Finn packs his van with his tools, leaving us without so much as a goodbye.

I return to the Annexe and re-read the messages Finn has sent me since our argument. I've reached the point where I don't know what angers me the most: that he wouldn't listen to me about Dave, that he thinks that dosing me up with antidepressants is going to solve everything, or that he's vocalised what we're all thinking but no one has said – I'm a useless mother. It's the latter that stings the most. I know I should have organised a therapist by now but I'm putting it off because I know they'll want me to relive these last few months again. It was and still is so hard to deal with first time around, let alone do it again. I expected Abigail Douglas's funeral to give me closure and let me focus on connecting with Sonny. Instead, it's been replaced by a need to learn what else Dave is keeping from us.

I need to find a way of embracing my baby and discovering the truth without neglecting either. But where do I start? And then it dawns on me: I'm alone in the house. The others won't be back for hours.

If I want the truth, I'm going to have to find it myself.

ADVERTISEMENT TAKEN FROM THE TELEGRAPH, 15 AUGUST 1946

'Luggage that is better travelled than you!'

It's a smart, fashion-forward family that knows the best holidays are the ones you take with your Portmanteau leather suitcases. France's best-kept secret is finally available in the United Kingdom and whether you are flying high or ready for an oceanic adventure, our stylish and durable box leather suitcases and beauty cases are perfect for the whole family. Their sturdy frames, covered by our patented hard-wearing leather, are airtight, tough and stain resistant, and come in a variety of colours. For men there's Deep Olive, Biscayne Bay and Marina Blue. And for the fairer sex, there's Dove White, Gentle Fawn and Dover Cream. Our cases can hold up to 60 lb in weight, which means you can take all your creature comforts on holiday with you – including the kitchen sink! With a Portmanteau suitcase by your side, everyone will know you are the smartest thing going.

CHAPTER 34
THIRTY-SIX YEARS EARLIER

'Are you sure you want to do this?' my grandmother asks as the taxi pulls away. I nod. She looks to my grandfather, their concern mirrored in each other's faces. He shrugs, cracks open the window and lights up one of the pre-made roll-up cigarettes he keeps inside a tin in his pocket. The smell reminds me of my mother and I hate it as much as I hate her.

I disregard their obvious doubts and focus my attention on the sudden rain lashing against the car and the road. If I'd looked at the weather forecast in the newspaper this morning, I'd have brought an umbrella with me. I don't want to smell like a wet dog on my wedding day.

I know what my grandparents are thinking, as neither has disguised their doubts that I'm making the right decision. It took weeks of persuasion before they agreed to sign the permission forms to allow me to marry at sixteen. But this is what I want, this is what I need, someone whom I don't have to share, who will always be there for me, no matter who or what I am. Or even what might lie deep inside.

I'm starting to develop these urges, you see. Cravings to do things that I can never tell another living soul about because they wouldn't understand. I don't even understand them myself. The person I'm about to spend the rest of my life with knows some of what goes on in my head, but only as much as I allow them to. The difference between me and my parents is that I can keep my urges under control, something they never managed. I'm counting on my spouse to help me become a better person. Once I'm married, they'll keep me on the straight and narrow and the cravings will disappear.

I wish George were with us. It's been five years since I saw him and I hoped he might have come back and found me by now. At eighteen, perhaps he's now enrolled in the army and unable to take leave because he's stationed somewhere else in the world? If I wasn't getting married, I might even be tempted to join myself.

You know what happened to him, a voice inside me whispers. I choose to ignore it.

I know that, if he were here, George would be cracking a joke to ease the tension and reassuring our grandparents that I'm doing the right thing. I wish he had never left. But most of all, I wish I had not let him down so badly.

We'd spent so much time together, partly because we were all the other had and also because my parents insisted on it. They enrolled us in activity groups together, church clubs, sports teams and the like. As the older sibling, it was up to George to single out a kid who fitted my parents' criteria and invite them back to our house to play. I'd join them in games of cricket or football in the garden and if my parents didn't approve of George's choice, Dad would offer the child a fizzy orange juice from his carbonated drinks maker. But if he or Mum took a shine to them, Dad would signal his intentions by offering our guest a cola.

Soon after, that child would fall asleep. Then he or Mum would carry them upstairs to the spare room and they'd stay with them behind closed doors as they napped. Later, they'd be driven home and Dad would explain to their parents they'd been poorly. And George and I were never allowed to return to that same club again. For a long time, we didn't understand why so many of our new friends became ill at our house. Eventually we accepted that it was just one of those things.

Because there was only a finite number of clubs locally that we could join, my parents used the caravan the house's previous owners had left behind and we spent many half-term breaks touring the country and staying at holiday parks and campsites. Much like at home, George was encouraged to make friends in kids' clubs or at the arcades. And after he brought one back to the caravan, we were sent out to play and the doors locked behind us. Before our new friends awoke, they'd be left unconscious somewhere like a roadside or car park and we were en route to our next location.

Our lives were cloaked in such secrecy that there was no one to tell us what our parents were doing was wrong. Yet somehow, we knew. But it was love, loyalty and fear of the unknown that prevented us from telling anyone. 'What happens in our house stays in our house,' Dad said. 'This family will not survive if people start interfering. We'll be broken up into pieces and you two will be separated and living in foster homes.' We had no reason to disbelieve him.

They scared us equally, but increasingly, it became Mum we avoided where possible. Her mood swings were becoming more frequent and more erratic. One minute she could be making you dinner, and the next she was scraping it into the bin because of a look you gave that she perceived to be disrespectful. She was also much freer with her aggression than Dad was. The gold rings she wore on three fingers gave her slaps extra clout, and the cigarettes she chain-smoked left nasty raised red welts on my arms and neck. When she wasn't enraged, she was lost in her own world, floating around the house wearing her melancholy like a housecoat.

I recall how the two years that separated George's and my ages suddenly expanded when he turned thirteen. He began spending as much time as possible away from home and away from me, creeping out at night as my parents slept and returning in the early hours stinking of beer and cigarettes. In hindsight, I can only assume he was developing a taste for normality and rebelling against our parents' strict rules. But this desire for freedom was pulling him away from me. When I begged him to take me out with him, he laughed. Rejected, I turned to my parents to fill the George-sized void. I wanted them to give me a purpose and involve me like they had involved him.

The beginning of the end for our family came when Martin Hamilton appeared in our lives – a new lad George had quietly befriended and who became the catalyst for everything that followed.

My grandfather's voice returns me to the present. 'We're almost here,' he says, stubbing his cigarette out in the ashtray. 'We'll ask you one more time, are you sure you want to do this?'

'Yes,' I say without hesitation. And for a moment I think that he has a hand on my shoulder. But when I look to it, it's bare. A comforting warmth spreads through my body when I realise that on the most important day of my life, my brother and best friend is with me after all.

CHAPTER 35

MIA, 2019

Dave and Debbie's home office is inside a partially converted double garage. It's windowless and stuffy and there's the waft of a sickly sweet cinnamon scent coming from a plug-in air freshener under the desk. The breeze-block interior has been whitewashed, giving it an even more sterile feel than if they'd left it grey. It's large enough to fit three cars, two side by side and one in front. In one section they store gardening tools like a lawnmower and hedge trimmer, and on the wall there are shelves for things like plant pots, secateurs and, bizarrely, what looks like a hunting knife.

Sonny is fast asleep so I've left him in his playpen in the kitchen. I tell myself that he's safe and I'm right next door and will hear him if he wakes up.

There's a line of dark-grey filing cabinets stacked along one wall, a chunky desktop computer, plastic filing trays and a line of shelves containing black ring binders. The other half of the room is packed to the ceiling with plastic containers and cardboard boxes, each labelled by name or by content. Some I recognise as belonging to Finn and me, but the majority of cardboard boxes are Debbie and Dave's.

I have no idea what I'm searching for, beyond anything that might give me more information or a better understanding of my father-in-law. His filing cabinets are the most organised part of this space so they feel like as good a place to start as any. I open each drawer and most contain historic invoices. Debbie is clearly old-school when it comes to organising Dave's accounts and prefers to keep them in a physical format rather than convert them into spreadsheets and store them in a desktop folder.

I turn on the computer but it's password-encrypted. I try the predictable combinations of names and dates of birth but I switch it off when I'm locked out. My attention moves towards the boxes of Finn's and my stuff for a moment. They're a bleak reminder that we still don't have anywhere of our own to store their contents. I'm tempted to flick through a book I find of our Maldives wedding photographs but stop myself. Images of happier days are only going to depress me.

I pick up an unlabelled box, which contains old road maps of towns from across the country and letters and invoices typed on yellowing paper. The dates start in the late 1940s and finish in the mid-1950s. Letterheads mention something about leather and luxury travel imports. How does this relate to Finn's family? Attached to one invoice with a paperclip is a scrap of typed paper with an address. I take a photo of it on my phone and replace the box where I found it and delve into another.

This one contains a collection of Finn's old toys and books. There's a Tamagotchi with no battery, a robotic dog, and a Stretch Armstrong and plastic dinosaurs. Sometimes you forget your other half had a life before you, and assume they arrived in your world fully formed. I briefly find myself softening towards him. I know that he only wants the best for me, but his approach has been clumsy. Perhaps I've been too hard on him. Maybe my current mindset has me wanting to make everyone else around me as miserable as I am.

I step into the house to check on Sonny but he is still fast asleep, curled up in a ball, his head resting on a Cookie Monster cuddly toy. *This is hardly spending more time with him,* my conscience reminds me, but it's his nap time regardless of where we are.

Behind Finn's container in the garage is a battered, water-damaged cardboard box. I pull out papers and schoolbooks that have also been badly stained, making some illegible. But I can read Dave's name in one. Inside, most of his grades are Es and the occasional U. His teachers' descriptions of his ability and attendance are all a variation of the same thing: Dave barely turns up; he can hardly read and write, so he has been placed into what they refer to as a 'remedial class'. I wonder for how much of his later life he has carried that kind of stigma.

I find a book used for handwriting practice. The water damage has washed away his name from the cover and the first few pages, but they're made up of basic exercises that begin with the alphabet and, over time, progress to short words. The back of each page is indented as if he has put a lot of pressure on the nib. There's something familiar about his writing, the way he has formed his M, the backwards S and the two bars through the centre of the E. I continue flicking through the book, and then another, trying to recall why the handwriting is recognisable.

I turn back to each letter and trace them with my fingertip. And then it hits me so hard that it almost knocks me off my feet.

CHAPTER 36

FINN

'It's your dad's writing on the skirting board,' Mia begins. She says it so quickly it takes a moment for me to register what she means. She is wired, her skin is flushed and her eyes are wide open like she's been necking espressos.

'What?'

'It was your dad who wrote the message in the house warning us what was hidden in the attic.'

'When?'

'When he was a boy.'

She's not making sense and, once again, I'm playing catch-up. Then she seems to recognise that she shouldn't seem so happy about what she thinks she knows and dials it back a notch. She hands me an old schoolbook and her phone. Online, she has found and saved an image of the words etched into the nursery skirting board. 'I will save them from the attic.' I can't deny that the H and the Es are similar to those in this book, and as I look more closely, so is the S.

'Every kid writes like that,' I counter. 'We all got our letters mixed up and back to front when we were learning.'

She snaps her head back and she looks at me like I've just slapped her across the face. 'Finn,' she says. 'Look at it! It's identical! Every single bloody letter. You need to consider what this means.'

All this proves is that my wife has found another obsession that isn't our son. After days of giving me the silent treatment, she called me when I was on a job, begging me to come home. When I asked if Sonny was okay, she'd already hung up, so I raced across town, flying through countless speed cameras, only to hear this.

I pretend that I'm considering it but I'm really just trying to find a frame of reference for her behaviour. I honestly don't know how to handle her. 'What do you think it means?' I ask, hoping that when she says it aloud and it's no longer a conversation in her head, she might get how crazy she sounds.

'It means Dave wrote that message,' she repeats. 'At some point in his childhood, your dad was in that house. I don't know if it was at the same time Abigail was there or even Precious, but he was definitely there. He knew kids were being locked in the attic.'

'When did you last sleep?' I ask. 'Have you had lunch yet? Let's go into the kitchen and I can make you something.' She's not listening.

'Why didn't he tell us he knew those girls?' she says in the same accusatory way as when we argued about Dad last time.

'He already explained it to you, remember? He barely went to school for years.'

'So where did he go instead?'

'How would I know?'

'So he could have spent time at that house. I bet Mark will get it out of him—'

'Mark Goodwin?' I interrupt. 'You want to call the police on my dad?'

'Unless you want to ask him why he's been hiding the truth from us?'

157

I can't listen to any more of this. 'For Christ's sake, Mia!' I yell and she takes a step back. 'Listen to yourself. I'm not calling the police on my own dad and neither are you. He was not in that fucking house, he did not scratch a message in the skirting boards and he didn't know those girls. The handwriting is a coincidence. You are searching for something that hasn't happened and you have to stop it.'

Mia looks genuinely hurt by my outburst, but not even her quivering lips and the threat of tears can stop me now. 'You're ill, Mia, can't you see that? Something isn't right in your head and you need help. Stop this witch hunt against my family.' I'm pacing the lounge and everything that's been troubling me since our last row is spilling out. 'We can't go on like this. We have been through so much together and survived it, but this, well, I'm scared it's going to break us. You seem determined to sabotage what we have. And I might be able to deal with all of that if I was convinced that Sonny was your main priority, but he's not.' I look around when something dawns on me. I make my way into the bedroom. Sonny's cot is empty. 'Where is he?'

Panic spreads across her face.

'Mia, where is he?' I repeat as she hurries to the door.

'He's in your mum's kitchen,' she mutters. I catch her up and grab her by the shoulder, spinning her around.

'Alone?' I shout and she nods. 'How long for?'

'I don't know . . . half an hour?'

As she tries to free herself from my grip I push her then let go. She loses her balance and falls into the wall. I'm too angry with her to check if she is hurt.

'I'll get him,' I snap and turn my back on her. 'He needs one of us to be a parent.'

CHAPTER 37

DEBBIE

I knock on the door to the Annexe but wait until I'm invited in. Mia opens it; Sonny's head rests on her shoulder. At face value, this looks perfectly normal. But she can't fool me. Her posture is statue-stiff, as if it's the first time she's ever held a baby and she's frightened she might drop him.

Finn told me last night Mia thinks Dave's been keeping secrets about that house and she's been poking around our garage. It's time for me to take charge of the situation before it escalates.

'How are you?' I ask. 'I've not seen either of you much the last couple of days.'

'We're okay,' she says.

'Are you sleeping any better?'

'A little.'

The bags under her eyes tell a different story. 'Can we talk?'

She invites me to sit on the sofa opposite her. I spot pillows and a folded duvet on the floor and I feel for my poor son, kicked out of his own bedroom.

'Has Finn asked you to come?' She can't hide the anxiety in her voice.

'No, but he's told me you two are going through a difficult patch and about your doubts over Dave.' Her face reddens. 'Finn is worried about you, Mia, as we all are.'

'I'm getting better.'

'But you're not, are you, darling? With the greatest respect, you can't kid a kidder. You may have your baby in your arms, but he's not in your heart, is he?'

'I love him,' she protests and clutches him like an expensive handbag.

'But is that enough? Finn told me you left Sonny in the kitchen unattended yesterday while you were in our garage trying to disprove what Dave told you. Why would you do that to your child?'

'I was only next door.'

'Mia, he is so low down your list of priorities that you forgot him. Can you not see that isn't normal behaviour for a new mum? He's supposed to be your *life*. Perhaps we expected too much of you . . .' I turn away and shake my head as if it's my fault.

She knows I'm right, I can sense it, but she isn't ready to admit it. I turn back around to face her. 'I hoped I was helping you out by taking care of Sonny when you were struggling, and that you and I had drawn a line under the way things once were between us. But it feels like Dave and I have done something to upset you. Nobody is keeping secrets from you, Mia. Ask me anything and maybe we can put this behind us.'

She's hesitant. With her free hand she rubs her fingers together.

'Did . . . did Dave tell you the truth about going to school with one of the kids in our house, and her friend?'

'Of course he did. He's my husband. We tell each other everything.'

'Then why didn't either of you mention it to us or the police?'

'Tell me one good thing that has come out of you learning about this.'

'It was our house. We had a right to know.'

'Dave didn't tell you because it bears no relevance to anything that's happened in the past or present. And we were concerned that in your current mindset, you might read more into it than there is. And we were right. Let me tell you something, Mia, that you might not know. My husband didn't have the world handed to him on a plate. Neither of us was born with a silver spoon in our mouths like you were. We had to work hard for everything we have. He had a terrible childhood so of course he doesn't want to be reminded of it. In the end, Dave went against the low expectations of him to become who he is now. My husband is a proud man, a devoted dad and a wonderful grandfather, but he is ashamed of what he was. It's hurtful when you rake up the past and accuse him of God knows what.'

'The skirting board . . .' she says, more quietly this time. 'It was his writing. I'm sure of it.'

'He's dyslexic. His handwriting looked like that of a much younger child's back then, so it could easily have belonged to one of those seven children in the attic. I'll say this once and once only: I swear on Finn's life that Dave never set foot in that house before you bought it. I'm begging you to stop this vendetta against him. There's enough pressure on this family already without you making everyone's lives more miserable. May I offer you some advice, woman to woman? Perhaps you should pay more attention to your marriage instead of coming up with these silly accusations. Dave and Finn are working their fingers to the bone to provide for us while you're busy searching for trouble where there is no trouble.'

Now Mia's face is filled with doubt. She looks away but not quickly enough for me not to witness her shame. I need to take advantage of the moment. 'What do you want from us, Mia?' I ask gently. 'We love you but it's clear that's not reciprocated by you. You took the house we wanted from under our noses and I didn't complain. You don't like living with us but you didn't care to accept our offer to help you buy somewhere else. I'm at a loss to know what else we can do. I know that we can't all go on living like this. So what will it take to make you happy?'

She hesitates before she whispers, 'I don't know.'

I have her on the ropes. I have waited months, years in fact, to have this conversation. 'Our offer still stands,' I say. 'We can remortgage the house to help you find somewhere of your own.'

'We can't take that money from you.'

'I think you'll admit, things have changed for us all. So we aren't offering it to you both any more. We are offering it to you only.' Her eyebrows knit. 'We will give you every penny of that money to buy yourself somewhere new. But it's on the condition that you leave my son and your marriage.'

'What?' she asks, thinking she's misheard or misunderstood me.

'I want you to leave Finn.' I place my hand gently on her fore-arm. 'I'm sorry to say it, but you bring nothing but unhappiness here. You are like a cancer in our family, Mia, eating away at us. Finn would be much happier if he had the chance to start afresh. I want nothing but the best for him, and the best does not involve you. So I'm begging you to take the money, move away and start again.'

A period of stunned silence follows before she speaks again. 'You are so desperate for us to split up that you'd pay me off?'

'I'm doing this for my own family, which you could have been a part of but have rejected every step of the way. If you knew anything about motherhood, you'd understand why I'm trying to protect my boys.'

'What does Dave say about this?'

'He is behind me one hundred per cent,' I lie. This is my own idea.

'And Finn? What's he going to say when I tell him?'

'I know my son better than you know your husband. In the end, he'll understand this is for the best.'

'You are unbelievable.' Mia rises to her feet still clutching Sonny and turns her back to me. I spot tufts of Sonny's dark hair and I'm desperate to feel them against my fingers. 'You pretend to be my friend when all you want is to control us all.'

'I might be unbelievable, but you haven't turned me down, have you? You haven't said no.'

She opens her mouth but she is unable to find the words. And in that moment, I realise that she is actually considering this. It was a long shot, but now I'm wondering if my plan just might work. I try to contain my excitement.

'Just take it, Mia,' I press. 'Admit it, you hate it here. You think you can do better than Finn and us. You're never going to like me, and Finn is never going to choose you over us. So this vicious circle of you and I trading blows is going to continue forever, if you let it. I'm giving you the power to change it all. Think about your old life in London – your friends, the buzz you got out of living and working there. You could use our money as a deposit on a flat. Start going back to your glamorous parties and celebrity clients. Be honest with yourself: you miss it all, don't you? So why not make it easy on yourself – on all of us – and leave?'

Now she is facing me. 'Just like that?'

'Just like that. We are perfectly capable of muddling on without you. We did it before you arrived and we can do it again. And when he's older, Sonny will understand.'

'Understand what?'

'Understand why his mum left him with his dad.'

'What did you say?'

'You don't expect us to let you take him with you, do you? Part of the condition of you moving away is that you leave my grandson behind.'

CHAPTER 38
THIRTY-EIGHT YEARS EARLIER

I look around the classroom at the rest of the pupils here and quietly pick them off one by one.

As our teacher Mrs Dennison continues talking about the earth's tectonic plates – something Dad taught George and I about years earlier in his homeschooling – I've drifted off into my own world, one that is partly a new creation and part of my parents' making. I'm splitting classmates up into categories of who Mum and Dad would've wanted me to bring home, those who they wouldn't care for, and others who would never leave *that room* again.

Suddenly I remind myself of where I am and who I am now. I don't have to think like this because I no longer inhabit that world. I am ordinary. Everyone in this class is safe because I am ordinary. I even sound ordinary, I have quelled my vocabulary so I'm more like them and less like my father. And now, if I bring anyone home with me, it will be to my grandparents' house. These friends will leave as they arrived, conscious and breathing.

My relationship with my grandparents has improved in the time I have been living with them. I remember how shocked they were when I turned up on their doorstep, introducing myself as their grandchild and begging for help. Before that day, they hadn't seen me – not by choice, apparently – since I was an infant. Attempts to visit had been rebuffed by my mother. The story of how and why I escaped, along with George's disappearance and everything else that went on under that roof, horrified them. But they never doubted me for a second.

My grandfather is far from being a little old man in a pair of slippers and puffing on a pipe. His faded merchant navy and prison tattoos tell stories he doesn't need to. My grandmother is his female equivalent. She doesn't suffer fools gladly but is perceptive of emotion – quick to offer hugs and just as fast to retract them if I recoil at her sudden movements.

Living with them means I'm having to change a lot of my mindsets and I don't need to analyse who I should be making friends with. I don't have to fear what mood they might be in when I return from school. Instead, I live a normal life now. Yet it remains stained by abnormal thoughts. I still fantasise about seeing new school friends slump unconscious over our dining room table, eyeballs rolling backwards, threads of drool falling from the corners of their mouths. Only now it's my grandfather carrying them over his broad shoulders and up the stairs.

If I hadn't been forced to attend so many clubs and groups, I might have found it difficult adjusting to school life and being surrounded by my peers. But the practice I had at befriending anyone means the transition has been smooth. The one and only time a group of boys tried to give me a hard time for being the new kid in class, I punched the ringleader so hard in the face that his black eye remained for a fortnight. He was too humiliated to tell on me.

I have even made a best friend, something I'd only ever had in George until I betrayed him. We spent much of the recent summer holidays in one another's company, and sometimes, when we played together, I mistakenly called him George. I don't think he noticed.

He made me wonder if making a connection with someone outside the family was what attracted George to Martin Hamilton. Because that's what I feel with my friend. We are already so close that I would kill for him if he asked me to.

It was soon after Martin appeared in his life that my brother wanted less to do with me. Our conversations were made up of 'Martin this' and 'Martin that' and the attention this stranger was getting far outweighed anything George gave me. By then, Mum was taking pleasure in pitting George and me against each other, praising one and criticising the other, encouraging us to snitch for even the most trivial of misdemeanours. So in retaliation against George's neglect and being desperate to find favour with Mum, I told her about the friend George had confided in me about.

And I knew I had done the wrong thing the second the words tripped from my tongue. Just how wrong wouldn't become immediately clear, though.

Mum and George rowed when he point-blank refused to bring Martin home, and it escalated later when Dad returned from work. My satisfaction at dropping George in it was so brief it couldn't even be accurately described as short-lived. I had turned on the only person in the world who cared for me. Eventually, two beatings later, George caved, but our relationship was irretrievably damaged.

Soon after, Martin regularly came around for tea. He was a funny-looking boy with a big goofy smile and protruding ears. He told silly jokes, did impressions of film and TV stars and I reluctantly found myself liking him.

Mum also showed a surprising amount of interest in him; much more than any of the other kids George had befriended. She'd ensure his belly was always full, heaping strawberry-flavoured Angel Delight dessert into his bowl while we had none, and giving him a snack to take home. My like of him soon turned to resentment. Martin's mum may have died while he was still a baby but that didn't mean he could steal mine or my brother.

Dad wasn't as drawn to him as Mum was. Quite the opposite, in fact. He seemed to grow tired of the boy's regular appearances, and during one particular visit – and to everyone's shock but Dad's – Martin fell asleep at the table. We all knew what was to follow.

I swear there were tears in Mum's eyes as she followed Dad carrying Martin in his arms into *that room*. When my parents reappeared shortly before bedtime, Martin wasn't with them. We never saw him again. That was the day everything altered. From then on, no child ever returned once they were carried away.

George and I never spoke of Martin again. When the police turned up at the house, as his dad knew he and George were pals, we didn't need to get the story straight between us first. We just knew what to do to protect our family. We said that while we played with him sometimes after school, he'd never been to the house before and they had no reason to think we were lying.

I wonder now how different my life might have been had Martin returned. Would I still have developed urges? Would there have been any necessity to save people? To save my brother? Because he was the one I let down the most.

My last memory of George is the following weekend, his desperate eyes locking on to mine when Mum caught us watching a video cassette labelled *Raiders of the Lost Ark* that we found lying on the floor by the machine that suddenly appeared one afternoon. But after loading it into the top, the snowy screen perplexed us when it suddenly showed *that room* upstairs and not the movie.

The only person on the screen at first was Martin. It was a close-up of his tearful face, his eyes full of fear and his arms above his head, reaching up high as if trying to touch the stars. The camera panned out to show a rope around his neck and attached to a hook in the ceiling. Then someone taller than him and wearing a jumper like Dad's appeared, holding a plastic bag in both hands.

We both turned our heads as fast as lightning bolts when Mum began screaming from behind us. We tried to run but she blocked the door, and when Dad appeared, George grabbed a cricket bat propped up against the sofa and hit Mum hard across the chest with it, sending her sprawling to the floor. My hysterical brother was yelling at the top of his voice, pleading with me to run to the village for help as Dad grabbed the bat from his hands and dragged him up the stairs by his neck and towards the open loft hatch and ladder. Terrified and confused, I hid away in my bedroom instead. *It'll blow over soon*, I kept reminding myself. *By morning, we'll be back to normal. Our version of normal.*

Later, and as the house quietened, I crept out and along the landing. They had left the ladder down and the key in the lock of the loft hatch. Just one turn anti-clockwise and I could release him. I could save us both.

But I didn't dare to do it. If I had and we were caught, we would both be in much more trouble than George was in now. Instead, I convinced myself that once tempers calmed, they would let him out and we could continue as we always did. So I returned to my room.

I must have drifted off because I awoke hours later to the sound of a heavy object being dragged along the landing. I opened my door a crack just in time to see Dad pulling his semi-conscious eldest son into *that room*. I panicked and ran towards them, stopping at the doorway. The orange sunset outside bathed the room in a soft light. Dad taught me to always frame beauty when I saw it, so that's what I did. Trapped in that picture was George, lying on his side, next to an open suitcase and a pile of his clothes.

Dad didn't reprimand me, he just slammed the door and a darkness smothered the corridor.

The final image of my brother was fleeting but one that I have spent time trying to both replicate and forget in equal measure.

'Where's George?' I asked nervously over breakfast the next morning. The table was only set for three.

'You were both warned what would happen if you were disloyal to this family,' said Mum, matter-of-factly, lighting up a cigarette. She wrapped an arm across her chest and held it there. 'Your brother threatened to tell other people about what happens here. We can't let that happen, can we?'

I shook my head and looked outside to Dad, stoking a bonfire in the garden. Next to him on the ground was a pile of empty coat hangers. His face was drawn and his shoulders hunched as he threw a piece of clothing into the flames. I recognised George's red and white jumper. I swallowed my tears. My brother had gone and it was all because of me.

Four years have passed and I miss him as much today as I did that morning over my first breakfast without him.

'BABES IN ATTIC' HUSBAND IS A SECRET LOVE CHEAT

BY CAROLE WATSON, CHIEF CRIME REPORTER

The husband who discovered the bodies of seven children in his 'house from hell' is harbouring his own dark secrets, we can exclusively reveal.

Finn Hunter, 30, has been spending cosy nights with his ex-girlfriend behind his wife Mia's back – and they have a daughter together.

Finn and Mia, who was once engaged to *Strictly Come Dancing* winner Ellis Anders, hit the headlines after discovering the bodies of the murdered children in the attic of their new home in March. Two adult corpses were also found in the garden last week.

But Hunter has been spotted several times since then sneaking into the home of his ex, Emma Jones, with whom he has a four-year-old love-child. He also has a baby son with Mia.

A close friend revealed how the Hunters have been living under huge strain since the grisly discovery in their loft.

'Mia will be devastated to learn her husband and Emma have not only kept in regular touch since they split up, but that they had a baby together,' said our source. 'He has been lying to her for years.'

Continued on pages four and five.

CHAPTER 39

FINN

Fuck.

CHAPTER 40

MIA

I'm relatively calm, all things considered. Those 'things' being that my husband is a lying, cheating bastard who has fathered a baby with his ex-girlfriend and continued their affair throughout our marriage. That my father-in-law is hiding what he knows about the house where the bodies of seven children and two decapitated adults were found. And let's not forget my snake of a mother-in-law who has tried to buy me out of my marriage and parenthood.

It's only 6 a.m. but for the umpteenth time this morning, I pick up the iPad to torture myself by re-reading the newspaper story describing Finn's secret life, word by word. They've printed a photograph of Emma, the woman they've branded my 'love rival', next to a child with a pixelated face riding a pink bike. Three other shots include her and my husband walking hand in hand and kissing on a doorstep.

Autopilot is how I'm functioning right now. I've had no sleep – not even a wink – and my empty stomach keeps gurgling like a drain. But I have no appetite. Even a mouthful of toast would make me sick right now. I do, however, have an insatiable thirst. I wonder if it's because of how much fluid I've lost from crying. Is that even possible? I make a mental note to google it. Then I ask myself why I care. My brain is firing in so many different directions right now that it's struggling to settle on any one train of thought.

I'm actually a little grateful it's behaving this way because, when I stop to take a moment, I'm reminded of ashen-faced Finn's appearance in the bedroom last night. He was so ghostly that I thought he was going to tell me that something terrible had happened to Debbie. And I'll be honest, I'd have needed to have pulled off an Oscar-winning performance to show even a little bit of grief now she's shown me her true colours.

Instead, he asked me to sit down on the bed as he explained how DS Goodwin had been in touch to warn him that a newspaper had contacted the press office. It was planning to run a story with photographs about Finn and was offering him a right to reply. It involved his ex-girlfriend.

'What photographs?' I asked.

'They're of me leaving her house.'

'When?'

'In the last couple of weeks.'

'How often?'

'A few times.'

'How many is a few?'

'Half a dozen or so. Perhaps more.'

My heart sank. I wasn't stupid. I knew where this was going. There's only one reason why he would be at Emma's house so often. 'How long has it been going on for?'

He struggled to look me in the eye. 'It never really finished.'

I had to process his words before I replied. 'You've been having an affair with her for the last six years?' He nodded. 'Why?' He shrugged. 'Not an answer, Finn.'

'I don't know why.'

'I repeat, not an answer. If you loved her more than me, why not just break things off with me? Why marry me? Why not marry her?'

He shrugged again and I dabbed at my glistening eyes with my sleeve.

'There's more,' he continued, and this time, he couldn't face me. He made his way to the window and spoke to the darkness of the garden. And that's when he explained how Emma fell pregnant a year after he and I married and how they have a daughter, Chloe, together.

I did the maths. 'So while I was in a fertility clinic having my eggs removed, while I was jabbing daily hormone injections deep into my body, making me feel constantly sick, while my moods were up and down like a yoyo, all for us to have a family, you'd already started one with somebody else?'

'It wasn't planned.'

'Then why the hell didn't you make her get rid of it?' I regretted how cruel the words sounded as I said them, but I didn't apologise. As Finn moved to the armchair with his head in his hands, I was up and about, pacing the bedroom like a chained circus bear and making a mental list of objects within reaching distance that I could hurl at him. But I held back. I didn't want Sonny to be woken by the sound of his parents' marriage falling apart. 'Were you ever going to tell me about Chloe?'

'I don't know,' he said.

'And your affair? Did you plan to continue that indefinitely?'

'I don't know.'

'Don't know much, do you? How long did you think you could play happy families with both of us for? I assume she knows about Sonny and I?' He nodded. 'And she doesn't care that she's having an affair with a married man?'

'It's not the ideal situation for her, no.'

'Oh, poor Emma,' I replied, my words dripping with sarcasm. 'Well, if there's anything I can do to make life easier for the poor girl, she only has to ask.' I thought of the countless times I'd scowled at Emma and Finn's prom night photograph in Debbie's dining room, and how I'd tell myself off for being so petty. His past was no more of a threat to our relationship than the boys I'd dated in my teens. How naive I was.

We went back and forth throughout the night until my iPad chimed with a Google alert message an hour ago, set up to inform me each time our names appeared in the press when it was in relation to the house. I never considered it might be used for something else. Finn guessed what I was about to do. 'Please don't read it,' he begged.

'Why, are there more surprises in here?'

'No, I've told you everything.'

'And you expect me to believe you?'

'Yes . . . no . . . I don't know.'

It was the photograph of Finn and Emma kissing that made this nightmare real. I repeated the same questions over and over again to try and catch him out. His answers always remained the same, never faltering. Eventually, I believed there was nothing else the stranger in the room hadn't told me. Because that's what he is to me now. A stranger. Finn is not the man I married.

I find myself hating the newspapers for making me out to be a victim again, even if I suppose that's what I am. I had enough of it when they exposed Ellis's affair with his *Strictly* partner. Now history is repeating itself. What the hell is wrong with me? I thought I had picked the opposite of Ellis with Finn. It turns out they're exactly the same. No, my husband is worse.

'This fucking family,' I said. 'You're as bad as each other. You're all liars. Did your mum tell you she offered me money to leave you and Sonny behind and start afresh somewhere else?'

177

He looked at me blankly. 'I don't think she would have . . .'

'I know exactly what I heard, so don't you dare tell me I've misinterpreted her,' I bellow. 'Don't you fucking dare!'

Half an hour of silence followed until I could take no more. Now, I lift a waking Sonny from his cot and leave the Annexe.

'Where are you going?' he calls after me. When I don't reply, he follows me to his parents' section of the house, where Debbie and Dave are already sitting at the kitchen table. She looks as if she's had about as much sleep as me.

'How long have you known?' I ask.

'I didn't know until last night,' she replies.

'Who did you tell first, me or her?' I ask Finn. His delayed response is its own answer. 'And that's definitely the first you knew about it?' I ask Debbie. She nods. I glare at her for tell-tale signs that she too is a liar, but there's nothing. She is as shell-shocked as me. The only saving grace in this whole mess is that Debbie is probably just as hurt as I am learning that her precious son has kept something so important from her. Not to mention she has been robbed of four years of being a grandmother. And I hope that it really, *really* wounds her.

'Finn and Emma together is everything you wanted, isn't it?' I don't give her a chance to reply. I return to the Annexe, Finn following me, head down, like a chastised dog desperate for its owner's forgiveness. He isn't going to get it.

My phone beeps – it's a text message from Lorna, checking if I'm okay. She must have heard the news. I bet I'm all over the internet again. The only good thing to come from any of the mess that started the day we bought that house is that she and I are in touch again. I tell her I am alright, and that I'll call her later.

'You better get ready for work,' I say to Finn.

He shakes his head. 'I'm not going in.'

'You can't afford not to. And I don't want you anywhere near me today.'

'Mia, we need to talk.'

'No, we don't. You need to leave me alone.'

'But—'

'If you have any respect left for me at all, that's what you're going to do.'

He opens his mouth but thinks twice about replying. Instead, he dresses and, without showering or cleaning his teeth, he leaves the Annexe, turning to look at me one last time, scared I might not be here when he returns. And the way I feel at this moment, he might be right.

CHAPTER 41

DAVE

I close the bathroom window and hold a towel over my mouth to quieten the noises I'm making as I retch. It falls to the floor when the vomit rises and I spew into the toilet. I cock my ear but I don't think Debbie has heard me from the bedroom. Twice more it happens before I study what's come out. The blood is bright red, and there's much more of it today than there was yesterday.

My bones and muscles ache and I don't need a doctor to tell me the cancer is spreading from my stomach to the rest of my body. I need more painkillers, but the last time I saw Jakub on site he explained his contact was searched by customs on his return from Poland and all his medications were confiscated. I've yet to find a new supplier. I have a half-full bottle of bourbon tucked under the passenger seat of the van. It'll do as a temporary fix.

Debbie knows nothing of my illness. I've kept it to myself. I watched as my wife was made to jump through hoops for months before the doctors told us she had Motor Neurone Disease. I'm not going through what she went through when I already know what I have. Every website I've visited lists my symptoms as stomach cancer. I don't have time to spend recovering from an operation or laid up in a bed for months sick from the chemotherapy, radiotherapy or any other kind of therapy they want to throw at me. I've had months to come to terms with it but I have no intention of telling Debbie that I'm slowly dying before her. She has enough on her plate without adding me to her list of worries. I can't watch as her heart breaks.

I climb into the shower and rinse away the sour, metallic taste with mouthwash. The sound of a jet of warm water offers a brief respite from overhearing Finn and Mia's arguing. Last night it was unbearably humid and we could even hear them above the noise of the fan on its highest setting. We tried not to listen but it was impossible not to.

I dry myself off but can't see my reflection in the bathroom mirror to shave, so I wipe it then open the window again and let out the steam. As the fog lifts, I catch my appearance from the neck down for the first time in weeks. I look worse than I remember. I've lost a lot of weight yet my belly has developed a prominent paunch and I don't know if the cancer or alcohol is to blame. Debbie has mentioned my weight loss and I've blamed it on skipping lunch breaks and more manually intensive labour. I'm not sure if she believes me.

When I'm changed I find Debbie in the lounge playing with Sonny. His hand fits neatly inside hers and they couldn't look more at peace despite the war raging between his parents.

I'm glad that Sonny is with us and not them. Some of my earliest childhood memories are of hearing my parents at each other's throats and hurling abuse or objects at one another, like balls in a coconut shy. When Mia reluctantly agreed to let us look after him, I noticed something pass between her and Debbie; a new, much deeper layer of animosity than I've ever seen before. Months after their truce, something has changed and it's more than what

Finn has been doing behind their backs. Debbie denies they've had words but I know when she's keeping something from me. However, I'm going to pick my battles, and this morning, I'm too tired to start one.

'Look how well he can hold his head up.' She beams at him. 'You're coming on so well, aren't you, my little man?' She turns to me. 'Is world war three still raging out there?'

'It's quieted a little. There must be a ceasefire.'

'What do you think they'll do?'

'I don't know,' I reply. 'I really don't know.'

Debbie doesn't have to say it for me to know how she hopes this will play out. Finn's lies have knocked the wind out of her sails. She has spent her life keeping him up there on the pedestal she's built for him, believing he can do no wrong. She assumed they had an honest, open relationship. It's a shock to learn he's been keeping secrets from her. And especially something as monumental as this. So naturally, she is just as hurt as Mia is by his deceit. The two women in his life finally have something in common, yet they appear further apart than ever.

I'm conflicted over how I should be feeling. I pity Mia for what Finn has done. I'd like nothing more than to tell her how sorry I am for having such a stupid, selfish lad. But I can't, because she has brought this all on herself. By poking around in my business and my childhood, she left me with no choice but to interfere.

Finn never confided in me about Emma and Chloe. I found out about it by chance. A couple of years or so after she and Finn separated, he borrowed my van while his was undergoing repairs. My vehicle is linked to an app on my phone that informs me of every journey it makes. And four times he visited the same address on an estate where I knew he wasn't working. The only way I can protect my family is if I know what they are doing, so when he returned the keys, I drove to the semi-detached house with a 'Let

182

By' board in the garden. I arrived to see Emma opening the front door and lifting a pushchair outside. Even before I spotted the little girl's dark hair, I knew who her father was. Birth certificates are public records so it was easy to check the online register office, which listed Finn's name as Chloe Jones's father. A former client who owns a property-letting agency confirmed the house was rented in Emma's name.

I held back from telling Debbie what I had learned. Finn's silence was his own decision. If he wanted to be with Emma and Chloe, he would be, but he chose to remain with Mia. It was not my place to interfere. So I kept quiet. At least until a few days ago, when I contacted the news desk of *The Sun on Sunday* to tip them off anonymously about Finn's double life.

I'm not proud of what I've done, but it will give Mia something else to focus on instead of me. If I have sacrificed her marriage to safeguard myself, then so be it. It's the lesser of two evils. And it will be something else to add to the long list of things I shall learn to live with.

CHAPTER 42

FINN

I remain in the van parked up the street from the house where we will never live. The coppers and forensic teams searching it come and go but no one pays me any attention. I'm past caring how long the investigation will take and what we'll do with the place once they give it back to us. They can bulldoze it as far as I care.

If the last few months have been hell, then the last few weeks have been spectacularly bad even by our standards. I have fucked things up royally, and it's all my own doing. Almost everyone in my life has good reason to hate me right now. A month after my secrets were splashed across the newspapers, Mum still can't look me in the eye because she's missed four years of being in the life of a grandchild she had no idea existed. Mia is livid because I had a kid with someone else and have cheated on her for almost our entire relationship. And Emma is furious with me for dragging her name through the mud in a national newspaper. A group of teenagers called her a 'slag' on the school run yesterday.

I know I've handled this badly, and if I could go back to when we found the bodies, the first thing I'd change is how we dealt with the press. Me, Mum and Dad were adamant that we didn't want anything to do with the media and couldn't understand their fascination with us. It took Mia with her PR hat on to point out that they were interested because she'd had a brush with fame and we were a young, attractive, pregnant couple who, through no fault of our own, bought a house where so many bodies were found. It was like the plot of a horror movie. But they kept harassing us for interviews.

Away from Mum and Dad, Mia tried to talk me into doing just one so they'd leave us alone. But even the fistfuls of cash they were throwing at us weren't enough to make me want that kind of exposure. She was used to it with that idiot of an ex of hers, but I wasn't. The house was the story, not us. But really, I was scared of what they'd dig up about me. Emma and Chloe are not the whole story.

I should have put the brakes on my second family immediately and kept well away to protect them just as much as my marriage. But then things started getting really bad with Mia's postnatal depression or whatever it is she still hasn't got treatment for, and when she pushed me out of the bedroom and made me sleep in the lounge, it was the final straw. I started seeing more and more of Emma. It was, well, familiar and comfortable, like slipping on an old pair of trainers you've had knocking around for years but don't want to wear every day. God knows I needed a bit of normality.

I thought interest in us had long passed, especially after I lost my rag on that fake broken boiler call-out by the journalist and photographer – so I stopped being so cautious when it came to going to Emma's place. How dumb was that? I pretty much gift-wrapped and handed them a much better story on a plate because everyone loves reading about a love rat.

None of this is Mia's fault. I'm the liar in this marriage, not her. And now I've just tossed away the last six years. The newspapers have got what they want: my relationships with the three women I care about the most are in pieces, and I have no idea how to repair any of them.

AUTOPSY REPORT ON TWO BODIES FOUND IN THE GARDEN OF 45, HIGH STREET, STEWKBURY

Body 1 –

These are the remains of a largely skeletonised adult human. The skeleton appears complete except for the skull and upper five cervical vertebrae. There is partial clothing present over the anterior aspect of the body but much of it has deteriorated. Some bloodstaining is apparent on the remaining blue shirt over the chest region and centrally a ragged defect noted. There are three major abnormalities of the bones. The first is a defect measuring just under one cm on the volar aspect of the right forearm; this could represent a defence wound. The second is an induration measuring 0.5 cm on the fifth rib; this is likely to be from a sharp force injury such as a stab wound. Finally, there is a healed fracture to the left tibia, which probably occurred many years prior to death. The dimensions of the hip bones are in keeping with this being a male and the state of the bones puts the age between seventy-five and eighty-five years. It is not possible to give a definitive cause of death as the skull and cervical vertebrae could not be examined; however, the injuries identified point towards the death being traumatic in nature, probably due to injury by a knife or other sharp object.

Body 2 –

These are the remains of a largely skeletonised adult human. The skeleton is complete except for the skull and the upper six cervical vertebrae. Remnants of clothing are present over the anterior aspect of the body including part of a dress and a cardigan, much of which appears bloodstained. The major abnormalities of the skeleton seen are multiple < 0.5 cm cut marks on the bones of the right radius, right humerus, right clavicle and also the anterior pubic rami; this is consistent with sharp force injury. In addition, there is also a left-sided Colles' (wrist) fracture which was probably sustained around the time of death. The dimensions of the hip bones are in keeping with this being a female and the state of the bones puts the age somewhere in the region of eighty and ninety. Although the lack of skull and cervical vertebrae preclude a definite cause of death, it is highly likely that death was traumatic in nature, probably from a knife attack. The fracture to the wrist could have occurred in relation to a fall or struggle around the time of death.

CHAPTER 43

THIRTY-NINE YEARS EARLIER

After extended periods of playing outside alone, I've learned to spend the first minutes of my return home standing quietly, listening to what the house is telling me. When the floorboards creak and the radiators gurgle it's like it is trying to talk. And today it wants me to know that something has happened while I've been chasing wild rabbits around fields. There is something here that doesn't belong. *Or someone.* I haven't seen who it is, but I sense their presence. In the stuffiness of the corridors and hallways I can taste them.

It's not Dad – the car he borrowed from the people who lived here before us isn't on the drive – and we don't get visitors, ever.

And then suddenly, warmth spreads through my small body. I know who it is. *It's George! He's come back for me on my birthday! I turn fourteen tomorrow and he remembered!*

Without thinking, I run up the staircase yelling his name. 'You're back!' I shout and try to open his closed bedroom door. Only it's locked. I rattle the handle but it won't open. 'Are you in there?' I ask hopefully but there is no response. I ask again as the rush of warmth cools and I worry that I've let my imagination run away with me. An aching to be with my brother opens up inside me again, so wide and so desperate to be filled. Then, just as I'm about to leave, I spot his shadow under the door. I hold my breath, waiting for George to turn the handle, open the door, leap out and shout, 'Surprise!' Instead, I hear a completely different voice. It comes from a girl. 'Help me,' she whispers.

Scared, I back away, turn and run downstairs as fast as my legs can carry me, but they buckle and I fall down the last three, scuffing my knees. I land awkwardly at the base. I pick myself up and hurry into the kitchen.

Mum is sitting at the table with her back to me, her posture rigid, head straight and focused on a blank space on the wall. I wonder if the house is talking to her as well. A cigarette has burned down to the filter, leaving a neat line of ash. *Back away now*, I tell myself. Her mood swings are becoming completely unpredictable. But there is someone upstairs and it's been months since they last told me to bring anyone back here. I have to know who it is.

'Who's in George's bedroom?' I ask quietly, but she maintains her silence. Nervously, I approach her and tug at her sleeve. The backhander she gives me is so unexpected that I'm sent crashing to the floor. Then she kicks her chair back as she rises to her feet and begins throwing anything at me that she can lay her hands on. She is hatchet-faced as I try to shield myself. Plates, a breadboard, a saucepan and a washing-up bowl fly into or above me. I wish I was big and strong enough to fight back like George did with her, but all I can do is scramble to my feet and run, only for her to grab me by the neck of my T-shirt and yank me backwards with such force that I feel my neck crick. I'm scared what will happen next, when the kitchen door suddenly opens and Dad appears. He's early, thank God. He glares at us: first her and then me.

'Get out!' she screams at me.

I run to the nearest safe place, the downstairs toilet as it has a lock on the door, and I drop to the floor, panting. Their voices are raised and I press my ear to the wall but they're too muffled to understand. With the door ajar, their words become clearer. They're not arguing over her treatment of me; instead, Dad is furious because, behind his back, she has two children locked upstairs.

Two, I repeat to myself.

Where has she found them? How did she get them here? And why didn't she ask for my help? Mum has never gone out on her own like this before. Since George left, I've always done everything they've asked of me and brought back someone whenever they've demanded it. I've added a few things together and guessed why I never see them again and for what purpose Dad uses the suitcases that keep appearing. But I've not asked where these children go next, or why my parents do this.

Suddenly it dawns on me that if my parents no longer have a use for me, then where is my place in this family? If I'm not a means to an end, then I am nothing.

The kitchen door opens and I close mine, and my father's heavy footsteps stamp up the staircase and into George's room. He is clutching a suitcase, like the one that was next to George the last time I saw him. I can't see from where I am, but I think Dad puts it in *that room*. Soon after, a shriek rings out across the landing before something is dragged along the floorboards and once the door slams, the house falls silent again.

Later, as my parents argue in the kitchen, hunger and curiosity get the better of me. There's a stash of KitKat chocolate bars under my bed I keep for when Mum forgets to feed me. I pad up the stairs, my feet astride each step to minimise the sound of creaking floorboards. I approach George's room but the door is open and his room is empty. The door to *that room*, however, is closed.

I lay my head against the floorboards and try to focus on the dim space under it. Nothing happens for a long time, but I've learned to be patient. Eventually and without warning, something on the other side flickers and I jolt backwards, hitting my head on the skirting board behind me. I return, closer this time, and spot the white of an eye staring back at me. It blinks twice but instead of shying away, I edge closer to it.

'Please help me,' a girl's voice whispers. I want to reply but I'm stuck for words. 'Has she taken you too?' she continues, her voice permeated by short gasps.

'Yes.' I don't know why I'm lying.

'Where are we?'

'In a house in a village, I think.'

'Where's my friend? Have you seen Abigail?'

'No. I'm sorry I haven't.' She doesn't need to know the truth and I want to change the subject. 'What's your name?'

'Precious.' It's an unusual but familiar name. I recall meeting a Precious at a church group my parents took me to shortly after George left. She made a point of approaching me and introducing me to her group of friends. I liked her; she was kind. I wanted her to live. So I didn't befriend her.

'How did she get you here?'

'Abi and I were walking back from choir practice through the park when a woman came from behind a car with a knife. She told us to get inside and we were so scared . . . she made us breathe in something from a cloth and then I woke up in here. Did she do the same to you?'

'Yes.'

I'm stunned by my mum's shameless approach. It goes against everything her and Dad have ever taught us. She is becoming more and more unhinged.

'What does she want?' Precious asks.

'I don't know.' I do know, of course, but again, the truth will do her no favours.

She starts crying again and I find myself feeling something for her that I haven't for any of the others George or I brought here. Pity. For the first time, I'm seeing one of these kids as another human being. So I try to reassure her that everything is going to be alright and that, soon, the woman who took us will set 'us' free.

I want to stay but I move away quickly when I hear my parents emerge from the kitchen. I listen from behind my bedroom door as Precious is moved up into the attic. I lie on my bed in the room below, hearing her pacing the floorboards for much of the night and wishing I could say something to calm her down. But my parents might hear me. It isn't worth the risk.

I am ordered out of the house for much of the next day, but to my relief, she is still alive the following afternoon and she is back in *that room*. 'You're safe!' I whisper under the door.

'Where have you been?' she asks.

'They locked me downstairs,' I say.

'Did you see Abigail?'

'No, I'm sorry. Maybe she escaped?'

'Do you think so? If she has, she'll go and get help for me. For both of us.'

'Me too?' I ask.

'Yes,' she says. 'We won't leave you behind.'

I'm temporarily silenced. I repeat it to myself. *We won't leave you behind.* She said it with such conviction that I believe her. Even though she doesn't know the first thing about me, she wants to help me.

In reality, it's me who can help her. And I want to. I failed George and I won't make the same mistake again. My mother is a danger my father can't control. Sooner or later, one or both of them

193

will turn on me. I need to get Precious and I out of here. I need to save her from what's to come because I am the only one who can.

My parents are still downstairs so I try to keep her mind off the present by asking about her family. She describes her mum and dad, her two cats, the cousins she plays with, grandparents she adores and the church she worships at. I wonder where her god is now. Or maybe he sent me to rescue her?

The more she describes her life, the more I want to know about it. The more I want to be in her world, and not her in mine. Later, when her voice fades, I assume she's fallen asleep, so I slide two KitKats under her door.

I stay awake for much of her second night here, coming up with ideas of how to help her. I must've drifted off because I awake suddenly the next morning, aware of a presence in my darkened room. I can smell the smoke on her clothes and my heart instantly begins to pound. But she has the advantage and I can't move quickly enough to prevent a hand from grabbing my throat and squeezing it hard.

'Traitor!' Mum snarls before dragging me by the arm on to the landing across the floor and then to the other room where she had been keeping Precious. 'You gave her food,' she continues. 'You don't feed the animals. You are done here.' And with a mighty shove that sends me to my knees, it's my turn to be behind the door.

'Dad!' I yell over and over again, banging on the door and hoping he can hear me. But if he's in the house, he's not responding. Later, and when the palms of my hands are too sore and splintered to continue, my heart sinks to a new depth. And I know there and then, that if Dad is not looking out for me, nobody is.

Hours pass as I pace up and down the bare floorboards hoping to be released. When I spot a rusty nail sticking out of a board used to cover the fireplace, I prise it out and absent-mindedly play with it between my fingers until it drops and rolls across the floor.

It comes to rest next to the skirting board. I pick it up and have an idea. Carefully I press it hard into the wood until I have spelled out the words *I will save them from the attic.*

If this is the last place where I will ever be alive and someone ever reads it, I want them to know that I tried.

CHAPTER 44

MIA, 2019

Sonny is giving me a wide, toothless smile as he sits on my lap and we rock gently back and forth on the swings in the playpark. I can't tell if he is grinning because he is enjoying this or because of the long fart he's just let out. But as long as he's not crying, I'm not complaining.

Throughout my pregnancy I looked forward to simple activities like this. Taking my child to a playpark, joining baby clubs and meeting up with other mums for playdates. I wanted to be one of those parents huddled over a table in Starbucks with a latte and a babycino, listening to one another moan about weak bladders and chafed nipples. Instead, I've never felt so lonely.

I use my feet to push the swing forwards and Sonny lets out a gurgling sound followed by a second, much louder fart. I can't help but laugh, my first one in days, I think. I go anywhere I can these days so that I don't have to spend time under the same roof as Finn and his family. If we're not wandering aimlessly around Milton Keynes's indoor shopping centre, then we're haunting one of the half-dozen playparks in the area with which we've become intimately familiar. I wear my sunglasses everywhere, even when it's not bright enough to need them, because I can't bear it when strangers recognise me and start giving me *that look*; the one that says 'poor cow' or 'I'm glad I'm not her' so clearly they might just as well have bellowed it out loud.

I'm happy Lorna and I are back in touch. When we met for coffee yesterday, she tried to say the right things, telling me I deserve better than Finn and his family. And I know she's right, but something stops me from extricating myself from this toxic situation.

Finn has moved out of the Annexe and into one of the spare bedrooms of the main house, no doubt much to Debbie's delight. I wouldn't know just how elated she is because she and Dave have been giving me a wide berth since the revelations of their son's affair were made public. I imagine Dave has had much to do with keeping Debbie away from me, because if I see even a hint of satisfaction in her face, I'll grab her walking stick and smack her around the head with it. Sometimes I even fantasise about doing that just for the hell of it.

How has my life come to this? I am stuck in a house I hate surrounded by people I don't like and who don't like me. I am the mother to a baby I'm still struggling to attach to and the wife of a liar who has no respect for me or our marriage. We have so little money that I cannot afford to rent on my own, and living out of a suitcase in a Holiday Inn with a baby is just about impossible.

I have considered packing Sonny's and my bags and catching a train to London. I still have friends there who knew me before I became this object of pity, friends who text me and email me and who give a damn about me even if I rarely respond because I am too down on myself to discuss my dire situation with anyone else. But who is really going to appreciate me and a child sofa-hopping in their one-bedroom apartment? And that's not fair on Sonny. So I'm stuck.

To describe Finn and me as not in a great place is an understatement. We are so far removed from 'great' that we might as well be orbiting different planets. I don't know if I still want to be married to him. If you'd asked me before Sonny was born whether I'd stay with a cheat, the answer would have been an absolute no. I didn't do it with Ellis. But there's no longer only me to think about. I have to put our child first. And because Finn is a far better parent than I am – it turns out he's had an extra four years of practice with Chloe – Sonny needs at least one of us to have our shit together. I love my husband but I hate him in equal measure. How do I move past that?

I have surprised myself in my willingness for him to continue seeing his little girl, because I could have been a real bitch about it. And perhaps if I didn't have Sonny, I'd resent Chloe and Emma more than I do already. But Finn has a relationship with his daughter and will do for the rest of his life, and it'd be cruel of me to come between them just because I'm jealous. However, it doesn't mean that I want to meet her. I've also warned him in no uncertain terms that he is not to go to Emma's place. And when she drops Chloe off at the house, Sonny and I remain in the Annexe. I'll let her see her half-brother soon, but not yet. Small steps, I remind Finn.

It's on days like this when I wish I had an ordinary mum and dad who'd come to my rescue and take over the adulting that I'm struggling with, not continue sailing around the world. When we finally managed to connect via Skype a few days ago, the excuse for their radio silence was that they'd been living and working for a wildlife charity in Tristan da Cunha, a South Atlantic island and one of the least-connected inhabited places in the world. And with a patchy GPS system, they assumed all the emails they'd sent me from the yacht were being received. They weren't.

To their credit, once I told them of the latest in my long line of dramas, they were adamant they'd be docking in Cape Town, South Africa, and flying home. But an Icelandic volcano spewing ash into the atmosphere has grounded all flights for at least a fortnight, so they are sailing to southern Spain instead and will drive the rest of the way here. Until then, it's just me and Sonny in our own little bubble.

In my darker hours I'm ashamed to admit that I have mulled over Debbie's offer to pay me to leave this all behind and start again. Who would miss me? Finn has a ready-made family he can move on with, Debbie would get the daughter-in-law she always wanted, Dave could go about his life without me questioning its gaps, and I wouldn't have to deal with their dysfunctional, co-dependent, claustrophobic crap. Even without knowing her, I'm sure Emma would probably be a better mum to Sonny than I am.

Perhaps Debbie was right when she described me as a 'cancer in their family'. They were ticking along perfectly well until I came along. Maybe I'm going to be equally toxic around my son, my negative energy damaging him in ways I won't recognise until he's older and it's too late to do anything about. If I took her money and left Sonny with them, perhaps he'd have a chance of normality?

But even imagining not being around my little boy is enough to bring me out in a cold sweat. My baby and I might not have connected, but by God I'm trying. I am confronting my fears about being a danger to him and wanting to protect him from the world in the belief that the final piece of the motherhood puzzle will eventually fit. It has to. I pull him in closer to me as the swing glides gently back and forth.

The buzzing phone in my pocket distracts me. Finn's face is lighting up my screen. Most of the time I send his calls to voice-mail, but I decide to answer this one.

'Hello,' I say, my voice emotionless.

'Have you heard the news?'

My heart sinks. 'What have you done now?'

'It's about the house. They've identified the bodies found in the garden.'

CHAPTER 45

DAVE

I lower the wheelbarrow of rubble to the ground, push up my hard hat and wipe the sweat from my brow. I take a look around. I don't think I've spoken to a single person on site all day. They're all at least half my age and they know about as much English as I know Romanian or Polish.

I can smell my own body odour through my T-shirt and it's unpleasant. I'm sure when I was doing this kind of labouring on the Youth Training Scheme back in the 1980s I wouldn't get as exhausted as I am now. I guess I feel old because I am old. This is a young man's game. My lower back aches, the burning finger of arthritis jabs at my shoulder, and I can't even self-medicate because I'm still out of pills. The foreman says lunch is at 1 p.m. today while we wait for the cement mixer to arrive, so that's when I'll drive into town and pick up a six-pack of beer and some Ibuprofen to keep in the cool box at the back of the van. My only saving grace is that the pain in my stomach has eased off since breakfast.

I should be grateful for any work I'm offered. It's cash in hand and there isn't much else coming my way. I've spent my working life providing for family and I'm too proud to sign on and claim benefits. So I have no choice but to suck it up and earn as much as I can before the cancer gets me. I've been slipping Finn cash here and there as he's struggling to support the two households relying on him. I still feel no guilt at throwing him under a bus driven by tabloid journalists. Of course I haven't told Debbie what I did or about the £7,000 the reporter paid me for the tip-off. That's rainy-day money, and something tells me it won't be long before the heavens open upon us again soon.

I look up and, as if by thinking about my son, I've summoned him. Finn stands twenty feet away from me, beckoning me over. What's he doing here? He can't have good news. When I reach him, he updates me about the two bodies recently found in his garden.

'Kenneth and Moira Kilgour,' Finn says. 'Did you know who they were going to be?'

'I had an idea,' I admit. 'I came across their names in some old paperwork.'

'Goodwin reckons they lived in the house until the mid-1970s before they disappeared.'

'Sounds about right. I don't think they were the only ones to end up like that.'

Finn looks panicked. 'In that house?'

'No, elsewhere. Other houses around the country. It's what they did.'

'Where?'

'I don't know. It was a long time ago.'

He rubs his face with his hands and paces in circles before returning to me. 'And is any of this going to come back on us?'

'I doubt it.'

'But is it possible?'

'In theory, yes.'

'When is this going to end, Dad?' Finn doesn't sound angry, just exhausted. I want to reach out and put my hand on his shoulder, but I hold back. That's not what he and I do. Instead, I shrug.

I don't tell him I have a plan and how, if pushed, it's the only way I can see that will keep him and his mum safe. Because that's all I've ever wanted. No matter what happens to me, I must protect them from the aftermath of the inevitable explosion.

CHAPTER 46

MIA

The car pulls up on the driveway behind mine and I recognise it as DS Mark Goodwin's. We exit our vehicles at the same time. All of a sudden I'm nervous, but not in a bad way.

'Did we have an appointment?' I ask, leaning back in to unclip a wriggling Sonny from the straps in his car seat.

'No, I was just passing and thought I'd call in to see how you are.' He swiftly corrects himself. 'How you *all* are. I mean, after the newspaper stories about Finn . . . well, I can't imagine that was easy to read.' Like me, he's a little flustered. It's endearing. 'Can I give you a hand?'

I pass him the nappy and food rucksack while I hold Sonny with one hand and search for the house keys with the other.

I assume Mark is driving an unmarked police vehicle because a boring estate like that doesn't suit anyone under the age of sixty. Unless he has a wife, 2.4 children and a Labrador at home that he hasn't mentioned. He doesn't wear a wedding ring – I don't know why but I've checked – I guess that doesn't mean much these days, as neither do I. It's lying in my bedside drawer until I've decided whether I still have a reason to wear it.

I assume that Mark and I are roughly the same age, judging by the stray grey hairs in his receding hairline and the light flurry of lines across his forehead. In all the times we've met, he has offered nothing about his life outside the police force and I guess I haven't asked. Yet I find myself thinking about him sometimes, probably more than I should, especially since the rest of my world is caving in around me. But he offers a welcome distraction and is about the only person who genuinely cares about our family's welfare. And God knows I can do with someone like that in my life right now.

He follows me into the kitchen where I lower Sonny into his high chair and put the kettle on. I'm quietly wishing I hadn't worn these tatty old sweatpants and the jumper with the holes in the sleeve.

'How have you been dealing with it all?' he asks.

'Not brilliantly, to be honest,' I say. 'Having everyone knowing your husband's a cheat and has a second child is kind of humiliating.'

'I can imagine.' I look at him with my eyebrows arched. 'Well, no,' he corrects himself, 'obviously, I can't imagine. But I do sympathise.'

I notice a soft lisp when he speaks that I've not heard before. And I've not spotted the brown flecks in his hazel-coloured eyes until now. It's because when I usually see him there are others around us, but today I have no distractions. It's only him and I. It's nice.

'Do you know how the newspapers found out?' he continues.

'I've wondered,' I say. 'I can't imagine they were following him on the off chance he might be up to something, so I assume somebody tipped them off.'

'That's usually the case. Money talks in situations like this.'

I pour him a tea and we chat about how things have been at home, the pending arrival of my parents and the police investigation.

'There's a lot going against us because of how historic the murders are,' he says, 'but now we have identified all of the deceased, it has opened up more leads.'

'Can I ask what you're working on at the moment?'

'Well, I've been tasked with trying to trace the origins of the suitcases the bodies were inside. There were quite a number of them, and they were not a bargain item. Very distinctive. We know the Portmanteau brand was popular in France before World War Two, and back then, they were built to last, made of strong wooden boxed frames, covered in leather and with padded handles. But the war damaged the travel industry and people didn't have the spare money to spend on luxuries, so they ceased production in the early 1950s. For our killer to have come into possession of this many of them, and to have relied solely on specifically this brand and model . . . we don't know what it means, if it means anything. But it's of interest, in any event. We're looking to see who might have exported them over here, but the conflict obliterated a lot of businesses and records. So it's a little like searching for a needle in a haystack.'

A little later, Mark receives a call and has to leave, and I find myself wishing he didn't have to go so suddenly. And maybe I'm imagining it, but I think he was also a little reluctant to go.

I am winding Sonny after his milk when the word 'Portmanteau' comes to mind. Why does it ring a bell? I'm sure I came across it recently. I rack my brains – was it in Debbie and Dave's garage? I swipe my way to the photos folder in my phone until I find the picture I took of an old invoice found amongst their paperwork. There it is. 'Portmanteau Leathers' and 'Luxury Travel Import &

Export Specialists'. My heartbeat switches up a notch. Is this a second link between that house and Dave?

I'm about to leave Sonny in his high chair and return to the garage, but think better of it. The last time I put my search for the truth above all else, Finn justifiably went mad. I take Sonny with me, but when I get to where I found the box of paperwork last time, it has vanished. In fact someone has tidied up everything in here since my last visit and has got rid of much of it. Even the water-damaged boxes containing Dave's old schoolbooks have gone.

I debate whether I should call Mark and ask him to come back. However, without physical proof, it's just a photo on my phone. I'm no expert, but even I know the metadata attached to the image describing where and when it was taken isn't enough evidence. And there are plenty of people around me who think I'm going mad without Mark jumping on the bandwagon.

I rifle through everything else that's left here, even though I'm sure they'll have removed anything incriminating, which is incriminating in itself. Nevertheless, I search the remaining boxes until I reach the back of the double-length part of the garage and reach a disused steel tank that once stored oil to heat the house. Dave and Finn installed a combi boiler a year ago and I wonder why they've kept this thing here when everything else has gone.

I try moving it and realise why – it is cemented into the floor. It's darker in this part of the garage so I illuminate my phone. I reckon it's about five feet by four feet in size and a section has been cut out but then used to re-cover it. It's loose and, when I look more carefully, there's something inside it. With Sonny still pressed against my chest, I lower myself to my knees and tug gently at the panel. It falls to the ground with a clatter and I shine the light inside.

It contains just one object.

A suitcase.

Not just any suitcase, but exactly the same shape and style as the seven used to hide the bodies of children in the attic of my home.

POLICE FEAR FOR MISSING WRITER

BY CLAIE WILSON

The family of a missing journalist is appealing for witnesses who may have seen her the day she vanished three weeks ago.

Freelance writer Aaliyah Anderson, 34, disappeared on Friday, 17 May after telling friends she was interviewing a subject for a book she was working on. Family and friends say that she has not been seen since.

Detective Sergeant Karl Stuart said: 'We are concerned for the safety of Ms. Anderson and we encourage anyone who might know of where she was going or who she planned to see to contact us urgently.'

CHAPTER 47

THIRTY-NINE YEARS EARLIER

When a bright but narrow light hits my face, I scramble backwards to the corner of the room like an animal seeking safety. I don't know how long I've been locked in this pitch-black attic. A day might even have passed without me realising. All I know is that they moved me up here from *that room* last night. The floorboards are cold and uncomfortable but I was so exhausted, I had to sleep. So I fumbled around and made a makeshift bed by pushing together what felt to my fingertips like heavy suitcases. I'm not sure how long I was unconscious but I'm awoken by the sound of the loft-hatch hinges opening and see a torch's light shining.

I recoil at my mother's voice. 'Downstairs, now,' she says gruffly, and I squint as I descend the ladder. I'm too slow for her liking so she shakes it and I lose my grip and slip down the last few rungs. She yanks me up from the floor by my T-shirt, her sharp fingernails digging into my shoulders as she directs me back into *that room*.

Mum slams the door behind me and locks it, leaving me alone. Then I hear a muffled cry and someone climbing up the ladder.

Unless they have brought someone else here, Precious is still alive. I'm not sure why. The attic hatch slams shut again and now it's her turn to be alone and afraid in the dark. Only she doesn't know the worst is yet to come. Unless I help her.

I press my ear to the gap under the door and, a few minutes later, I hear Mum and Dad talking as they leave the house. I think they're going out by the back door. I hurry to the window and spy on them. Mum is carrying a handful of plastic bags. It must be Saturday morning and they are going out to do their supermarket shop. They are leaving us alone in here – one locked in the attic, one locked in this room – and will pretend to the world how ordinary they are.

This is my opportunity. I look around, searching for a means of escape. I push hard on the door but I'm not strong enough to break it open on my own. Two of us might manage it though.

My attention turns to the fireplace and I recall it being nailed shut to stop soot falling from the chimney. 'The chimney,' I whisper. I'd forgotten that Dad took a section of it apart in the attic when something became lodged inside it and died, its rotting carcass causing a stink. He cleared away the remains of a crow but never got around to repairing the brickwork.

Using all my strength I pull at the board until it comes free. Clouds of soot and dirt pour into the room, making me cough and splutter. I wait until I can breathe again before I shout 'Can you hear me?' with my head in the hearth, my voice carrying up the chimney breast and flue. There's no reply. 'Are you up there?'

'Yes!' she replies to my relief. 'Where are you?'

'I'm in the room downstairs. I think I know how we can get out of here. You need to follow the sound of my voice until you reach the chimney.'

'It's so dark in here,' she says. 'I can't see anything.'

'Be careful,' I say. 'Go down on your hands and knees and move slowly as I talk.' She follows my voice until I hear a clunking sound and a yelp. 'What was that?'

'I hit my knee against something. It feels like a hammer.'

Dad must have left it up there. 'Bring it with you.'

As her voice grows louder, I know she's reached the opening Dad made. 'Stand up and feel for a hole, then drop the hammer down it so we know how far down it is,' and again, she does as I say. I move my head just in time for the hammer to land on the grate with a clank. The drop is too steep for her to jump without getting hurt. I look around the room, at the leather straps attached to the ceiling, a camera tripod, the plastic bags in the corner of the room and the mattress from a single bed. I reach for the latter, use my body weight to fold it in two and cram as much of it as I can into the hearth. 'You need to lower yourself into the hole and let yourself drop. There's a mattress here to break your fall.'

'I can't do that,' she protests. 'I'll hurt myself.'

'If you don't, we're going to die,' I say bluntly. 'I don't think you've heard from your friend because she's already dead. And if we don't get out of here, we'll be next.'

'Please don't say that!'

'We don't have time to argue about it. Just trust me. Lower yourself in, count to three and then drop.'

I pause until I hear a brief whoosh before her feet hit the mattress with a muffled thump. Her clothes, face and braided hair are covered in a fine coat of soot and I try to wipe some away. 'Are you okay?'

'I . . . I think so,' she replies, and then turns to give me a tight and unexpected embrace. Now that I see her in the flesh, I know for sure that we have met before. Thankfully she doesn't appear to remember me.

'What happens now?' she asks.

'Stand back,' I say, and then I swing the hammer as hard as my skinny arms allow against the door handle. It takes two more blows before it breaks into pieces and falls. She puts her hand through the hole to push the other handle to the floor, then her fingers grasp the rim and she pulls the door towards us. It opens and now we are out of *that room* and on the landing.

I am going to save her. I am going to save both of us.

She looks around her, confused as if something is only just registering. 'I saw them go out,' I explain before I take her arm and encourage her down the stairs with me. We run to the front door but my parents have locked us in. We hurry through the kitchen and find the back door also locked. So together, we take a dining room chair, swing it back and forth, then let go and cover our faces as it smashes through the bay windows at the front of the house. Carefully, she climbs through the frame first and jumps to the lawn below. She's free.

'Hurry up,' she yells and I scramble out from the frame and we make our way along the driveway.

'Where are we?' she asks, glancing up and down the high street.

'Follow me, I'll get you home,' I say, and the two of us run as fast as our legs can carry us, out of the village and towards the horizon. But her lack of food, water and sleep means she soon flags, stumbling through the fields as we leave the outskirts of my village.

'I want to phone my mum,' she pants, and I slow my pace so that I don't leave her behind.

'As soon as we reach town, we'll find a phone box.'

'How much further is it?'

'You see over there?' I point at a high-rise block of flats. 'I bet we'll find one there.'

'But it's so far.'

We continue at a reduced pace, me with no idea of where I might go after we reach those flats and her preparing to return to the life she was snatched from. I'm pinning my hopes on her parents taking pity on me and being so grateful for saving their daughter's life that they'll allow me to stay under their roof and I can experience what it's like to live in an ordinary family. I could go to school, make more friends, stop living in fear and stay in a house that doesn't talk to me. I can't stop the smile from spreading across my face.

But by the time we reach the outskirts of an industrial estate, I too am beginning to flag. A cramp in my leg is tightening the muscles but I don't want to stop. However, Precious can't continue. Her pace declines to a walk before she sits on the kerb, her head in her hands. She has a stitch and complains of feeling sick. There is no greenery around us aside from overgrown grass verges. All that surrounds us are offices, warehouses, lorry parks, wide roads for large vehicles and closed gates. It's Saturday so there's no traffic or workers. Just us. 'I don't think it's much further, I promise you,' I say.

'I need a rest.'

As desperate as I am to continue, I can't and I won't leave her alone. So I wait with her, holding her hand, nervously scanning the roads.

We suddenly hear a car behind us, its engine growing louder as it speeds. I'm on my feet, pulling at her arm, ready to run, terrified it's my parents hunting us down. But it's the wrong colour. It passes us, its tyres screeching as it hurtles around a sharp corner a little further down the road.

'Where were you?' she asks, still struggling for breath.

'When?' I reply, pushing at my knotted calf muscle.

'That first day, when you were talking to me in that room, where were you?'

'Next door,' I lie.

She thinks before she answers. 'You were talking to me from under the door. You must have been on the landing.' I can't think of another lie quickly enough. 'What were you doing out there?'

'They let me out for a few minutes.'

'How did you know there was a hole in the chimney to climb down?'

'I, I . . .'

'And where the back door was? You ran straight for it.'

My throat dries up. She has seen through me.

'You live in that house, don't you?'

'I . . .'

'Who was the woman who took us?'

'My . . . my mum . . . but you have to let me explain.'

'No, no, no . . .' Her eyes are wide with fear. And without giving me the chance to come up with an explanation, she is back on her feet. The only person who has ever looked at me before with such betrayal was George after I told Mum and Dad about his friend Martin. My self-loathing returns in earnest.

With a renewed burst of energy, Precious starts running along the road, around a sharp bend and out of view. I sprint after her, the cramp in my leg burning and pulling with each movement. As I turn the corner, I see her again and shout her name as she approaches traffic lights.

'Leave me alone!' she turns her head and screams. And even from this distance, I can feel her terror. She has tarred me with the same brush used to paint my parents.

'Wait, please,' I yell, my pain escalating. The cramp is getting worse and it's slowing my pace. I can't keep up with her. Now my mind races with how the next few days will play out, how the police will be searching for me and how I'll end up in prison if they find me. 'Please wait!' I repeat but my words are in vain. My fate is sealed. I have jumped from the frying pan and into the fire.

'No!' she shouts and turns to look at me again. 'You are a very bad—'

She doesn't finish her sentence and turns her head at the sound of a fast-moving car's engine. She's like a rabbit caught in the headlights as the car that passed us minutes earlier completes another lap. Only this time, the driver appears to lose control because it clips the kerb as it turns and then hits her, hard enough to send her crashing over the bonnet and off the windscreen before she lands on the verge in a heap of twisted limbs.

CHAPTER 48

MIA, 2019

I don't know what to do. One of my hands is firmly attached to Sonny and the other clutches the handle of the suitcase within the disused oil storage tank in Dave and Debbie's garage. It's definitely a Portmanteau; it has the red embossed P logo on the bottom right-hand corner and is identical to those in the attic. And as with the others, this one could also fit a child's body. Where did it come from? Why the hell does Dave have it? But more importantly, is there something inside it?

Again, I know I should call Mark but something stops me. If I were watching this scene play out on a TV drama, I'd be screaming at the actress playing me to call the police and get the hell out of there. But this is real life and, if I'm wrong, it would kill what's left of my marriage. As much as I hate living with a family I don't trust, there really is no going back once I involve the authorities. Would Finn be any use if I contacted him instead? Or would his head remain buried in the sand about his dad and what this might mean? I can't be sure. The only thing I know is that if I leave this garage, that suitcase won't be here when I return. Things have a habit of disappearing quickly from this room.

I make my decision. I remove a blanket from a box and lay Sonny on it. He huffs his displeasure but stops short of a cry. Then I pull at the suitcase, wincing as it jars my recently repaired wrist, before it eventually comes free. It's heavy so I know there's something inside it. I lay it down in front of me, then slowly unclip the latches. They aren't stiff like the ones in our attic Finn prised open. This has been unlocked more recently. My heart races and I squint as I pull the lid up, prepared for the worst.

But inside, and to my relief, there is no body. It contains nothing but reams of paperwork, some of it clamped together with bulldog clips, others loose leaf. I sink to the floor, my back against the wall, trying to regain control of my pulse. I take a closer look at these decades-old import and export documents, receipts and orders. The names attached to the company are Kenneth and Moira Kilgour. It takes just a second to remember who they are – the former owners of my house and the headless corpses buried in their own garden for forty years. Did Dave unearth all of this while he was working on the house, or did he take it all those years ago when he was carving a message into the skirting board? None of this makes sense.

There's an address printed on the invoices: a storage unit. It's so old, the postcode contains only two letters and a number. Google only recognises the area and Street View doesn't register it at all.

I pack up the suitcase carefully and place it all back inside the tank. Dave cannot know I have been in here again or what I have found. Not yet, at least. Not until I'm ready.

I pick up a still-grumbling Sonny and begin to make my way back to the door when a fluorescent-pink ball of paper catches my eye, trapped under the wheel of Dave's office chair. It's next to an empty wire wastepaper basket and I assume its failure to reach the bin went unnoticed. As the room is now so devoid of anything else out of place – suitcase aside – curiosity gets the better of me.

I pick it up and uncrumple it. It's a Post-it note. On it, there's a telephone number that's been scribbled over several times. But when I turn the paper over, I can make it out. It also contains the initials CW.

I withhold my number as I dial, and it's answered in three rings. '*Sun on Sunday* news desk, Carole Watson speaking,' says a voice in a north-east accent.

I hang up quickly, recognizing her name immediately as the journalist who wrote the exposé about my husband's affair. I shake my head. There is only one meaning to take from Dave having written down this woman's number. He called her. He was her source.

If Dave is willing to do that to his son, what else might he be capable of?

◆ ◆ ◆

I assume I'm at the correct address. It was only when I left the car and peered down the hill that I could make out a cluster of roofs on buildings enveloped by trees. You'd have to be really searching for this place to find it, like I am. Even now, I'm unsure why I'm here or what I'm expecting to find.

I take a photo of what I see in front of me, then send it to Lorna along with the postcode and a message saying *Just in case. Will explain all later.* I don't want to tell her what I'm up to now because she'll try to talk me out of it. I raise her suspicions though and she rings me immediately anyway, but I reject the call.

Is Sonny okay? I text to Finn instead. He thinks I'm out shopping. He replies a minute later with two photos – one of our boy in his pushchair watching intently as his dad feeds carrots to horses in a field. The second is of him sleeping on Finn's chest. I think Finn purposely included himself in the picture to elicit an emotional tug of seeing father and son together. For an uninvited moment, I wonder how often Finn took selfies with his daughter and Emma. I wonder if somewhere on his phone lies a misleadingly titled folder that contains pictures of the three of them together. A pang of jealousy strikes before my focus returns.

I make my way to a wooden gate. There's no lock so it swings open with a creak, and I begin my descent down a steep dirt track. The gradient isn't easy to negotiate in these pumps and neither are the potholes. Twice, I stumble. The closer I get to the buildings, the more insistently my inner voice begs me to turn back. However, another voice – one that tells me I need to see this through for the sake of my sanity – is much louder.

At the bottom of the hill I count eight buildings, all separate from one another but roughly equal in size and appearance. They are made up of brick bases about five feet in height and framed windows that reach rusted, corrugated-iron roofs shaped like bars of Toblerone. I assume this to be an incomplete, decades-old industrial estate. Most of the buildings have gone to rack and ruin, with cracked windows, missing guttering and giant leafy weeds growing from the inside out. None have numbers or signs attached to them.

There is one exception and I'm counting on it being the place I'm here to find. It also has damaged panes of glass but they have been patched up with grey tape. I peer inside but they are thick with dirt on both sides. Wiping them with my hand makes little difference. Overgrown hedges and bracken have been cut back to allow a rough path to reach the door. It's locked.

I take a step back and size up the place. I wonder if Debbie knows about it. She is responsible for Dave's accounts. But anything related to the import of suitcases was purposely kept out of the main filing cabinets and hidden away; so I'll give her the benefit of the doubt. The way she so emphatically denied that it was Dave's writing on the skirting board makes me think she is as blinkered – or as gullible – as Finn.

Two other sides of the building are too overgrown to walk around, but when I reach the fourth, I spot the branch of a tree that has grown through a window and partially broken the pane. Dave cannot have noticed it or he'd have likely repaired it. Carefully, I slip my hand through the hole in the glass and feel around for the handle. After several yanks, it judders open. It's a tight squeeze and, with my heart pounding, I carefully push myself through the open window head first until I reach a table. I push myself across it using my hands and my belly until I'm in completely, then swing my feet around until they reach the floor.

It's dim in here but just light enough to note layers of faint and fresh footprints on the dirty floor. There's a desk with clothes and empty bottles of rubbing alcohol, packets of wet wipes and lint rollers. There's a long line of shelving running the length of the building. I can't make out what it contains so I move closer. Lined up is suitcase after suitcase, stacked side by side and with a gap between each one.

Most are kept under plastic sheeting, weighed down by decades of dust. There must be at least a hundred of them. I move slowly and hesitantly, lifting some sheets and sneezing when I inhale too quickly. I nervously stretch out my hand and pick one up – to my relief, it's light. Each one is embossed with the Portmanteau branding, a red P. I keep picking up random cases just to reassure myself they are empty until I reach the end of the line and turn a corner to a second aisle.

It's darker over here so I use my phone to illuminate the shelving. These suitcases are uncovered and spaced further apart. And there's something in front of each one, stacked into a small, neat pile. They are children's clothes and shoes. I swallow hard as I pick one up. They are all vacuum-packed like the ones we saw in my attic. My body wants to fold in on itself because I know without looking what the cases contain.

I count them. There are forty in total. The ones towards the end are less dusty, suggesting they're more recent. I should get out of here but I have to see this through. I reach out to grab a suitcase and pull it to the floor. It's heavy and, as the latches pop open, I prepare myself for what I'm about to witness.

'I don't think you should do that,' comes a voice from behind me.

CHAPTER 49

DAVE

Mia lets out a shrill cry and turns quickly. Only she loses her balance and her legs fold beneath her like a newborn lamb's. Her phone falls from her hand, but its torch is still bright and it shines on her face from where it landed beside her. Before I have time to think about how it will appear to her, I stretch out my hand to help her back to her feet. But of course she's petrified, and instead of taking it, she scuttles backwards. Even in this gloomy building, her eyes clearly reflect the fear she has of me. Then they dart around the room as if searching for an escape route. I could tell her there is none; that this place was built before buildings regulations required more than one entrance and exit. I could tell her that I have her cornered, but I don't want to scare her any more than I am already. Not unless I have to.

She opens her mouth then closes it just as quickly, repeating the action several times before she finds her words. They're released in short sharp bursts.

'What . . . what are . . . inside the cases?' she asks.

'I think you know the answer to that.'

'But there are so many of them.' This time I don't say anything. When she processes what this means, she's predictably appalled. 'Are they all children?' she asks. Again, I remain quiet. 'How . . . how long has this . . . ?'

'More years than I care to remember.'

'Why?'

'It's not something I can explain, or that you'll understand.'

'And Debbie? Does she know?' I shake my head. 'But what about the bodies in the attic? You're too young to have been involved in those murders.'

The chime of a bell rings out – it's her phone, she's received a text message.

'Slide it across the floor to me,' I say.

Her fingers wrap around the device but she is too quick for me to stop her from throwing it at my head. I move just in time for it to hit a shelf, and in that second, she is on her feet and running down the aisle. She doesn't know where she is going so I charge along a third aisle and cut her off. I grab her arm but she fights back, biting and scratching and clawing at me like a feral cat. I don't want to hurt her, I really don't, but I can't see another way so I use what little strength I have left to strike her hard across the face. She loses her balance for a second time, but now as she falls, she hits the back of her head on a shelf and slumps to the floor, her eyes rolling and then snapping shut.

I curse aloud and drop to her side, place my arm under her head and say her name over and over again. My arm feels damp, and when I look at it, I realise she is bleeding from a wound to the back of her head. All I have to stem it is the T-shirt I'm wearing. I take it off and use it as a compress.

'Jesus *Christ*!' I shout against the pain that has emerged in my stomach. It's so sharp that I have to look down to convince myself Mia hasn't stabbed me. I want to double over and roll about the

224

floor, as this is worse than it's ever been before. Instead I hold firm for as long as I can until it subsides and I push myself back up to my feet.

Debbie once told me in no uncertain terms that she thought Mia was like a cancer, eating away at this family. However, Mia isn't the cancer. The rest of us are. And one by one we have all taken a bite out of this girl. But today it's cancer's turn to take its biggest bite, out of me.

My only saving grace is that I won't have to watch her suffer for much longer.

CHAPTER 50

MIA

I'm woozy. The back of my head is pounding. What the hell happened to make me feel like this? I blink and squint and take in my surroundings before it hits me with the force of a speeding train. I remember everything, all at once.

Quick as a flash I'm sitting upright on the floor, but I can't climb to my feet because there's something attaching my wrists to the leg of a bench. I'm aware of a compress of sorts that's wrapped about my head. I can just about reach to tug at it. Its fabric smells of body odour and cheap aftershave.

Only then do I see Dave.

I break into a cold sweat and now I feel my pulse throbbing in both temples, escalating my head pain. I eye him up and down as he sits on a chair by a desk. His face is slightly illuminated by his phone as he quietly taps something into it. He is bare-chested and I'm taken aback by how skeletal he is. The tongues from his steel-capped work boots hang loosely. He has removed the laces and used them to secure me. I wonder why he hasn't killed me yet.

'How's your head?' he asks, without looking up. If I didn't know he was a multiple murderer, I might actually believe he's concerned. He places the phone screen-down on the desk and approaches me with something in his hand. I flinch, only relaxing my shoulders a little when I recognise it as a can. 'Sorry, there's no water, it's all I have.' From the smell, I guess it's beer. I shake my head and he takes it away.

I look around, searching for a potential escape route. Ahead is the window I entered. It's tantalizingly close, but I don't know how I can free myself. Suddenly, I'm overcome by nausea. I turn to the right and I'm sick over the floor and the leg of my jeans. Dave takes an old newspaper from the table and covers the mess I've made. Then he uses a section of it to wipe the vomit from my leg. He's gentle, surprisingly so. Then he's looking me in the eye as he does it, stroking me as you would a kitten, and leaning closer. I recoil from him with short, sharp breaths, terrified of where he might take this. He appears to read me, as he regains control of himself and backs away, returning to his chair.

I am scared and frustrated by how much control he has over me. Sonny's and Finn's faces burst into my head and I want to cry because I don't know if I will ever see them again. There are so many mistakes I've made with my baby – not getting help when I knew something was wrong with me, putting my need to find the truth ahead of his well-being – and now there's every chance that I won't be able to make any of it up to him. My imagination plays a cruel trick and fast-forwards to after my death and I want to be sick again when I think of Finn and Emma playing happy families with my son and their daughter.

Then my fear makes way for anger. I'm annoyed that I put myself in this position but I'm more furious at the man holding me prisoner. My life is going to end in this warehouse; my final resting place will be in a suitcase on a shelf. So I vow that if I am to die in here, I'm not going to make it easy for him. My last breath will be a scream.

'Why haven't you killed me yet?' I ask. 'Or do you only murder children?'

'I need you to know that I am sorry for everything that's happened,' he says, then winces and grabs at his stomach. He takes a long gulp from his can. 'This is not how it was supposed to be,' he continues. He takes a deep breath and releases it in a sigh. 'I've done many things I'm not proud of.'

He blanches again. Whatever is wrong with him is escalating. He turns his back to me to try and hide it but I know that he is clutching his stomach again.

'How did you pick them?' I continue, but he says nothing. 'How did you kill them? Did they suffer? Were they in pain? Is that why you did it? Did you abuse them first?'

'Shut up!' he yells. 'Of course I didn't! I'd never do that to a child.'

'But you'd kill one.'

'I didn't have parents who cared about me like you did, Mia.'

'A lot of people don't. But they don't go on to do what you've done.'

He drains the can and then pulls another one from the desk drawer and snaps open the ring pull.

'Why, Dave? Just tell me why? Help me to understand.'

He shakes his head. There is so much that I want to know but there is so little he seems willing to tell me. I note the large number of empty cans stacked neatly on and under the desk and the many, many footprints on the floor by the chair. 'You come here a lot, don't you? Why?'

'To think.'

'About what?'

'Everything.'

'Why do you keep their bodies here? Why not leave them somewhere for their parents to find?'

'Parents don't always deserve their children.'

I let out a huff. 'That's not your decision to make.'

'If someone had noticed I shouldn't have been left with mine, my whole life could have been very different. We wouldn't be where we find ourselves today.'

'Please Dave, enough of your "woe is me" act. I get it. Finn told me they were junkies and that you practically brought yourself up.' He raises an eyebrow as if surprised his son would admit such a thing about him. 'Were you jealous of these kids because they had something you didn't?'

He shakes his head. 'We've all been let down,' he says.

'By who?'

'By those who should have cared.'

'What happened to Precious Johnson?'

'Precious,' he repeats, and sorrow washes over him as if he's picturing the face of his bright young classmate. His hand returns to his stomach. It's like, each time a disturbing memory surfaces, it develops into a physical pain. Dave removes something from his pocket, holds it in his hand and stares at it. And for a long moment, he loses himself. Eventually I see it's the photograph I stole from Abigail Douglas's wake, and which he must have taken from where I left it, in my jacket.

'People talk about how they'd do things differently if they could go back to a time of their choosing,' he continues. 'But I'm not sure I could do any better the second time around. We are who we are destined to be. No matter what decision I made or path I took, I'd have ended up here in this moment.'

'What are you going to do with me?' In spite of myself, my voice breaks. 'I assume you're not going to let me go home.'

He finishes the contents of his can, stacks it neatly with the others and shapes his fingers in front of his mouth like a steeple.

'I'm sorry, Mia, I really am,' he says before rising to his feet again. He approaches me but this time the light catches a silver blade. I recognise it as the hunting knife from the wall of his garage.

This is it, I think.

I use my legs to kick, trying to catch him anywhere. But despite his sickly appearance, a life of manual labouring has made him strong. He mounts me, pinning my legs down with his. I smell the booze on his breath as he leans in against my ear and pauses for a second. Then he takes the knife and lunges forward to my wrist.

He's slashed one of the laces tying my hand to the shelving. Now he returns to the desk but remains on his feet.

What trap is he laying here for me? I reach to untie the other lace but it's too tight for me to loosen with just one hand. I look to him, more confused than ever.

'Did you know that at the turn of the century, doctors believed that a guilty conscience could manifest itself with physical ailments?' he asks. 'Even today, it hasn't been proven completely untrue. There's pain and penance the size of a fist inside my stomach that's developed into a physical cancer which is slowly killing me.'

That takes me aback. My immediate reaction is to say I'm sorry, but I stop myself when I realise that's what I'd say to the old Dave. I don't know this Dave. This Dave deserves no sympathy.

'When you first learn you're dying, you wonder "Why me?"' he continues. 'Then your conscience reminds you how much you've allowed it to be weighed down with decades of remorse and you think, "Why *not* me?" Mia, I want you to know that I did try to be a good man, I honestly did. I tried to live a normal life, providing for a family I love. I let Debbie keep the baby she always wanted so that she'd get the happy-ever-after she deserved. But it wasn't enough. I failed as a husband and a dad because I'm not like my wife or son. So this is the only way. Do you understand me?'

He's talking in riddles. I realise that Dave is crying and now I am too. 'I don't think I do,' I say.

He looks almost disappointed, as if he was counting on me getting it.

'One person's death can mean another person's rebirth,' he continues. 'This is the only way that Finn and Debbie can start again. Debbie has been everything to me. She has saved me, and now I must do the same for her. Please tell them that I am sorry for what I've done.'

Dave takes my phone and slides it across the floor to me. It stops at my legs. 'Call for help,' he says. 'It'll take the nearest station about fifteen minutes to get people here.'

Then I watch helplessly as he takes the knife, holds it up to his neck and closes his eyes.

'No,' I gasp, both transfixed and dumbstruck.

After three deep breaths, he howls as he uses both hands to push the blade into his skin and, in one swift movement, slits his own throat.

CHAPTER 51
THIRTY-NINE YEARS EARLIER

He is distraught and his words are hard to make out between his sobs and struggles for breath.

'I can't understand you,' I say. 'Speak slower.'

His face is pale like snow. 'I've killed her . . . I've killed her . . . I've killed her,' he says over and over again. We are both kneeling by Precious's body, searching for signs of life. Her arms protrude at irregular angles and she is bleeding from the back of her head. I use the palm of my hand to try and make it stop. It's surprisingly warm on my skin and makes something in me tingle.

For two, maybe three seconds, her eyes open widely and she stares at him first. Then her lips part as if she wants to say something. But everything snaps shut at the same time and this is how they remain.

I look around to see if I can locate an adult who can help us, but it's the weekend so the industrial estate is deserted. There's only the three of us here now: me, her and the one who has left her like this. A few feet away is the car that, moments earlier, lost control and clipped her, pushing her over the bonnet, on to the windscreen and into the verge in a tangled heap. The car screamed to a halt and all four doors opened. Five exited and four ran in different directions. The fifth, who was behind the wheel, remains with me here.

'I'm sorry,' he says, still crying. 'When I hit the kerb I couldn't keep the car steady. I didn't see her until it was too late.'

'She needs an ambulance,' I reply. 'You need to get help.'

He turns his head from side to side. 'How?'

'There must be a phone box around here somewhere. Go find it and I'll stay with her.'

'Okay, I'll be back, I promise,' he says and I believe him. 'I'm sorry.'

As he runs off and out of sight, I turn back to look at my friend. It isn't just his fault she has been left like this, it is mine too. If it hadn't been for me, she would not be lying here so injured. But then, she wouldn't be alive, either.

This is the first time I have watched someone dying. It should frighten me, I should be just as panicked as the person who knocked her down, but I'm not. I'm weirdly calm and morbidly curious. Is this how my parents feel when they've had enough of playing with the kids in *that room*?

My hand is still clamped to the back of her head when, without warning, her eyes open again and she lets out an agonizing scream. 'Please, stay calm,' I beg. 'Somebody has gone to get help. The ambulance will be here soon.'

Precious's expression contains nothing but hatred. I feel flushed, like my face is burning and I want to rip off the skin that covers my shame. 'You,' she manages to whisper between gasps. 'I know what you are.'

'I'm your friend,' I reply. 'I'm just a kid, like you.'

But I'm not convincing. Her face winces as a fresh burst of pain travels through her. 'You're one of them!' she cries.

'What they do isn't my fault,' I say. But I know that, some-times, it is.

'I'm going to tell everyone you're evil.'

I take a step back, crestfallen that she can't see me for who I really am. I wipe at my eyes with the back of my hands.

'Please don't,' I beg. Everything I daydreamed about evaporates just like that – her family's gratitude for saving Precious's life, invit-ing me to stay with them, attending school, making more friends, no longer living in fear – all gone in the blink of her eye.

I rise and her blood drips down my hand and fingertips and on to my jeans. I stand over her. 'I was only trying to help,' I remind her. 'I wanted to save you.'

I've tried to make her understand, but she doesn't want to listen. And now I'm scared what will happen when the lad returns and the ambulance arrives. I can't go back to that house and I can't go to prison, so I have no choice but to run away. I hurry along the path ahead, unsure of where I am and where to go next. There are no road signs, only large warehouses, electricity pylons marching into the distance and parked-up lorries. I start to believe I could be trapped in this grey, concrete maze forever. It's as bad as the jail I'll be sent to when Precious tells everyone who I am.

It's right then, when I'm at my most hopeless, that a light shines upon me and stops me in my tracks. I look up to the sky, blinded by the sun as it finds a crack in the clouds. This is a sign, an answer to my problems. There is a way to save Precious and myself too. A one-size-fits-all solution. And after all I have been through, I deserve a shot at happiness. I am owed it. I cannot let Precious rob me of the rest of my life.

I turn around and make my way back to her, picking up a plank of wood from a broken pallet discarded on a verge. As I reach her, I raise it above me and wait for a moment, giving her one last chance to change her mind and tell me that she will keep my secret and that we really are friends. Instead, she screams.

Then I apologise and, before she can shield herself, I hit her, once, twice and then a third time until something cracks. I have killed her. And in doing so, I have saved us both. Me, from exposure so that I can go on and be anyone I want to be, and her from the guilt of surviving while Abigail died. She will never feel physical pain or mental anguish again, she will never fear the known or the unknown. I have freed her from herself. I have *saved her*.

I throw my weapon over a fence into a rubbish skip behind me as fresh blood begins to ooze from a separate wound to the side of her head. I listen closely just to check that she is no longer breathing.

This is not how I wanted our journey to end but it was the right thing to do. I kneel back down by her side and the blood has formed a halo around her head. She looks so serene and so, so beautiful. I take in every inch of this scene, framing it and storing it to memory. I uncurl my fingers to feel her blood's warmth again but retract them quickly as the car's driver reappears, red-faced and wheezing.

'Is she dead?' he blurts out.

'I think so,' I reply.

The front of his jeans darkens and I realise that he is so terrified by what he thinks he has done, he has wet himself. I feel for him. I'm also aware I need to take control of this situation. 'Have you called an ambulance?' I ask and he nods. 'Then we need to get out of here.' He glares at me, puzzled. 'But I've killed your friend.'

'She's not my friend any more,' I say. 'If we don't go now, you'll be arrested. The car – is it stolen?' He nods. 'So they'll charge you for that as well as murder. Do you want to spend the rest of your life in prison?'

He shakes his head.

'Then we need to get out of here. What's your name?'

'Dave,' he says.

'I'm Debbie,' I offer. Then I grab his arm and pull him away from Precious. Now, it's him and me running together. To where, I don't know yet. But with Dave, I already feel safe.

PART THREE

NEWS ALERT, *ANGLIA FREE PRESS*

BY EMMA LOUISE BUNTING

The funeral of the man described as Britain's most prolific child killer has taken place in a private ceremony.

David Hunter, 55, who admitted causing the deaths of at least forty children over four decades, was cremated yesterday, a police spokesman confirmed. His family are not thought to have attended.

Thirty-two of the forty bodies of the children hidden in suitcases and discovered in Hunter's warehouse have now been identified as the investigation continues.

According to an inquest held last week, he took his own life during a confrontation with his daughter-in-law Mia Hunter, 32, who had uncovered his crimes. He used a hunting knife to sever the major arteries of his neck.

While it was widely reported that Hunter believed he was suffering from terminal cancer, an autopsy revealed his condition to be a treatable stomach ulcer.

CHAPTER 52

MIA, FIVE MONTHS LATER, 2020

I take a deep breath as I approach Debbie's house from the pavement outside. After all these months away, the very sight of this place fills me with apprehension. I cannot recollect one moment of pleasure I've had in there. And knowing that I lived under the same roof as Dave, someone capable of such evil, makes my dislike of it even more intense.

I don't know how Debbie returned here once the police gave her back the keys. I'd never have set foot in that house again. And I told Finn that I was reluctant to let Sonny visit. But he keeps reminding me that in the five months the police CSI team spent examining that house and garden, they found no bodies and not a shred of evidence to suggest that any of the forty victims had ever been there. However, it still makes me uneasy.

You can't see the driveway since the new gates were fitted. But from this angle you can still spot the gravel underneath it and the faint scorch marks where vigilantes set fire to Dave's van.

The last time Debbie and I came face to face was at the police station two days after he killed himself in front of me. For a woman with her disabilities, she was surprisingly agile as she kicked and beat me with her walking stick until officers dragged her away and into a cell.

'You killed him!' she yelled. 'You killed him! Murdering bitch!'

DS Mark Goodwin asked me afterwards if I wanted to press charges against her for actual bodily harm, but I declined. As much as I detest the woman, Debbie needed someone to blame for Dave's death and it was never going to be the culprit. Five months have passed, but her opinion of me won't have changed. It will always be my fault. The fact that he killed himself rather than publicly confess to all those child murders has escaped her.

Sonny talks to himself and chews on a rubber giraffe designed for teething babies as I carry his car seat. He is a year old and has now lived more of his life with his parents apart than he has with us together, and while it saddens me, I know it's for the best. Together, Finn and I no longer work. We played at being a happy family for a few hours on Christmas Day by spending it together for Sonny's sake, but once that passed, we returned to our new routine.

I'm here, I text Finn and, moments later, the new gates slide open and he appears, traipsing up the driveway until he reaches us. I leave the car and grab Sonny's bag. It contains his food amongst things like nappies and spare clothing.

For a moment, I find myself ogling Finn like the night we first met at the bar in London. *Christ, he looks handsome.* Back then, he was in a relationship with Emma which, as it turned out, they never quite ended. Now they are officially together again. He has been living with her and their daughter for a few weeks now, a reconciliation I quietly predicted but which still felt like a kick in the teeth when it arrived. He catches my lingering gaze.

'You alright?' he asks.

I retract my stare and nod. 'I changed his nappy an hour ago, his lunch and dinner are in the blue Tupperware pots and I'm trying to cut down his morning nap before he starts nursery. So don't let him sleep for too long.'

'What time shall I drop him off?'

'I start my new hours this week, so about 5.45 p.m. if the trains are running okay.' I offer him an olive branch. 'You can stay and bath him if you like?'

'I'd love to, but I can't this time,' he says, which I translate to mean, 'I have commitments with my other family.' Sometimes I still hate him for what he did to us, and on other occasions, after all that's happened, I feel like the luckiest woman in the world to be free of that family.

'How's Chloe?' I ask.

'She's good,' he says.

'And Emma?'

'She's being supportive.'

That was something I struggled to be in the aftermath of Dave's suicide and a huge part of why Finn and I separated. I couldn't pretend to be sorry for the death of a man who murdered so many children, even if he was my husband's father and Finn was hurting. It was impossible and we both knew it.

'How about Debbie?'

'She's struggling,' he says, 'but she's not doing much to help herself. You know how stubborn parents can be.'

I do, because I'm back to living with mine and, with the exception of Christmas Day afternoon, they point-blank refuse to let Finn set foot over the doorstep. They finally returned to England a day after Dave's death. And it wasn't a moment too soon. They quickly put the wheels in motion of renting a property for us all to stay in a few miles from here, far enough for me not to bump into Debbie but close enough for Sonny to see his dad. I never thought for a moment I'd be a single parent in my thirties relying on Mum and Dad to put a roof over my head, but that's how the dice have landed. I'm not fretting about it because it won't be like this forever. And to be honest, I'm kind of enjoying being parented.

'I suppose Debbie still blames me for everything.' I glance up at her bedroom window while he looks down at his Converse. *I bought them for your birthday*, I think. *In fact I bought you most of what you're wearing. I wonder if Emma knows that?*

Eventually he nods.

'Don't you think she's being unfair?'

Again, he agrees. Quietly, I wonder how much he has tried to defend me to her or whether he remains tied as tightly as ever to those apron strings.

'You're not to blame for what Dad did,' he says eventually.

'And how are you dealing with things?'

'You know,' he says, but I don't. We haven't spoken much about Dave since the immediate aftermath. But I still care about how Finn is processing everything. He reaches for his son and kisses his head, effectively shutting down our conversation.

'Promise me something,' I ask before he goes. 'Promise me that you'll get help from someone who understands.'

'I don't recall you doing that when Sonny was born.'

'But I did in the end. You need someone to talk to, someone qualified who can help you to deal with what you're going through.'

'I don't think there are many therapists out there whose fathers are serial child killers,' he deadpans.

'You know what I mean.'

He shrugs. 'I have Emma, she gets it.' I don't know if it's a deliberate dig or accidental. Either way, it bruises, but not as much as it once might have. 'What about you? Are you still seeing a therapist?'

I nod. I don't tell him who else I confide in though.

We say goodbye and I climb back into my car. I watch as he throws Sonny's backpack over his shoulder and carries him towards the house. And as the gates close, I realise something. Whenever we go our separate ways, I usually shed a tear or two for what we've lost. But not today. Today, I'm strangely optimistic.

CHAPTER 53

DEBBIE

Look at her, shamelessly flirting with my son as if butter wouldn't melt in her mouth. I can tell she wants him back by the way she plays with her hair and cocks her head as Finn speaks, giving him her undivided attention. She is so brazenly coquettish that it makes me sick. She might as well be standing there with her knickers around her ankles. She lingers with the perseverance of a cold sore. I only hope Finn is strong enough to see through her facade.

I remain motionless in the bedroom I shared with my husband, hidden behind the wooden blinds, watching her. I can't face sleeping in here alone, so most nights I stay in one of the spare rooms. There's a framed photo in here of Dave and I together, on a shelf, the only one from our wedding day and the only picture I have at all of my grandparents. I want to pick it up and hurl it at the wall. Instead, I ball my fists as tightly as my ailing body will allow and, even though I'm alone, I suppress my urge to scream at the top of my lungs. My feelings towards my husband alter from day to day. I ache for him, mostly, but at this moment, I hate him for leaving me.

Why did he kill himself when he could so easily have killed Mia? It's a question I can't stop asking myself. She was restrained in a warehouse only he and I knew existed. Her body was unlikely to have ever been found. He could have got away with it. So why did he sacrifice his life for hers? What was he thinking? Did he die to protect me like he always said he would, or was this his way of forcing my hand to stop? My final kill was that boy in the field two years ago, but because my activities were no longer discussed, Dave wasn't to know that. In trying to save Mia and protect me, he has destroyed everything.

For months after his death, I paced the room in the bed and breakfast hotel I was forced to stay at, trying to imagine his final moments and what Mia must've said to him to drive him to such extremes. I've read her police statement over and over again and I don't believe a word of it. That cancer rubbish . . . it only proves how willing she is to lie to mask what really went on in the warehouse. But the not knowing is eating me up. I can't ask her about it because, firstly, she'd lie, and secondly, I can't face even being in the same room as her. If I was, I'd find a way to kill her with my own bare hands for what she's done.

Try as I might, I cannot picture Dave on the last day we were together. I can't remember the clothes he wore, if he kissed me goodbye, what he ate for breakfast, or our conversation. I had no opportunity to frame him and return to him whenever I like. Yes, we had decades together, but at no point did I ever anchor him to a moment or a place. And I hate Mia for depriving me of that too.

I remove the phone from my pocket and look at the last message Dave sent me, moments before his death. Littered with his dyslexic errors, I know why he sent it. He knew that it was going to be discovered by police and therefore help to exonerate me from the investigation. I don't know why I need to read it again, because I know it off by heart.

*My darrling Debbie. I am so sorry. I never meant to hurt any
one. But now Im left with no choice. Iv spent my life looking
after you so let me do this 1 last thingg too protect you and my
Finns. Pleese forgive me. D x*

If only Dave had found it in himself to imagine how our world
could be without Mia. But he was more fragile than I am. After my
parents' victims were found in the attic, he kept fretting the police
would unearth a link to me. He drank more, ate less and his weight
plummeted. However, it was easier to turn a blind eye to it than
confront him. So I said nothing. I wish I could turn back the clock.

Every now and again, outside, Mia's head tilts upwards. I think
at first she's spotted another bloody journalist's drone before realising she's looking in my direction because she senses that I'm watching her. I'm sure she actually wants me to see her with Finn, the
little bitch.

Mia eventually returns to her car and pulls away. What I
wouldn't give for a speeding lorry to plough into her right now.
We might not have come face to face in months, but I still have
her in my sights. More often than she realises.

Finn keeps trying to convince me that Dave's suicide wasn't
her fault, but I'll never see it that way. It's because of Mia that I'm
a widow, that I'm vilified every time I leave my house; that Dave's
van was set alight on our driveway; that my MND is now so bad I
can't even pick up either of my grandchildren without fear of losing
my balance and dropping them. Washing and dressing is taking me
longer and longer, and the continuous pain in my legs is spreading
to the muscles in my back. My specialist admits stress has likely
triggered my decreasing mobility.

Mia is to blame for it all.

I recall watching her and Sonny on the lawn last summer; he
must have been only a few weeks old and was lying on the tartan

picnic blanket under the shade of an umbrella. Mia's wrist remained in plaster. Even then she was only playing at parenting. She was going through the motions of feeding and changing him, but there were none of the little unspoken actions – stroking his cheeks, rubbing noses, playing with his toes – that reveal a mum's love for her baby. She was, and remains, as cold as an Antarctic winter. I thank God that I can only see Finn's features when I look at Sonny. If he resembled her, I honestly think I might struggle to be around him so much. I didn't even get to spend Sonny's first Christmas with him because she insisted they did it at her parents' house. And they barely knew the boy!

That detective Finn didn't like asked if I wanted any of the evidence the police seized returning, including the boxes from the garage. They don't know Dave removed and destroyed anything incriminating after the internal security cameras recorded Mia's first visit.

Mia blundered from one misperception to another. She poked through a box of old water-damaged schoolbooks, the top two belonging to Dave but the rest were mine that my grandfather had brought back from my parents' house. Mia, not knowing a flood had erased the names on my books, had assumed them all to be Dave's. Then, putting two and two together from *that* error, she convinced herself that his handwriting matched what had been etched into the skirting board, when it was mine. While I wasn't dyslexic like Dave, Dad's homeschooling concentrated more on the arts than basics like handwriting.

If only I'd remembered doing that, maybe none of this might have happened. But so much was happening in those two days – thinking my mum and dad were going to kill me, rescuing Precious, thinking I had killed her, meeting Dave and starting my life again with my grandparents – it's not surprising that I forgot.

However, Dave's ultimate downfall was forgetting about the suitcase of invoices hidden in the oil tank. If he'd destroyed them, Mia would never have discovered the warehouse. In the end, we all answer to our mistakes one way or another.

Finn tells me Mia's mental health has been improving. She has been seeing a therapist for her postnatal depression and she has also been diagnosed with Post-Traumatic Stress Disorder, that trendy ailment that celebrities blame for their bad behaviour. She can fool my son and her idiot shrink, but she won't fool me. It's obvious what she's up to. You don't have to be stung by a scorpion to know it can kill. She's inventing conditions for sympathy.

Emma and my son have always been a much more natural fit. But they will need my help if they're to remain that way. I know Finn better than he knows himself and I can tell when he's not putting his heart and soul into something. I fear he is only going through the motions with Emma. He needs to be patient and give them time and eventually he will see what I do. She is compliant and devoted and easily malleable. Relationships have been built on far weaker foundations.

Little Chloe has never questioned my sudden appearance in her life and she's adapted to it with ease. However, I'm aware that we are strangers to one another. We have missed out on four years of each other's lives, and I don't know how we can make up that time.

A rush of air from the opening of the front door brushes against the back of my neck, and for a moment, I imagine it's Dave's breath. Then I feel his arms around my waist, his lips pressed gently against my ear, telling me that he loves me and that, despite everything, I am a good person. Today's rage towards him slowly begins to evaporate. But I know that tomorrow it will return. It always does.

Sonny's laughter echoes around the house and brings a rare smile to my face. I make my way out of the bedroom and remind myself how lucky I am to have him, considering the circumstances in which he made his unscheduled appearance.

My only regret – aside from causing the events that led to George's disappearance – is shaking Mia's ladder to distract her from urging Finn to open those suitcases. Their discovery was just as much of a surprise to me as it was to everyone else, and I panicked.

When I first discovered that house was up for auction, I knew we had to buy it. Finn had no idea it had been my home for a while. The plan was for Dave to renovate it and we'd sell it on for a profit. And we could eliminate any secrets lingering under its roof as and when we found them. But when Mia made such a fuss about wanting the place for her and Finn, we had little choice but to let them buy it. At least with Dave project-managing, we could keep a close eye on it. However, I had no idea about the secret room in the attic. And when I saw the suitcases inside, it was obvious what they contained.

If Mia and Finn hadn't been there, I could have warned Dave and we could have moved them elsewhere. But there they were, and I panicked. Shaking the ladder was only supposed to scare Mia into climbing down, but instead she lost her balance and fell.

Would I have forgiven myself if I'd hurt Sonny to save the rest of my family? I've asked myself this a lot and the answer is always the same – yes. At the time, he was only a blurred, pixelated cluster of cells on an ultrasound screen, a print-out on a piece of paper. I hadn't held him, wiped his tears, watched his personality develop or grown to love him. Now that he is a living, breathing human being, I will do anything necessary to protect him. Like I did with Finn.

Anything at all. And that means saving him from Mia. I will not let her take anyone else I love away from me.

There is one victim we all seem to forget in this terrible story – Debbie Hunter. When the man she loved for more than forty years took his own life, he abandoned her to the condemnation of the world's press and social media. It is unlikely she or their son Finn will ever escape his legacy. But the real shame is that this woman – this tragic character – who lived under the same roof as him, didn't see what he was capable of.

I believe she may be suffering from the psychological condition *folie à deux*. It's a shared psychosis of people with too close an emotional tie. It allows delusional belief to be transmitted from one person to another. From meeting at a very young, impressionable age, Dave began pulling her strings and made this gullible woman believe they were a normal couple. And her submissiveness fed into his desire for control. All she wanted to do – all he had *trained* her to do – was to support him in his endeavours, such as starting his own business. Even though she was responsible for his accounts, she didn't question why he didn't win any of the contracts he told her he had meetings for out of the county and when he was actually kidnapping and killing children. She just accepted his trips because he had schooled her into being unsuspecting.

One well-known example of this behaviour can be found in the case of Dr Harold Shipman and his wife Primrose. She steadfastly refused to believe anything negative about her husband or the two hundred deaths he was implicated in.

Debbie has since claimed to accept her late husband's guilt, but, like Mrs Shipman, she has spent her life unable to see her husband's flaws. It's more likely Debbie is paying lip service to this concept. However, I believe she should be pitied, not pilloried.

CHAPTER 54

FINN

Mum comes downstairs when she hears me playing peek-a-boo with Sonny. She acts surprised that he's here already and pretends she hasn't been watching me talk to Mia outside. I don't call her out on it because she's like a loaded gun ready to fire whenever I mention Mia. Even though Mum has got what she wanted and I'm with Emma again, she's still worried that Mia and I will find our way back to one another. I'm sure it's why she keeps hinting how Emma and I should think about having another baby and asking when Mia and I plan to legally separate.

Sonny giggles again and flaps his chubby arms wildly when he sees his nana. He's the only one who can cheer her up when she's spiralling and there has been a lot of that lately. I can't blame her. Her whole life has been ripped apart and she has lost the only man she has ever loved. And while none of that is Mia's fault, our family imploded because of what she did.

As much as I still love her, I wish she'd left things alone. If Mia hadn't interfered, I'd still have a dad, Sonny would have a grandfather and we wouldn't be the most hated family in the country. But unlike Mum, I don't over-dwell on what happened. Dad made his own decisions and blaming Mia won't change a thing. So to move forward, I've let it go.

When I ask Mum if she'd like to hold Sonny, she shakes her head. I assume it's because her MND is pretty bad today. It saps her of her strength, which embarrasses her. She can't walk the length of the house without a stick now, and sometimes she slurs her words. She's pencil thin because she's not eating properly and she is pale because she gets so little sunlight. All she does is stay indoors, staring blankly at the telly but rarely paying attention to anything on it. She is dying in front me, a prisoner of this house.

The last time she was out in public, I had to rescue her from Tesco after a group of people started hurling fruit at her in an aisle, yelling 'child killer'. She has also faced harassment at the bank and in her car waiting at traffic lights. Even though I begged her not to go, she insisted on attending Dad's public inquest, where a furious crowd made up of relatives of the dead children screamed at her on the steps. Even most of her post is hate mail.

'Are you hungry, baby boy?' Mum asks Sonny.

I unzip the largest of the pockets of Mia's bag and start removing the food Mia's made.

'He's not having any of her processed rubbish,' Mum sniffs, and once I place him in his high chair, she shuffles over to the fridge, takes out a small portion of homemade chicken casserole, heats it up in the microwave, then joins him at the kitchen table and helps load food on to his spoon.

Earlier, Mia asked me how I was and suggested that I should find someone professional to talk to like she has. I told her that I had Emma, but that's a half-truth because I can't talk to her about what my life has become. There are things I know that I can't tell anyone about. And it wouldn't be fair to start offloading on to Emma. She is already guilty by association because she is living with

Dave Hunter's son. Most of the school-gate muffia have shunned her and Chloe is no longer invited to birthday parties. She recently turned five and keeps asking us if we are sure Grandad is dead because a girl in her class told her he used to eat children. It breaks my heart to hear how frightened she is. At least Sonny is too young to know what social pariahs we are.

I'm not going to lie – I miss Mia like mad. But our relationship is what it is now and we both agreed that too much had happened for us to stay together. And it's because I struggle to function on my own, because I need to be surrounded by the familiar, that I fell back in with Emma. I'm a selfish bastard for using her, but perhaps she is doing the same with me. Maybe she needs to be one half of a couple to feel whole. Or maybe she loves me so much that she would turn a blind eye to anything I did. One day I might have to test that theory.

I've tried to keep a low profile since the accusations against Dad became international news, but it's tough when the paparazzi are camped outside your front door or taking pictures of you while you're working. I've lost half of my contracts and I'm considering going to Saudi Arabia to work for a while. A friend of a friend says he can get me a job on a new hotel complex. I don't want to leave Mum or my kids but my choices are narrowing.

I look to Sonny and wonder, if I accepted the job, could I be without him for six months? He is so happy and carefree, sitting there with the remnants of Mum's casserole spread between his fingers and smeared across his face. I don't know what I'm going to tell him about his grandad when he is old enough to understand. But if I don't say something, someone else will.

All I want is for him to be able to enjoy his innocence for as long as possible, and not have his childhood corrupted. I don't want him to grow up like I did.

CHAPTER 55

MIA

DS Mark Goodwin is already waiting for me at a table in the garden centre's coffee shop when I arrive. It's his day off so he's dressed casually in a white T-shirt, grey hoodie, skinny black jeans and a pair of Adidas trainers. He looks good. Each time we meet, it always surprises me when he's in civilian clothing. It's like being a child and bumping into a teacher at the weekend. You forget they have lives beyond their jobs and uniforms.

'Hey,' he begins with a smile and rises to his feet. We give each other a peck on the cheek and I inhale him. Finn douses himself in Lynx body spray like a teenage boy on the pull. But Mark's a cologne man and I immediately pick out notes of cedarwood and sage in his aftershave. And for a moment, I'm reluctant to pull away.

'I'm sorry I'm late,' I reply and he holds his hand out to invite me to sit. There's a pot of tea on the table and two cups, along with a jug of milk. He's also bought us a couple of flapjacks because he's remembered I have a sweet tooth. I'm flattered.

'No Sonny today?' he asks as he pours us both a cup. I notice his hands. Finn's job means they're rough and callused and his nails are always dirty. Mark's are clean and, for a moment, I want to feel how smooth they are pressed upon mine.

'He's with his grandparents,' I say.

'Ah, I was looking forward to seeing him again.' He opens up a messenger bag lying by his feet and slides it across the table. 'It's nothing special,' he says, his face reddening. 'It's a toy tractor because you told me last time how much he likes them.'

'That's really sweet of you.'

Something quietly and not altogether unpleasant bubbles away inside me as I wonder how on earth Mark is still single. Lorna thought the same when I confessed our meetings to her. She tells me I should make my move, as Mark is clearly interested. I'm tempted but I can't leap into something new until I know that something old – i.e. Finn – has completely left my system. I'm certainly moving in the right direction though.

'Does it feel weird when Sonny's not with you?' he continues. 'I know what it's like when I take my boy back to his mum's after having him for long weekends. I really miss him.'

'I'm getting used to it. He's a year old now so I can't have him with me all the time, especially as I'm back working in London twice a week.'

He nods his understanding. 'I thought about asking for a transfer to the Met a couple of years ago, just for the experience. But I didn't fancy commuting every day and it's above my pay grade to afford anywhere decent to live down there.'

'I didn't realise how much I'd missed it,' I admit. 'But it's very different to how it was before. A lot of my friends are still single, and even though I guess I am now too, I have Sonny to come home for. And I don't have that desire to go out at night, drinking and being stared at by strangers.'

'Is that still happening?'

'Yes, even in here. There's an elderly woman about four tables behind you who keeps looking in our direction. She's doing it now.' I stare back at her, then wave my hand. Her cheeks flush and she averts her gaze towards her mug. 'It won't be like this forever though, I'm sure. Now that Dave's funeral and inquest are over, we just have to get the public inquiry out of the way before people eventually start forgetting who I am. Or, if not forget, then at least get used to seeing me around.'

'That's a healthy attitude.'

'Believe me, it's taken a lot of therapy to get there. When I thought he was going to kill me, all I could think of was never seeing my son again. And I promised myself that, if by some miracle I survived, then I'd be a better mum. There's only one thing I have to thank Dave for, and that's for making me take ownership of my postnatal depression. But I admit the PTSD diagnosis took me by surprise. However, I guess it makes sense after the last twelve months.'

'You're a great parent.'

It's a nice thing to hear and we unwrap our flapjacks and pull chunks from them. Aside from Lorna and my counsellor, who is paid to listen to me moan, Mark is one of the only people I can talk to when I need to rant or cry or tell someone how unfair it all is that my life has turned out like this. And as I gradually pull myself together, my needy moments are becoming fewer and further between.

I'm also thinking there's more to whatever is going on between us than either of us has admitted to the other. We WhatsApp on his private number and sometimes when my parents and Sonny are asleep, we'll FaceTime for a while before bed. There's nothing sexual about it but I'd be lying if I said it hadn't crossed my mind.

And lately, it's crossed my mind a lot. We haven't stepped over the line but that line is growing fainter every time we meet.

Mark seems like the perfect man, but I find myself holding back. I thought the same about Finn, so perhaps I can't trust my own judgement. Today, each time we place our cups of tea back on to the table, our fingertips inch a little closer to one another's until finally they meet. And there they stay.

I move the conversation to Mark's life. He was mountain biking last weekend in the Pennines, and for the rest of the week, he has his young son staying with him. He told me once that earlier this year, he lost his dad, his only remaining parent, to cancer. And I'm ashamed to admit that my first reaction was quiet gratitude, because if he and I did go any further, I wouldn't have to deal with any more insane in-laws. That selfish thought also serves as a reminder of how much work I need to do before I can toss my baggage away completely.

'There's something I need to talk to you about,' Mark says, his eyes looking dead into mine. My heart flutters like a teenage girl's. Is he about to ask me out on a proper date?

'Okay . . .' I reply.

'It's about the investigation into your father-in-law.'

Oh, I think. *That'll teach me for getting my hopes up.*

'There's something about his confession that doesn't add up and it's bothering me.'

'Which part?'

'Well, all of it actually. If what you say he told you is accurate – and I'm not doubting you at all – there isn't a moment where he actually admits to what he's done.'

He pulls from his bag a copy of my police statement. I shrink back into my seat. Is that why we are here today, for work?

'I don't understand,' I reply. 'You found his DNA all over that warehouse.'

'But not on the suitcases, clothes or the bags they were in. They'd all been wiped clean; even the more recent victims had no fingerprints, fibres or DNA on them. According to your statement, Hunter said, "I need you to know that I am sorry for everything that's happened. This is not how it was supposed to be. I've done many things I'm not proud of." Is that correct?'

'Uh-huh.'

'But he never said specifically what he was sorry for?'

'Mark, it's obvious. He was referring to the forty bodies in that warehouse. And what about his suicide text message to Debbie?'

'Again, he never specifically admitted to any criminal act. You said he became agitated when you asked why he targeted kids, if he abused them, and you said that he told you he'd "never hurt a child".'

My hackles twitch. 'You sound like you're doubting me.'

'No, not at all. For decades he got away with it. There were no eyewitnesses, no descriptions of him, no car registration plates reported, he wasn't captured once on CCTV even though every one of those kids was abducted in plain sight. He covered his tracks so well. So why did he wipe clean the bodies, the suitcases and the clothes but not the warehouse? It troubles me that maybe his confession wasn't a confession at all.'

'Then what was it?'

'A distraction. Could he have been trying to divert us from what really happened?'

'Who else shares this opinion?'

'I haven't voiced my concerns to anyone else yet. But are you sure there's nothing else he said that might be relevant?'

I fold my arms. 'I'm sure. I was there, alone in that room with him. He had guilt written all over his face. He might not have gone into detail or answered all my questions, but in his own way, there was stuff he wanted to get off his chest before he killed himself. If you were there, you'd know exactly what I mean.'

'Think again, think back. A word, a line, something casual, something throwaway that came to you later and that you didn't think was worth mentioning at the time.'

'There's nothing.'

'Close your eyes, maybe try to put yourself back into that warehouse.'

'No Mark, I don't want to,' I say, my impatience growing. 'I did that for my police statement and I did it again for therapy and you have no idea how many times I've done it on my own when all I can picture is Dave slitting his own throat in front of me. So you'll forgive me if I don't want to think about being tied up and surrounded by dozens of dead children while I'm in a bloody garden centre tea room.'

He knows he has gone too far. 'I'm sorry,' he says. 'I didn't mean to upset you.'

'Well, you have. I don't know why, when your bosses have closed the case and an inquest decided Dave was a serial murderer, it's not enough to convince you? Are you feeling guilty or something for not having looked into his background earlier? Is that what this is all about?'

'No, not at all.'

'Then what is it?'

'I can't explain it. It's an instinct. It just doesn't sit right.'

I push my cup to one side and rise to my feet. 'This is a bad idea, Mark,' I say, feeling utterly foolish. 'Me and you . . . whatever the hell we are doing here . . . I need to leave.'

'No please, Mia, don't go,' he protests. 'Not like this.'

I leave the toy tractor on the table and don't look at him again as I make my way out of the café and through the main store. I ignore a man in a wheelchair pointing at me and muttering to his wife. Outside, I climb into my car and slam the door closed.

How dare he! I think. *He knows how far I've come and how much I have sacrificed to get here. And now he's questioning me like I've got something wrong?*

Turning the music up loud, I reverse on to the main road and do my best to accelerate away from Mark and my whirling thoughts.

It doesn't work. The fact is, on hearing Mark reading aloud my statement months after I made it, I find a small part of myself able to understand why he has his suspicions. *Had* that been a confession from a psychopath, or had I heard only the ramblings of a suicidal man? Mark was right: at no point did Dave ever admit guilt. But surely there was enough evidence stacked against him without the need for him to say the actual words 'I killed forty children'.

'Fuck it!' I shout aloud and slam my fists down so hard on the steering wheel that I accidentally blow the horn.

Just when I was starting to believe there was a light at the end of the tunnel, it's extinguished and I'm back to fumbling around in the dark.

BABES IN THE ATTIC EPISODE –
PART 2 OF 3

Hi there folks, Caroline Mitchell here. I'm an ex-police detective and crime thriller author and today I'm bringing you part two of my theories behind the unsolved case of the Babes In the Attic.

In the last episode, I told you the incredible story of what happened after the seven young victims were discovered, and how the killings of the original elderly homeowners that preceded those slayings remain unsolved. Today, I'm going to offer my theory on what happened to that couple – Kenneth and Moira Kilgour – whose skeletal remains were discovered in a grave in the garden, forty years after they were killed and dismembered.

They had lived in the village for at least two decades. Neighbours describe them as pleasant but private. Nobody recalls any children or extended family members visiting. By the mid-1970s, they were in poor health when a second family moved in, a young couple with two children. Soon after, the Kilgours were not seen again. Given their age and health, this aroused no suspicion; it was simply assumed they had moved to a smaller property or a care home.

But my research reveals this isn't the first time that an elderly couple has vanished under these kinds of circumstances. I've spent many hours searching through cold cases and I have found many more spread across the UK that mirror and pre-date the Kilgours. Each time, the residents who vanish are elderly, in poor health, live in large properties, and have very few, if any, relatives. They are never seen again and there are no official records of their deaths. More than that, a family of four always replaces them in their home and, despite the couple's absences, their bank accounts are gradually drained until nothing is left.

I believe the cuckoos in the Kilgours' nest not only murdered the seven children found in their attic, but are also likely responsible for the deaths of at least twelve more adults. Some of these bodies have yet to be discovered.

In the early 1980s, this mysterious house-hopping family vanished too. We may never know who they are, why they stopped killing or what happened to them. But in my experience, people like this don't stop killing out of choice. In the next episode, I'll discuss the various scenarios of what might have happened to them that ended their reign of terror.

CHAPTER 56

DEBBIE

My watch pings with an alarm reminding me to take my medication. I swallow a couple of tablets I slipped into my pocket earlier. I try and outstretch my fingers and toes but they feel rigid, like claws curling in on themselves. I check the time and realise it won't be long before my company arrives: the only light in my darkness. I can't let them see me like this, puffy-eyed, thin-lipped and so worn. Perhaps some fresh air will help to blow the dark clouds from my sky.

Walking stick in hand, I wander slowly into the garden. It's safe out here now, much more secluded since Finn erected seven-feet-high wooden fencing around the perimeter. It keeps me caged in but shelters me from the world. Outside it, I am persona non grata, abandoned without exception by all of my neighbours and friends. And I'm too stained to make new ones.

For my whole adult life, I made my home in the shadows, but Dave's suicide has forced me centre stage. Now I'll be forever judged, always a punchbag for the strangers I shy away from. I'm not allowed to be a grieving widow because I cannot be seen to be mourning the death of a child killer. I can't appear to be happy that he's dead, either, or I'll be viewed as callous. And if I behave like nothing's happened, I'll be judged for my indifference.

Finn and I tried making a public statement, expressing our disbelief – but acceptance – of Dave's abhorrent behaviour. We talked of the pain we felt for the families of those he'd killed. But it had little effect on public opinion. I know that it was right to put that carefully worded document on the record, but it hurts me to think nobody will ever know Dave the way that Finn and I knew him.

I sometimes allow myself to wonder how different my life might have been had Dave and I not met. Might fate have brought us together another way? I can't help thinking we were two lost souls always destined to be together. But in a different life, perhaps our alliance wouldn't have been based on a lie. I exploited his guilt over the fatal injuries he thought he'd inflicted on Precious Johnson by using it to tether us and promising to keep it a secret. The same instinct that warned me I was going to die at the hands of my parents in that house told me that Dave was as damaged as I was and that he could save me.

We stayed awake for most of our first night together, on the cusp of a new world and comparing notes about the last. We hid behind the closed bedroom door of the residential drugs den in which he had been left to raise himself. All night, through the holes in his bedroom door, we watched spectral figures glide by as though roaming the halls of a hotel for the dead.

There was no judgement when I confessed to him what my parents made me do or about the role I played in George's disappearance. And it was Dave who encouraged me to locate my grandparents. The following morning, I arrived on their doorstep, expecting them to turn me away or accuse me of having a wild imagination when I described my life with their son, my father. But they doubted nothing and I am forever grateful for that. I can still smell my grandmother's rose-scented eau de toilette as she pulled me into her chest and told me I was safe when she settled me in to my new bedroom. I can still feel the weight of the thick quilt she tucked me under that night and how I noticed that this was a house without locks on the outside of each internal door.

I also spotted Dave that first night, sitting under a streetlight on the opposite side of the road. My heart flutters even now when I think about him wanting to make sure I was safe, protecting me in his own way.

It was something he never stopped doing, even years later when he discovered I shared more with my parents than just DNA. He hated that I killed; he tried reasoning with me, begging me to stop, fearing I would be caught and that he would be left alone again. And for a time, I really did try to adapt to his will. But eventually my need to protect the vulnerable became bigger than the both of us. And he understood that he would lose me if he didn't accept me for who I was. He just didn't want to know about it.

After my escape from home, my grandparents argued behind closed doors about how best to help me. They didn't know I felt no empathy towards the children Mum and Dad hurt. Perhaps Grandad had his suspicions, as he wanted to find me professional help. But Grandma was doggedly against it. 'If she says one wrong word about her old life, they could take her away from us,' she warned. 'All Deborah needs is stability and love. Her parents have already put her through too much.'

I often worried about Mum and Dad turning up on our doorstep or at the school gates ready to drag me home. But as the weeks stretched into months and they failed to appear, I concluded the cuckoos had nested elsewhere. It was a mixed blessing, a combination of relief yet abandonment. I waited until after my grandfather died years later and there was a brief clearing in the fog of my grandmother's dementia to ask why she thought they never came for me. 'They didn't have the chance to,' she said, before revealing that my grandfather and a group of close friends had ensured my parents could never hurt another child again. Then he paid a crematorium attendant to open up after hours and dispose of their bodies.

'But Dad was your son,' I said.

'Which is why we were duty bound. We brought him into this world so it was our responsibility to take him out of it.' One solitary tear fell from her cheek and caught in a deep-set line. I wondered how many of those creases Dad was to blame for. I also realised that, between my grandfather and my parents, I was now a third-generation killer.

I can only assume it was my grandfather who also disposed of their caravan, video tapes and camera, and sealed the seven suitcases containing the bodies behind a brick wall in the attic. Perhaps even his crematorium associates couldn't be bribed into incinerating that number of children. But despite this, I learned more in my time with my grandparents about the need for a moral compass than I ever did from Mum and Dad. They demonstrated that even good people like them – *like me* – can kill out of necessity.

When my grandmother too passed away a month before I turned twenty-one, I discovered the paperwork and address for the Kilgours' warehouse and import company. And over the years, I'd visit it to plunder the suitcases as and when required, returning each case when it was filled. Dave could read me like a book and knew without asking if I'd filled another case. Then he'd go to the warehouse, clean each body and piece of clothing with the precision of an undertaker, before storing them on a shelf. It's a near-impossible task finding forty different locations to bury bodies without the danger of them being discovered. That's why keeping them all together in one secluded place removed the risk factor.

My phone buzzes and the screen reveals camera footage of a figure outside the gate. My heart tightens at who it is. I buzz them in, apply some lipstick, flatten down my hair and take a deep breath.

These clandestine visits are all I have to look forward to, the only positive thing to come from this mess of Mia's making. And I look forward to them more than anyone could ever know.

CHAPTER 57

MIA

Much to my frustration, the train I'm travelling on from London to Leighton Buzzard has been delayed again. I've been trapped in here like a tinned sardine for forty minutes, squashed up against the window even though I have a seat. And experience makes me think the conductor's warning about the delay being related to overhead wire issues means we won't be moving any time soon. I'm not sure how much longer I'm going to be doing this commute anyway, because if what they're saying is true and this Covid thing continues to spread, I might be working from home for a while during a lockdown.

I text Mum to ask if she can bathe Sonny, give him a snack and put him to bed, as it's unlikely I'll be home in time. She says yes and sends a baby emoji. I've enjoyed watching her and Dad spending time with him over the last few months. I hope he has a closer relationship with them than I did. They might not have graduated from their 'how to be an attentive parent' class, but they've excelled at grandparenting. Maybe they are trying to make up for their mistakes with me by being more attentive with Sonny. Many times, I've wondered if I should bring up my memories of my own distanced childhood with them, but I'm not sure what good it would do. They are here now and that's what counts.

The woman sitting next to me keeps reading my text messages. She thinks she's being subtle, but I catch her reflection in the window. I don't know if she is showing interest because she recognises me, or if she's bored and just wants to take her mind off this interminable wait. Only when I slip my phone back into my handbag does she close her eyes and drift off to sleep.

I swap the phone for my iPad and open the Notes application. At the top of a long list of reminders and work drafts is a file containing the names of some of the forty young victims found inside Dave's warehouse. Almost all have now been identified. Some were easier to trace than others, thanks to name tags sewn into their school clothes followed by family DNA tests. Others have been determined through public appeals in which hundreds of relatives of missing children offered their DNA for testing.

There has been very little contact between myself and Mark since we met for coffee. He has texted several times over the weeks to apologise for questioning the accuracy of my police statement. My responses were curt. He thinks he's offended me, and yes, at first, he really pissed me off. But our blurred lines distracted me from remembering that, first and foremost, he has a job to do. And if I'm being honest, I'm also embarrassed for considering there might be something between us aside from our stated roles as victim and police liaison officer.

But my awkwardness hasn't stopped me from dwelling on the point he was making. I've since replayed my conversation with Dave hundreds of times over in my head, asking myself if I've missed something; if there is a key piece of information I have subconsciously blocked out or failed to recollect. After all, there was a lot to process and digest in that warehouse in a very short space of time.

I've also re-read my witness statement many times and Mark is right – despite the overwhelming evidence, nowhere does Dave actually admit that he was a killer. 'A dog doesn't have to bark for you to know what he is,' my dad countered when I mentioned it to him. But I can't get away from the niggling thought that, for a confession, Dave didn't admit to very much at all.

There's something else puzzling me. Two names in my Notes file don't fit the pattern of all the other kills. A brother and sister disappeared together in February 1990: a four-year-old girl, Tanya, along with one-month-old William. I switch screens to remind myself of their heartbreaking story and re-read a saved newspaper clipping. Both children were in their family garden when they were abducted. Their mum left them alone to go inside and make up a bottle for William, and when she returned five minutes later, the gate was open, the pushchair empty and both of her children missing. Police and neighbourhood search parties combed the area for weeks but no clues were ever found. I remember watching a documentary about it on YouTube before Sonny was born and it scared the hell out of me.

Anyway, a week ago, Tanya's body was identified as one of the warehouse suitcase victims, but William was not among them. This appears to be the only time Dave ever deviated from his pattern of kills. Although a police statement said there was always a possibility other bodies were hidden in an alternative location, no such site has been discovered.

I remember Dave being a creature of habit. Day in, day out, he ate the same foods, drank the same brand of beer and of bourbon, his tools were hung up in his shed and outlined with a marker pen so he knew exactly where to replace them, the petrol gauge in his van was never allowed to dip below the half-full limit, and he mowed his lawns on the same day each week, rain or shine. Each suitcase – even the empty ones – was perfectly spaced apart from its neighbours, arranged with the precision of a window dresser. Dave was not a man who liked change. So why would he hide one sibling in the warehouse and another elsewhere?

This prompts me to recall something else Dave said . . . something in my own statement that returns to me so clearly, it's as if he's sitting next to me and whispering in my ear.

I shake my head. No, I'm being ridiculous. It's a ludicrous idea, isn't it. Isn't it? But it's possible. It's actually possible.

The enormity of what I'm considering jolts me back into my seat so suddenly, the whole row of chairs judders and I wake up the dozing woman next to me. I lose my grip of the iPad and it falls under my seat. I'm all fingers and thumbs as I pick it up and, somehow, I've clicked on to my photo reel. It's gone as far back as when renovation work started on the house.

The last image is a clip I recorded. I know from the holding shot exactly what it is before I open it. I have not watched it before. But today, a masochistic side of me makes me press play and I once again relive the moment we found the suitcases in the attic. A few minutes into the recording, I started to feel faint and my legs began wobbling, which is when I dropped the phone on to the rim of the loft hatch.

But I didn't realise the phone continued to record, and now, for the first time, I see what the lens continued to capture from its new position. Below us, a split second before I fall down the ladder, is Debbie. And she looks as if she is shaking it. No, I correct myself, she doesn't just *look* like she is shaking it, she actually *is*.

I replay it several times to make sure my eyes aren't deceiving me, but they're not. She is the reason I fell.

CHAPTER 58

MIA

'Hi,' says Finn, removing his paper mask and placing it and his coat on the bench. He tilts his head and moves to kiss me on the lips like old times. Then he stops himself, remembering that we're only just coming out of a national lockdown. Just as importantly, we are no longer a couple and not yet friends and thus existing in a no-man's-land. So it's inappropriate for all kinds of reasons.

He takes a seat on the bench next to me in a park opposite the Grand Union Canal. He asks how I am and I tell him I'm fine, though I'm far from it, actually. I'm so nervous that I want to walk away from him right now. But I hold it together and bring up a couple of anecdotes about things Sonny did that morning which amused Dad. He asks after my parents, but I don't reciprocate and ask about Debbie. Not tonight.

I try to figure out how to begin the conversation I need to have with him. I've tried rehearsing it ever since I texted him asking to meet, but I'm still struggling to engineer a jumping-off point. I just need to get on with it.

'There are some things I need to talk to you about,' I say eventually.

'What's up?'

I start tapping my foot against the bench leg. Both things I'm about to say are of equal importance and I'm not sure which one to begin with.

'I found something on my phone,' I say, my voice low. 'Something your mum did.'

'What?'

I slide the phone towards him and press play on the video. When it's over, a second after Debbie shakes the ladder, he does a double take. He watches it again.

'You saw it, didn't you?' I ask hopefully.

'If you're going to say what I think you're going to say, then no, you're wrong.'

'I fell because she shook the ladder.'

Finn grimaces and closes his eyes. 'It was already moving and she was trying to steady it.'

'Well she didn't do a very good job because, a second later, Sonny and I almost died.'

'You really think she'd want to hurt you and Sonny?'

'I don't know what your family are capable of any more,' I reply without thinking. For a moment, he looks hurt, as if I'm including him.

'There's something else,' I say and take a deep breath. 'It's about your dad and something he said to me in the warehouse that afternoon.'

He leans forward. 'But you've already told me everything, haven't you?' I nod. 'Then . . . ?'

'I met with Mark Goodwin recently.'

'Is he still sniffing around you?' Finn says sharply.

I ignore his disdain. I once almost told Finn that Mark and I had met for coffee a couple of times to prove that my life, like his, had moved on. I decided against it for fear of it sounding like I was trying to make him jealous.

'We were discussing my statement,' I tell him, 'and he pointed out that nowhere does Dave admit he killed those children.'

'He didn't have to.'

'No, but—'

'Then why are you bringing it up again?'

'Do you think it's possible that he might not be guilty? Or that he might not have done it alone? That he could be trying to protect someone?'

'Who?'

'I don't know.'

'Mia, what's this really about?' My foot-tapping picks up pace. 'Well?'

'There's something else your dad said that doesn't make sense. He told me: "I let Debbie keep the baby she always wanted."' I leave this hanging, waiting for him to catch up with me.

'And?' he asks.

'Don't you think it's a strange thing to say? What do you think that means?'

'I don't know, maybe he meant he didn't want to have his own children because he was worried he might hurt them too. But then, when Mum got pregnant, he realised there was nothing to worry about. He never laid a finger on me.'

It's plausible, but I know better.

'The pathologist measured his blood,' he adds, 'and he was three times above the legal drink-drive limit. He just wasn't making sense.'

'Finn, we both know that he could handle his alcohol, and I can assure you he definitely wasn't drunk. He knew exactly what he was saying.'

276

His tone cools. 'And what are *you* saying? Because you clearly have something else to get off your chest.'

I reach out my hand to place it on his. 'What if he meant that you weren't biologically his or Debbie's, and you came into their lives another way?'

Finn spits out a laugh. 'Are you mad?'

I hesitate. 'I asked Mark if he could DNA-test you and Dave to see if you really are father and son.'

He snatches his hand back. 'You did what?'

'He said that legally, he wouldn't be allowed to, as it wasn't pertinent to the case.'

'Good! What the hell were you thinking? Don't you think I'd know if we weren't—'

'So I organised two tests myself.'

His jaw drops like a stunned cartoon character's. I count the seconds before he registers what I've said. Seven pass. One for each suitcase. 'You did what, exactly?'

'I organised a DNA test on your behalf. I let myself into Debbie's house when she was out with Sonny and sent stubble from your dad's razor and some hairs from inside one of your baseball caps. And I also used a lint roller to remove hairs from clothes in Debbie's wardrobe.'

It's only when revealing the lengths I've gone to that I become aware of how crazy I must sound.

Now Finn's expression is paralysed. 'I can't believe this,' he says finally. I don't think I have ever seen him this shocked at something I've done since I told him I was pregnant.

'And do you have the results?' he asks.

I nod, and take out a white envelope from my handbag, sliding it across the bench to him. He glares at it with the intensity of a man whose past and future are about to collide.

CHAPTER 59

FINN

What the hell has she done? My head is spinning and my hands are shaking and that's before I even pick the envelope up. She's tested my DNA behind my back! I look at Mia in utter disbelief: why would she want to put me through this? Does she really hate me that much? I've just about come to terms with Dad's suicide and now she's telling me we might not even be related? And Mum too? I thought Mia's therapy and antidepressants were helping her return to her old self. But from what I'm hearing tonight, she is worse than she ever was. She's delusional. I shove the envelope back towards her.

'No,' I say. 'I don't know why Goodwin's been filling your head with this kind of shit.'

'It's not shit, I promise you,' she says, so calmly that I believe that's what she thinks. I should show her compassion, but I can't. Instead, I want to be cruel and hurt her as much as she is trying to hurt me.

'Is it not enough that you've torn my family apart once already?' I growl. 'What's next? Are you going to tell me that Sonny's not mine? Are you going to try and turn Emma against me? Chloe too? Look, I'm genuinely sorry for what I did to you and for what Dad put you through. But attacking me isn't going to make your life any better.'

She takes something else out of her handbag and I pull further away from her until I see it's a packet of paper tissues. She passes them to me. Only when I feel wetness on the corners of my lips do I realise I have been crying. I wipe them away with my cuff. We both remain where we are, maintaining our eye contact but saying nothing. She is perfectly composed, calmer in fact than I recall ever seeing her. I'm desperate for her to admit this is a sick joke, that she is mistaken. But she isn't going to, and a chasm opens up inside me. She is calm because she knows what the contents of this envelope say. I lean over and take it. Inside are two sheets of A4 paper with the words 'Helix Labs' and a graphic across the top. I begin to read.

'A comparison of the DNA profiles of Finn Hunter and David Hunter does not support the hypothesis that David Hunter is the biological father of Finn Hunter. Based on testing results obtained from analysis of the DNA loci listed in the technical data, the probability of paternity is zero per cent. This testing is based on information provided by the client.'

The next sheet says exactly the same thing, except about Mum. Both are caveated with the warning: 'The identity of the sample donor and chain of custody of the samples cannot be guaranteed; therefore these results are not admissible in court.'

'See?' I say. 'They say this isn't admissible in court, so even they know they can't prove it's true.' Even as I'm saying it, I know I'm clutching at straws because straws are all I have.

'Mark says it might be enough evidence for them to carry out a controlled test to compare your DNA with the family of a boy who disappeared back in 1990,' Mia says, still calm, still refusing to fight fire with fire.

'You've told Goodwin about the results?'

'Yesterday, when they arrived. I didn't know where else to turn.'

'And that boy?'

'He went missing at the same time as his sister.'

'What happened to her?'

Mia's eyes move towards a narrowboat slowly chugging its way along the canal. I know what the answer is before she tells me. 'She was in your dad's warehouse. But her brother's body was never found.'

Now she shows me a newspaper story about the siblings' disappearance. William Brown had dark hair and dark eyes like me, features I don't share with either of my parents. I make a note of the article's date and count back – this boy and I were both a month old when he vanished.

'And you think . . .' My voice trails off. I don't want to say it aloud.

'I don't know what to think.' But she does and she's sparing my feelings. She believes I was taken from another family by Dave and raised as his own. I don't know in what order to start putting my thoughts together. If any of this is true . . . I . . . I . . . I can't bring myself to consider it.

'When we were going through IVF, I remember your mum telling me how hard she found it to conceive,' Mia adds. 'What if they never managed to? What if they couldn't have a baby, so Dave took you from another family?'

'So you think Dad came home from work one day with a kid and said, "Look what I've found, he's ours now"? And Mum didn't bat an eyelid? That's ridiculous.'

'I don't know what happened. But if you are William Brown, then Debbie was complicit in a crime. And if that's the case, it's also feasible that she could know more about Dave's killings than she's letting on.'

I need some space to process what she's telling me but she won't shut up.

'Aside from his DNA in the warehouse, have you wondered why the police can't find any links between Dave and how those children were kidnapped and killed?'

'Mia,' I mutter.

'What I don't understand is the link between Dave and the children found in our house and the couple in the garden. And why did he write "I will save them from the attic"? Or if he was locked up there at some point, then how did he escape?'

'Mia,' I say a little louder, but she's not listening.

'I just keep thinking that your mum must know more than she is letting on . . .'

I can't listen to any more. 'For God's sake just shut up!' I shout and slam my fists down on the bench as I stand up. Her face reddens and two women a couple of benches away from us stare at me. 'You've made your point. Or are you about to tell me another way in which you're planning to destroy my life?'

She doesn't respond, and anything else I have to say about Mum or Dad snags in my throat. 'Just leave me the hell alone,' I add, finally. 'Because I don't know how much more of this, of them, of you, I can take.'

I grab my coat and mask and leave her there.

CHAPTER 60

DEBBIE

I can't stop crying. My tears are a toxic combination of rage and disappointment at what I've just witnessed. Only, tonight, my frustration and anger aren't directed towards Dave. They're at Finn.

I called him earlier to see if he could come over and help me move a chest of drawers from my and his dad's old bedroom and into the spare room. And I knew immediately from his tone that he was hiding something when he said he was busy seeing friends.

So I followed my instinct and my son, and now I'm sitting in my parked car close to the canal and park where he and Mia have enjoyed a clandestine meeting. I have watched from a distance as they cosied up to one another, at one point even brazenly holding hands. For what seemed like forever they remained like this, her probably reminding him of old times and convincing him how they are better together than they are apart. He dabbed at his eyes so I think she must have said something to upset him or put him on another one of her guilt trips. And he was sucked in by it.

They left separately – him first and then her. My heart bleeds for Emma, being treated like this again. I remain where I am, but my hands are clamped on the steering wheel too firmly to drive. I am nothing short of devastated. How can he be so stupid as to fall for Mia's lies? She killed his father, for God's sake! He might not have died by her hand, but certainly by her tongue. The thought of Finn and her recoupling makes me ill. Them, together. Her turning him against me with her wicked words and deeds, edging me out of their lives, out of the life of my grandson . . . it's all too much.

That poor little boy. I'm constantly worried about Sonny. Finn asked me to look after him yesterday afternoon, and when I changed his nappy, I was horrified by the glowing red rash between his buttocks. He was raw and almost bleeding. If that were the only sign of neglect, then perhaps I'd accept it as an oversight. But when I weighed him on the kitchen scales and checked the results online, he was only in the fourth percentile. Mia is literally starving him. And as for the bruises on his legs, nothing will convince me these are from regular spills as he learns to crawl. Mia can't even perform her most basic motherly duties by keeping him safe, nourished and clean.

I've tried talking to Finn about it but he's blinkered. Tonight, I want so badly to give him the benefit of the doubt and hope that common sense has prevailed and he has spurned her advances, but how can I after what I've just seen? He kept Chloe's existence from me, and now he's lying about Mia. I cannot trust him to know what is best for himself. Mia can't be allowed to keep ruining people's lives without punishment. She needs to pay for everything she has done – and will continue to do, if not stopped.

I try to think calming thoughts, returning to my favourites of the forty mental pictures I created at locations around the country over the decades. I placed suitcases in woodlands, warehouses, under bridges and sunsets, in snowfalls, on deserted beaches and lake shores. Eventually those special memories are just enough to subdue my rage.

Then, without fanfare, something unexpected happens. An idea develops, slowly and quietly at first, like an animal waking up from hibernation. I assumed it was something I'd put to bed after my last kill. But it has returned because it senses an urge, no, *a need*, for me to take matters into my own hands. To regain control over myself and those around me. And to fulfil my destiny of helping those who can't help themselves. For the first time, I must intervene in my own family, because we cannot continue in this vicious cycle. It will take all my strength but Finn needs to learn the hard way that I will do anything – anything at all – to protect him. He has and will always come first, no matter what.

Taking my phone from the door pocket, I make a call I never considered might be necessary. It is answered within three rings. And I don't need to fake my tears for them to hear how upset I am.

I knew who they were talking about as soon as the news started to spread. This isn't a large village so most of us know one another by sight at least. They came in here at least once a week after picking up supplies in the shops and taking their boat back home. To look at them, there was nothing unusual and they appeared perfectly at ease in one another's company. They were always friendly with the rest of my customers and none of us had any reason to believe there was anything wrong with their set-up. I can't believe anyone could do what he did to another human being. It's almost inconceivably cruel.

CHAPTER 61

MIA

The pads of my thumbs are sore, as I've been rubbing them against my index fingers so often. It's a habit I've had since I was a child but lately it's getting worse. As I've been nothing but anxious for the last year, it's a wonder I have any fingerprints left.

A lengthy, pounding headache meant I only dozed for much of the night and it isn't helping my state of mind this afternoon. The body in that attic suitcase used to be the first thing I saw in the morning and the last thing at night. But it's been replaced by the equally grisly image of Dave slitting his own throat. I remember the spray of blood against a suitcase, how he remained on his feet for what felt like an age before he collapsed to his knees. I recall his hand clasping at his throat and the fear in his eyes as he knew the end was imminent. I can still hear his rasping and my own screams as I watched him die before my eyes.

Liz, my therapist, tells me it's all part of my PTSD, and she's given me some coping strategies to use when it all gets too much. Being aware of the present and what surrounds me can distract me from remembering what upsets me.

However, Dave's ghost is persistent and has chosen this afternoon and the moment I woke up from a nap for his second appearance of the day. Sonny is also down for his sleep in the nursery so I make the most of the quiet and shut my eyes again, taking in the aroma of the beef and Yorkshire puddings cooking in the oven and wafting its way up the stairs. Eventually, Dave returns to his box and I secure the lid. For now, at least. Because he always finds his way out.

'What do you think of this kidney bean and quinoa casserole recipe?' Mum asks when I eventually make my way downstairs and into the kitchen. She shows me a page in a Joe Wicks baby recipe book with a dozen Post-it notes protruding from it. She's very excited about it.

'I'm sure Sonny will love it,' I say. He took to weaning like a duck to water and, to date, there's nothing we've presented that he hasn't wolfed down. The doorbell chimes and Mum answers it, returning with a face like thunder.

'It's *him*,' she growls, and I know she's referring to Finn. She barely forgave him for cheating on me but has point-blankly refused to even say his name since he moved into Emma's house. 'I've left him on the doorstep where he belongs, next to the wheelie bin. He likes to recycle, doesn't he?' It takes me a beat to identify this as a thinly veiled dig at his and Emma's reconciliation.

Sonny is to have his first sleepover at his dad's tonight. I want him to spend time with Finn but not at Debbie's house, and on the strict provision that she goes nowhere near him. So I've swallowed my pride and allowed him to stay at Emma's place. Now that I know Debbie has been lying to Finn about his parentage, I don't trust what else she might be hiding or what she's capable of – such as her awareness of Dave's crimes. Until I know she can be trusted, Sonny is not to be left alone with her.

Finn didn't take much convincing, which says something. He's told her that Sonny has chickenpox and, with her poor health, she could develop shingles if they're together. But this can't go on forever; he's going to have to tell her the truth soon. And her reaction is no longer my problem.

The only times Finn and I have crossed paths in the fortnight since we met at the canal have been by text and all have been Sonny-related. Despite my best efforts, he's refused to engage in conversation about anything other than our boy. Maybe I did go too far by organising the DNA tests, but I'd want to know if someone had lied to me my whole life about my heritage. However, at least I know for certain he isn't that stolen baby, William Brown. I spoke again with Mark to tell him about Finn's DNA test results, and he pulled up Finn's birth certificate. William was born two days before Finn in a different hospital 100 miles away. So the mystery of Finn's biological parents remains – along with why Dave and Debbie's names are printed on his birth certificate when they aren't related.

I brace myself as I approach the door. My headache won't allow for us to argue again.

The moment our eyes lock, I know something's wrong. Finn is unshaven, his hair is scraped back into a messy ponytail and there are dark rings surrounding his eyes. He looks as exhausted as I did in the depths of my postnatal depression. 'Come in,' I offer and lead him into the conservatory, closing the double doors behind us. There's a bulging bag weighing his shoulder down. He opens the clasp and pulls out leather-bound diaries with different years embossed on each cover, along with the letters DH – Dave's initials – in gold lettering. He spreads them out across the coffee table.

'They're Dad's appointment books from the late 1980s onwards,' he begins. 'He wrote down every meeting he went to when he was tendering for contracts.'

'Didn't the police take them away when they searched the house?'

'They must have missed them,' Finn says but doesn't elaborate on where he found them. 'Look at what's inside.'

I flick through the pages. Most are blank, but some contain the location and time of Dave's visits, the name of the person he saw at each company, and a date when he was expected to return. Attached to each of those pages, he had stapled a sheet of A4 business notepaper with a preliminary quote and his signature.

'That's not his signature,' Finn says. 'It's close but not identical. And one in every ten companies he was supposed to have visited doesn't exist. I've checked each one listed here. For every date he is supposed to be at one of these made-up businesses, a kid went missing. Including that boy William and his sister in Ipswich.'

My mind races as I digest this new information.

'Mark says you and William were born two days apart,' I blurt out suddenly.

I wait for him to fly off the handle at me having discussed this with Mark again. Instead, he doesn't really react and flicks through one from the 1990s and then a handful of others. They're all notably empty until they suddenly begin again.

'There were no appointments or missing children found in the warehouse for almost five years after I was born,' he says. 'None of the forty kids disappeared in that time. And look at the signature on this one. It reads "D.R. Hunter".'

'What about it?'

'Dad doesn't have a middle name. But Mum does. It's Ruth. Deborah Ruth Hunter. She has slipped up; she used her own initials instead of his. These diaries are in Dad's name but filled in by her. It wasn't Dad travelling from county to county, it was her. She did his accounts, didn't she? She managed his diaries. *These* diaries.'

I clasp my hand to my mouth. 'You think it was Debbie and not Dave who . . . who . . .' I can't even finish what I'm trying to say, but he knows what I'm asking. He shakes his head but he means the opposite.

'I don't know, Mia. I just don't know. What am I supposed to believe? This is such a headfuck.'

'Have you told her about the DNA results yet?'

'No, I haven't said anything. I needed time to deal with it myself first.'

We turn as Mum enters the room without knocking. She's put out by his presence inside the house. 'Why is he still here?' she asks me. 'He'd best not be upsetting you.'

'He's not, we've just got a few things to talk about. Could you wake Sonny for me, please?'

'Sonny?' she asks, puzzled. 'He's not here.'

'He was upstairs napping. Has Dad taken him out?'

'No, Debbie came an hour ago while you were asleep. Said she was picking up Sonny for Finn.'

My posture stiffens and my muscles tense as I scowl at Finn. 'I told you I don't want her anywhere near him. Why did you send her here?'

His face pales. 'I didn't,' he replies.

CHAPTER 62

DEBBIE

I'm pushing Sonny in his buggy, struggling with the uneven stones and thick-stalked weeds growing out of the path. Several times I lose my balance and think I'm about to fall, only to recover in the nick of time. Finally, we reach our destination and I take a seat. The rainwater pooling on the bench seeps through my trousers and dampens my legs. I don't care.

My grandson is sucking the life out of a rubbery toy giraffe, which is supposed to soothe children's inflamed gums. Salts or a gel is what he needs, not another fad bought into by a mother who hasn't got the first clue about parenting. He removes the toy from his mouth, waves it in his hand and smiles at me, a proper, heartfelt grin that radiates as much from his face as it does his heart.

'Nana,' he chirps, 'Nanananananana,' and it almost breaks my heart at how beautiful, wide-eyed and innocent he is. It's like going back in time and watching Finn all over again. And, like Finn, I want to keep Sonny this way forever, stainless and bursting with wide-eyed joy at everything and everyone around him. Only I know it's not possible because, if I don't intervene now, Mia will corrupt him as she corrupts all men. I am the only person who can save Sonny from that black widow.

The churchyard we're in contains centuries-old gravestones, so eroded by weather and time that the names etched into them are indecipherable. Around us are towering, grey stone walls and the remains of a small chapel that burned down back in the 1980s. I scouted this place years ago as a potential location for one of my children, but only a twenty-minute drive from home, it was too close for comfort.

After a brief respite from the rain, it begins to drizzle again so I zip up Sonny's puddle-suit and pull his hood over his head. We continue to the far end of the graveyard and stop under the long, sweeping branches of a willow tree. I place a plastic bag on the ground, remove Sonny from his pushchair and slowly lower him and myself on to it. There, I locate a small mound of slightly raised earth. An urn containing Dave's ashes lies beneath it. Finn and I buried it here ourselves after he was cremated. On police advice, we didn't attend his funeral for fear of making the newspapers once again. If my son has ever returned, he's yet to mention it.

Until I know for sure that Finn's telling me the truth, I have to assume everything he tells me now is a lie, like his claim of Sonny having chicken pox so I can't see him. I followed his other grandmother as she pushed him around Sainsbury's until I got a good-enough view of him to see his unblemished skin.

'She won't keep you from me,' I tell Sonny, now. 'Nobody will.'

Without anyone's knowledge, I've brought Sonny here a handful of times with posies of flowers that we leave for his grandad. Then I tell him all about Dave and what a wonderful man he was. I know Sonny can't understand me but it's important he knows who Dave really was and not the monster the world assumes they know.

I love him like no other person ever did or will do. But I can also see now how much internal conflict my love brought him. He made the ultimate sacrifice for me and he deserves to rest somewhere that will bring him peace.

Taking a step back, I watch Sonny rub his fingertips through the wet soil, then scoop up handfuls and chuckle as he throws clumps back to the ground again. I cry and smile at the same time, taking one of my mental pictures of the only person in the world who has yet to let me down. As I frame Sonny here under the tree, his head turns to make sure I'm still there, offering me his complete trust. For a moment, I truly believe that he knows I am here to rescue him from a weak father and a mother who only has her own best interests at heart.

I close my eyes and the image of Sonny is as clear as if they were still open. A beautiful warmth spreads through every vein in my body, as if I've just stepped into the sun after years trapped under ice. I am alive again.

I know that I will return to this picture many times over in the limited number of years that I have left, especially when this cruel disease robs me of everything but my memory.

Physically, it's a struggle, but I manage to pick Sonny up again and hold him close to me, his head pressing tight against my chest. 'I'm sorry,' I whisper in his ear, and squeeze him harder and longer than I ever have before. And will ever do again.

CHAPTER 63

MIA

I push a button to wind down the window and allow cool air to reach my face.

My throat is dry so I grab a metal flask from the cup holder in Finn's van, not caring what it contains. I don't know if it's travel sickness, my headache or fear that's making me queasy. It doesn't matter because, moments later, I have to push my head out of the open window and vomit on to the passing road beneath us.

'Shall I pull over?' asks Finn.

'No, no,' I say and take another swig of something fizzy from his flask to wash the acrid taste from my mouth. 'How far away is this place?'

'Another five minutes.'

'And you think they'll be there?'

'The house was empty, so it's the only place I can think of.'

Earlier, he told me about the informal ceremony he and Debbie held after the funeral directors sent them Dave's ashes. Early one morning, away from public view, they had used a trowel to dig a hole and buried Dave's urn under a tree in the grounds of a forgotten cemetery. There's some logic behind the choice to visit this cemetery now, but it seems horribly short of a certainty that we'll find Debbie and Sonny there.

I'm petrified but I'm angry. I hate myself for not sharing my suspicions with my parents or Mark, or showing anyone but Finn that Debbie caused my fall down the ladder. If I had said something, Sonny might still be at home with us, not God knows where with his psychopath of a grandmother.

'What if she's hurt him?' I say.

'She won't have,' Finn says, but his tone doesn't reassure me.

'You can't know that. If you're right, she has killed forty children already and let her husband take the blame. She's capable of anything.'

'Sonny is different: he's her grandson.'

'Who she tried to kill while he was still in the womb!' I yell. 'Surely you believe me now? And he's not her grandson, is he? Not biologically. If her motives are innocent, then why did she say you'd sent her to pick him up?'

He accelerates by way of reply. He is just as terrified as I am. We spend the rest of the journey in a nervous silence, each praying for the best-case scenario but quietly fearing the worst. Finn is too busy concentrating on the bends of the country road to see me with my phone in my left hand, texting.

'It's here,' Finn says, pointing to the remains of a church just ahead. He brakes sharply, and even before the car reaches a standstill, I have opened the door and am running towards a set of open gates.

The grounds are large and overgrown and remind me of when we first bought our cursed home. It's hard to see past overgrown hedges, grasses, weeds and trees. I can't see Sonny or Debbie. 'Where are they?' I shout in panic.

'This way,' says Finn, and I start running after him. And there, by the edge of the cemetery underneath an enormous willow tree, I spot Debbie sitting on a bench, a pushchair by her side, a plastic cover protecting Sonny from the rain. I let out a breath I've been holding ever since we left the house.

'Mum,' Finn yells, but the word sounds awkward coming from his mouth. We both know it no longer fits. I don't think she's heard us, so I shout her name. This time, she turns.

It's the first time I've seen her since our altercation in the police station and I'm startled by her appearance. Her grey roots make up half of her once-blonde hair, she is not wearing make-up and there are more lines on her face than I've ever noticed before. Her shoulders are hunched and her body shrunken. Grief is wearing her away.

As I approach her, she lifts her walking stick above her head, ready to strike me if I get any nearer. Her arm is trembling and the threat is pathetic. I don't care if she hits me; I just want to hold my baby again. However, Finn grabs my arm and keeps me where I am. 'I want my son,' I say firmly.

'Why, what do you think I'm going to do to him?'

'We know, Debbie,' I say. 'We know what you've done to children just like him.'

'What's she talking about?' she asks Finn.

I watch as he opens his mouth, but suddenly, it's all too much for him. Her lies have sapped every bit of strength from this man. He doesn't know where to start, so I fill in the blanks.

'We know it was you who abducted those children, not Dave. We've found your diaries.'

'What the hell are you talking about?'

'No more lies, Debbie. You're the one who's been killing for all these years. You slipped up, you put your own initials in one of the diary entries.'

'Are you going to let her talk to your mother like this?' she asks Finn. 'Where's your backbone?'

'And we know you're not his mother,' I snap. The words hang there for a moment. 'Finn is not your son.'

This accusation wrongfoots her more than the first, which surprises me. 'What . . . what are you . . . ? Of course he's my son,' she stumbles.

'We've done a DNA test and he's not related to you or Dave.'

The colour drains from her face. She looks to Finn again and his stony expression tells her that he knows everything.

Finally, Finn speaks. 'Who am I?'

Now Debbie is lost for words. 'It . . . it . . . it just happened. All of it . . . *everything*. It just happened.'

'It never "just happens",' he says. 'Everything in those diaries is planned and listed, the address and date of every town where a child disappeared. It was all premeditated. You were too careful to allow something to "just happen". You did your research. So who am I?'

CHAPTER 64

DEBBIE

He knows, he knows, he knows. My worst fears have been realised. All these years of pretence have come to a swift and sudden end.

I assumed – and hoped – that Finn might guess I was here, but this is not the conversation I was expecting or have rehearsed. I don't have a prepared lie to reel off. When he was a little boy and he fell from his bike, I'd comfort him with a cuddle and a stroke of his head. Before me now is the same little boy, hurting all over again, but now I'm the cause of his pain and I can't take it away. And he doesn't know the worst of what I have done to him yet.

Finn's parental revelation is her doing; I can sense it from the smug, self-satisfied look when she told me he knew. Finn would never have questioned his lineage, let alone have taken a DNA test of his own accord. I want to lurch forward and strike her, but I'm struggling even to hold this walking stick above my head. Damn that bitch and damn my failing body.

'Who am I?' Finn repeats.

'You . . . you are . . . your name is . . . was . . . William Brown.'

His brows knit and he and Mia look to one another. If I'm not mistaken, they recognise the name. 'That's not possible,' he says, turning back to me. 'I was born before him.'

'Your birth certificate isn't yours,' I reply.

'Then whose is it?'

I don't want to talk about this, I really don't. But I have no choice. Finn is forcing open a valve and I can't prevent the air from escaping.

'Finn Hunter was my biological child. He died a month before I found you.' If I close my eyes tightly, I can still feel my baby son's slowly cooling body in my arms before Dave took him away from me. 'I'd suffered many miscarriages before he was born, each of which almost broke me. With each came an enormous emotional impact as powerful as grief. And then a miracle happened. We managed to go full-term with a wonderful, beautiful little boy,' I continue. 'We immediately fell in love with each and every tiny bone in his body until he was snatched away from us three days later. Cot death, we assumed, as there could be no other explanation for it. But we never reported it or told another living soul. Neither of us trusted the authorities. I was convinced they were going to blame me for doing something wrong, and then somehow find out about the suitcases in the warehouse. Your dad had only just registered Finn's birth, but neither of us could bring ourselves to register his death.'

For weeks, I didn't know whether I was coming or going. I didn't call friends back who'd left answerphone messages to see if I'd had my baby yet. I lay in bed holding on to Dave, desperate for him to bring my Finn back. And when I accepted there would be no miracle, the only way I could regain any part of my old self was if I could do what I knew best. I couldn't save my own baby, but I could save somebody else's from this cruel, spiteful world.

I remember that day still with such clarity. I'd slipped away from Dave and driven to Ipswich, a place I'd visited once but had yet to choose a child to rescue. I gravitated towards a harassed young mum pushing a baby in a battered old pram. Following her a few steps behind like an afterthought was a young girl, the heel on one of her trainers flapping as she walked, her T-shirt stained and unwashed. At intervals, her mother turned around to bark at her for being too slow.

Later, the girl was left to keep watch over her infant sibling outside a supermarket as she went inside. I will never forget how soft her long dark curls felt against my fingertips as I brushed past her. But there were too many other people about for me to help her.

I clear my throat. 'You caught my attention from your pram,' I direct to Finn. 'You had these rich, dark eyes, and a mop of thick dark-brown hair. Then your gaze locked on to mine and something inside my head clicked into place. You and I belonged together.'

'But I wasn't yours to take,' Finn says quietly.

'Dave's text message to Debbie that was read out at the inquest,' Mia says to him. 'He wrote something like, "let me do this one last thing to protect you and my Finns". "My Finns", plural, not "my Finn". I assumed it was a mistake, but I think he meant he wanted to protect you and the child they lost.'

'I followed you home,' I tell him, 'and I stayed out of sight in the alleyway behind the house. You were all in the garden, but that woman was ignoring you both while she smoked and read a magazine. Then she got up and went inside, leaving you alone. It was a sign. So I crept in, scooped you up into my arms. The little girl was old enough to know something was happening that shouldn't be. I told her that I was a friend of her mummy's and did she want to play hide and seek with me? She had been so starved of attention that she agreed. So the three of us ran to where I'd parked my car by a bank of garages. And with you and her inside, I drove away.'

Even under his coat, I catch Finn's chest rapidly rising and falling. He is hanging on to my every word. Mia is watching him closely too. I bristle when she takes his hand and entwines her fingers around his. He doesn't try and brush her off, only adding to my resolve. I have done the right thing. Very soon, she will pay for this.

'What happened to Finn's sister?' asks Mia.

'I did what I went there to do, and then I drove home with my new baby son wrapped in a travel rug in the passenger footwell. There's never been any doubt in my mind that I was the mother Finn needed.'

'But he already had one,' says Mia.

'I gave him a better life than she ever could have given him,' I snap. 'Or than you could ever give him, the pathetic excuse for a wife you are.'

Mia brushes this aside. 'And Dave didn't ask any questions when you returned home with a baby?'

'Of course he did.'

'But he agreed to let you keep it?'

'He loved me. He would've done anything for me.'

I will never forget my husband's face when he returned from work later that night to find me in our bedroom, cradling a baby he had never set eyes on before. At first he couldn't make sense of the scene. 'What have you done?' he eventually asked.

I explained to him that day's events, including the fate of Finn's sister. He muttered the word 'no' over and over again and quietly left. I found him later in the hallway of the flat where we were living. He was leaning against the wall, forehead pressed against it.

'I don't know if I can take any more of this,' he said and pinched the bridge of his nose.

His despondency frightened me. I had pushed him to the very edge. I couldn't live without Dave, but I couldn't give up this child who needed me so badly. I'd already been robbed of one baby, I couldn't allow a second to be taken from me. 'I'm not asking you to do anything but to love him and be his father,' I told him.

'But you've stolen him!' Dave shouted. 'There will be police and search parties out looking for him; it'll be all over the news. We are going to be arrested for this! And what if they discover . . .' As always, he couldn't put my other activities into words.

'They have no reason to believe this boy is here,' I assured him, 'a hundred miles away from where he vanished. And we can easily pass him off as our own. I'll tell our friends I've not been in touch since he was born because I've had the baby blues. It won't be that hard. And we already have a birth certificate.'

Dave's head turned sharply. 'What?'

His swell of anger took me aback, but I persisted. 'We can use Finn's. Nobody will know.'

'You can't just erase our baby and replace him with another one!'

'I'm not.'

'You are. And you don't know the first thing about this boy. What he likes or dislikes; if he has any medical conditions; how often he sleeps and what he eats. What's his name? How old is he? What's he allergic to?'

'I don't know.'

'Because he is not our son and he never will be. If you know how it feels to lose a child, then you know the hell you're putting his mother through. We could have tried for another baby . . .'

'No. Losing Finn almost destroyed me. *Did* destroy me. I can't go through that again.'

'We could have looked into adoption.'

'What, and have strangers poking around in our backgrounds, sticking their noses in where they don't belong? This little boy is our last chance to have a family of our own. And I'm sure that me saving him means I won't need to go out there and save another child, ever again.'

That stopped Dave in his tracks; the suggestion that this changeling could bring to an end the side of his wife he reluctantly accepted but never truly understood.

'He's all I'll need to fill the void,' I continued. 'You'll see. Please, don't take him away from me. I'm begging you.'

Mia's voice snaps me back to the present. 'Did Dave help you kidnap and kill, or just hide the bodies?'

'I work alone,' I say to her. It hasn't always been the case, but she doesn't need to know that.

'But he knew what you were doing?' Mia presses.

'We didn't talk about it.'

'That doesn't mean he didn't know. So he could have stopped you at any time.'

Oh, this woman. This woman. 'I've seen how you treat my son, so I wouldn't expect you to understand how marriages work,' I say. 'Dave's only crime was loving me too much and wanting to protect me.'

'No, they weren't his only crimes. Not by a long shot.'

I look to my son, hoping that he doesn't disappoint me again by allowing Mia's animosity to cloud his judgement. But he can't look me in the eye. 'I accept the way you came into our lives wasn't typical,' I say to him, 'but you *know* me, Finn. I am your mum. I love you every bit as much as if I'd given birth to you. Don't let Mia turn you against me.'

There's a pause that lasts a lifetime before he speaks. His words are carefully chosen.

'But you didn't give birth to me, did you? Somebody else did. And you took me from her and killed my sister.'

'You've manipulated him his whole life,' Mia adds. 'But this is where it ends.'

'No,' I spit. 'It ends when I say it ends.' I already know before the second act of our story plays out that this is it for us. I can taste the poison on my tongue as I point to Mia. 'You think I'm the manipulator here? Well take a look in the mirror. I've watched the both of you, messing about behind Emma's back, putting your own needs above Sonny's. He doesn't deserve a mother like you, Mia, and while it pains me to say it, you don't deserve him either, Finn.'

He shakes his head. 'He doesn't deserve any of us,' he replies.

I regard my son one last time, hoping that I have misread him, giving him a final opportunity to realise what he is throwing away for her. Because in the next few minutes, he is about to lose everything. I prepare my parting shot. 'You know, there's one question you haven't asked me, Mia.'

'What's that?' she says.

'How long ago my last kill was.'

'And?'

'And what?' I reply. 'Ask me.'

She sighs. 'How long ago was your last kill?'

Suddenly, everything inside me calms. The anger, the frustration, the shock, the upset, the longing and the spite – they all disappear within the time it takes to slowly turn Sonny's pushchair around to face them.

CHAPTER 65

FINN

I stare at Sonny's pushchair for a long, long moment before it registers.

It is empty.

There is nothing under the plastic cover that's supposed to be shielding him from the rain. My little lad is not here.

'Where is he?' Mia finds her voice first. 'Where's Sonny?'

There's a strange smile creeping across Mum's face, one I've not seen since I was a kid. It's as if someone else is controlling her expressions and a glacial chill hits me.

'He's gone,' Mum says matter-of-factly.

'Gone where?' I ask.

'I've saved him.'

'From what?' I continue.

'From her,' she says. 'From you.'

'You're not making any sense. Where's my son?'

'I'm sorry, Finn, it's too late.'

'What is she saying?' shouts Mia, her fingers no longer wrapped around mine and clutching my arm instead.

'You know what I'm saying,' Mum says to Mia. 'By turning Finn against me, you have taken away something so precious. So I have done the same to you.'

'What's she talking about, Finn? What the hell does she mean?'

I take a step closer to Mum, a new, raw fear rising up inside me. I'm confused and I'm scared and her riddles are frustrating me. 'Where is Sonny?'

And then she gives me that smile again, the one that frightened me as a boy and frightens me now. 'You've brought this on yourself,' she says. 'Both of you have. You're a bad fit and I couldn't sit around and do nothing as you reunited and destroyed that little boy's life. I love him too much.'

'But we're not together,' says Mia.

'Liar!' Mum yells. 'Don't take me for an idiot. I see things, I know things. You're only saying that so I'll tell you where Sonny is.'

'We're not!' says an exasperated Mia. Tears are streaming down her cheeks, snot running from her nose. The rain is dripping eyeliner down her cheeks. 'Debbie, I promise you.'

'Your promises are worth as little to me as your lies.'

'I don't care what you think about me, I just want to know where Sonny is.'

'Why would I tell you? Why would I want to relieve you of even a second of what you're feeling right now? Or, for that matter, the pain you're going to suffer for the rest of your life? And believe me, Mia, it is going to hurt. It is really going to hurt like nothing else has hurt you before.'

I can't hold back any longer. I lurch towards Mum, grabbing her by her bony shoulders and shaking her like a rag doll. 'If you love me then tell me where he is.'

'I'm sorry, Finn,' she says, her voice rattling as I throttle her. 'But it's too late.'

She turns her head and looks a few feet away to where she buried Dad's ashes. It's only then that I see it. A neatly folded set of baby clothes inside a shrink-wrapped bag placed upon the ground.

CHAPTER 66

MIA

Finn turns to me, his eyes as wide and full of disbelief as I have ever seen them. I cover my mouth as if trying to hold back a scream that's trapped in my throat. *She can't have*, I think. *She wouldn't hurt someone she loves so much.*

Finn and I race towards the pile of clothes and drop to our knees before them and tear it open. It's made up of a pair of brown chinos and a dinosaur-patterned jumper, white vest and light-blue socks with cartoon crabs on them. It is the outfit I changed Sonny into this afternoon before Debbie took him.

We pass them between one another, one of us hoping the other will tell us we've made a mistake and these don't belong to him. I hold them to my nose to try and get my son's scent.

'My baby,' I cry out. 'What has she done with my baby?' I turn to Finn and grab the cords hanging from his hoodie, dragging his face closer to mine. 'Where is he?!' Now I'm pushing my fingers deep into the flesh of his forearms, desperate for him to assure me that not even his monster of a mother would do this to a baby.

However, Finn's face tells me that, long before this moment, he accepted Debbie might be capable of anything.

I take my hands off him and look around the cemetery. If she has buried him here, he could be anywhere. But he could also still be alive, as she can't have been here for long. A patch of earth nearby catches my eye; it contains no weeds and looks as if it has been cleared recently. I use my fingernails to claw at the ground. I sense she has moved towards us. I feel her eyes above me, I sense her cruel mouth as I tear at the wet soil, creating small mountains of it, going as deep as my fingertips will allow until suddenly, I reach something. 'Help me!' I scream at Finn and now I'm digging frantically until I realise what I've found. It's an urn, and likely the one containing Dave's ashes.

I search for somewhere else to gouge, anywhere, yanking out clumps of grass, my fingers stinging with the pricks of thistles, repeating the action over and over again in different places. I only stop to brush away my tears and I feel mud caking my face. I don't know whether to be relieved or scared that there is nothing here. I'm suddenly aware I'm doing this alone and that Finn isn't helping. I turn to yell at him again, but he's slowly rising to his feet, his hair wet and loosened from its top knot, hanging over his face.

Then, within a blink of an eye, he launches himself at his mother. They fall to the ground together, him with his large hands around her narrow neck, strangling her as her weak limbs flail against the gravel pathway and weeds. This is a Finn I have never seen, one acting on pure, naked impulse. There's a side of me that wants him to strangle her, that wants him to snuff her out like a candle flame. But she is the only person who can tell us where

Sonny is. 'Finn, no!' I shout, but he can't hear me. Instead, he keeps shaking her, banging her head on the ground.

His mouth is close to her ear and he is saying something to her, but his voice is too low for me to make out the words.

'Finn!' I continue and pull at his shoulder to try and turn him around, but he holds firm. He is going to kill her.

CHAPTER 67

DEBBIE

I'm sprawled across the ground, struggling to breathe as Finn's hands maintain their vice-like grip around my neck. My vision is blurred and I'm dizzy from where I've hit the back of my head, over and over. Even if he wasn't choking me I doubt I could inhale under his weight as he sits astride me.

My instinct is to gasp for air and try to grab at his arms to push him off me. But I fight that impulse, not my son. I don't want him to stop. I'm ready to die. I want to be with my Dave and as far away from this world as possible. I want peace, I want quiet; I want to be buried under that carpet of soil beneath the willow tree with my husband.

I look Finn in the eye as he strangles me. And I can tell he has it in him to kill me. Nurture has won out. He wants nothing more than to end my life for what I have done to him, Mia and Sonny. And who can blame him? This is what I deserve. But it's what they deserve too. In being kind to Sonny, I had to be cruel to them.

'Finn, no!' I hear Mia shouting and I want her to shut up. For once, I need her to stop meddling and let this play out to its natural conclusion and as I intended.

I know how long this will take because I'm seasoned. Perhaps it will take a little longer with an adult than it does with a child, but surely, if Finn continues applying this degree of compression, I will black out very soon, and it will be over in less than a minute after that.

'This is what you've always wanted, isn't it?' he hisses into my ear. 'Another generation of killers in the family.'

I'm physically unable to reply. He is right, but regardless of how he has made my heart bleed and how we have arrived at this point, Finn is still my greatest accomplishment. For a long time it was my first kill, by the canal. I staved in the head of Justin Powell for Dave.

He had pointed Powell out to me in a shopping centre one Saturday, weeks earlier. With my encouragement, Dave had returned to school but he was behind his old classmates. There, a new, young teacher spotted his handwriting and reading struggles and, after testing, diagnosed him with a then rarely discussed learning disorder called dyslexia. A wonderful, exciting development.

Of course, Dave's diagnosis didn't stop Powell and his gang from bullying him. Why would they allow something like that to interrupt their fun? They kept at it to the point where, by the time Dave pointed him out to me, he was ready to quit school again.

I couldn't have that. *Wouldn't* have it. Finding Powell alone a little over a week later, and with no witnesses, I seized the opportunity to protect the boy I loved.

Weeks later, Dave found in my schoolbag a metal badge that had fallen from the boy's blazer and on to the towpath. It was a magpie-esque response to pick up the shiny keepsake with Powell's name and Head Prefect title upon it. I was too tongue-tied to lie convincingly. I watched Dave's face gradually alter from curiosity to confusion and finally shock as the realisation of what I was capable of dawned on him.

I expected that to be the end of us. Instead, he took me in his arms, hugged me tightly and he didn't let go until the day Mia killed him.

Years later, I had already delivered six young faces into a better life when Dave stumbled across my deceased grandparents' paperwork for the Kilgours' warehouse and its contents. I assumed they'd taken it from the house along with my schoolbooks and anything that tied me to it. I denied any knowledge of it but he could read me like a book. Behind my back, he went to see it for himself, opening up a couple of suitcases I'd removed empty and returned full. To his horror, he learned Justin wasn't a one-off.

He locked us away in our flat for days as I tried to explain what compelled me to kill those children. And of course, he attempted to convince me how wrong it was. But I remained convinced I was doing the right thing. I was saving children like Dave, like me, kids destined to fall through the cracks. Had he and I not found one another, I shudder to think what might have become of us.

Eventually, while he would never agree, he was forced to accept how determined and passionate I was. He needed and loved me too much to turn me in to the police. I had shown my loyalty by killing for him, and protecting him from what he had done (well, what he thought he had done) to Precious. He knew I would always belong to him. It was then that I knew there was nothing I could do to make him fall out of love with me. He would die for me. And he was a man of his word.

So for decades, and in return for his blind eye, I promised him I'd not take any unnecessary risks or discuss with him what I did. I would also not give in to my urges the moment they surfaced. Instead, I'd pace myself and hang on as long as I possibly could, then I'd take my mental picture and place their bodies where no one could hurt them again, safe in the warehouse nobody but us knew existed.

Now, as I inhale the tiniest morsel of air for the very last time, I picture Dave and how he will smile at me when we are reunited once Finn has finished killing me. My body is becoming limp and darkness is descending. My life has been well lived and now my expiry date approaches.

My darling, I whisper to myself. *I'll be with you soon.*

PART FOUR

TWO YEARS LATER

CHAPTER 68

MIA, 2022

A montage of familiar video clips is playing on several wall-mounted televisions when a young floor assistant appears.

'Good luck, hun,' says Lorna and gives me a virtual hug from her end of our video call. I wish she'd been allowed here in person to give me moral support on today of all days, but Covid restrictions are still in force in this television studio even though we're out of what will hopefully be our last lockdown. The masked assistant guides me from the green room and along two corridors, through a double set of doors and into the main studio. I keep catching glimpses of other screens en route. They are filled with images of Sonny, Finn and I, then Dave, and finally *her*. I know the gist without having to hear exactly what the muffled voiceover is saying.

Two breakfast television presenters sit behind their desk and turn their heads as I enter. We have met several times before and, as always, they offer me warm, sympathetic smiles. One of the pair, Kylie Pentelow, reaches over to touch my hand but then withdraws it, remembering the two-metre rule. 'It's so lovely to see you again,' she says with a sincerity I believe.

'And we're back in five . . . four . . .' comes the voice of a person I can't see behind the bank of cameras. Then a hand shoots up to count the final three numbers manually. Bob Gadsby, Kylie's co-anchor, reads from a rolling autocue fixed under a camera, filling the viewers in on the significance of my appearance today.

'Welcome, Mia, on what we know must be an emotional day,' he begins.

'Thank you,' I reply.

'It was two years ago today when you discovered your mother-in-law, the now-infamous multiple child killer Debbie Hunter, was also responsible for the disappearance of your little boy, Sonny. And you have been working with police artists to come up with an image of how you think Sonny might look now?'

'Yes.' On a screen I catch an image of a boy I both do and don't recognise. He has my son's eyes and lips, but he has longer hair, a mouth full of teeth and a slimmer face. 'This is what the experts think Sonny might look like now, as a three-year-old. And I'm appealing to anyone who thinks they might recognise him to contact the number on the screen.'

'Can you remind us what happened the afternoon he vanished?' asks Kylie.

As I do so often when I'm making public appeals like this, I slip into autopilot and recount the events of the day that ripped my world apart. The only part I don't discuss is Finn strangling his mother. That, we have kept between ourselves.

'And to this day,' Kylie continues, 'you still have no idea what happened to Sonny?'

'No. It's still an open case with investigators attached to it.'

'Tell us what the aftermath of Sonny's disappearance was like for you. Because I cannot even begin to imagine the pain you must have gone through.'

'It's hard to explain,' I say. 'It's like I've been split into two halves. Part of me is still grieving an immeasurable loss, but at the same time, I have to hope that he is alive. And appeals like this might just bring him home.'

'According to a story in yesterday's *Daily Mail*,' says Bob, 'the police are also looking into child-trafficking organisations Sonny could have been sold into.' A shiver spreads across my chest and shoulders at the horrific implications. 'But what do you think happened to him?'

'The best-case scenario is that Debbie gave him away to punish us and that he's being raised by someone who loves him,' I reply. 'And while that breaks my heart, at least it means he is out there. But based on what we know about the extent of Debbie's previous crimes, there is every possibility that he's not. There have been no confirmed sightings of Sonny at all since he vanished, and the police have no evidence to suggest he is alive or otherwise.'

I am filled with tears and I dab at them with my fingers until someone off-camera passes me a box of tissues.

'The last time you were here,' says Kylie, 'you told us that you hadn't spoken to your ex-husband Finn since your divorce. Are you still estranged?'

I silently recall the last time Finn and I were in the same area together, four months after the events of that afternoon. I'd created a support bubble with my parents, so we were in the garden, and a few metres away was Finn and the new family liaison officer we'd been appointed after Finn had refused to deal with Mark any longer. Even from a distance, I smelled alcohol on Finn's breath and clothes and we argued when he accused me of having an affair with Mark. I was furious with him. The last thing on my mind was a relationship when my son was missing.

In hindsight, I understand that Finn was lashing out, his grief and anger merging into one. He had lost everything – his son, his mother, his father and even his identity. His relationship with Emma was the last thing to leave his grip when she couldn't cope with any more revelations about his twisted family. She ended it, only allowing him to see his daughter at court-appointed times. His lockdowns were spent in solitude. As guilty as this made me feel, I couldn't take on Finn's problems and guilt on top of my own. And each time I was around him, all I saw was the son of the woman who stole my baby. I resented him, even though it wasn't his fault. I'll always feel guilty for abandoning him, but I had to put myself first.

'We're in a better place now,' I tell Kylie. 'We stay in touch by text message when it's relating to the case. I hope that one day we can be friends again.'

'Is it ever possible to get back to a sense of normality after living through what you have?' asks Bob.

'I don't recognise normal any more, but I've had to find a way to survive. I couldn't continue my PR job because the media were more interested in me rather than my clients. So I've put my marketing skills and knowledge about missing persons to work, for a charity. We present cold cases of vanished children which we believe deserve further investigation to various police forces around the country. There are thousands of parents whose children have been missing for much longer than Sonny. So, if I can use some of what I've learned to help them in any way, then I will.'

'What are your thoughts regarding Debbie Hunter now, Mia?' Bob asks. 'Have they changed over time?'

I think back to her narrowed, serpent-like eyes as she watched the realisation of what she had taken away from us sink in. There was nothing left of her but spite. 'No, they haven't changed,' I say. 'I still believe that she is a monster.'

'Can you ever forgive her?'

'I wish I could be a better person and say yes, but until I know where Sonny is or what happened to him then, no, I can't.'

I hate that she is still alive.

'Have you had any contact with Debbie at all?'

'Only through her lawyers. And she still refuses to say a word about what she did.'

'What would you say to her now if she's watching?'

'I'd ask her to give us back our son. She has punished us for long enough. We just want to bring him home.'

POLICE REPORT: EYEWITNESS ACCOUNT FROM FORMER BROADMOOR PSYCHIATRIC HOSPITAL PATIENT, TRACY FENTON

Hunter is kept away from the others in a section for vulnerable patients because of what she did and her disability. She was being escorted from her cell to recreation time outside when she was knifed. I was coming back with the food trolley from the officers' room when her attacker ran past me, grabbed a knife from one of my trays and started stabbing Hunter. Even though the officer with her was quick to act, Hunter had already been slashed across the face and stabbed in the shoulder and arm. There was loads of blood but she wasn't screaming or anything. She didn't even try to fight her off; she just lay there, letting it happen. I asked around and apparently the attacker was related to one of the kids she'd murdered. So you can't really blame them, can you? She should have been given a medal, not an attempted murder charge.

CHAPTER 69

DEBBIE

I'm normally a bundle of nerves waiting for his arrival. But today I'm unusually calm. They've upped my medication and prescribed me painkillers, and the two together are giving me a gentle buzz. I'm also eager for my visitor to see the dressing that covers the wound to my face. I'll make sure to mention the injuries that can't be seen, under my shirt and sling.

I have no idea who my assailant was; she'd only been admitted two nights before she struck. I've since heard on the grapevine that her niece was one of the children I saved back in the early 2000s, which explains why she had it in for me. If only she'd put as much effort into protecting that girl as she had avenging her. She should be thanking me.

I pat my bandaged wounds. There are five in total – four shallow cuts and one a little deeper in my arm. My attacker also slashed my face, narrowly avoiding my eye. The gash has been stitched up but I've been warned I'll be scarred. In time I could have plastic surgery, but what'd be the point? The nurses who patched me up said I'm lucky to be alive because the blade could have easily nicked my carotid artery and I might have bled to death like my Dave. Not so long ago, I'd have been over the moon with that result.

When I was first transferred into the secure unit of this psychiatric hospital, I fought against the drugs they forced me to take. My stress manifested itself in torrents of physical and verbal abuse aimed at the staff, nurses and sometimes the other patients. I was frequently sedated because I no longer had control over my own behaviour. But since my Motor Neurone Disease symptoms worsened and I take meds to help me get through even a good day, I'm no physical threat to anyone. I'm no longer angry to be alive.

And now I have something to live for.

I scour the room to ensure none of the officers in the visiting room are watching, and then flinch as I squeeze the wound under the bandage. I'm counting on a few droplets of blood emerging from between the stitches and revealing themselves in the padding. It'll emphasise my trauma. The MND makes my fingers tremble as I do it. It's also been leaving my body weaker than ever of late and I struggle to move from place to place without the help of an officer. My speech slurs more often, as if I'm drunk, and I shudder to think what I will be like a year from now.

A trickle of people arrive as the doors to the visiting room open. Covid means the times are staggered so that only five of us 'high security risk' patients are allowed in here at any one time, and spaced well apart. I lean forward in my plastic chair, squinting at the door, until I see Finn. Every butterfly in my stomach rises at once when he approaches me. His hair has been cut short since I last saw him and it suits him. His temples are flecked with grey and, for the first time, I notice the lines at the sides of his eyes thickening. I hope he is getting enough sleep.

I'm unsteady as I stand, leaning towards him and hoping for a hug. He sits down, two arm lengths away from me and offering no physical contact. His hands remain firmly by his sides. I had hoped this visit might differ from the others. Then I remember that of course we can't. Bloody Covid.

'You were supposed to be here a week ago,' I begin. My voice remains raspy from the permanent damage he caused to my vocal cords when he strangled me. 'You have to stick to the agreement. You know what happens if you don't.'

'I've been busy.'

'Doing what?'

He scans my arm in its sling and I touch the bandage on my face, wondering if any blood has leaked yet. 'Does it hurt?'

'Not now, although it did at the time. The woman who attacked me was crazy.'

'Aren't you all?' he replies and I pretend to laugh.

'Did you deposit the money into my account?' I ask.

'No.'

'Oh. I was going to order some of those nice biscuits I used to buy your dad from M&S. Do you remember, the ones with cranberries and chunks of white chocolate in them?' I forget that Finn no longer responds to small talk. 'When do you think you'll do it?'

He shrugs.

'Finn, it was part of our agreement.'

'Things change.'

'Does Mia know you're here?' I ask instead, her name catching sharply in my throat. He shakes his head and I can barely conceal my joy. 'Good,' I say. 'Probably best to keep it that way.' It pleases me immensely that he is still keeping secrets from her. 'How's work?'

'The business has folded.'

'When?'

'A few months ago.'

I think I've misheard but his expression says not. 'And you didn't think to mention it?'

He gives me a look as if to say 'there's a lot I don't tell you', which unnerves me. 'What happened?' I continue.

'What do you think happened? Having a parent who's a child killer is a fast way to derail a business. So I'm doing odd jobs until I can find something else.'

'You were good at woodwork at school, weren't you? You made me that lovely doorstop and keyholder. Perhaps you could retrain in carpentry.'

Finn looks elsewhere, scanning the room for anything to focus on but me. He doesn't humour me when I recall stories from his childhood. That's the hardest part of being in here, being alone, having no Dave or Finn. There is no one to reminisce with. No one to share a long-forgotten re-emerging memory. No one to hug. And no one to feel loved by.

'How's Chloe?'

'Fine.'

'Can I see a picture of her?'

'You know I can't bring my phone in here.'

I'd forgotten. 'You could print me out some and bring them with you next time,' I suggest. He stares at me peculiarly and I struggle to read him. 'Or even better, perhaps you can bring her to see me one day.'

'You are kidding, right?'

'No. If it's Emma you're worried about, you don't need to tell her.'

He glares at me as if I'm stupid. And then the penny drops.

'Oh, it's because of *Sonny*,' I say, almost triumphantly, as if I've just answered the winning question on *The Chase*.

Finn closes his eyes and shakes his head. 'No, it's because you're a fucking psychopath who's killed forty kids, made her grandson disappear and is spending the rest of her life behind bars in a madhouse.'

The harshness of his tone is a little unwarranted, but I can't argue with the facts. 'Well at least I get to see *you*,' I add. 'You wouldn't abandon your mum, would you?'

'Except I do want to abandon you, and you're not my mum, are you, Debbie?' His use of my name cuts deeper than the knife used to stab and slice me. 'You and I aren't family. Chloe and Sonny are – and so is Lorraine.'

That unfamiliar name catches me off guard. 'Lorraine?' I repeat. 'Who is Lorraine?'

'My mother.'

'I'm your mother.'

'No. You're the person who stole me and lied to me my entire life. Lorraine is my birth mother.'

I inhale sharply. 'You've met her?'

He cocks his head. 'You look surprised. Why wouldn't I want to get to know her? It's not as if she willingly gave me up.'

'When did this happen?'

'About eighteen months ago.'

'And I'm only hearing about it now?'

'You never asked.'

My rage rises so rapidly that even I am taken aback by it. I want to speak but it comes out as a slur, so I swallow hard and try again. 'I rescued you from the awful life she was giving you and offered you a better one,' I protest. 'You wouldn't be who you are now if it wasn't for me. I gave you everything. I taught you everything.'

He leans towards me, his voice low but pointed. 'What kind of mother teaches their son how to kill?'

I'm unsure what he expects me to say. He was a teenager when we stopped working together for a common goal. I know that he made the choice not to continue, but it's unfair to throw it back in my face and suggest what we did together was so wrong.

'You'd take me out of school to join you on your trips,' he continues. 'You taught me which children to choose, how to approach them, what to say, how to lure them back to the car . . . I was eight years old when I helped you to abduct that girl in Leicester. *Eight years old.* What kind of mum encourages their child to do that, Debbie?'

'Stop calling me Debbie!' I shout, and my raised voice claims the attention of the other patients. A guard waves his hand to warn me to lower the volume so I falsely lighten my tone. 'I didn't *make* you do anything. You were fourteen when you came on your last trip with me. You were almost a grown-up, not an impressionable child.'

'I did it because I thought I had to, because I thought you were my mum. You manipulated me into believing we were saving those children.'

I don't understand why Finn wants to deliberately hurt me like this. I know I'm not like other mothers, I know I was overbearing at times. But I loved this boy with all my heart.

'What I encouraged you to do brought us closer together. You were the only person in the world with whom I shared my secrets in such detail because I trusted you with my life. Maybe I've always feared that, because I didn't give birth to you, you'd grow up to realise we were different people. That was my way of ensuring we bonded.'

'You did it so we could bond?' He laughs. 'Why not teach me how to swim? Ride a bike? Draw, paint, play tennis, garden, watch Disney movies together, grow vegetables, bake, play board games? That's how you bond, not by showing me how to fold a kid's body into a suitcase. Spending time together like Lorraine and I do, that's how you make a connection.'

'How often do you see her?'

'Fairly regularly. And I also have a sister, aside from the one you murdered. Gemma. She's five years younger than me. We're close.'

'Close enough to tell her what you really are?'

He ignores this. 'They are my family now. And Mia, of course.'

The mention of her name is like hearing fingernails being dragged down a blackboard. 'I saw the interview she did on that breakfast programme last month, making sure she stretches out her fifteen minutes of fame for as long as possible. She's still revelling in the attention.'

'Our marriage couldn't survive what you put us through. However, you'll be pleased to know I've recently found a way for us to be in one another's lives again.'

A sour taste rapidly rises up my throat and stalls at my mouth. I swallow hard. 'I told you that I don't want you seeing her again.'

'You can't tell me what to do.'

'Oh really?' I let the words hang for a moment to emphasise how I can, I am and I will, before I continue. 'You're weak around that woman, Finn, you always have been. And I bet she enjoys egging you on, trying to turn you against me.'

'What?' He laughs again. 'You take our son away from us and you're still blaming Mia for turning me against you? Listen to yourself. You are responsible for all the shit that's happening to you in here. And while Dave didn't physically kill anyone, he was just as guilty for enabling you. You call me weak around Mia, but he was *pathetic* around you.'

'Finn!' I exclaim. 'How can you say that?'

'Because it's true. He let his wife manipulate him into bringing home a stolen baby to raise as their own. When he saw those suitcases filling up on the shelves in the warehouse, why didn't he do something about it? Why did he never question where you were taking me on trips, and why wasn't I allowed to talk to him about where we'd been or what we'd done? How many lives could he have saved, how many families could he have prevented from being ripped apart because he wanted to protect you?'

The tape that secures the bandage to my face pulls as my jaw tightens. 'And what about you?' I ask. 'Because for most of your life you've known what I do. If you were so upset, why didn't *you* do something about it?'

'I did. I gave your appointment diaries to the police.'

'But not because you disapproved of what I did. When you found out you were chosen—'

'Stolen, not chosen.'

'—you did it out of revenge.'

'What the fuck did you expect?'

'I expected you to be loyal to your family. You knew where I hid the diaries under your dad's name – diaries *that he agreed to me keeping* – to protect me if I was ever caught. You should have honoured his memory and left them where they were. Not turned me in.'

'Honour? There's no honour in this family.'

'We all lie to protect the ones we love, and you did exactly that with Mia. Need I remind you about Emma and Chloe? Or when Dad explained to you about my relationship with that house after you found the suitcases – yet you chose not to tell her?'

'I lied because I loved her. You lie because you don't know any better. But I don't have to put up with it any longer.'

'You don't have any choice. You need me.'

'No, I don't. And after today, I won't be seeing you again.' He sits back and folds his arms, almost as if he believes what he is saying.

'Oh, you will, Finn.'

'You're wrong.'

'If you don't keep coming to visit me, I'll make sure you never receive another new photograph of Sonny again.'

CHAPTER 70

GEORGE LEWIS, NORWAY, TWO AND A HALF YEARS EARLIER

I didn't recognise my sister Debbie when I first caught a glimpse of her on the television screen.

They say no man is an island, but I am mine. And on this island I have no TV, phone line or internet connection. So when the story about the suicide of a man in England thought to have murdered forty children became international news, I had no knowledge of it for weeks.

I was at a bar on the Norwegian mainland enjoying my second *akvavit* – a reward for finishing my weekly shop for essentials – when the screen on the wall caught my eye. It showed footage of a woman with a walking stick leaving a police station and being ushered into a waiting car. It was her slender frame and stoop that kept my attention more than the story. Her rounded shoulders and furrowed brow as she stared briefly into the lens of the camera gave me chills, reminding me instantly of my mother. But when the name Debbie Hunter appeared on screen and the location of Leighton Buzzard, my heart skipped a beat. Her Christian name and the last place I'd lived in England were too much of a coincidence to dismiss.

I quickly took out my phone, a basic gadget but with some internet capabilities, and spent the rest of the morning catching up with the rest of the world about the bodies found in one of my childhood homes and Debbie's husband's horrific crimes.

For much of my life, I had pushed Debbie and my parents to the back of my mind. The only way to move forwards was to never look back. Now suddenly here she was, the sister I had so loved but been estranged from for forty years, caught in the eye of a storm. And the bond we once shared rapidly rose to the surface, as strong as it had ever been, despite our distance. Instantly, I wanted to protect her.

I used my motorboat to return to my island, ten minutes south-east of the coastline. After packing a bag, I returned to the mainland, mooring at a dock and hitching a ride on a friend's fishing trawler to the Scottish coast. From there, I hired a car and made the nine-hour journey to the home town I escaped.

Finding Debbie's address was easy, but on my early evening arrival, a handful of journalists and photographers were still camped outside her home. What must it have been like for her, living here at the story's peak, I thought. I held back until after dark when most dispersed. I didn't want those remaining to catch me knocking on her door and to ask me questions, so I climbed fences and crept through neighbours' gardens until I reached hers. From a copse at the back of the property I spotted her in the lounge with someone I assumed to be the son I'd read about. It was only when he left and she came outside that I nervously made my approach, my heart in my mouth. As soon as she saw a random stranger on her property, she grabbed her walking stick and hurried away.

'Debbie!' I shouted.

'I'm not talking to the press so don't come any closer,' she yelled without looking back. 'Leave me alone or I'll call the police.'

'It's George,' I replied. She turned her head but carried on moving. 'Your brother.' She stopped in her tracks and eyed me up and down, still from a distance.

'How do you know about George? The newspapers don't know about him. Who told you about him?'

'Nobody has. It's me.'

'George is dead,' she said firmly.

'Is that what Mum and Dad told you? I'm not, I'm here.'

'Stop saying that! I've had private detectives try and find him.'

'Then they've been looking in the wrong places, Debbie. For years I worked on farms in Scotland, then the fishing trawlers in Scandinavia. Eventually I bought my own place near Store Brattholmen in Norway, where I've lived for nearly twenty years.'

I'm unsure for how long the two of us remained in a stalemate before she spoke again. 'You don't sound like George,' she said hesitantly.

I could only shrug. 'I'm a mongrel,' I said. 'I've spent most of my life in northern Europe, so I've absorbed all kinds of accents. But I promise you, I am your brother. Ask me anything about our childhood.'

She paused and then fired out a question only she or I could answer: 'Who was the last boy you brought to the house before you disappeared?'

'Martin Hamilton,' I said without thought. His death is the reason I have never made a true friend, forever believing I am a danger to anyone who comes close to me. His face remains as clear now as it ever was. 'I'll never forgive myself for what they did to him.'

'Neither will I,' she whispered, knowing I was telling the truth. Her legs began to shake and, before I could reach her, she fell to her knees, her hand covering her mouth, sobbing. I joined her on the ground and held her in my arms, and there we remained for a long time.

'Why didn't you come back for me?' she cried.

'I promise I wanted to, but I had no choice but to keep away,' I replied. 'Dad told me he would kill you if I ever came back. If I couldn't protect you in person, I had to protect you with distance.'

Eventually we made our way inside, where I recounted the events of the night I vanished from her life. I recalled how, when I woke up in the spare room of the house, Dad and I were alone. He warned me that if I didn't stay silent and climb into the open suitcase next to him, he wouldn't be able to control what Mum might do to me. 'She has episodes I can't manage,' he admitted. 'So you need to go tonight.'

I had little choice but to obey. And wearing just the clothes on my back and with no other possessions, I was dragged inside the case downstairs and into the back of the car. Then he drove me to the train station and bought me a ticket to Glasgow, where I was to be met by an old acquaintance of his. I did as I was told, and from there, I explained to Debbie, I was driven to the Hebrides to live and work on a farm with Dad's friend's family. 'I was told to learn the accent quickly and that if I ever told anyone who I was, including the police, Dad would find me and kill me himself. I was fourteen and had no reason to disbelieve him.'

'I searched for you for so long,' Debbie explained. 'Please, you have to believe me, I never wanted to give up on you.'

'I do, I do believe you.'

I told her more about my life, how in my early twenties I traded farming for the life of a trawler man, eventually finding a home in Sweden, then Norway. I recalled how, for years, I moved from town to town, never settling anywhere and always preferring my own company. And how eventually I saved up enough money to buy an island of my own. I'd never married or had children.

In turn, she explained how she too had believed she was going to die at my parents' hands, which prompted her escape and new life with grandparents neither of us knew. I felt nothing but relief at hearing of Mum and Dad's deaths. I hoped each was lingering and merciless.

Debbie admitted shortly that, after she married Dave, she discovered he too possessed a dark, cruel side, a relic of his own atrocious upbringing. He often became violent towards her for no reason but she believed that she could change him. They tried for a family but failed to conceive, and eventually, specialists informed them he was infertile. He took to drink and made her life hell. But everything changed when, one day, he appeared on their doorstep with a baby boy. 'He wouldn't tell me where he found him, only that he was now ours,' she recalled. 'I begged Dave to return him, explaining how much trouble we could get into, but he refused. He told me the child would make us a proper family. He said he knew that he had been an awful husband but he could be a better father. But if I didn't let the boy stay then he would have no choice but to "dispose" of him rather than hand him back. And I truly believed that he would. I couldn't live with that, so, despite knowing how wrong it was, I went along with it.'

It was only years later, when the contents of the warehouse were discovered, that she realised Dave had also murdered Finn's sister. 'I didn't want to believe he was responsible for the deaths of any of those children,' she wept, 'but deep inside I knew what the police were telling me was true. And it was all my fault.'

'How could it have been?' I asked.

'I was his wife. I was aware of how cruel and manipulative he could be. I should have known what else he was capable of. Instead I buried my head in the sand to try and make my marriage work and to provide a safe home for Finn. If only I'd had you to turn to. If only you'd come back sooner, then you could have protected me

335

like you did before and things could have been so different for me. For the both of us.'

I had never felt a guilt like it. Debbie didn't mean to make me feel this way, but it was instant and immeasurable. I held her tighter than I had when we were frightened children, hiding from Mum and waiting until her boil reduced to a simmer. Debbie was every bit as delicate now as she was then. And I vowed never to let this beautiful soul down again, like so many others – including me – had done before.

CHAPTER 71
DEBBIE, 2022

Finn is glaring at me, but I don't linger on his face for long. Instead, I'm drawn to his hands. His fists usually remain clenched for the duration of our monthly meetings, his forearms tense and his gaze steely. His body language oozes rage and his dislike of the things I've done.

Today, he is none of those things. Instead, his hands are pressed palms down and flat upon the table that separates us, indicating that he is hiding something. I skirt over it for the time being.

For a moment, I remember I'm not supposed to be here, that I should be long dead. But I hadn't counted on Mia interfering in my life one last time. En route to the cemetery, she had texted DS Goodwin for help and, shortly after my world turned black, he appeared with his team and dragged Finn off me. It was Goodwin who resuscitated me with his own breath, and I have cursed him every day since.

Later, when I eventually came to terms with the continuation of my life, I found a way to keep my son close. In return for his monthly visits, I rewarded him with one brand-new photograph of Sonny. It would be taken every month after Finn's appearance and sent by text to his phone. This was on the strict provision that he didn't inform the police or Mia of our arrangement. She had to believe that her son was likely dead. If I had a reason to think anyone other than Finn knew he was alive, one call would ensure Sonny would never be seen by him again. Finn had little choice but to accept. Even with the odds stacked against me, I found a way of maintaining control over my boy. This way, he would remain my whole life.

'My health isn't good, Finn,' I continue. 'Everything is seizing up; I'm on so much medication that I rattle when I walk. God knows where I might be this time next year.'

'Are you looking for sympathy?' he asks. 'Wrong audience.'

'No. But when I die, that's when Sonny will be returned to you. Not a day sooner. And until then, you have to keep visiting me.'

Finn nods his head and then folds his arms. A smile creeps across his face that's not mirrored by his eyes. It makes me nervous and I'm aware my mouth is dry. 'I don't need to wait until you die before I see my son again,' he says.

'What makes you think that?'

He glances around the room to ensure we aren't being seen or overheard. Then he slowly pulls up the sleeve of his jacket to reveal a large watch face that takes up most of his wrist. Only he isn't wearing just one. He slides it up his arm ever-so-slightly to reveal he is hiding a second watch beneath it. This one is a smartwatch and he angles it so that only I can see its digital display. Then the fingers of his other hand slide across the table and he touches the screen.

A blurred, pixelated image appears. Slowly it comes into focus. I recognise the figure immediately and the bottom falls out of my world.

CHAPTER 72

GEORGE LEWIS, NORWAY, THREE WEEKS EARLIER

The waves are choppy this morning, splashing our faces and the dog's fur as the boat ploughs through the sea. The cold I felt from an oppressive wind evaporates under peals of laughter that warm my bones. It's hard not to laugh along with his infectious giggle. For two years, he has been my everything. And I have my sister to thank for this precious gift.

I recall how Debbie and I stayed up talking for most of the first night she and I were reunited. As the dawn broke, I left the way I came, scurrying through her neighbours' gardens, away from the press, which was soon to return. We made our meetings regular occurrences. Every evening after her son returned to his girlfriend for the night, I appeared. Finn didn't know his mother had a brother, and Debbie insisted on keeping it that way. As much as I'd have relished getting to know my only nephew, I respected her wish to keep her two worlds from colliding, at least for the present. Eventually, I returned to my Norwegian island, but once I got a phone mast erected, we remained in close contact, talking every few days and regularly texting one another. She filled a part of me that I hadn't wanted to accept was empty. She was my history, my present and now my future.

I wanted so badly for Debbie to come and see where I had made my home and experience the peace of heart that she deserved. But by then, complications resulting from her Motor Neurone Disease were escalating and making travel uncomfortable. She was also too nervous to leave her home for long. Despite an unhappy marriage and a psychopathic husband, those bricks and mortar remained a fortress that made her feel safe.

So I regularly travelled to visit her instead. I had no passport, but many friends and contacts in the trawler business helped me to slip in and out of Scotland without question.

Over the months, Debbie and I became close, maybe even closer than we had been as children. There was nothing we wouldn't do for one another. And then came the telephone call that sent my life moving in yet another different direction.

'I need to see you,' she said tearfully.

'What's wrong?' I asked, immediately concerned.

'It's Finn.'

'Is he okay?'

'No, he's not, and I'm worried for my grandson.'

I took the first boat I could catch to Fraserburgh and then I drove to Milton Keynes for a clandestine meeting in a hotel car park. There, she broke down and told me what she had learned about Finn – she had unearthed diaries kept hidden by Dave for decades that revealed how Finn had known all along about the murders his father had committed, and he had even accompanied him on abductions and kills.

'Are you absolutely sure?' I asked, aghast.

'I'm positive. I've never wanted to admit it, but I've always known there's a darkness in him like his father's. He has a violent streak; I've witnessed him slapping Sonny, and when I stepped in, he hit me too. However, not for a minute had I ever considered he might have been a party to Dave's awful crimes. This is all my fault.'

'Of course it's not!'

'It is, George. I wasn't the mother he needed me to be. I tried my hardest to bond with him, but every step of the way, Dave created a distance between us. It's as if he just wanted him for himself. And now I know why. What am I going to do?'

'What we should have done to our parents when we were children – tell the police. Tell them everything.'

'But I can't. Who would look after Sonny if his dad goes to prison? Mia's mental health is getting worse. Remember what Mum was like? Mia is the same – she's either depressed or paranoid or angry, so she can't be trusted to raise him. And he has no living relatives who could take him. You know I would, but look at the state of me. I'm finding it harder and harder to look after myself, let alone a toddler. Plus I'd be arrested and charged with knowing Finn was stolen from his biological parents and not reporting my husband. I'd never survive prison, I'm too fragile.'

'Perhaps I should confront Finn? Make him see sense.'

'No, please don't do that. You're approaching sixty. He's half your age and stronger than you. I'd hate for him to hurt you too.'

'Then what can I do to help?'

'Can you stay nearby until I figure it all out? Knowing you're close after all those years without you is a huge help.'

'Of course,' I replied, and held her tightly. Once again my heart bled for my poor sister.

I checked into a nearby hotel and waited for her to call. After three long days, she finally texted me, asking to meet within the hour and sending me a map. She was in a cemetery with Sonny. There had been an almighty row between Finn and his wife that had turned violent. Debbie had whisked the boy to safety, and when I arrived, she was close to hysterical.

'I didn't know who else to call,' she said. 'I need to get him away from them. I'm scared of what will happen if I don't. You remember what it was like for us growing up in such an awful environment. But if I contact the police, they'll call social services and I can't bear to see Sonny in foster care.'

An idea came to me. 'Come back to Norway with me,' I said. 'Both of you. If we set off now we can catch a boat first thing in the morning. Text Finn and Mia to say that you're taking him away for a few days until things calm down. Tell them it'll give them a chance to sort things out.'

'Oh George, I wish I could, but I'm not fit enough.'

'I'll look after you. I'll take care of you both.'

'Even the ferry journey would cripple me.' Debbie hesitated and wiped her eyes. 'But you could take him for me.'

'Me? Alone?'

'Yes.' She nodded.

'But I can't. I'd be kidnapping him.'

'Sonny is a wonderful, intelligent little boy who needs someone to look after him and offer him a safe environment. From everything you've told me about your island, it sounds idyllic.'

'I don't know the first thing about looking after a little boy.'

'You looked after me before you left. You'll learn as you go along and, as you said, it'll only be for a few days.'

'Debbie, this is too much . . .'

'Do you remember how bad it was in that house with Mum? I didn't want to tell you this, but after you left it got worse. A hundred times worse. The physical violence escalated and they . . . Oh God, this is so hard for me to admit . . . they *did things* to me, George. Horrid, unspeakable things. And without you there, I had to face it all by myself. I have never asked you for anything in my life, but I need you now like I did back then. Your nephew needs you. I've changed him out of the clothes he came here in and under the pushchair is a bag with a few days' worth of food, nappies and clothes. They should last you until you reach home.'

I continued to come up with reasons why I couldn't do this. But Debbie had suffered blow after blow because I had neglected her for so many years. I'd been too gutless to face up to the past, too weak to return and rescue her. I couldn't turn my back on her again, and on this little mite as well. So, finally, I agreed. She hugged me and kissed her grandson and placed him in my arms. 'Don't try and get in touch with me,' she added. 'I'll contact you when it's safe for him to return.'

Decades after I was smuggled out of the country to start a new life, history was repeating itself. Only now I was the smuggler.

Over the next few days, my island for one became a home for two – me and a child I didn't know the first thing about. To my escalating concern, Debbie failed to call and I didn't contact her, as per her instruction. I could only assume the situation had grown even worse over there. Meanwhile Sonny and I muddled along together, me gaining a gradual understanding of what made him tick and him slowly learning not to scream every time I approached him.

It was on another trip to the mainland when I learned my once-estranged family was making headlines again. My body went cold as I read in a newspaper how Debbie had now been charged with the forty murders the police had believed her husband guilty of. I wanted to be sick. Of course she couldn't have done something like that! What was wrong with the authorities over there? Why would they think she had? It didn't make sense until I thought about it carefully. My beautiful, sweet, caring sister was sacrificing herself for the sake of the stolen son she loved so much. By admitting guilt, she was ensuring the finger of suspicion never pointed towards Finn. She would rather suffer than watch her son do the same. Debbie was the true definition of what it meant to be a parent.

Back and forth I went, debating what to do. I gave serious consideration to returning to England to tell the police what I knew, that my sister was a victim, not a killer. But would this be in Sonny's best interests? What would happen to him then? My conscience wouldn't allow me to return him to Mia, by all accounts a mother to rival our own. So I decided to put Sonny's needs first and keep him safe with me.

Weeks later, Debbie was able to call from another patient's contraband mobile phone at the psychiatric hospital she was being held at. She explained why she had taken the blame and it was for the reasons I suspected. And I could never bring Sonny home, not even after her cruel disease killed her.

Even then, she continued to put Finn's needs above her own. She asked me to text him a photo of Sonny every month, then destroy each phone afterwards so we couldn't be traced. I did as she asked, and Sonny, who I'd renamed Andreas so as not to rouse suspicion on my mainland trips, and I continued our new life together, away from the madness of home.

Now, Debbie and I have not spoken in so long but she still trusts I will do the right thing for him, and I will never let him down as I did her.

Tomorrow will be my birthday and Andreas and I will celebrate with cake and tea at the café in town. We live a simple life together on our island, drawing, painting, sailing, hunting, going on adventures and exploring the mainland with Oscar, the dog I bought him. I am giving Andreas the father I never had and the one he deserves.

He is fluent in both Norwegian and English and recently we began the thrice-weekly commute from our home to the mainland nursery, as I am conscious he needs to be around children his own age and not just me. He is a happy, well-rounded three-year-old, and although he knows I am his uncle, he chooses to call me *Pappa* like the other children in his class call their fathers. One day he will want to know where he came from and I will either lie to him to spare his feelings or tell him the truth. I haven't yet decided which path to take.

It's the little, everyday things about him that fill me with pride, like now, for example, as he thinks he is taking control of the boat's rudder to guide us to the mainland. For so many years I feared having a family of my own might unleash in me a genetic remnant of my parents. But now I'm a father, I'm confident that I am nothing like them. Andreas is like Debbie and me, and we are good people. I lean over and kiss the back of his head.

'What's that for?' he asks.

'Just to remind you that you are loved,' I say, and he beams.

Later, when he is in nursery, I make my way back to our island. Our home comes into view but there's a boat already docked at the pier. I don't get visitors very often, and as I draw closer, it looks as if they travelled here on one of those crafts Bjarne Johansen rents to tourists.

I have no idea who has come to see me, but I don't have a good feeling about it.

CHAPTER 73

DEBBIE, 2022

The first few images to appear on Finn's watch are of my gentle, kind brother, staring beyond the camera, the wind caught in his hair. His brow is knitted like it so often was when we were children, a giveaway of something troubling him. Now something he is looking at is making him uncomfortable. It gradually dawns on me that the cause is the person behind the lens.

It is Finn.

It has taken him two years, but my son has tracked George down.

Finn's fingers tap the screen again and, now, George is lying on something white and wooden, his head tilted to one side, his eyes open, and streaks of blood line his face. I clamp my hand to my mouth but it's not quick enough to suppress a cry. The third and final image is a video clip that lasts just seconds but breaks my already fragile heart.

'How did . . .' is all I can say before I realise I don't need to finish the sentence. I don't need to know the whys and the wherefores.

'He didn't think like us, did he?' Finn says. 'He wasn't as careful as you and I would've been. Over the last two years of taunting me with photos of my son, he left fragments of info here and there in the background about their lives. A section of a car registration plate, a partial shop sign, a radio transmitter in the distance, a hill with an unusual-looking peak . . . there are plenty of amateur desktop detectives on Twitter who have been more than willing to help a stranger solve a puzzle. Then all I did was turn up in the town and ask a few questions. He wasn't hard to find.'

'Where is Sonny now?'

'You only need to know that, for the first time, I am in complete control of my life. Not you. And after today, you will never see or hear from me again.'

It's all falling apart around me and I don't know what to do to make it stop. I'm flustered, I can't think straight, and in the heat of the moment I go on the attack and blurt out the first thing that comes into my head. 'I'll tell the police you helped me abduct those children. I'll tell them how we did it together. Then you'll never see Sonny or Chloe ever again.'

He breaks into a laugh. 'Really?' he asks. 'And who do you think will listen? You waited until a week into your trial before you pleaded guilty on the grounds of insanity, and now you're locked up in a fucking nuthouse. Who's going to believe you over me?'

'Then I'll write to Mia and Emma and tell them.'

'Be my guest. I'll even send you a pad and pen if you like. They know how you lied and let the world believe Dave was a killer. And now I have Sonny back, they'll think you're trying to find a new way to get revenge.'

Damn it! Why did I threaten him? All I've done is antagonise and alienate him further. I could never throw my son to the dogs like that. But it hurts that he would so willingly discard me like he's threatening to.

'Please, Finn, don't stop coming to see me,' I beg. 'You're all I have left. You don't even have to visit every month. Just a couple of times a year, how does that sound?' I reach out to try and touch him but he recoils.

He stands up and I am filled with a dread the like of which I have never experienced before. And I realise I have never had call to frame Finn before. I have never had call to doubt he would always be in my life. Now my panicked eyes take him in from top to toe, trying to put to memory every inch of the man I love now and the boy I ache for. He looks at me, but there's no connection between us as there was that first day we met.

I am staring at him so hard that my eyes are burning, like they have grit in them. Only a mental block is preventing me from framing him and I desperately need that image before my disease robs me of everything but my memory. But Finn doesn't understand, and turns away from me.

'Stop!' I scream. 'I need to put you in a frame!'

He doesn't know what I mean. 'Goodbye Debbie,' he says matter-of-factly, and turns his back on me with the ease of someone ignoring a charity worker's rattling collection tin.

'Turn around,' I beg, 'just for a moment. Please turn around, Finn!'

'It's William now,' he adds without turning around. 'The name my real family calls me.'

He leaves by the door he entered, the back of his head all I can see of him. That's the image that's now locked in and I don't want it to be. That is what I'll keep returning to and I don't want to because it's so awful. My chair swallows me, my body folding in on itself as I double over in pain.

The guard who escorted me in makes his way towards me, takes my arm and I try to get up but my legs buckle and he's not quick enough to catch me. I land flat on my face, my wounded cheek smacking the floor. I feel the stitches burst and my blood feels warm against the cold floor. I hear voices but I can't concentrate on what they're saying because the only thing that matters is that I have lost Finn. He is gone forever, and I wish I was too.

CHAPTER 74

MIA, TWO AND A HALF
WEEKS EARLIER

Finn is waiting for me by the doors of a specialist unit inside Oslo's Gaustad Hospital.

Too anxious for pleasantries, I hurl a torrent of questions at him. 'Where is Sonny? Is he okay? What did the doctors say? Did that bastard hurt him?'

'He's fit, he's healthy, he has been looked after, he's just very confused,' says Finn. I stare at every inch of his face to see if he's keeping anything else from me, but I don't think he is.

'When can I see him? I want to see him now.'

'His psychiatrist says we can go in this afternoon.'

'That's hours away!' I protest. 'I caught the first flight here so that I could be with him now.' I begin to cry and Finn draws me in to his body. It feels familiar, it feels safe. It feels good.

It was last night when he called me with the news. It had been almost a year since I'd actually heard his voice. 'I'm in Norway,' he said. 'I've found Sonny. You need to get here now.'

I assumed he was drunk. I barely remember a time when he wasn't, in the aftermath of Sonny's disappearance. Like father, like son: both men driven to the same crutch by the same woman. 'Finn, you don't know what you're saying,' I told him. 'Call me when you've sobered up.'

'Mia, listen to me. *I have found him*. I'm at a hospital in Oslo where the police brought him. The first thing they did was a DNA test confirming he's ours.'

I froze, unable to process or react. I glared wide-eyed at Mum, shaking my head, saying the same thing over and over again. 'Sonny . . . he's alive.' She took the phone from my hand and spoke to Finn. It was only when she started sobbing uncontrollably that I accepted I wasn't dreaming.

My boy is alive.

Sleep was not on the agenda last night. Instead, I kept calling Finn for updates until the airport opened. It was then that Finn admitted to how he had been receiving anonymous text messages with photographs of Sonny for almost two years but was powerless to tell me or the police as it would risk our son vanishing for good. I couldn't believe that he had lied to me again, and this time, about something so much more important than an affair. I wanted to yell at him, scream at him, swear at him, call him every name under the sun. While I was going out of my mind imagining the worst, he at least had a shred of comfort knowing that Sonny was still alive. But I held back. Now wasn't the time to berate him, and really, what would I have done in his place?

He explained how, once he'd tracked down Sonny's kidnapper to Norway and located his home on an island, the man had already fled without our boy. So Finn returned to the mainland to report him to the police. And it being a small town, they knew who the man was, that he had a young son called Andreas matching Sonny's description and that the boy went to a local nursery.

They interrogated Finn and contacted their British counterparts to verify his claims. And when the results of the expedited DNA test came back, both father and son were taken separately to Oslo where specialists have set about learning some of what has happened to him in his short life.

Now, outside the hospital, Finn warns me that when we do see him, we can't expect miracles. He was fourteen months old when he was stolen from us and is unlikely to remember much, if anything. He won't be the same son we lost.

'It took me so long to bond with him, and you're saying he won't even remember who we are?' I ask.

'It's a possibility. We have to tread very carefully, Mia. We can't go charging in there expecting the loving little boy we lost to come running into our arms calling us Mummy and Daddy. He's led a completely different life away from ours for two years. So we have to be guided by what the psychiatrists advise us.'

'What if he hates us?' I ask. 'What if that man told him we didn't love him and that we gave him away? God knows what he thinks.'

'Then we'll deal with it together. If it takes months, or weeks or years, we'll show him how loved he is. He's still just a little boy. Eventually he will come around.'

I hope Finn is right. I don't want to think the worst, but I can't help it, my thoughts veer towards the dark side: what if Sonny has been physically, sexually or mentally abused? How bad did it get for him on that island with just a stranger for company? The not knowing tears at my insides. Finn senses my apprehension and hugs me again then takes me to a cafeteria. I order a black coffee, my stomach too unstable to eat and keep food down.

On the way here, a nasty little voice in the back of my head using Debbie's voice keeps asking me if I even deserve to have Sonny back in my life. Parents are supposed to keep their kids safe. His dad and I failed to meet this most basic of needs. Even before that, my postnatal depression came between us, followed by my obsession with finding out the truth about Dave then Debbie. How much of what happened next did I bring upon all three of us?

'Do you want to see some pictures of him?' Finn asks tentatively. I nod and he removes his phone from his pocket and shows me the photographs he has been sent over the past two years. There's Sonny with a fish on the end of a line, wearing a life vest on a motorboat, walking confidently across a steep hillside, nursing a steaming drink in a café. I burst into tears at seeing my son growing up in monthly instalments, even as I feel a wave of relief that he looks happy.

'I am so sorry that I didn't tell you about them,' Finn says. 'But you and I know what Debbie is capable of. I didn't doubt for a minute that she would cut off all contact with him if I told anyone. At least this way, we had a chance.'

I still don't know if I can forgive him as it's all too raw, but I understand his reasoning. And the end result is that I'm soon to be reunited with my child.

'What was the island like where they were living?'

'It looked nice, actually. They lived in an old stone building. When I looked inside, it had an open fire, two bedrooms, a kitchen and a bathroom. It was clean and tidy. There were plenty of toys scattered about the place and the shelves were well stocked with food. Outside there were fishing rods and a boat. They compared DNA taken from his house with Debbie's and, like I said, it looks like they're related. Probably brother and sister. She never mentioned him.'

'And when you went to his house, he wasn't there?'

'No.'

'But his boat was?'

'Yes.'

'So how did he get off the island?'

'When I arrived at Store Brattholmen, I showed some of the locals Sonny's photo and they identified him as Andreas and told me where he and the man they assumed was his dad lived. He must have been tipped off that someone was asking about him and left with him.'

This recollection is the only time in our reunion that Finn can't look me in the eye. I wonder if he's telling me the whole story. But before I can press him further, two women wearing lanyards and jackets approach us and introduce themselves as doctors and part of the care team looking after Sonny. They offer to take us to see him.

As we sit in the briefing room, my heart beats so loudly I think everyone around us can hear it. The doctors reiterate what they told Finn earlier today and that we must enter with no expectations. And soon after, we follow them into a viewing room where we watch Sonny in a playroom pushing toy cars along a rug. Next to him lies a small, sleeping terrier.

Despite having seen the photos sent to Finn, it takes time for me to connect this little boy with my lost baby. He left us a tot and now he's a walking, talking person. I can't hold back any longer and I start crying again for all I've missed.

'Andreas has been reacting very well to his new circumstances, but understandably, he is quite confused,' explains a psychiatrist in fluent English. 'He's been asking for his pappa a lot, but I'm afraid he isn't referring to you, Finn. He knows the man who was looking after him was not his actual father, but there was obviously a bond of trust between them because he tells us he chose to call him that. He insisted his dog came with him and although it's against hospital regulations, an exception has been made for a highly irregular case. But on the whole, he appears to be a well-rounded child who has been loved and nurtured.'

My skin prickles at this. Of course I'm relieved he has not been the victim of abuse, yet it hurts to learn someone else was doing what I should have been doing. I hate that man for taking him away from me, but I know how incredibly lucky I am to have Sonny back unharmed. So many of the families I try and help in my work will not be as fortunate as we are.

'For now, you'll just go in and say hello. You can introduce yourselves by name and wait for him to invite you to play with him if that's what he wants. If not, just sit and watch. I know that it's going to be difficult not holding him or telling him you are his parents, but if we take small steps now, it will help in the long term.'

'Okay,' says Finn. 'We can do that.'

'Are you ready?' the psychiatrist asks, and a rush of blood shoots to my head so quickly that I'm scared I might pass out. But I have to be strong. I am never letting that boy down again.

Finn and I look at one another and nod together. And without either of us speaking, we reach for each other's hand. We want to be a united front the first time our son sees us. This will be a new start for us all.

EXCERPT TAKEN FROM
INCOMPLETE MANUSCRIPT
BABES IN THE ATTIC – THE
FAMILY BEHIND BRITAIN'S MOST
INFAMOUS CHILD KILLER, BY
AALIYAH ANDERSON

Little is known about the background of Deborah Hunter (née Lewis) aside from living at 45 High Street for several years up until the 1980s. Despite a forty-year absence from that property, her fingerprints, only taken after her arrest, were eventually matched by chemical enhancement with prints she left as a child in the property. However, hers were not found on the attic suitcases or in the warehouse.

Hunter's birth certificate reveals the names of parents Samuel and Alice Lewis, but there is no record of employment for either of them. No death certificates have ever been registered. They are, however, assumed by police to be dead.

Along with Debbie, they are also believed to have had a son, George Lewis, who was not registered at birth, did not attend a school and does not have a National Insurance number.* It is not known when he left the family or where he went, only that he resurfaced in Norway approximately twenty years ago. Since the kidnapping of his nephew Sonny was revealed, he too has since disappeared.

Finn Hunter, née William Brown, has refused all approaches to be interviewed for this book, but questions have been raised about his role in the sudden disappearance of George Lewis. In a statement, Finn told police George Lewis's house was empty when he arrived on the island, yet George's boat remained at the dock. So how did he depart, as no one has so far admitted to picking him up and the distance is too far to swim?

Can Finn be trusted?** He has been previously publicly exposed as unfaithful in his marriage to Mia by fathering a child and having an affair with his ex-girlfriend. Is it inconceivable he was also dishonest about what really happened on that island that day?** Visitors' records at his mother's prison hospital confirm him having been to see her on twenty-three occasions over a two-year period. Could he know more about Sonny's kidnapping than he is admitting to?** Was he in on it?** Just how many more of his family's secrets is he hiding?**

* Speculate as to why
** Needs checking by libel lawyer.

EPILOGUE

FINN, 2023

I must have had my mind on other things because I missed the sound of the pips announcing the news bulletin. I usually turn off the radio as soon as I hear them.

'The house where the bodies of seven children were found murdered is to be demolished tomorrow,' begins the newsreader. 'The property, which is located in the village of Stewkbury, Bedfordshire, belongs to the son of Britain's most prolific female serial killer, Debbie Hunter, and is set to be turned into a pocket park . . .'

I switch it off. I don't need to hear any more. I don't listen to the news or read the papers any more, not since I found Sonny. It was relentless for those first few weeks after Debbie's sentencing, and again after we got Sonny home. We've turned down massive amounts of money for interviews and book deals because we want privacy and for Sonny to have some normality again. Thankfully, interest is waning.

Mia told me last night that she's changed her mind and wants to watch as the house is being bulldozed. She asked if I'd go with her, but I declined and offered to look after Sonny instead. She didn't seem surprised, nodding her head as if she expected me to say no. It might give her closure, but it won't change anything for me. The sooner that place is a pile of rubble the better. Once the council made us an offer for the land we said yes without hesitation. We've still lost a barrel of money on buying the place and the renovation work, but neither of us cares any more. We just want rid of it.

I think back to when I first saw those suitcases in the attic. I knew straight away that Debbie had a history with that house. It explained why she was so eager to buy it and was so reluctant to let us bid for it instead. But I didn't get to confront her or Dad about it until days later because Mia's and Sonny's well-being were my immediate priority after her fall.

I was fucking livid when Dad eventually confirmed that she'd lived there as a girl and they'd kept it from me for months. Years ago, she'd already told me about the things her parents did, but she swore blind she didn't know there were bodies up there. However, she must have suspected that place had something to hide or why would she ever want anything to do with it again? She might've suspected there were skeletons in her closet but maybe not in the attic. Immediately, it was as if I was being dragged back into a world I'd rejected as a teenager.

And when I told Dad this, he knew exactly to what I was referring. It was an admission that he knew what Mum had involved me in. I lost any respect I had for him there and then. He could have saved me from her if he'd wanted to. Instead, he turned a blind eye.

The car's sat nav says I'm about eighteen miles from a house I'm going to view in neighbouring Buckinghamshire that I saw on Rightmove. It's sixty years old and needs a total refurb, but nowhere near as much as the other place. I can do a lot of it myself. The garden is big enough for Sonny and Chloe to play in when they come to visit, and Sonny's already made sure there'll be a section where he can start growing his own vegetables. Mia and I don't have a single green finger between us so I assume he got them while he was living in Norway. If I can convince Mia that this is the perfect family home for us, then maybe she'll finally take me up on my offer to start afresh.

My phone beeps – speak of the devil, it's her. I'll read her message later. We're in a good place now. Much better than we have been in years. It's taken us a long time to get here and there's stuff she will never completely forgive me for, like my affair and Chloe. But she's found a way to live with it and I'm determined to win her back and not mess things up again.

However, not telling her that I knew Sonny was still alive will always be the biggest wedge between us. She gets why I had to keep it from her but, regardless, for two years I still let her think he might be dead. If the roles were reversed, I might feel the same towards her. She argues if I'd told the police they might have found him sooner. But I know Debbie. If she had the slightest inkling I'd told anyone about Sonny, she'd have been true to her word and I'd never have seen him again. Once Mia understands that, I'm sure she'll give us another go. To use one of her PR buzzwords, I've promised 'absolute transparency' from here on in. Well, transparency within reason. I can't let her see everything, can I?

Emma and I are still only talking through lawyers but at least I get to have Chloe every second weekend. She's a lovely kid who Sonny adores and Mia has grown fond of. It was Mia's idea that she and Emma meet in person. It wasn't an easy couple of hours, Mia admitted afterwards, and they didn't walk away best mates, but at least they're civil with one another. I even caught Mia texting Emma a photo of Sonny with Chloe at Whipsnade Zoo, which was sweet. Emma's got a new bloke now, Chloe tells me. He works in finance and it sounds like he treats her well. She deserves so much better than me. They both do. But if he hurts either of them, I'll make sure he only does it once.

Sonny is still in therapy. Post-Covid, appointments were back-logged but we finally found a psychologist and she tells us he's dealing with his kidnap and return home well, probably better than Mia and I are. I still dream about the first time we saw him in that hospital room and how he smiled as soon as we entered. *He remembers us!* I thought, and I wanted to wrap my arms around him and make up for two lost years. But when he grinned at a nurse in exactly the same way, I got it. It's just what he does. He's a polite little lad. I hate that we can't take any credit for that.

We did what the experts told us to do – we put no pressure on him, we let him come to us when he was ready, we played with him and we stayed in Norway for another twelve days, building up his trust, until he was ready to leave with us. On the day before we travelled back to England, he asked if we could take him to the island he called home for two years. Reluctantly we agreed.

We were all dead quiet on the police-escorted boat ride and throughout the hour or so we spent there. Andreas, as we were advised to call him then, showed us around his home and his favourite fishing spots. But he became upset when he thought he might never see his 'pappa' ever again. I hate that he thought of someone else as his dad, and even now, the P word puts me on edge.

But I have to admit, that island was a beautiful place for a kid. And as I scanned the darkness of the water, I wondered how far my Uncle George's body had washed away or if it was still weighed down on the seabed by the rocks I tied to his arms and legs with rope. He regained consciousness during our boat ride but his pleas were unintelligible under the gag. I didn't much care for what he wanted to say to me, so I rolled him overboard to his grave without so much as a goodbye.

Since I've got to know my biological family, I have a rough idea how it must feel for Sonny. Mia has nothing to draw from like that so she finds it tougher. She's also wrestling with all kinds of guilt from her postnatal depression days. But she's never caved in front of Sonny, not once. Out of me and her, she's been the stronger one.

Fourteen months have passed and Sonny still has a few hangovers from his time with George. I hear the odd Norwegian twang in some of his words. He's much more outdoorsy than us and he's always nagging us to take him hiking or on mountain bike rides. He'll be five on his next birthday and there is no end to his energy. Sometimes we struggle to keep up. But Mia and I never forget how lucky we are to have him.

I take a diversion from the sat nav's route and leave the dual carriageway, making my way towards an out-of-town retail estate. On the way, I'm reminded of a voicemail I received yesterday. Every time the phone rings and it's a withheld number, I assume it's going to be staff at Broadmoor Hospital telling me Debbie's dead. I've kept to my word and refused to have anything to do with her. There was a voicemail recently which I'm sure was her, but it was impossible to make out what she was saying. Her MND must be so advanced now that, when she speaks, it's hard to understand her. She's becoming trapped within herself and she deserves every moment of that living hell.

Mia asked me once how I'm going to feel when she dies. Relieved? Yes. Sorry? Not at all. Will I miss her? No. Do I forgive her for what she involved me in as a kid? Again, no. She robbed me of my biological family, my childhood and normality.

I've thought about it a lot over the years and I still don't understand her boundaries when she'd take me out to a kill. She'd insist I join her in tracking the kids she picked, and sometimes it was down to me to lure them back to our car. I was expected to help stuff them in suitcases, organise the location the suitcases were positioned in and then I'd watch as she'd slip into this glazed, trance-like state, staring at them.

But I was never allowed to watch them die. She made me face forwards in the front passenger seat, eyes fixed on the glovebox, the only sound that of shoes scraping against the leather seats as they struggled to free themselves from her vice-like grip.

Maybe she didn't want to share her ritual or, in her own twisted way, she might've been trying to protect what was left of my innocence by not allowing me to witness the conclusion of our task. Or perhaps she was quietly ashamed that she couldn't control herself.

I can't tell you how I knew, but I was always aware that what we were doing was wrong. I never enjoyed going on those trips with her as much as she enjoyed taking me, but I went because you do what your parents ask of you. Like her, I convinced myself we were doing something good in helping those kids escape their shitty childhoods. But as I got older, I realised she was kidding herself in thinking she was doing it for them and not herself. And I didn't want to be a part of it any more. I didn't tell on her because, despite all that, she was a good mum. A day didn't pass when she didn't remind me how much she loved me.

As the years went on, I wondered if she was still killing but I never asked her about it. I guess I didn't need to know. I never asked Dad either. Like him, I buried my head in the sand. And then when she was diagnosed with MND I just assumed she couldn't physically do it any more. She could barely wrap her hands around a mug, let alone a child's throat.

It's only from spending time with my biological mum Lorraine that I can see what a very different life I might have had. Not necessarily the greatest life, but a normal one at least. Lorraine's by no means perfect and if I could choose any parent, she wouldn't be high on my list. But there's no pretence with her, and most importantly, no manipulation.

We meet once every couple of months – not as regularly as I told Debbie we do. I know Lorraine would like to see me more often, but that doesn't suit me and I'm done with putting mothers first. She's clingy, but so are Mia and I with Sonny, we never want to let him out of our sight and I guess Lorraine feels the same now she's got me back. My younger sister Gemma and I no longer have a relationship after she sold her story and photos of us to a newspaper.

I pull into a cul-de-sac and park outside a sign that reads 'Storage and Lock-Up – Competitive Rates'. I take the suitcase from the back of the van: it weighs very little. I know who it contains so I didn't need to look inside when I dug it up from the cemetery where he was buried for decades before Dave joined him. Inside is the body of my brother, the original baby Finn. In the other hand I carry his shrink-wrapped clothing containing a perfectly preserved Babygro and blue hat. Debbie explained that was the outfit he wore the night he died. I can't help thinking death was a lucky escape for him.

She told me where to find him in a letter. The cemetery had not been officially used in fifty years and because there were no living relatives to object, it's going to be turned into a new housing development. Debbie begged me to move him and eventually I agreed he deserved better than an unmarked grave or being concreted over. So a couple of days ago, I dug up the suitcase, clothes and Dave's urn and brought them here where they can remain together, far from Debbie's influence.

The window of the rear passenger door lowers. 'Can I come too, Daddy?' asks Sonny.

'Okay but we can't stay long,' I reply, before unclipping him from his child seat and lifting him out. He helps me to carry the case.

Mia and I rented a container in this lock-up years ago to store all our stuff when we were moving into the Annexe. Mia doesn't know that I haven't given notice on it. Inside, I type my code into a security pad and the door rolls up from the ground. I turn on the fluorescent strip lights and close it again behind us. I take a moment to scan the shelves I've installed in here. There are about a dozen or so suitcases sitting on them, empty ones that were in the warehouse where Dave died and which the police eventually returned to me. Mia doesn't know about them.

Or that I've already filled two.

After George's drowning, my first solo kill on home territory came three months later, a freelance journalist and author called Aaliyah Anderson who wouldn't leave us alone. I remembered her from the bogus boiler call-out a couple of years earlier. Her first few approaches were polite, asking for our help with a book she planned to write about Debbie and Dave. Mia and I turned her down. But she was persistent and began doorstepping both Emma and Mia at their homes and approaching them on school runs, offering thinly veiled threats of how she wouldn't paint them in a good light unless they spoke to her. A letter from our lawyer threatening a restraining order fell on deaf ears. And when she turned up at my house, she found me alone. This time, she was invited over the threshold.

Then, a week ago, I filled a second case with Mia's friend Lorna Holmes. I was in Mia's parents' lounge playing with Sonny when I overheard them talking in her kitchen. Lorna was trying to talk a wavering Mia out of giving me another chance, reminding her it would only be a matter of time before I cheated, lied or hurt her again. She said she'd be better off with that copper, Goodwin, which threw me, as when I'd asked her about him before, Mia was adamant they were no longer in touch.

I confronted Lorna soon after to talk her into changing her mind. Instead, she vowed that if it was the last thing she did, she would try and keep me apart from Mia. I didn't set out for it to happen but I lost my temper and it *was* the last thing she did. She's now an official missing person and Mia's and Lorna's parents are worried for her safety, especially with her history of anorexia and self-harming. No more harm can come to her now that she's separated limb from limb inside a suitcase.

There's a third waiting to be filled and I have an idea who I'm saving it for. I've downloaded an 'invisible' app on Mia's phone which allows me to read all her incoming and outgoing text messages on my own device. That snake Goodwin is still squirming around, making it pretty clear that his interest in her is less than professional. She hasn't told him no but she hasn't told him to piss off either. She's tempted by him, I can tell, and that concerns me. I have put too much work into getting my wife back for him to get in the way. I have his address and, if the need arises, I'll be paying him a visit.

'Can you open them, Daddy?' asks Sonny, pointing to three cases at the end of the aisle, separate from the others.

'Just the one, as we're pressed for time,' I say and slide the barrels of the combination lock until the bar opens. I place it on the floor and he eagerly opens the lid like he is unwrapping a Christmas present. Inside are four human skulls that belong to the owners of several houses Debbie's parents moved into and killed. Every time I bring him here and show him them, he's as fascinated as if it's his first time.

'And they were inside people's heads?' he asks in amazement for the thousandth time. He lifts one up and holds it up to the light.

'Yep.'

'Tell me again what happened to them?'

'They were bad people who did horrible things, so your great-grandma and grandad made sure they couldn't do it again.'

'Were the people as bad as Scar in *The Lion King*?'

'Yes.'

'What about Hans in *Frozen*?'

'They were even worse than Hans.'

'Oh wow. They were really naughty.'

'And what do we do to naughty people?'

'We punish them!' he says enthusiastically.

I was only a few years older than him when I became fascinated by the different shapes, sizes and textures of all twelve skulls in this and another suitcase. I'd found them by chance hidden in boxes in my parents' garage. But when I asked Debbie who they belonged to, she didn't lie to me like I've just lied to Sonny by telling him they belonged to bad people. She told me straight but warned me not to tell anyone else, not my friends, my teachers or Dave.

I'd spend hours playing with them, lining them up and talking to them, imagining they were replying to me, pretending I was the teacher and they were students, dressing them up in sunglasses and hats or wrapping them up in scarves so they wouldn't get cold. I never did ask Dad if he knew about them, or if they were another thing he conveniently ignored in return for an easier life.

I look at my watch – it's time to leave. I help Sonny to pack away the skulls and tell him we can come back again soon, but only if he promises again not to tell anyone, especially his mum. I remind him it's our secret and that if Mia ever found out, he would be sent back to Norway and we would never get to live together as a family. He hates the thought of that not happening.

I lower the shutter, lock up and we make our way back to the van. Then I continue to follow the sat nav directions to view our potential new home. I suddenly remember Mia's text from earlier.

I know it's silly, but don't forget to check the attic.

I'm sure it'll be fine, I reply.

Her immediate reply: *Finn, humour me.*

Of course. Love you.

She replies with a smiley emoji and an X. It's not quite an *I love you too*, but I'll win her round eventually.

'You shouldn't text and drive,' says Sonny.

367

'Sorry,' I reply and put the phone down. 'Right, let's go and see this house, shall we?'

'Yeah!' he chirps.

'And don't forget to tell Mummy how much you love it and that you want us all to live there together, okay?'

'Yes.'

'I mean it, Sonny. It's really important.'

'If we buy it, can we get another dog?'

'That's up to you and how well you do with Mummy. Don't be scared to cry a bit if you need to.'

I am reminded of his Norwegian pet Oscar who we brought back to England with us. Sonny was heartbroken when he thought the dog had escaped from his grandparents' garden weeks later, and, as I hoped, turned to his mum and I for comfort. Nobody knows that I took the dog and left it tied to a tree in woodland a few miles from here. I saw on a local Facebook group that someone had found him and taken him in. I know it wasn't the dog's fault, but it was George who gave it to him, not us. And every time I walked, fed or petted that animal, it reminded me too much of Sonny's life without his mum and dad. And I need us all to forget that period of his short life as soon as possible.

I rub his head. 'Daddy!' he complains and I hesitate when I realise today is the first time he has started calling me Daddy and not *Pappa* since he came home.

I love this kid like I've loved nothing else in this world, even Chloe. Perhaps it's because we were apart for so long that makes me resent being away from him for even a night. Or maybe I want us to have the relationship Dave and I never had.

One thing is for sure though. I'm not going to manipulate him like I let Debbie manipulate me. I'm going to teach him how to be his own man, to follow his own path and to protect himself from anything that threatens to interfere with that. Only if he is at risk will I step in and do whatever is necessary to safeguard him, like any decent parent would. I will never let him down again.

I'm still bound to Debbie and always will be, even if I'm not her son any more. I don't tell anyone that a small part of her clings to my darkest corners and shapes my decisions. The only thing I have to thank her for is teaching me to kill without remorse. When you do it for a reason, you do it without conscience. I may have felt guilty about the kids I helped her to find, but not the lives I have since taken. Her lessons and her nurture of me will help me to protect Sonny. But I promise I won't involve him in what I do like Debbie did with me.

Not until he's much older than he is now. Not until he is ready.

ACKNOWLEDGEMENTS

This is my ninth novel and the first one in which the core idea came to me in a dream. (You wouldn't even want to be in my head at the best of times, let alone at night and in the dark . . .) I remember waking up at about 1 a.m. and dictating as much as I could remember into my phone, and trying not to wake my husband up. My subconscious stopped once we reached the suitcases in the attic, then I had to consciously figure out the rest.

My rollcall of thank yous begins with John Russell for trying to keep my office Elliot-and-Oscar free while I was writing. At times it failed and resulted in you three playing with Thomas the Tank Engine toys while I was sitting with my back to you, writing about cutting up bodies to stuff into suitcases.

There are many people who have helped with this book. I'd like to thank *CSI* and author Kate Bendelow and Christopher Allen of GL Law. My gratitude also goes to Benjamin P. Swift and Dr Katherine Brougham, Jo Richardson, Mark Williams, my former editor Jack Butler, RIP (he's not dead, he's just moved publishers), along with my current editors Victoria Haslam and David 'Interstitial' Downing, Sadie Mayne, Gemma Wain and all at Thomas & Mercer and Amazon, including Nicole Wagner and

Eoin Purcell. Thanks for your continued support with each and every one of my books.

Thanks also for your constant support to my mum Pamela Marrs, Queen of the News Kylie Pentelow, Darren O'Sullivan, Louise Beech, Carole Watson, Wendy Clarke, Emma Louise Bunting, Mark Fearn, Bob Gadsby-Fowler, Rosemary 'Mother' Wallace, Denise Stevenson, Michael Bartowski, Kate Thurston, Caroline Mitchell and Gabby Gibson. Also thanks to Mark 'Mr Pineapple Head' Goodwin for letting me borrow your name. Sorry the seal never reached Mia's port. And, as always, to Tracy Fenton for one of your finest cameos to date.

Huge gratitude goes to my old Chron colleague Richard Edmondson and Sergio Di Rienzo for their invaluable help in walking me through a crime scene. Any police procedural errors made in this story are my own.

To approach writing some of these characters and their emotions, I read *Love as Always, Mum*, by Mae West, daughter of Fred and Rosemary West.

As ever, thanks to the book bloggers, Tweeters, Instagrammers, TikTokers, Facebookers and Snapchatters amongst you for talking about my books.

And last but not least, to my loyal readers. You dark, dark souls have stuck with me for ten years now, and for that, I thank you from the bottom of my cold, merciless heart.

ABOUT THE AUTHOR

Photo © R. Gershinson

John Marrs is an author and former journalist based in Northamptonshire, England. After spending his career interviewing celebrities from the worlds of television, film and music for numerous national newspapers and magazines, he is now a full-time author. Follow him at www.johnmarrsauthor.co.uk, on Twitter @ johnmarrs1, on Instagram @johnmarrs.author and on Facebook at www.facebook.com/johnmarrsauthor.